THE GOSPEL
ACCORDING TO
SLIM
G-ZUS

THE GOSPEL ACCORDING TO SLIM G-ZUS

JAMES R. LONG

Bannockburn Press
Vancouver, WA

Bannockburn Press
drutledge@bannockburnpress.org

Ten percent of the proceeds from the sale of this book will be donated to Forgiven Ministry (www.forgivenministry.org), a not-for-profit organization that allows inmates to have a day-long visit with their children via its One Day with God program.

Paperback edition ISBN: 978-0-9963351-1-9

Cover and interior design: Gary Palmatier, Ideas to Images

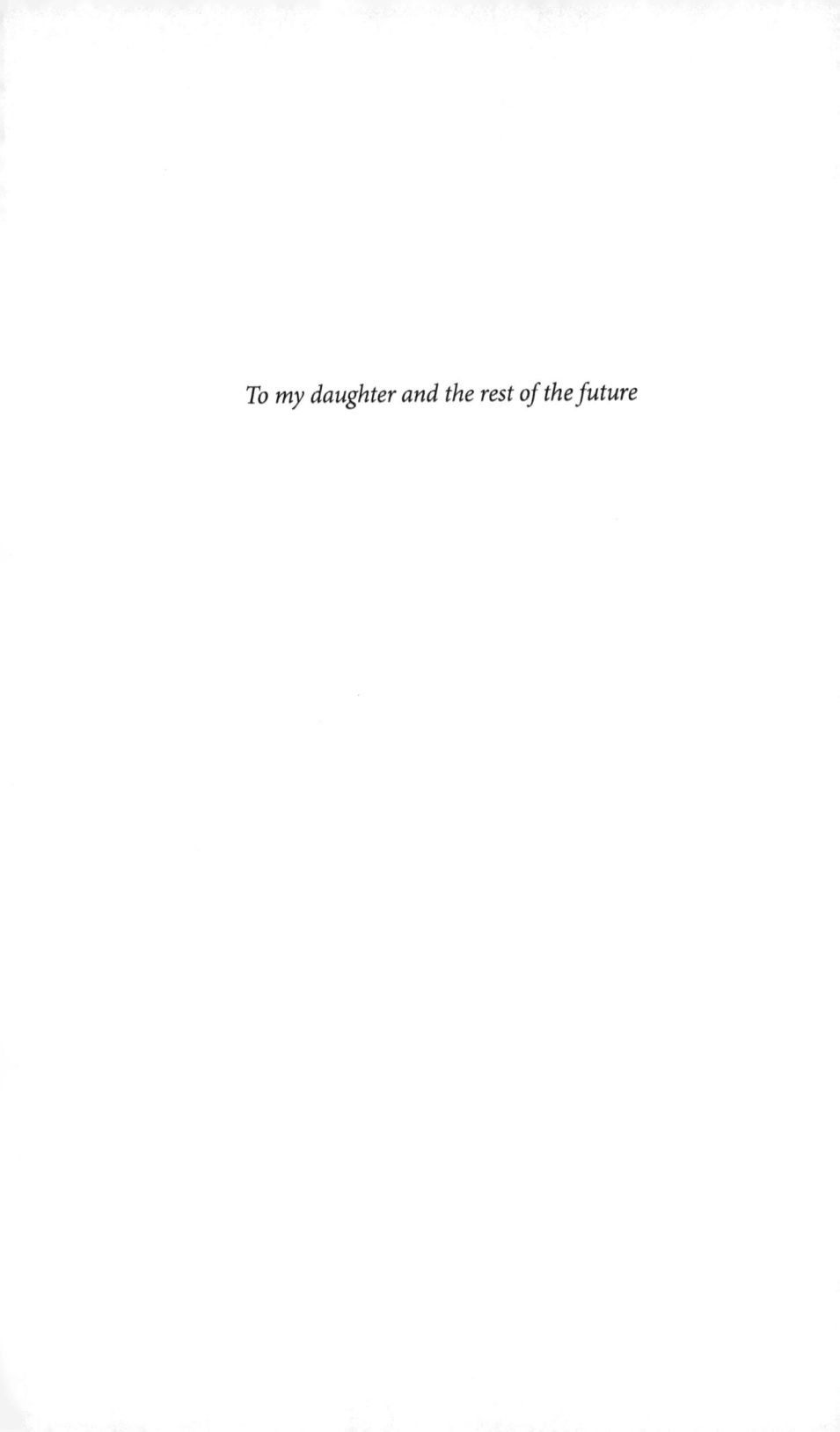

To my daughter and the rest of the future

Part One

Barbarism is always waiting in the wings,
and civilization is simply 'a thin crust over a volcano.'

—THOMAS SOWELL

CHAPTER 1

Russell McCann sat at his desk rummaging through his backpack, feeling for the Cliff Notes to *I, Rigoberta Menchu*. He turned to Cordell on his left and lifted his chin, "Got those Cliff Notes?" Cordell smiled. Gleaming white teeth the size of a man's thumbnail. A hard contrast to his ebony skin.

Cordell shook his head. "Tess ain't today, bro. I was bullshittin'." Russell kept on elbow-deep in his bag trying to play it off as he felt his ears heat up.

"I know it ain't," said Russell, "just trying to find 'em."

Cordell exhaled sharply, "Pssshh."

Russell felt something small with a smooth cover and pulled it out. The 2014 Football Factory Junior College program. Cordell said, "You still got that?" Russell slid it back in his bag ignoring the question. He leaned back in his chair. It was the fifth week of the spring semester at Northside Community College of Houston. But it might as well have been fifth grade all over again; Cordell pulling a prank about a test, the exposed fluorescent lights, the corkboard ceiling like they used to launch their pencils into, and the rubbery, ash-white tile floor and colorless walls... All of it represented a lack of progress at best.

Cordell cleared his throat. Russell looked up. Destiny Jenkins was strolling in graceful and confident. She took her customary seat in front of the teacher's desk. She wore a pearl-white button-up blouse and a gray knee-length skirt with white stockings. Almost as dark as Cordell, her skin was a satiny chocolate that Russell figured tasted as good as it looked. He'd never seen her wear any makeup. No need to mess with perfection. Tall and classy, she looked like Gabrielle Union with short hair and a curvier body. Neither he nor Cordell had approached her. "She's almost as tall as me," was Russell's excuse. Cordell's was, "She dark. Probably only like bright niggas." But they were really just intimidated. Destiny wasn't community college material. They'd learned that she'd been at Texas A&M on an academic scholarship, but had come home to take care of her grandmother. Ten-year-old Cadillacs and fifteen-year-old Mustangs with suped-up engines worth more than the car itself weren't going to impress her.

Other students continued filing in. Russell and Cordell used facial expressions to grade each of the girls as they walked into the classroom. There were no A's or D's or number grades either. Just pass or fail. And when you're nineteen, you don't flunk too many women.

The teacher for Sociology 101, Madison Templeton, walked in and closed the door behind her. A pasty white face appeared in the door's thin vertical window. A look of feigned outrage on the boy's face. He opened the door and smiled at Ms. Templeton, who completely ignored him, and found his seat.

Looking down at her desk, Ms. Templeton gathered her light brown hair behind her head. "Okay," she said, as she released her hair and looked at the class. "Everyone should be finished with *I, Rigoberta Menchu*. About 25 percent of the multiple-choice and short-answer questions on your test will come from Ms. Menchu's book. And at least one essay question. The rest of the questions will come from your textbook, chapters 4–8. We're going to spend the first half of class today discussing *I, Rigoberta,* so if there's anything you didn't understand about the book, this is your chance."

Destiny sat with perfect posture. Her legs crossed, one hand in her lap, the other in the air. Ms. Templeton smiled cautiously, "Yes, Ms. Jenkins?"

Destiny cleared her throat, "I found some stuff on the Internet. This guy, I forget his name, wrote a whole book basically saying that Rigoberta Menchu lied. He said they found her brother alive, he was not burned to death by the Europeans. And that her dad did go to jail but it was over a disagreement on some property. Not for political reasons. It basically said she made the whole thing up."

Ms. Templeton clasped her hands in front of her, pursed her lips, and in the most feminine of ways, leaned her head slightly to the side. "Well," she said, "I'm not sure where that... *information* originated from, but you have to remember that when the dominant culture merely feels like its institutions are being threatened, it is often reactionary in its response. Certainly Ms. Menchu, in her book, causes us to question things like capitalism and private property. But rest assured, Ms. Jenkins, that what Ms. Menchu claims happened to her people is very real and very true. Indigenous people the world over have been brutalized time and time again. Even if that doesn't fit some revisionist historian's version of the truth."

Now Destiny pursed her lips. Russell was pretty sure she was not satisfied with that explanation. They went through something like this every time the class met. Russell yawned, regarded Cordell. Even though their skin colors were polar opposites, they wore identical standard-issue H-Town uniforms: ice-white t-shirts, baggy jeans, retro Jordans, and 10-karat gold chains—Russell's a Figaro, Cordell's a Byzantine link.

Russell was on the verge of checking out. Going through the usual cycle of regret that almost always centered around his time at Football Factory Junior College when a car backfired and grabbed his attention... only the parking lot was too far away for him to have heard a backfire. He and Cordell glanced at each other, brows pinched. Russell surveyed the faces of the other students. Another loud bang. His pulse quickened as he sat up in his chair. He turned and locked eyes with Cordell... *Naw, ain't no way.*

Russell stood as sweat popped up on the back of his neck. A wave of heat passed through his chest as he headed for the door.

Russell opened the door and looked to the right. What he saw made his stomach flip. About fifty feet down the hallway was a dark-haired man in a black jumpsuit pointing a gun at someone on the ground. The gunman looked up at Russell, and Russell recognized his face. The gunman left his victim on the floor and ran towards Russell. Russell slammed the door and threw the lock home.

"Guy's gotta gun," he said. He stepped back, oblivious to the rectangular window on the right side of the door.

The shooter shook the door violently. Russell snapped to and moved out of his line of sight. Two shots burst through the window as Russell scrambled away on all fours. Most of the students had already moved to the left side of the room away from the door as the gunman's hand came through the window firing repeatedly.

Russell crouched at the far end of the teacher's desk and leaned his shoulder into it. An elephant roared as Russell drove the desk across the tile floor like a blocking sled. He squatted and jerked the desk up on its end, grazing the gunman's arm in the process. The door rattled. The desk took a couple of slugs.

Russell turned around. Cordell had one hand under Destiny's back and the other on her chest. Russell could still hear shots ringing out, but they were fading as the shooter abandoned his assault on their classroom. Russell's hearing came back in waves of sobbing and screams for help.

Russell hurried down the center aisle towards the large window in the back of the classroom. He snatched up a desk and spun 360 degrees, launching it through the window.

Cordell Youngblood was tying a sweatshirt around Destiny's chest when the window in the back of the classroom exploded. He looked up. Russell was punching out shards of glass the desk didn't take with it. Some of the students were still frozen with fear. Unable to move. Scarcely breathing. Others were up and over the window sill as soon as the glass hit the ground outside. As far as he could tell, only Destiny had been hit.

Cordell lifted Destiny off the floor and carried her towards the back of the classroom. She was rasping breaths through her nose and clenched teeth, the sound chilling Cordell to the bone as he lumbered forward.

Outside, the sidewalk to the parking lot had to be about fifty yards long. The cool, dry air, a rarity in Houston, stung Cordell's lungs with every labored breath. He laid Destiny down as gently as he could on the grass behind several rows of cars. Everyone in the parking lot was on their iPhones or Galaxies flooding the dispatch office at HPD.

Cordell was scared to look down at Destiny. Shots rang out in the distance at a steady pace. He dug under her back with his left hand and covered the exit wound. He placed his right hand over the hole in her chest. Ms. Templeton kneeled across from him, tucking her hair behind her ears. Destiny's shoulders jerked off of the ground and fell back flat again. She coughed and sent a spray of blood onto Cordell's face. He turned away and retched. Ms. Templeton moved in and placed her hands where Cordell's were. Cordell leaned forward dry-heaving, not sure if it was from the blood on his face or the lack of oxygen in his lungs. The tears in his eyes weren't helping. *Please, Jesus,* he thought.

Russell felt a bit of relief blooming, then shame as he looked at Destiny. *Please, God, stop this,* he prayed to himself. Pacing, he tried to catch his breath. Fists clenched and fighting back tears, Russell's shame turned to anger. Anger to rage. Like many warriors before him, the distance from the battlefield was emboldening.

Russell placed his hand on Cordell's shoulder. "Dell, you alright?" Cordell was bent over coughing and heaving. He nodded his head and straightened up, sucking air hard.

"Oh my God!" cried Ms. Templeton. Russell looked down at Destiny. Blood erupted from her mouth as she coughed, then flowed down the side of her face like lava from a volcano. Russell and Cordell turned away, eyes closed.

Russell grabbed Cordell by the arm and said, "You gotcha shit?" Cordell stared. Blinked once. "Yeah."

They stared for another moment before breaking into a jog for their vehicles.

Russell reached under the driver's seat of his gray Olds 98 and pulled out his .40 caliber Smith & Wesson. He ejected the clip and thumbed a hollow-point round he and his dad had reloaded in their garage, then rammed the clip back in. Russell looked back at the crowd as he chambered the round, then tucked the pistol into the waistband of his jeans.

Cordell opened the console in his white Ford F-150 and grabbed his 9mm Beretta. Left to him by his father, the Beretta 92F was a special Desert Storm commemorative edition. Identical to the one his old man carried in the cavalry in Iraq. He pulled the slide to ensure a round was in the chamber, then lifted his shirt and slid the pistol into his jeans waistband. He felt the reality of its cold steel, both comforting and frightening all at once.

The sirens from the police and other emergency vehicles were getting louder as Russell and Cordell navigated through the panicked crowd stampeding down the sidewalk. As the herd thinned, Russell said, "It was one guy. One gun."

"Yeah," said Cordell.

Russell was careful to make sure the pistol's grip was concealed from the students he was dodging, as shots continued growing louder.

The Northside campus is seven large, red-brick buildings that sit equidistant from one another. The sidewalk Russell and Cordell were on ran like a spine between them. Three buildings on the left, four on the right.

Their pace quickened as a police officer began yelling through a bullhorn. They were wearing their game faces—a contradiction Russell was sure belied the creeping doubts they both felt. Turning back now wasn't an option. This had become the most righteous dare in the history of dares.

The shots seemed to be coming from the last building on the right, the one that contained the cafeteria and gymnasium. Russell and Cordell stepped off of the sidewalk onto the grass and headed for the corner of the second-to-last building. They edged along the west wall before coming to a halt and peering around the corner. The south wall of the cafeteria had lightly tinted floor-to-ceiling windows. They could see shadows darting back and forth through the glass. The gunshots, especially at this distance, were sobering. Russell wondered if firing a few shots in the air would distract the shooter from his killing spree.

Russell pulled his pistol from under his shirt. Cordell did the same, flicking the Beretta's safety off, then back on again. Russell looked at Cordell. "S'go in by the gym," he said. Cordell nodded.

Russell took off running, white-knuckle gripping the pistol in his right hand. Cordell followed behind as they headed for the building's west-side entrance.

Russell held his hand up to his brow like a visor and peered through the glass door into the building. The hallway to the cafeteria looked much shorter than he remembered—even more so as they inched down it, gunshots going off ahead of them.

The hallway was about ten feet wide and doorless at the end, where it led into the cafeteria's south end. Russell stopped at the end of the hallway and squatted down. The coppery smell of blood was thick in the air.

Russell leaned carefully from the safety of the hallway and looked into the cafeteria. The gunman had his back to him. He was firing methodically at the thirty or so people he had corralled into the eating area. People were running back and forth in desperate attempts to avoid the shooter's hail of lead.

Russell pulled back and closed his eyes, bowing his head for a beat. *I gotta do this,* he thought. *My idea... People are dying...* He stood, looked at Cordell and said, "Dell, I'ma go for that cash register." Cordell looked away and widened his stance, then looked back. Jaw muscles flexing. Nostrils flaring.

"Say, man..." Cordell said.

Russell didn't like the idea either, but it was the only one he had, and there was no time for talking it out.

Russell peered around the corner again. The shooter still had his back to them. Russell was pretty sure it was a Glock in his hand. Damn. Glocks were known for their high-capacity clips. They could hold twenty or more rounds in a single magazine. Sooner or later, though, he would have to reload. Russell took a deep breath and exhaled slowly. He dipped low and bolted for the cash register.

Cordell flipped the safety off and stepped up, both hands on the pistol. He aimed it at the gunman, bracing himself against the corner while keeping most of his body concealed in the hallway. He knew he could not hit him from this distance, but if Russell missed and the gunman turned around he'd at least be able to keep him from getting to Russell.

The counter that the cash register sat on was about four feet high and eight feet long. As he knelt behind it, Russell swallowed hard and realized how dry his mouth was. He looked back at Cordell and saw the Beretta aimed around the corner. Russell bobbed his head above the countertop. Same scene. Pure carnage. A human turkey-shoot. *I gotta do this now.*

Russell rose up and laid his arms flat across the countertop. His heart banged hard in his chest against the gray particle-board of the countertop. He struggled to keep the three dots of his site lined up. Shallow breaths. Steady. Steady... Squeeze...

The gun nearly jumped out of his hands when it fired. The gunman stumbled forward as the bullet punched through the right side of his torso. Russell stood and started around the counter, but the gunman did not go down. Russell doubled back, squatted and aimed—and fired again. Another hit. The shooter fell to a knee, then flat on his face, his gun firing into the ground. Cordell blew by Russell, arms extended and aiming the Beretta at the floor. Russell stood. Cordell raised his right foot and brought it down on the gunman's hand. Another shot. "Dell!" shouted Russell. Cordell lowered the Beretta's barrel to the gunman's temple and pulled the trigger.

A few days later the news media commentators were making their pronouncements. On American Public Radio, Nancy Garza filed this report:

> Another school shooting has come and gone. The lives of twenty-six young people lost forever, including that of the troubled gunman, Jon Loc Tran. I must admit, when I first saw Tran's picture, my heart stopped. His broad face, weary eyes, and brown skin made him appear Latino. And with the immigration debate raging, I just knew the nativists and their allies would seize upon this tragedy and use it to further their agenda of exclusion and bigotry against undocumented workers. When I saw that his name was Tran, I joined in with the rest of my people in a collective sigh of Brown relief. Knowing that the "gringo" militias along the border who hunt the undocumented immigrants like animals and their counterparts in the talk-radio world wouldn't be able to blame

this one on us is cause enough for celebration. But we should also rejoice that three more merchants of death, handguns, are off the streets. One that belonged to the gunman and two that belonged to the two students who killed him. Some have attempted to make Cordell Youngblood and Russell McCann into heroes. This is folly. Were it not for someone carrying a gun on a school campus to begin with, we'd be twenty-six young people stronger today. The concealed-carry crowd will never understand that Youngblood's and McCann's guns also took a young life, as all guns have the potential to do. We all know what the Second Amendment says, whether we agree on what its wording means or not. But we also know that the Constitution was written by and for rich White men. Am I wrong to question whether or not such a document should be an authority for today's America? Would it be wrong to ask a group such as gun owners, whose membership is almost entirely made up of the privileged, to give up so little? Can't hunters slaughter enough Bambies without handguns or assault rifles? The N.R.A. can blowhard all they want about how a bad guy with a gun can only be stopped by a good guy with a gun. The truth of the matter is that no matter how many good guys there are with guns, guns allow bad guys to be much worse than they could ever possibly be without them. Mass shootings will continue to be a regular occurrence in American society until we go door-to-door and take up every one of these hideous creations.

Nancy Garza, American Public Radio

Brian Hunt editorialized on a cable news network:

The mass shooting at a community college in Houston last week took one of our worst nightmares and made it into reality. Jon Loc Tran, who came to America as a seven-year-old, murdered twenty-five innocent students. We've since learned that he had close to a hundred more rounds of ammunition on his person. There is very little doubt what would have happened had it not been for two brave nineteen-year-old men and the bravado that they are so famous for. A bravado that those on the left are constantly trying to tame. Our politicians are promising they will gather and act. I thank

God Russell McCann and Cordell Youngblood didn't see fit to call to order a committee to discuss how they should act. To Congress I say this: There are already millions of firearms on the streets, and there is a constitutional amendment protecting their being owned by our citizens. Grandstanding to fire up your base with impotent promises and idle threats about disarming the American public will not improve upon our very real problem: evil. It has been with us since the dawn of time, and like tyranny and backaches, probably always will be. The question is, what can we do to lessen the chances this particular form of evil is visited upon us again? Congress can meet and debate ad-infinitum. The evidence before us is not going to change. This madman was only stopped because two young men had the means to stop him. Congress has the ability to equip every school with those same means, whether it be in the form of a security guard with a gun or properly trained teachers or students with concealed guns. Unfortunately for the American public, these courses of action do not offer our pols the emotional satisfaction their pandering tirades do.

CHAPTER 2

I t wasn't his gun. His daddy owned that gun. S'in his name." Sandra Youngblood's eyes sharpened as she looked at Ronald Elston across his huge mahogany desk. She had never seen the inside of a law office before. Never had reason to. Her late husband Tobias, God rest his soul, had seen to all the family's legal matters. Lord, how she needed him now. This was definitely not income taxes or family budgets being dealt with here. This was serious. If only Tobias had not taken that security job. He would have never gone to Iraq. He would be here now. Together they would handle this.

"Mrs. Youngblood? Mrs. Youngblood, are you okay?" Elston's voice was slow and deep.

"Yes, I'm fine," her voice was thin and shaky.

"I was saying that this crime carries a mandatory minimum sentence. There is nothing I or anyone can do about it."

Mrs. Youngblood uncrossed her legs. Recrossed them. She looked at Elston with cold determination. "Are you telling me, Mr. Elston, that my only son has risked his life to save countless people he doesn't even know, and now he is going to go to prison for it?"

Elston looked at Cordell, "Yes ma'am, unfortunately, that's exactly what I'm telling you."

"Well then," she said, fear giving way to anger, "maybe we need to talk to someone else. A White lawyer perhaps."

Cordell sunk lower in his chair and closed his eyes. Tried to think of something he could say to calm his mother. Her fear now greater than his own.

Elston held his hands palms up. "If that is what you think is best for you and your son, Mrs. Youngblood, by all means. You're going to hear the same thing wherever you go. But let me remind you that Cordell will be eligible for parole when he serves half of his sentence, in this case eighteen months. I can represent him at his parole hearing, and if he stays out of trouble, I think he has a good shot."

She shrank into the rustic brown-leather chair. Reality rushing in. Fear and pain finally winning out. She tried to speak. Instead of words, Sandra Youngblood found only tears. Cordell leaned down and wrapped his arms around his mother's shaking body.

Julisa Washington-Kenyetta, czar of the Houston Police Department's Office of Community Relations and Outreach, sat alone in her office clicking through interdepartmental memos dealing with the recent mass shooting at the Northside Community College of Houston. Police interviews with individuals who knew Tran painted a picture of a young man who was resentful and contemptuous. Writings of Tran's recovered by investigators were filled with anti-American invective. *Releasing this information isn't going to improve the relationship between communities of color and the majority,* she thought. It would only subject those who were already marginalized to adverse treatment. On the other hand, maybe Tran's writings could be used to increase awareness about the plight of people of color in America. But no, she decided, whitebread world still was not ready for this. She began typing an e-mail to the chief, advising him about the potential ramifications of releasing this information.

The McCanns lived in a three-bedroom house off of Aldine West-field in a neighborhood bookended by two trailer parks. It was a real improvement over their first home in Cloverleaf on the east side of town. Darren McCann, Russell's father, was a private man, especially when it came to his religious beliefs. His family attended a small Presbyterian church sparingly. Mostly around the holidays. When his wife, Judy, told him earlier in the week that she'd invited their church's youth minister and his wife over for a visit, Darren planned to be in the garage reloading shotgun shells full-bore after dinner. Since his memory was not what it used to be and he'd gotten caught up in a really good rerun of Duck Dynasty, Darren was jarred from his Lazy Boy by the knock at the door. Scrambling to reach the garage from where he sat, he realized he was too late. His wife was already welcoming in Tom and Patricia Doyle.

Darren and Tom shook hands. Tom pointed to one of the many trophies mounted on the dull brown wood-paneled walls. "Darren," he said, "that rack looks a little too big for that buck."

"Buddy of mine did that one before he finished taxidermy school."

"Oh, well, I guess that explains it." Tom thrust his hands into his pockets and looked admiringly at the rest of the mounts.

Judy said, "Patty brought peach cobbler," and held up a dish covered in Saran Wrap.

Darren smiled, "Boy, howdy, I bet it's good."

Judy yelled down the hail, "Russ, the Doyles are here!"

Russell was sitting on his weight bench, wearing his battle-red Rahim Moore jersey, listening to some old Slim Thugga when he heard his mom's voice. He had the Football Factory Junior College program opened to page 14, the defensive backs. Number 34, Russell McCann, six foot three inches tall, 210 pounds, North Side High, Houston, Texas. Like so much else at the school, those numbers were a willful exaggeration. He was barely six foot even and only 200 pounds. His was the only White face on the page. Small green eyes far apart and wolf-like. Just a year ago he was going to be the next Pat Tillman—a safety who tackled like a linebacker. Now he was a hero unable to talk, thanks to a gag order from the judge, and on his way to prison for three years. Russell tossed the program on his unmade bed and stood. Better to go on out there before his dad started calling for him.

Russell smiled as he walked in to the living room. Mr. and Mrs. Doyle stood up to greet him. Mrs. Doyle hugged him tightly and Mr. Doyle shook his hand and clapped him on the back like the good ol' boy he was. "How are ya, sir?" said Russell.

"You know, Russ, I'm only about five years older than your brother."

Still standing, Tom offered up a brief prayer. Russell bowed his head and looked at their yellow-brown shag carpet, forty years old and flattened out like those fake alien crop circles. He closed his eyes and prayed in earnest. Tom finished and everyone said amen.

"Well, Russ," asked Tom, "you talked to Cordell lately?"

"Yessir." Russell hoped the shorter his answers, the shorter the visit. He knew there was a God and that the Bible was His written word, but he wasn't looking for any spiritual guidance or support.

"He doing all right?" asked Tom.

"Oh, yeah. Yeah, he's a'ight."

Mrs. Doyle and his mother were smiling and nodding approvingly. Darren looked like he was contemplating an attempt at turning Duck Dynasty back on.

Mr. Doyle looked at his wife and grinned. "Patty, why don't you tell Judy what you found out."

"Well," Patricia said proudly, "I got ahold of the head chaplain in Huntsville. Real nice man. He said Russell would be able to keep a Bible, and that most units have at least one Protestant service a week. I asked about the all-Christian unit we talked about last time. The one we saw on the Internet? And basically he said that there's a real long waiting list for that one, but that most units have a separate area—he called it a faith-based wing—and that it was the warden's discretion who got to live there."

Judy nodded. "That's about what I got from that ombudsman person I talked to. They can't tell us what unit Russell will go to, but we're hoping that because the D.A. is writing a letter on his behalf, he will go somewhere decent."

Darren chimed in, "We're hoping they will put him and Cordell at the same one."

Russell winced. Every time his dad said that, it was as if he thought Russell couldn't handle himself—a sentiment Russell had felt often enough throughout his life. His dad and older brother Mitch were every bit of six foot three inches tall and 230 pounds. Despite this Mitch was never an all-district first team selection after leading the team in total tackles. Mitch played tight end and didn't even start until his senior year, never making much of an impact on the game. And yet, Russell could not help but think if he were

working on a drilling rig out in the gulf and Mitch was on his way
to prison...

Mr. Doyle started a lecture on the book of Job. It wasn't
supposed to sound like a lecture, and actually it wasn't half bad.
Eventually they got into a conversation that was only a few clicks
short of gossip about other members of the church, and Russell was
able to excuse himself. Darren had already made his escape to the
garage, using a trip to the bathroom as his exit strategy.

Sandra Youngblood sat in the same seat in the same pew that she'd
been sitting in since the family joined Northside Baptist Church
over fifteen years ago. She watched the pastor intently as he gave his
sermon but her mind was elsewhere. It had been over a month since
her visit to the attorney's office and she still had not accepted the fact
that her son was going to prison. She reflected on everything she
and her husband had done in an effort to spare their son from this
particular fate. She thought of all the difficulties in their lives they
had overcome. Tobias joining the Army to get out of Brewster Park
in Fifth Ward. How she had joined the National Guard to escape
Garden City apartments (a.k.a. the bricks) in Acres Homes. The
sense of accomplishment she felt when she got her degree from U
of H and they had left Havastock Hills apartments in Greenspoint
and bought their home on Veterans Memorial. There were still
White folks in the neighborhood then. How had they come to this?

Cordell saw the distance in his mother's eyes and put his arm
around her. Since the visit to the attorney's office, he had taken on
the role of comforter, as if the roles had been reversed and his mom
was the one about to do a bid.

The pastor asked the congregation to take out their hymnals.
The Youngbloods had no need of a hymnal, they knew every song
in the book by heart. The organ came alive. The congregation stood
and began singing: Trust in Him, thy Lord. Trust in Him, thy Father.

The McCann men never completely finished the deck they had
begun building in their small backyard, but they had finished

enough of it to assemble a mismatched set of folding lawn chairs and a barbecue pit that Mitch had welded together himself.

Tonight, five young men and two young women, all friends since junior-high, sat around the unfinished deck. Megan Laughton sat to Russell's left. She was the closest thing he had ever had to a girlfriend. Her eggshell cheekbones and delicate dimpled chin were framed by long dirty-blonde hair. She kept her hands tucked into the sleeves of her thin white sweater, while her legs stayed crossed in a pair of jeans that fit but didn't require any gold-medal gymnastics to get into. Russell had his arm around her and was planning on trying to pull her into his lap later. He figured that if she didn't resist, she might be up for sneaking in through his bedroom window later that night.

To Megan's left was Mike Ellis. He wore his hair just long enough to comb to the side but, of course, never parted it. This transgression of the Code of the Bald Fade brought numerous Justin Bieber barbs his way, but, just like most things with Mike, they slid off like water on a duck's back. His white T wasn't the iciest of white and his jeans weren't made by a rap label. Still, the garb was technically sound, the Polo boots putting it over the top.

To the left of Mike and directly across from Russell was Terrance Corbin in a deep steel-blue Deandre Hopkins jersey. He held his Motorola Droid with both hands. Thumbs flashing across the keyboard. Terrance and Cordell had been the starting wide receivers at Northside High their junior and senior years. Cordell the Z, Terrance the X. Criminally baggy Rocawear jeans and custom Nike Air Force Ones in Texans colors covered his lower half.

On Terrance's left was Demetrius Hixon. He was brushing his always-fresh-from-a-wave-cap cinnamon-colored hair from back to front. It was said that the waves on his head would get a sailor seasick. Damn Chris Rock and his hatin'-ass movie, Demetrius had Best Hair. That hair, along with his brown eyes and square pit-bull jaw, attracted so many ladies that he could keep his dress strictly regulation. Tonight he sported a shimmering white t-shirt, a pair of starched and creased jeans, and the all-white '95 patent-leather Jordans.

In between Demetrius and Cordell was Natasha Saunders. Cordell's version of Megan. Caramel skin and braided hair in a bun, with two errant locks dangling beside her heart-shaped face. She wore a black cardigan over her Target work uniform. Red polo shirt and khaki pants.

Russell sensed an uneasiness in everyone there. No one seemed to know how to act. He couldn't decide if it felt like a funeral or a going-away party. He said, "Anybody ever hear about Kelvin and Jason? They got five years each, right?" Kelvin Montgomery and Jason Larue tried to rob an armored car their junior year at Northside.

Terrance lifted his head, "What's-his-name said they were in Indiana. You know that shit was Fed right?"

"Yeah," said Russell, "well, whatever. Fed, state, it's still prison. My lawyer said that state has parole, Feds don't."

Russell and Cordell spent the entire evening trying to reassure their friends, and themselves, that they weren't worried about driving to 1301 Franklin Street in downtown Houston the next morning to start their three-year sentences for possessing firearms in a gun-free zone.

"All's I know," said Cordell, "is that if Jason and Kelvin went in and they're still alive, we'll be alright too."

Silent nods all around.

Megan asked, "Hey Russ, didn't you say that the D.A. was gonna make sure y'all went to the same unit?"

"Yeah," answered Russell, "that was one of the first things we discussed."

More nods.

"And he's gonna write a letter to the parole board as soon as we're eligible. About a year," Cordell added. It was actually a year and a half, but there was no need to tell everyone all that.

Natasha broke in, "Shouldn't be going at all."

"Already," agreed Demetrius.

"Yeah," said Cordell, "but it coulda been worse. They coulda hit us with another charge. We both underage. Supposed to be twenty-one."

Natasha put her head on Cordell's shoulder and her hands around his right arm. Russell squeezed Megan's hand, thinking this might be a good time to pull her into his lap. Megan placed her hand on the back of Russell's and held it in her lap.

Mike said, "Didn't y'all say they got college in the joint?"

There was a pause as Russell and Cordell enjoyed the moment with their ladies. Finally, Cordell answered, "Yeah. And they're supposed to have some kind of program where you don't have to pay for it till you get out."

Russell said, "See, they got different kindsa prisons. Me and Dell ain't got much time, just three years, so they're liable to send us somewhere where, you know, fools are playing golf and shit."

That got everybody smiling.

Mike said, "Shit, I don't even know how to score golf."

"Me neither," said Cordell and Russell simultaneously.

"Check it out y'all," said Terrance holding up his Droid.

"What's that?" asked Russell. "You put the pics on your Facebook page?"

Everyone smiled. They all got the joke. No one their age used Facebook anymore. Even though they all still had their pages up from high school, it was all about Instagram now. Which was where Terrance had been uploading the pics he'd taken of them earlier. Terrance passed his Droid to Mike who nodded his head and passed it to Megan. She smiled and showed it to Russell. *Perfect opportunity,* he thought. "My eyes ain't that good," he said as he grabbed her by the waist and pulled her up towards his lap. She didn't resist, but she didn't exactly jump into his lap either. She stood and gently backed down onto his lap.

Russell blushed at the awkwardness of his move. He looked to see if anyone noticed. The replay was inconclusive. Megan had never been much for cuddling. She settled into Russell's lap and passed the phone to Cordell. Russell wrapped his arm around her. Inhaling the fresh smell of her hair, he was beginning to like his chances for tonight.

Demetrius asked, "That gag order shit over with yet? Y'all gonna talk to that writer and try to get paid?"

Russell said, "Texas has a law where you can't make money off your crime. We don't know yet if we can do a book deal like ol' boy was talkin' about. Or even if we can do interviews."

Natasha asked, "What about that guy who killed his wife and put her in the freezer? They made a movie about him."

Mike said, "Yeah. *Bernie.* My dad said Hollywood likes that kind of story 'cause it's weird. And they're all weird in Hollywood."

The screen door squeaked open, and Russell's dad informed Cordell that his mother had called and that she was ready for him to be getting home.

Darren said to Cordell, "I would like to talk to you and Russ before you head out."

Demetrius stood, brushing his hair. He and Russell began the slap and grab handshakes that morphed into half hugs. Promises to write and visit were given. Everyone drifted to the gate that led out front. Cordell handed Natasha his keys.

Russell whispered to Megan, "I'm gonna leave my window open tonight."

"Mmm, okay," she purred, "thank you."

Everyone was gone and the backyard was quiet. Fireflies lit up the evening sky. Russell and Cordell sat down as Darren pulled up a chair and sat down across from the two of them. Darren looked at Russell and said, "Russ, your uncle Robby was in TDC for two years back in the Ninties. We told everyone that he was back up in Odessa. The oilfields. He had gotten hold of some guy in a bar and put him in the hospital. You know he was always a little too good with his hands. Anyway, wasn't the first time, and the judge got tired of fiddlin' with him and sent him to prison for two years. Never made parole 'cause he kept getting in fights. Did the whole sentence day for day."

Russell was surprised, but not shocked. His dad went on: "Robby and I talked about y'all. He said when he was down there, the White boys and the Black boys... didn't really..." His dad came as close to fidgeting as Russell had ever seen. Russell and Cordell looked at each other.

"Dad, we know. Even though they kept us separated from most everyone else in the county, we could tell it was kinda... messed up."

"Robby said where he was on the Ferguson Unit, they had separate benches for everybody to sit on. Said they had some trouble sometimes."

The three of them sat silently in the dark. Moments passing. None of them knew how to prepare for what was coming, and certainly couldn't express it in words.

"Mr. McCann," said Cordell, "me and Russ been knowing each other, like, all our life." Russell nodded. Cordell continued, "That's them down there with that." It was Darren's turn to nod. Men of few words understand one another.

Darren said, "y'all know how to defend yourselves. Cordell, you better get on the road. You've got two women waitin' on ya."

They all stood and Darren shook Cordell's hand. "Son, you're a hero like your daddy was. I promise ya he's up there watchin' over ya. Over all of us. He'll keep you safe."

"Thank you, sir." Russell couldn't remember a time when his dad had tried harder.

Russell walked Cordell around the garage to his truck. Natasha leaned against Cordell's F-150, thumbs ablaze on her iPhone. Russell said; "Say, Dell, you know I'm joining the Nazi Brotherhood soon as we get there, right?"

"They ain't gonna let you. Done seen your picture with mine on the TV."

"Oh. Yeah."

"Yeah, you're outta there wigga."

"You gettin' down with the Black supremacist gang?"

Cordell frowned, "We ain't got them."

Russell laughed, "Yeah, well..." They shook hands, Russell looking up; Cordell looking down. In a hushed tone so that Natasha couldn't hear him, Russell said, "Case we don't catch each other in the morning. Whatever happens down there we keep it between us. Like Vegas, ya feel me? I doubt we'll get into a jam. Probably going to some place they send all the famous people. Martha Stewart and shit."

"Yeah," said Cordell. "But just in case..."

"Yeah, I gotcha."

"Alright then."

"Alright, bro." They shook hands again.

Russell said, "You could always tell them fools you had to start slingin' dope or jackin' 'cause they quit making *Fast and Furious* and *Transformers*. You can't sing no more."

"You back on that again?"

"Say..."

"You could say somebody jacked your grill and you shot 'em. Been awhile since you had a hit," said Cordell.

Who you think gets more cred down there, Paul Wall or Tyreese?

"What's Wall without a grill, though?"

"We fiddin' to find out."

CHAPTER 3

Russell was in the county jail for nine days before he was hand-cuffed to another inmate and put on what looked like an old school bus that had been painted white and blue. The "chain bus" drove them all to the Byrd Unit in Huntsville. A half-mile concrete corridor with perpendicular hallways or "lines" extending from it like vertebrae that contained three tiers of cells. Built in the 1930's, the Byrd Unit was one of the only units not named after one of the state's governors. It was the intake unit. Inmates were photographed, fingerprinted, tested for intelligence as well as a variety of diseases, and sheared for lice.

Strict adherence to the Code of the Bald Fade already had Russell's hair so short that the clippers hummed quietly over his entire head without incident. After a wash off in a drizzle of cold water, he was sent into the main hallway. *Here we go*, he thought. His cell line and number, K111, had been written in black marker on the left shoulder of his white sleeveless jumper. A middle-aged Black woman with curly, highlighted hair sat behind a tall wooden desk to his right. Inmates were coming and going in both direc-tions. The guard glanced at the writing on his jumper and thumbed him south without ever making eye contact. The cement floor was heavily waxed and lanes on each side of the hallway had been created by yellow striping paint. Foot traffic flowed in different directions, depending on which side of the hallway you were on. Only the guards were walking down the middle of the hall.

Russell stood in front of cell 111, on the third row of K-Line, almost 30 feet off of the ground. He was ready. Stomaching the butterflies that were rising up within him. The door slid sideways automatically, and he stepped in. A young Black female guard came down the run and slammed the door behind him. There was someone on the bottom bunk, asleep under a sheet until the door got slammed. He jerked his head up from under the sheet and looked at Russell with bloodshot eyes. Russell stood stock still. A two-inch toothbrush in one hand and a paper cup of tooth powder in the other. The two bunks were against the wall to his left and a combination sink and toilet were directly ahead on the back wall of the cell. All together it was six feet by nine. Maybe.

"What's goin' on, man?" the guy asked.

"What's up?" replied Russell, still standing by the door sizing up his potential opponent.

"Where'd you come from?" *This dude is nosey,* Russell thought. He answered anyway, "Houston."

"Harris County, huh? Heard we had it pretty bad in there."

Russell didn't know what to make of the "we," or the "bad." The guy stood up from the bunk wearing only a pair of thin white boxer shorts. He was pasty white, with hardly an ounce of muscle tone on him. He extended a hand for Russell to shake and said, "Yeah, we're lucky here. They only put you in a cell with your own. I'm Nelson. From west Texas, but I fell outta Amarillo up in the panhandle. What do they call you?"

"My name's Russell."

Nelson rubbed his eyes as he sat down on his bunk. "I just came from a transfer facility. You got lucky coming here straight from the county. Transfer facilities suck. Like a homeless shelter, man." Russell nodded his head. He'd never been in a homeless shelter, but Harris County wasn't exactly a Holiday Inn. "I gotta dime. You gotta lotta time, man?" Russell had been considering telling anybody who asked him that question that he had a life sentence for killing a cop. He figured that would get him the most respect from the inmate population. But he decided against that here, not too worried about his chances with Nelson should they get into it.

"I got three years," said Russell.

"That's all? That'll fly right by." Nelson gestured to his bunk. "Wanna sit down, man?" Russell put his toothbrush and tooth powder on the light-blue cracked vinyl mattress that lay on the top bunk and sat down. "That ag or nonag?" asked Nelson.

"Ag. Gotta do a year and a half before I'm eligible."

"Yeah, when it's ag you gotta pull half to come up. Nonag's like twenty percent."

Russell nodded. Nelson stretched; he looked comfortable, like all of this was no big deal. "Me and my fall partner had stole probably twenty-five cars. Laws only got us for eight of 'em. I was on probation for some pills, handlebars. D.A. offered me that nonag ten, and I said 'where do I sign.' I come up in two months. They'll probably give me a set-off, but I ain't trippin.'"

"So you've already done two years and you're just now getting here?"

"Yeah, pretty much. I was in the county for a year and then Garza East and West for a year." Russell nodded, thinking. Nelson pointed to a locker above the door. "I got some commissary in there, man. Some peanut butter and crackers. You hungry?"

"Nah, I'm cool," said Russell.

Nelson grinned. "You know you ain't gotta worry about me tryna put you up in some game, right? If you're hungry, it's cool." He grinned wider, exposing two yellow front teeth. "I ain't gonna try and tell you you owe me them same crackers back, or whatever. Know you probably heard stories in the county about all the game these dudes try to pop down here." Russell continued looking ahead. He pushed down into the mattress, flexing his horseshoe triceps. He turned to Nelson and said, "I wasn't worried about that. Just not hungry." Nelson smirked.

Russell looked at the wall. It was covered in gang graffiti from floor to ceiling. Nelson said, "Where I just came from all the guards are Mexican. Here, they're damn near all Black. They do feed better on this unit, though."

Russell asked, "Is the food here really better than in the county?"

"Better than any county I was ever in." Nelson blew his nose into some toilet paper. "East Texas shit messes with my allergies."

Russell took in more of the cell. Nelson continued, "You must've had a high-profile case. Or you tried to escape. Something."

Russell asked, "Why you say that?"

"Cause they normally don't send you straight here. Most go to Holliday, Garza, one of the transfer facilities." Russell knew not to mention the D.A.'s help. That would make him look like a snitch. Since he wanted the knowledge Nelson's experience had brought him, he needed to keep him talking. "I got caught with a pistol on a college campus. Gun-free zone. I'm in..." Russell shrugged. Nelson looked like he wasn't satisfied.

"You try to escape?"

"Nah." said Russell.

Nelson shook his head. Russell wondered if Nelson might tell some of the other inmates that his story didn't add up. That could be worse than letting everyone know he wasn't a criminal. Russell said, "You remember hearing about a school shooting in Houston? 'Bout a year ago? At a community college?"

"Yeah. Think so."

"That was me and my boy, Dell, who shot that fool."

"You shot who?"

"Tran. The gunman. I shot him in the back. Dell shot him in the head."

"So you don't have three years for a pistol case?"

"Yeah. We pled guilty to that."

"Oh... So why didn't you just say so?"

Russell held his palms up, then stood. "I don't know," he said, "shouldn't I say something like I'm in here for beatin' a cop?"

"Not unless you're in here for whippin' a law. Hell, naw. You know all our info is on the TDC website. All's you gotta have is someone's name and anyone can find out what you're in here for."

Russell's eyes widened. Nelson said, "If what you say is true and all you got is a pistol case, that is all it's gonna show when you get to your unit. Some of the other Whites are probably gonna check that out. You know, to like make sure you're not a cho-mo or somethin.'"

"Hell is that?" asked Russell.

"A cho-mo?"

"Yeah, what the hell is a cho-mo?"

"A child molester."

"I sure as hell ain't that."

"That's mostly what they're looking for. Families won't take rapists, either. At least they're not supposed to. You gonna stay solo?"

Russell said, "Yeah, I guess. I'm not gonna join a gang if that's what you mean."

"Yeah. Down here they usually call them families," Nelson grinned. "It's like some politically correct penitentiary shit."

Russell didn't say anything. He was thinking. Cho-mos, rapists, families. *It probably won't be like that where I'm going,* he thought. *Me and Dell's gonna get moved into the same cell and go to college for a year and a half.*

Russell sat back down on the bunk. "What you said about the other Whites. What if I just don't talk to anyone? The D.A. said he'd get 'em to put me and Dell on the same unit. Me and him will probably just kick it together."

Nelson stood and reached up into his locker and took out a sleeve of Ritz crackers and a jar of peanut butter. "I've never heard of anybody getting sent to the same unit as their fall partner. Least not on purpose. Depending on what unit you go to, you might be able to just stay to yourself. I seen some churchy dudes do it on Garza, but they were older." Nelson spread some peanut butter on a cracker with a plastic spoon. He offered it to Russell. "Sure you're not hungry?" Russell was. He took the cracker and put the whole thing in his mouth while Nelson made another one.

"Most units," Nelson said, "somebody is gonna want to take a look at you. Sometimes it's the 'woods, the independent Whites, sometimes it's the Blacks, and sometimes it's the Mexicans. Even if you just stayed to yourself, you'd eventually have to fight somebody. Whoever is doing the checkin' on that day. Some places rotate; Blacks one day, Mexicans or Whites the next."

"Yeah," he said, working the last of the peanut butter from the roof of his mouth, "I heard about that in the county. If you don't fight you're a ho, can't have nothin' or whatever."

"Yup," said Nelson. "If you catch that pussy, whoever you refuse to fight pretty much owns you. Some guys try to catch out, but a lot of the laws will tell 'em to go back and fight."

"What's a catch out?"

"It's when you go to the laws and tell them to lock you up 'cause your life's in danger."

Russell was confused. "But, you're already in prison."

Nelson looked up at him. "They put you in another building. Sorta like solitary. When they let you out they put you on a different wing, but it doesn't matter. Wherever you go, you'll be a ho. None of the other Whites will back you, and what's worse is that all the Blacks and Mexicans will know it. They'll be able to do whatever they want, clique on you, steal your shit, rape you, whatever."

"But if you fight?" asked Russell.

"The saying goes that as long as you fight, you'll be alright." Nelson handed Russell a second cracker with another generous dollop of peanut butter on it. Nelson had a look of deep thought on his face before he said, "Basically, you can whip somebody's ass, get your ass whipped, or get your ass fucked." Nelson smiled, happy with himself.

Over the next week Russell and the other inmates at the Byrd Unit were interviewed by physician assistants, psychologists, and chaplains. They were given IQ tests, tuberculosis, HIV, and hepatitis tests. Russell got a 106, negative, negative, and negative, respectively. He then went before a classification committee and was told he'd be going to the Acirema Unit in Bee Ef Eee, which was in deep South Texas. Nelson gave Russell his last stamped envelope to write home with.

Dear Mom and Dad,

They just told me I'm going to the Acirema Unit in Bee Ef Eee. I heard it is in South Texas, about four hours from Houston. I should leave here any day now. My IQ is six points higher than average and I don't have AIDS, TB, or hepatitis. Have y'all heard from Cordell's mom? I haven't seen him come through here yet but this place is real big. Let me know if y'all hear anything. When I get to Acirema I'll be able to go to commissary and get some stamps and envelopes. I'll write y'all again then. Everything is fine. Walk in the park.

Love,
Russ

Part Two

Pity the nation divided into fragments,
each fragment deeming itself a nation.

—Kahlil Gibran

CHAPTER 4

Bee Ef Eee, Texas, had a post office, a Piggly Wiggly, and a gas station. When Russell first spotted the Acirema Unit, riding downhill on the chain bus handcuffed to some dude that kept falling asleep, he couldn't help but think it looked like a really clean version of some East Coast housing project. Like on that back-in-the-day show, *The Wire,* or that old school Nas cover. The four largest buildings were perfectly square blocks of concrete. There were several smaller buildings in between, all varying in size, but all made of the same smooth, light-gray cement that skateboarders sold their souls for. The ten-foot-tall chain-link fences topped with spiraling razor wire looked brand new in the bright, midmorning sunlight and wrapped around the entire compound. Twice.

That is the right word, too. Compound. Acirema looked more like a military base than it did a prison. Russell thought of Pat Tillman. Then the old familiars crept in, too. He'd gain enough weight to play linebacker. He wouldn't have to hear that nonsense about not being able to turn and run with the receivers. He snapped back as the bus pulled inside the back gate.

All right, Russell thought, *most of these guys on this bus ain't much bigger than me... Half of them are saying this is their second time down... I won most of the fights I had as a kid... Kelvin and Jason were younger than me... but they're not White... Christ, I'm thinking like one of those White supremacists already.*

The Acirema Unit, and a dozen or so like it, were mostly built in the 1990's under the reign of governor Ann Richards. They were cookie-cutter. Identical inside and out, each holding approximately three thousand inmates. Previous Texas prisons, like the Byrd Unit, were all one long hallway with smaller bisecting "rows" three or four tiers high. Everything was contained inside the building. Chow halls, the library, et cetera. The only time an inmate went outside was for recreation or if his job required it. The modern units, like Acirema, were completely different. All the buildings were independent. There were buildings for housing, religious services, medical, and so on. To get anywhere on the unit you had to go outside. They were built this way in order to keep riots from spreading so quickly or easily. The fact that these new-styled units lead the system in riots each year, as well as in overall violence, is only a small disappointment to the politicians and administrators in Austin and Huntsville.

Russell and three others were given their housing assignments and escorted to four building by a portly, middle-aged Hispanic guard with a shiny name tag that read *E. Zamora*. The button-up jumper that Russell had worn on the Byrd Unit had been replaced by a white pullover shirt with a v-neck and white pants with an elastic waistband. The guards' uniforms were all gray with blue piping. They all wore black leather belts with handcuffs, pepper spray, and flashlights dangling from them. Not to mention the giant brass keys that chimed as they walked.

Zamora strutted proudly, greeting the officers he passed as well as a few inmates in Spanish. The sidewalks had yellow stripes on them like the hallways at the Byrd Unit. Inmates were coming and going, seemingly as they pleased, with an occasional guard screaming about staying on the "right side" of the yellow line. It was obvious Russell had just arrived, yet the hard stares he'd been expecting from the Acirema veterans weren't there. He got a quizzical glance here and there, but that was about it. None of the inmates he saw looked intimidating. A warm September breeze alerted him to the sweat on the back of his neck and on his palms.

After walking across what must have been half the unit, they arrived at four building. The inside looked a little more worn than the outside. Other than that, it was what he'd expect a modern prison to look like: concrete, steel, and plexiglass, all at right angles, everywhere he turned. The ceiling had to be thirty feet high. To the right of the front door was a cheap-looking desk; stained yellow and shaped like a horseshoe. A guard with skin as pale as Russell's sat behind the desk with his hands behind his head and leaning back in his chair. He said something to Zamora in Spanish.

In thickly accented English, Zamora asked, "Which one of you's McCann?"

Russell stepped forward. "I am, sir," he said with his hands behind his back, holding onto his only possessions: a few letters from his mom.

"You're going to F-Pod, twelve cell," Zamora pointed to the far hallway. "That's F-Pod. Twelve cell. Got it?"

Russell turned and made his way around the desk and headed for the pod, where he hoped he'd find twelve cell. He came to a stop in front of a door that was solid steel from the waist down and foggy plexiglass from the waist up. The guard at the desk behind him said, "Let the waydo in twelve." Russell looked back and saw that he was speaking into an intercom. The door in front of him rolled sideways with a mechanical whir. He took three steps forward to an identical door. As the first rolled closed, the second rolled open. He wondered if this was how it worked on submarines.

As the second door rolled open, Russell was faced with the pod's control center. Eight feet of cinder block gave way to yet more plexiglass where a dark-haired female was enclosed in a twelve-by-twelve cube watching the goings-on of the three sections of F-Pod. Russell was taking it all in, working to hide the mix of emotions. The set-up, the architecture, was like nothing he had ever seen before. The dark-haired guard looked down at Russell and pointed him to his left. He turned and saw another half-steel, half-plexiglass door rolling open. Above the door in black stencil: F-Pod 1 Section. He walked through the doorway and into the dayroom.

There were about twenty inmates standing around watching a couple of guys shadow-box, another dozen or so playing dominoes. A few people were sitting on steel benches in front of the dayroom's two TVs. It felt a little like walking into a locker room, only this one was full of running backs and defensive backs. There were only a handful of guys who could've been linemen. The cells were along the walls, with eight on each tier, for a total of twenty-four in the section. The cell doors weren't made of bars like those at Byrd. They were solid steel with two narrow slits of reinforced chicken-wire for windows. Between the windows the cell numbers were stenciled in black. Russell scanned for twelve, and found it upstairs on the second row. As he started for the stairwell in the corner, he saw a Black inmate near the crowd elbow another inmate. He felt them staring as he started up the steps.

He stood in front of twelve cell and waved at the guard in the picket. She sat in a chair eating something out of a bag, completely ignoring him. Russell peered through the grate. Nobody was home. He slid his letters under the door and headed back to the dayroom. Coming towards him were two Black inmates. They wore no shirts, and they had lots of tattoos. Wearing white shorts and white sneakers, with smiles on their faces. Russell figured they recognized his face from the TV or newspapers. *They probably saw me and Dell's picture together and know I ain't with that Nazi shit,* he thought.

They stopped about three feet from where he stood. The one on his left was short and ripped up. The letters *B.K.* tatted in Old English across his throat. *A scatback,* thought Russell. The one on the right was light-skinned and sucking his gold teeth. He had to be about six foot three. Definitely a wideout. He lifted his hands out to his sides, "Whatcha gon' do, whiteboy?" Russell stiffened. Not what he was expecting. He knew this was a challenge and that he had to accept, but he wasn't exactly sure how. Russell wanted to sound sure of himself but not overconfident. The adrenaline was doing its job. He swallowed. "If anyone wants to fight me 'cause they think I'm weak, I'll fight 'em." The scatback on the left backpedaled and said, "Catcha shower on three row."

The showers were in the middle of three row. About the size of a walk-in closet, they had small black doors that swung open and shut like the saloon doors in old Western movies. The short one slung the door open and stepped in. His entire back was covered by a tattoo of a faceless man being crucified, the words *Only God Can Judge Me* were tattooed above it. Russell wondered if he should mention that he, too, jammed that old Tupac. Probably not.

Russell swung the door open and stepped in. His opponent feigned a left. Russell raised his fists and jerked back. A hard right in his gut doubled him over and took most of his wind. Russell stumbled forward and hurled an overhand right that missed. An uppercut stood him up. A hook rocked his jaw. Russell's vision constricted into the narrowest of tunnels. He threw a right as more of a stiff arm than a punch, trying to create space. His adversary weaved right then skipped forward landing a left, then a right. The first of these landed squarely on Russell's chin; the second, on his forehead. His knees buckled. Still conscious, he started to fall forward. He reached up and grabbed his enemy's shoulders, catching himself, then driving his head into the guy's gut and pushing him into the back wall.

They locked up. Russell was getting manhandled by a guy who had to be twenty pounds lighter than him because he'd left his shirt on. They spun around, switching places and trying to land punches. Russell heard, "Say, my nigga. Dis bitch tryna wrastle." Then a voice from the door: "That White ho tryna wrastle? Strawberry blon' bitch! Do dat ho, my nigga! Break dat bitch wit dat strawberry blon' hur."

Russell had come out of his daze. Punches were coming hard and fast from east and west, pummeling his ears and temples. Russell sprang up at the waist and hammered down with his forearms, striking his opponent in the crooks of his elbows. He chucked a right that landed on a cheekbone. Then a left that glanced off of the guy's forehead as he weaved to Russell's left. Russell saw black with flashes of white light as what he figured were punches landed. His knees buckled again. He felt himself collapsing in a heap, his ass slamming into his heels.

Russell snapped back into consciousness as his head bounced off of the concrete wall. He looked up. Standing over him was a blurry version of his opponent hollering, "You gon ride? You gon ride? Bitch, is you gon ride?" Russell stared, trying to process, unable to answer the question even if he wanted to. A strange voice came from the dayroom: "Een an oww." Then the familiar voice from the door, "There go the law, C-Life. He doin' an in-and-out."

C-Life turned and slipped out of the shower and said over his shoulder, "We ain't done, ho." Russell felt around his face. His jaw wasn't broken and he was pretty sure he wasn't bleeding. He tried to stand but crashed into the wall, his equilibrium not back to normal yet. He rested on a knee for a second, blinked his eyes, and tried to catch his breath. He could hear cell doors slamming shut. He knew he had to make it down to two row, twelve cell. He reached out wide and braced himself against the walls, got to his feet, and lumbered out of the shower.

Russell exhaled as the door locked behind him. He stepped up to a mirror that belonged in a carnival funhouse, and assessed the damage. Red marks here and there, especially on his ears, and a swollen jaw. He stared. A seething voice came from the door, "See yo' bitch ass went in the house. You know what it is when this doe roll." Russell turned and looked as C-Life walked away.

Russell stood there. He had no idea what to do or say. He wasn't going to cry uncle, but depending on when that door opened again, he might not be able to defend himself for very long. He sat down on a stool that was bolted to the floor. He looked around the cell. It was a lot bigger than the one at Byrd Unit, with the bunks running across the back wall instead of from front to back. There were pictures of half-naked women on every wall. Some of them had the oddest of things strategically placed on their bodies, probably to get past the mailroom censors. IceT's wife, Coco, seemed to be featured the most. Russell continued looking. Maybe there was something he could make a weapon out of.

He stood and looked in the mirror again. The swelling was getting worse. He didn't know what to think. He'd won the few fights he'd been in up to this point in his life. He and his opponent standing toe-to-toe, swinging until someone folded up. But this C-Life wouldn't stand still, and he seemed to know ahead of time when and where Russell was going to punch.

A female voice came through a speaker outside the cell. "Twelve top, McCann. They want you up front."

Not good. No way these guards would miss his face. He wasn't sure, but from what he'd gathered during his short stay in the county and from talking to Nelson, getting a disciplinary case for fighting would affect his chances at parole.

The door rolled, and Russell stepped out onto the walkway. Down in the dayroom the section door was opening. A male guard walked through, looked up at him, and said, "You twelve top? McCann?" Russell nodded and headed for the stairwell, pretty sure the welcoming committee from earlier wasn't going to do anything with the guard standing right there.

"Go to one building for... hey, what happened to your face?" the guard asked as Russell slid by him and out the door heading for this one building. Wherever the hell it was.

The pale guard at the desk was cramming tortilla chips in his face. With his mouth full, he said, "What happened, waydo? They want your chooz?" Russell looked down at his retro Jordans and deliberated. *Should I tell this guy anything?* he thought. *It might be snitchin'; better not.* Russell pointed at the guard coming from F-Pod. "He said go to one building. Where's it at?"

"Go towards the shou hall." Russell didn't know where the chow hall was, but he was ready to try and find it.

CHAPTER 5

ussell stepped into a small white room with a low ceiling and bright fluorescent lighting. A large guard with two stars—or were they flowers?—pinned to the collars of his starched uniform sat between two women who looked like politicians behind an uneven table made of particleboard. An irritated voice said, "McCann?"

"Yessir," replied Russell.

"Sit. I'm Major Robledo."

The major was built like a lineman—a short lineman. He was fat but solid through the arms and shoulders, or maybe his shirt was just real tight. Russell recognized the look on his face immediately. It was the emperor with unchecked power, the same look he saw on the faces of the few bad football coaches he'd had. The women were both thirtyish and overdressed. They each wore expensive-looking pantsuits. One had fake eyelashes, the other penciled-in eyebrows. They both had fake nails.

The women were writing in earnest on some forms; neither had looked up at Russell yet. The major folded his arms and said, "This is your assigned unit. You're about to be given a handbook. You must learn it. Miss De La Garza, does he have any medical restrictions?"

"No. None," she said, still looking down at the form she was filling out.

"Miss Torres, make him an SSI. McCann, you're a Line One with no disciplinary. You're gonna be on minimum custody. Any questions? No? Good." The entire time the major had been staring at Russell's face without even the slightest acknowledgement of anything being wrong with it.

Torres looked up. A pained expression came across her face. She unwound a finger and pointed it at Russell, palm up, revealing a tattoo of the star from the state's seal on the inside of her wrist. "What happened to your face?" she asked. De La Garza looked up and recoiled, the look on her face equal parts disgust and embarrassment, like she'd witnessed a crime but wanted to move on without being bothered about it.

Russell slid his jaw forward, then back. "Uh," pain drummed his head.

The major frowned. "Who beat you up, waydo?" as if he was frustrated he had to waste his breath. *And what is this waydo shit?*

Russell looked down and said, "I slipped and fell in the shower." Torres sat back, frowning, and folded her arms.

Robledo said, "Are you going to continue to fall down?" Russell folded his arms and spread his legs a little wider. Robledo cocked his head to the side, his frown stretching. "Go pack your shit, waydo. You're moving to another pod. Hopefully, they won't beat you up over there."

Russell stood before the one section door on D-Pod, clutching his letters. Déjà vu. His head had swollen even more over the last hour or so, and he was actually wondering if he could be beaten to death. He imagined the headlines: "School Shooting Hero McCann Killed First Day of Incarceration." He liked that word *hero*.

Russell took a deep breath. His head throbbed. The door opened. He headed up the stairs to three row, twenty-one cell. Everything looked identical to F-Pod, the architecture and the inmates. Russell slid his letters under the door and turned around. Coming from the stairwell was a stocky Hispanic, or maybe a tan White guy. Broad shoulders, thick traps and arms. Tats everywhere. *A fullback,* Russell thought, *probably not that quick.*

"'Sup, dude? They call me Itchy Foot." He extended his hand. Russell shook it, remembering at the last second not to dead-fish it.

"'Sup, man," said Russell. "McCann."

"You get into it with somebody?"

"Yeah, man. Two guys asked me what was I gonna do. We went and fought in the shower. Fool was—"

"You got cliqued on?" asked Itchy Foot, his face screwing up. Russell had heard the word *cliqued* before in the county.

Russell said, "You mean—"

"Did they jump on you at the same time?"

"Nah." Russell shook his head. "I fought one in the shower while the other one stood outside."

"Who was the dude? Was it a tode? Was he Black?"

"Yeah, he was Black."

"Where was this?" asked Itchy Foot, clasping his hands behind his back.

"Uh, F-Pod."

"F-Pod? What section?"

"One."

Itchy Foot shuffled his feet and leaned in, all energy. "You don't know the dude's name?"

"I think they called him C-Life." Itchy Foot closed his eyes and dropped his head for a beat.

Itchy Foot asked, "Real cut-up tode? B.K. on his throat?"

"Yeah, pretty sure that's him," said Russell.

Itchy Foot's eyes narrowed. "Fuckin' piece a shit Crip from Dallas. I was on Beto with him." Itchy Foot studied Russell's face. "You sure you didn't do anything to disrespect him?"

"I was standing in front of my door, just like this," said Russell, lifting his arms.

"Come down to the dayroom, dude. They're not supposed to be trippin' like that." Itchy Foot turned for the stairs. Russell followed.

In the back of the dayroom about fifty feet from the door Russell had just walked through was a heavily barred window about five feet from the floor. In front of it were three White convicts. Two of them had their backs against the wall, the other stood facing them.

Itchy Foot said, "Lookout, y'all. This dude just got here. What's your name, dude?"

"McCann."

"Right. McCann. McCann, this is Big Body Slim, Youngbuck, and Slim Jesus." The last name threw Russell for a loop, but he didn't say anything. Big Body Slim grinned and said, "Name's Wallace." Youngbuck was giving Russell the once-over. Slim Jesus kept his head down, reading a large book.

Big Body Slim was exactly what Russell expected a White guy in prison to look like—Mr. Clean with tattoos. A little over six foot, he was keg-chested and had to be every bit of 240. *A linebacker,* thought Russell. *Probably in his mid-thirties.*

Youngbuck was a couple of inches shorter than Russell with impossibly broad shoulders. *A running back,* Russell thought. His chest and delts were covered with tats, and his brown hair was cut in a bald fade like Russell's. Despite his name, he didn't look much younger than the big one.

Itchy Foot said, "Dude claims C-Life just dry-tripped with him. They got their paper in the shower."

Slim Jesus jerked his head up and came off the wall. He was several inches taller than the others, and his name fit better. He looked like he'd just got done working out. Shrink-wrapped skin covering square muscles and thick veins in his arms. He had tats on his delts and the words *Blue-Eyed Devil* on his left pec, though his eyes looked a little more gray than blue. It was hard to tell. They were small and deep-set. Combined with the board-straight eyebrows above them, they made for the hardest stare Russell'd ever seen.

Russell gave them all the run down. When he finished, they all shook their heads. In a soft baritone, Slim Jesus said, "What was Stallion doing?" Russell shook his head slowly, confused.

"Shit," said Big Body Slim. "Stallion ain't no 'wood. Told me he ain't even White. Said he's an eye-talian."

"Aw, fuck," said Youngbuck. "When we was the only two honkies on L-Pod and they was stealing shit left and right, he was a 'wood. That ho-ass bitch."

Slim Jesus said, "Y'all know how that goes. Got over here and didn't want the responsibility. Convenience 'wood, not a peckerwood."

Russell was pretty sure he hadn't done anything wrong. Whatever the problem was, he felt almost certain he wasn't going to have to fight anyone else that day. Slim Jesus shook his head and rubbed his eyes. 'What's your name, kid?" Russell didn't know what to make of the *kid*. Slim Jesus didn't look much older than him.

Russell widened his stance, "McCann."

Slim Jesus said, "Check this out, McCann. We need to holler at everybody, all the other 'woods on the building, about this. If they call noon rec tomorrow, be ready to fall to the yard. See what's up." Still confused, Russell nodded his head anyway. Slim Jesus nodded at him and the others, then leaned back against the wall. Youngbuck and Big Body Slim edged closer to him.

Itchy Foot said, "Come on, dude. You play Moon? Forty-two?"

"Nah," Russell said, "I'm not that good at dominoes."

Itchy Foot raised his eyebrows, "Oh... uh—let's gamble then." He smiled and clapped Russell on the back. They came to a table where three Whites and one Hispanic were playing bones. Itchy Foot pointed, "That's Larson. He's a foreigner. From Arizona or California, he can't decide." Larson set down the dominoes he held in his right hand and extended his middle finger to Itchy Foot without taking his eyes off of the action. Itchy Foot pointed again. "That's Jew Boy... he's a real Jew. You know they own the media, right?" Jew Boy snorted and looked up at Russell. "No, *I* own the media." He had a Star of David tattoo covering his left pec, just like the White guy in that Tupac movie *Bullet*. "That's O.T. She stockpiles hemorrhoid cream, foot cream, and some young man cream, so you better watch out." The old timer had a tree trunk for a neck. He said to Itchy Foot, "If I's younger, I'd cream your face."

Itchy Foot backhanded Russell's shoulder. "See whatta mean? She's a freaky old thang." Russell swallowed. Itchy Foot pointed, "And that's Stain Wood right there, that's Campos. We let him come and visit from the barrio every now and then." The middle-aged Hispanic man smiled. He had a pair of praying hands tattooed on the left side of his neck. He set his bones down, grabbed one and flipped it over, then flicked it to the middle of the table. "I come to take you *cavachos*' money. I tole you, Mexicans won't gamble me no more." Larson looked up at Russell. "You been squabbling somebody, youngster?" He had curly hair and a little muscle to him. Kind of like a swimmer.

Russell stared at the table, hands behind his back. "Yeah," he said, "I had to catch the shower on three row." Russell impressed himself with that one, the lingo flowing naturally.

Itchy Foot said, "I'll run it down to y'all later."

Russell sat down with Itchy Foot on a steel bench against the wall. Russell said, "That guy calls himself Slim Jesus?"

Itchy Foot chuckled. "Yeah. Only he spells it G, that line deal? Z, U, S." Russell nodded once, not sure if a different spelling made it okay. "Slim G-Zus got the hoe squad to lay it down—that's refuse to work. Somebody said he was tryna be the Savior. It's a long story. He's been gone about fifteen years, since he was nineteen." Russell looked at the trio by the window. Slim G-Zus was talking with his hands, gesturing excitedly, as the other two nodded their heads.

Itchy Foot pointed to a table where two Black inmates were playing chess. "That's your celly. The bald-headed one. Goes by Adisa. He's real smart and shit. Fucks with Slim G-Zus real tough. They mess with the stock market. He's a Muslim, but not the kind that hates honkies." Russell looked. The guy was about his size. Probably in his thirties.

Itchy Foot sat cracking his knuckles, his left foot sliding back and forth. Russell figured that must be where his nickname came from. Russell rubbed on his jaw, opened and closed his mouth, and took in the scene. Itchy Foot said, "See 'em two on the wall between seven and eight cell?"

Russell leaned left, "Yeah."

"That's Damn Fool and Yella Fella. Two biggest pieces a shit in here. Yella thinks his shit don't stink 'cause he's from Louisiana. Damn Fool's a booty bandit. Yella probably is, too. Birds of a feather, ya know whatta mean? They're not gonna fuck with you, they see you with us. Try and stay away from 'em anyway."

Russell wasn't here to make friends, but he knew how Whites stereotyped Blacks as thugs and predators all too often. His sociology teacher at Football Factory Junior College once showed the class a video where people were placed in a simulator that mimicked the conditions cops often faced when pursuing suspects. The people in the experiment were given a gun and told to shoot at unfriendlies. The results showed that images of Blacks were more likely to be fired upon than any other. It hit home with Russell. Made him think about Dell, Terrance, and Demetrius. Then, to add insult to injury, some White dude went to saying that since the Black participants were just as likely to shoot at the images of Blacks as the Whites had been, racism or bias by the Whites couldn't be to blame. That it was the high crime rates of Blacks that made the participants shoot at the Black images more often. Russell was embarrassed. Luckily the teacher dressed the guy down. Told him something about checking his privilege, and didn't let him talk anymore.

Russell knew where he was, though, and knew who he was dealing with. He didn't say anything back to Itchy Foot. Just looked at the two bogeymen. The big one was a defensive lineman. The other, who looked like an angry Nelly, was an every-down back. Arian Foster.

CHAPTER 6

R ussell was ready to be locked in a concrete and steel cage when the guard came in at 10:30 p.m. and hollered, "Rack up." He was relieved to hear the door close and lock behind him, knowing it wouldn't open again until breakfast. His new cell seemed cleaner than the one on F-Pod. There were books neatly stacked on the corner of the desk and on one of the shelves above it. Instead of a collage of naked women, the walls had a Houston Texans calendar and a page from a newspaper that read *Investor's Business Daily's Ten Steps to Success.*

His cellmate was down on a knee, shuffling newspapers and folders that were on his bottom bunk. He sat down on a cleared space, interlocked his fingers in his lap, and smiled. Russell was still standing by the door when Adisa said, "What's up youngster? Slim G-Zus told me you had some trouble on F-Pod." His face had the kind of round features that, regardless of the expression it dialed up, were incapable of leaving behind creases or wrinkles. He looked young but had the body of an older man. Not fat, not skinny, perfectly average. Russell couldn't see him fielding a position. Maybe a punter.

Russell said, "Yeah, man," and rubbed his jaw.

Adisa said, "Slim G-Zus told me it was a Crip." Russell nodded. Adisa shook his head and mumbled something about gang members.

"What they call you?"

"McCann."

"McCann, huh?"

"Yeah."

"My name is Adisa."

Russell squinted his eyes, "Uh-*dee*-sel? Like Vin Diesel?"

"Nah. Uh-*dee*-suh. Adisa."

"Oh," said Russell, still not ready to try it again. Adisa just smiled and nodded his head. He couldn't have been more laid back. Russell hoped this wasn't too good to be true.

"Where you from?"

"Houston."

"Where 'bout?"

"Northside. Off Aldine Westfield."

"Oh, okay." Another smile and more head nodding. "I'm from Hiram Clark."

"Oh, yeah? Vince Young's hood, huh?"

"That's right. Man, I sure wanted the Texans to draft him."

"Yeah, me too. Whole city did. But they were right. Mario was better."

"This your first unit?"

Russell nodded, "Yeah. Just got here today."

"You gotta bunch of time?"

"Yeah. Three years."

Adisa's smile widened before he hung his head and laughed. "You think three years is a lot of time?"

Russell sat down on the toilet. "I'll be twenty 'fore long." Russell turned his hands palm up. "If I do the whole three that'd be thirty percent of my twenny's." Russell shrugged.

Adisa looked up and tilted his head, "Hmm... Well, I've been down here since I was twenty. I'm thirty-nine now." Russell stared, clenching his jaw. "So I've done your entire sentence, day for day, almost seven times now." Adisa said this without a grain of malice, just a statement of fact. Russell raised his eyebrows. "How much time you got?"

"I had a ninety-nine with a fifty stacked when I came down. I gave the fifty back—you used to could get cases overturned back in the day. Anyway, I came up on the ninety-nine four years ago, gave me a three-year set-off. Came up again, got a two-year set-off."

"Why'd they give you set-offs?"

"Oh," Adisa closed his eyes and shook his head. "That parole board's somethin' serious. They gave me two 'nature of the offences'— even though their own rules say they can't do that."

"Do what?" asked Russell.

"Set you off for the same thing twice."

Russell didn't like the sound of that. He rubbed his jaw.

Adisa said, "I got some non-aspirin Tylenol. Want some?"

"Yeah, man. I guess I better." Adisa took a white plastic mug off of the shelf and dumped its contents on the desk. A couple of well-worn erasers and a pencil sharpener fell among a dozen or so white packets of pain reliever. Adisa slid two packets toward Russell. "There ya go. It's two in each one."

"Thanks."

Adisa said, "I noticed you didn't have anything. No commissary or nothing. I gotta extra tube of toothpaste and some soap. You can use my shower slides."

Russell tossed two Tylenol in his mouth and hit the button for the water, which came out with the weak pressure of a city water fountain.

"This is a pretty good unit," said Adisa. "They don't sweat too much. Most of the pigs are real lazy. Cuts both ways." Adisa shrugged. "You can get away with a lot, but they also don't do the in-and-outs on time, and it takes 'em forever to clear count."

Russell said, "Do they have college here?"

"Yeah. First two years. You can get an Associates."

"How do you get enrolled or whatever?"

"Put in an I-60 to education." Adisa opened the locker beneath him, took out a piece of paper the size of a greeting card, and handed it to Russell. He explained how to fill it out and handed Russell a pen.

Adisa said, "You goin' to breakfast?"

"Yeah. What time do they run it?"

"Anywhere between 2:30 a.m. and 4:30 a.m."

Russell exhaled. "I was hoping they only did that at Byrd. Makes it hard to get some sleep. Let your muscles recover."

Adisa grinned. "Yeah, I filed a sleep-deprivation lawsuit on 'em years ago, but it didn't go nowhere." Adisa pointed, "Put that I-60 in the education box when we go to breakfast. S'right next to the mail box."

"All right. Thanks." Russell nodded at the Houston Texans calendar on the wall. "You like them Texans, huh?"

"Most definitely. I think this is the year."

"Yeah. I thought when they got Ed Reed that would put them over the top. Didn't exactly go down how I figured."

"Yeah, man, last year was rough." Adisa scooted forward to the edge of his bunk. "You know what I really wanna see?" Russell lifted his chin. Adisa grinned and said, "I wanna see the Rockets, Texans, and Astros all win a championship in the same year."

Russell cocked his head and half smiled "Yeah, that would be nice. Dwight Howard and them might. I think it'll be awhile for the Astros though." Adisa conceded as much, reluctantly nodding his head.

Adisa said, "I gotta type a couple of motions I drafted earlier so I can send them out in the morning. You don't need the desk, do you?"

"Nah," said Russell.

Adisa pulled a clear plastic typewriter out from under his bunk and laid it on the desk. "I got some sports pages from the *Chronicle*. Wanna check 'em out?"

"Yeah," said Russell.

Adisa pointed to his bunk as he sat down at the desk. "That's Saturday, Sunday, and Monday right there. Slim G-Zus's mom mails 'em. Subscription down here'll cost you like four hundred bucks to have it delivered. You can sit on my bunk."

Russell inhaled deeply as he stood and took a seat on the bottom bunk. The tension was fading. Adisa seemed like a normal guy, certainly more normal than the Whites he'd met in the dayroom. And now he had a *Chronicle* sports page in his hand. A large picture of J. J. Watt, head back, screaming with his arms flexed was under the headline "Raiders Wonder WATT Hit Them." A day that couldn't have started much worse had now come to a decent end.

CHAPTER 7

I had just heard they whipped a ho-ass whiteboy down there on F-Pod when they moved the bitch in twenty-one cell. It took me a minute but I snapped. He's the one all them Rush Limbaugh hoes been crowing about on the radio like he's some kinda hero. He came in here sporting a bald fade, stealing our shit, trying to be like us. I seen him and that Black-ass oreo nigga he had with him in the newspaper. I can't believe they put that ho on this unit. And as soon as he came through the door, a Crip nigga got right on his ass.

They call me Yella Fella. I came over from the Boot during Katrina. I started out in H-Town but moved to Dallas. I had me a White bitch getting scripts, boosting shit, and whatnot. I was about to have that ho trickin' when a law man got in my business. I shot that ho four times but he lived. The nigga that was with me signed a record deal and went Mariah Carey on my ass. I ended up coppin' for a sixty piece on attempted capital murder of a peace officer. I come up in eighteen years. I'll be fifty-one, but I ain't trippin'. Long as I keep my body like it is, I'll always have a bad ho. I can get a woman when I can't get nothing else.

It's fucked-up how much time they gave me. If I'd have been a whiteboy and murdered fifty people like that one in Colorado, they'd have said, "Oh, he's crazy. He had a bad childhood. We'll just send him to the crazy house." But every nigga in here had a worse childhood than any bitch-ass whiteboy. I hardly ever had my pops around. They locked him up so much I just thought prison was where Black men ended up. My moms got hooked on drugs Ronald Reagan put in my community. Then they took away the midnight basketball, supposedly to save money, but really so niggas would start trippin' and get locked up. They used the same M.O. when it came to the levies in my city. The army engineers half-assed their construction, supposedly because of the budget. On the real side, though, they just wanted niggas to drown. That's how Amerikkka works.

Think about this: I'm in here for shooting a motherfucker that got in my business. The fool didn't even die. George Bush bombs a million people for getting in the US's way—or really having some oil he wanted—and what does he get? Prison? Hell, no. He gets reelected. He blew up Iraq, Afghanistan, everywhere they don't accept Bush's religion and banking system. As you can see, I'm not one of them niggas who spends all his time watching them forty-million-dollar slaves run around on TV, chasing a ball for these White folks' entertainment. And that's not hatin' on a nigga that's getting paid. I'm just saying, I see through all this shit they use to keep a nigga pacified. I'm concerned with the least among us. The most disgruntled.

I have knowledge of self, and I study. If you do your research and learn why the world looks like it does, you can get yourself out of the bubble. You got to learn why it all happened. It started with White supremacy. When the White man crawled out of his cave and started going around stealing all the cultures. That's what Thanks-giving really commemorates. White people can't create things on their own. That's why you hear Rush Limbaugh saying "shout out," a hip-hop phrase created by us, like all music and language were, and you see Nike making their shorts long. Whites always wore short shorts because most of their culture comes from Greece, which was a bunch of faggots. Niggas, the original man, got everybody wearing long shorts, headbands, all that shit. We're the natural leaders of mankind.

When they found the Indians, they didn't enslave them. They just took everything they had and went to killing the ones who resisted. When they came to Africa, they invented slavery because they saw how superior we were and knew they could get rich off of us. It's right there in William Easterly's *White Man's Burden*. When they first saw the Indians naked, they didn't trip. When they saw us naked, they got scared because they knew they couldn't compete with us. Michael Moore, about the only whiteboy I got any respect for, even made a cartoon about this. I seen it on Oprah back in the day. Moore's got a book called *Stupid White Men* that's pretty good. It says all White folks should breed with non-Whites so they'll take themselves out of the gene pool, like a voluntary genocide. I can do White hoes, and you know they love niggas, but I don't think we need Yacub's devils mixing with us. They're all wicked and weak.

Speaking of White hoes, that Mobb Deep nigga Prodigy got strained up by the laws in New York because Nicole Kidman and Linsey Lohan was trying to fuck him. The bitch-ass detective told Prodigy he was sick of seeing White girls go to rap concerts and fuck niggas. So he was trying to lock us all up because they can't compete with us. It's all in Prodigy's book, *My Infamous Life*. Like a lot of rap niggas, JayZ, Nelly, Ice Cube, Prodigy's got that knowledge. He's read Dr. York, Minister Farrakhan, all that there.

So these whiteboys can't enslave us no more, because they know we'd go Nat Turner on that ass, and because they make just as much money off us as athletes and musicians. So they created the prison industrial complex to keep us from competing with them. If you can make them some money, like Allen Iverson or Tupac (R.I.P.), they'll get you out. But, if you just an everyday street nigga, the penitentiary is your home. They built it for us. You got to read Michelle Alexander's *The New Jim Crow*. In it, she tells you that the first inmate in the Federal pen was a nigga. And she's a law professor at Ohio State University, so you know she knows her shit.

Inventing the penitentiary for us, just like they invented slavery, wasn't enough. They saw Wilt Chamberlain and Rick James fucking all them White hoes and knew they couldn't compete. So they created the war on drugs. Michelle Alexander can't give you the details raw and uncut like I just did because she's in the public eye at Ohio State. So she says, basically, the White supremacists who came up with slavery and Jim Crow came up with the war on drugs because they needed a system that would hold us down without looking racist from the outside. And that's all true. But when dealing with devils, the devil is in the details. Specifically, it's whiteboys being scared of niggas taking all they hoes. Notice I been saying whiteboys. White girls have always helped us. Even today,

Hillary Clinton admits the justice system is racist. I guarantee you she done fucked with some niggas.

President Obama, who a lotta niggas say is Tommin' (he ain't), has tried to point this out, but he can only go so far. Them whiteboys will kill his ass if he tells it how it really is. But he had the nuts to say there's Scooter Libby justice for some (whiteboys), and Jena justice for others (Blacks). The problem is, the system's so entrenched, even he can't do much about it. At least not directly. He's letting all them pyahs stay because, eventually, they'll all be able to vote, and they're going to vote Democrat. That's a long-term strategy, but it'll work.

If you doubt they made the prison system to keep us from taking over, think about this: Africa was all Black and it never had one penitentiary. Not one. Which tells me, this shit in Amerikkka—having all these prisons packed with Blacks—ain't our fault. It's the system. We only make up 13 percent of the population, but everywhere I look in here it's majority Black. That's by design.

In Africa, we had everything we needed. We were a communal people. We had large families with multiple wives because that's how kings live. If not for the system and whiteboys making laws to keep us from marrying more than one woman (most whiteboys can't even satisfy one female) we'd have been done out-populated them. But they destroyed our families by locking us up and forcing us to live a European lifestyle of monogamy.

All this shit's been going on for four hundred years. That's why, on most units, every whiteboy coming through that door gets beat the fuck down. And when a nigga breaks one of them hoes, that's that nigga's property. He gets whatever that whiteboy's got. Including that booty. You got some booty bandit niggas in here love takin' that White booty. I done been knee deep in some ass, but I ain't really out there like that right now. I'm chillin'.

This unit's fucked up. They been letting these whiteboys make it. When I first got here from Cofield, I asked these niggas, "Why don't y'all smash these whiteboys when they pull up?" And they was like, "Yeah, Yella, ain't nobody really trippin' like that 'cause it'll start some shit." Like these whiteboys ain't trying to hear it. We outnumber them hoes like, five-to-one. Let them start some shit.

But that nigga C-Life come from Clemons, where they check all the whiteboys and make the ones who get broke ride with the nigga that broke them. I heard he dropped that ho, but they didn't get to finish. I hope C-Life pushes the issue. If he breaks that ho, I'll pay him whatever he wants to have that ho in my cell for a night. Niggas got cellphones galore around here. Female guards pack them in they pussies and sell them for about five hundy. I'll get one with a camera on it and film that whiteboy getting dicked down by somebody like my nigga Damn Fool. You'd have to be careful not to show too much because they could identify a nigga butt, man. Have that whiteboys face on YouTube? While he's taking the meat like a champ? "Here's your hero Amerikkka!" But that'd be too much like right. Hey, a nigga can dream though. A nigga can dream.

CHAPTER 8

Russell held his hands out to the side, a little uncomfortable, as the guard performed a pat search. He stepped outside onto the four building rec yard and began eyeing the cluster of machine weights next to the chain-link fence. There was a bench press, a military press, leg press, and separate cable pulleys: one high with a wide bar for lat pull-downs and one low for curls or rows. There was also a dip and pull-up bar. Not bad. Nowhere near as good as free weights, but it would have to do. To his right was the basketball court: two baskets without nets, and an aluminum canopy shielding it from the sun. Past the court was a patch of grass and dirt with a sagging volleyball net staked in it.

Straight ahead, about fifteen yards past the weight pile, was a concrete wall that had to be every bit of thirty feet tall. There was about a dozen inmates, White and Hispanic, standing around throwing a couple of blue racquet balls against it and then slapping the ball with their hands back into the wall. Russell scanned the yard. Pretty much everybody was in color-coded groups, just like the dayroom. The whole thing was about half the size of a football field. Between the handball court and the weights stood Slim G-Zus, Big Body Slim, and some other Whites Russell figured lived on E- or F-Pod. He headed that way.

The guy Slim G-Zus seemed to be most engaged with turned to Russell as soon as he arrived. "This him?" he asked in the thickest east Texas drawl Russell had ever heard, and that was saying something, considering his dad's side of the family was from Orange, outside of Beaumont. Slim G-Zus said, "Yeah, that's him. Hey, kid, this's Sidewinder. Lives down there on F-Pod, three section."

Sidewinder grinned and extended a thick paw. "Hey boy," he said. Russell shook his hand firmly and said, "McCann."

Sidewinder was built like a fire hydrant. Maybe five feet seven inches and every bit of 220 pounds. *A one-cut, downhill back,* Russell thought. Sidewinder had some tribal tattoos on his chest and shoulders that kind of looked like knife blades, and a dark head of hair just long enough to be combed and parted.

Slim G-Zus pointed. "This is Ogre. He's on E-Pod." A tall burly guy wearing a white t-shirt with red suspenders painted on it gave Russell the once over before extending his hand. Russell gripped it and nodded once. "They cut for the 'woodpile 'cause they prospect from it. So even though you ain't one of his bros, he's out here gettin' the run down. Lotta times when it's racial shit, the 'woods and families come together." Russell nodded, pretty sure he understood all that.

Big Body Slim stood with his arms folded, looking on through a pair of all black Oakley sunglasses. Slim G-Zus thumbed left. "That's Walker and Squirrel. They're over there with Sidewinder, F-3." Russell shook their hands. Walker looked like he was in his thirties. Average-sized with a little muscle tone, like he did a bunch of push ups. He had *1488* tatted on his right pec, an angry-looking eagle on his left. Squirrel was short and ripped up, like an Olympic gymnast, only covered in ink.

Slim G-Zus stepped back, peering over all their heads. "Lookout, Young," he hollered. Russell turned to look, startled. Youngbuck jogged over from the handball court. Russell was going to have to get used to the word "lookout" being substituted for "hey" when trying to get someone's attention. Youngbuck put his arm around Sidewinder and mocked his drawl, "'Ay, Boyz."

Slim G-Zus said, "Itchy and Jew Boy got stuck?"

Youngbuck said, "That bitch Alvarez running the kitchen today. Makin 'em stay till after count." Slim G-Zus frowned and looked away.

"Alright, y'all," said Slim G-Zus, "check this out. Now that everybody knows what went down with this kid, we gotta make some decisions. I see Stallion's ho-ass didn't even come out, so he knows what time it is. Somebody said he ain't claiming 'wood, but that's bullshit."

"Hell, yeah, that's bullshit," said Youngbuck.

"He just don't wanna fade the heat. What we gotta figure out is, after we smash Stallion, what are we gonna do with C-Life? He's Black, he's a Crip, they outnumber us two-to-one, blah the fuck blah." Slim G-Zus nodded towards Sidewinder and Walker. "Y'all are down there. Maybe one a y'all takes Stallion, one of us takes C-Life. Regardless, I can't see lettin' this slide. We need to make an example outta both them hoes."

Russell looked to his right. There was a large group of Black inmates standing in a circle on the small patch of grass by the volleyball net. He saw C-Life and the other one from the day before, standing next to each other.

Sidewinder said, "They're gonna try and say it was a one-on-one, 'this is the penitentiary,' all that there."

Slim G-Zus shook his head, Big Body Slim said, "I'm with Slim. Can't let 'em get away with it."

Walker said, "Me and C-Life's about the same size. Why don't we tell whoever his O.G. is, I wanna one-on-one with him, 'cause they dry-tripped. If they can do it, so can we."

Slim G-Zus nodded. "Right," he said. "Let's go try that out. They're all over there, pow-wowing too. Say, Young, who's C-Life's O.G.?"

"Murder Worth," said Youngbuck.

"That's right," said Slim G-Zus, nodding his head and pursing his lips. "Yeah, let's go see what's up. C'mon, Walker."

Youngbuck said, "I'ma roll with y'all."

"Yeah, so am I," said Big Body Slim.

"Nah," said Slim G-Zus. "y'all stay here. Just keep an eye on us."

Russell was aware no one had asked him anything, and it didn't bother him that much. He watched Slim G-Zus and Walker stride across the yard. They stopped at the edge of the grass. Slim G-Zus said something and C-Life came away from the circle in an all-business strut. A guy about the size of Big Body Slim, sporting as much of an afro as TDC probably allowed, followed close behind. Russell turned to Youngbuck and asked, "Guess the big one's Murder Worth, huh?" Youngbuck spat and nodded his head once.

Their conversation didn't last long. Slim G-Zus and Walker were heading back now. Slim G-Zus looked seven feet tall with his perfect posture and chest stuck out. *Must've went okay*, Russell thought.

Walker looked at Sidewinder and shook his head. Slim G-Zus stepped to Russell. "Did you fold up in that shower?"

Russell blinked, then glanced at the others. Disapproval on every face. "What do you mean?" asked Russell. Squirrel dropped his head, then shook it. Sidewinder frowned, exhaling through his nose, his brow knitted up.

Slim G-Zus widened his stance and raised his voice. "Did you give up? Did you quit swinging?"

"Nah," said Russell, his chest tightening.

"He's tryna say he broke you and you're Crip property."

Russell lost his breath. His heart punched his rib cage like a battering ram. He stepped back involuntarily and looked toward the mob on the grass.

Big Body Slim asked, "Did he drop you?"

Russell said, "Yeah, but..." He felt more helpless now, trying to defend himself with words, than he had the day before using his fists.

Slim G-Zus said, "What'd you do when he dropped you?"

"He left."

"He left?" asked Slim G-Zus.

"Yeah. One at the door said the guard was coming to let people in and out, and he left out the shower."

"At no point did you say, 'Alright,' or some shit like that?"

"No. Hell no. I..." Russell shook his head, bewildered, unsure of himself, wondering if maybe he did cry uncle.

Slim G-Zus looked at the others then back at Russell, his brow pinching, those grey-blue eyes burning a hole through Russell's face. He exhaled sharply. "Shit shoulda never happened anyway."

Sidewinder stepped to Russell, "S'gonna be awright, li'l dawg. We ain't gonna throw ya to the wolves."

Slim G-Zus said, "You willing to fight him again, right?" Russell's heart and pride wanted to answer that question with a "Hell, yeah!" but his brain informed them it didn't have a new plan that would lead to a different outcome. Still, Russell said, "Yeah, I'll fight him again," heart and pride winning a two-to-one vote over brain.

"Alright, then," said Slim G-Zus. "Check this out, potna. I'ma tell 'em you need a few days to heal up. And that if C-Life wants to finish that, he's gotta fall outta place to do it. You ain't going down there or fighting him out here where you can get caught. He's gotta come to us on D-Pod." Slim G-Zus turned and spat. "We're gonna tell 'em he was in the wrong, okay? But if they don't accept that—and they probably won't—you may have to fight him again, alright?" Russell nodded.

Slim G-Zus looked at the others. "We drawin' straws on smashing Stallion or what?"

"No. I got him," said Walker.

Squirrel reached up and rested his hand on Walker's shoulder. "I'll go with him," he said. Slim G-Zus looked at them and nodded a couple of times. "Alright, then." He turned to Russell. "Let's go tell ol' boy the bidness."

C-Life and Murder Worth peeled away from the hive as they approached. Slim G-Zus mumbled something about Yella Fella being a shit starter. "He ain't even a Crip."

Slim G-Zus stood opposite Murder Worth, Russell opposite C-Life. Slim G-Zus said, "Kid says he ain't fold. That the law came in for an in-and-out," he gestured to C-Life, "and he left out the shower."

Murder Worth was a couple inches shorter than Slim G-Zus, and about fifty pounds heavier. He had three teardrops tattooed on the right side of his acne-scarred face and *MURDER WORTH* on the right side of his neck.

C-Life shot Russell an enraged look that said, "I know you didn't." Russell met his stare with everything he had, narrowing his eyes and sticking his chin out defiantly. C-Life said, "Where was you when I left?"

Russell answered, "On the ground."

C-Life raised his arms, an *I told you so* expression on his face, as he turned to Murder Worth.

Slim G-Zus said, "He wasn't through with it. He was gonna keep going, but the law—"

"Keep going?" snapped C-Life, eyes bulging.

"—but the law came in and you left."

C-Life leaned towards Russell, "What was you gon do?"

"I wasn't gonna quit—"

"Getcha ass beat some more, whiteboy?"

"I'm not afraid of you," said Russell. It was all he could think of.

C-Life leaned in closer, twisting his head, "You ain't afraid of me?"

I'm sitting here watching these two ho-ass whiteboys try to look hard, and I'm thinking, *look at all these niggas out here. It ain't but, like, ten of them, and it's about a hundred of us. Why is there any talking going on? All these Crips. All us street niggas. We ought to be running this shit.* That tall one they call Slim G-Zus, standing there with that mask on his face like he's square business. If he ever cuts out of line with me, I'll beat the breaks off that bitch. I can't believe none of the Gods ain't smashed that ho for having that *Blue-Eyed Devil* tat on his chest.

It's just a soft-ass unit. Anywhere else these hoes would be getting broke as soon as they came through the door and wouldn't nobody be saying anything. Here, half these niggas are walking around saying, "Oh, that's messed up how they did that whiteboy." C-Life went easy on that ho. Whiteboys been murdering niggas for four hundred years! How these Acirema niggas ever agreed not to check these hoes, I'll never understand.

Russell was tempted to try and talk sensibly: "I don't know why you wanna fight me," or maybe, "I've never done anything to you." But somehow, he knew better. This world didn't make sense, and that wasn't about to change because he had entered it.

"I ain't afraid of nobody," said Russell.

C-Life said, "If you wasn't afraid you shouldn't been on the ground."

"Everybody's been on the ground before," said Slim G-Zus. "If not, you're pickin' and choosin' who you fight."

"WHAT?" barked C-Life.

Slim G-Zus ignored him and turned to Murder Worth. "I know he ain't been here that long," he said pointing at C-Life, "maybe he didn't know we don't play the checkin' thing here. If that's the case, somebody shoulda laced him up."

Poker-faced, Murder Worth said, "That shit's dead." C-Life pivoted ninety degrees, his mouth open, staring at Murder Worth. "We ain't trippin' like that, cuz," said Murder Worth. "Long as y'all through wit it, we through wit it."

Slim G-Zus looked at Russell and said, "Let's go ahead and drop this, potna. Bet?"

Russell nodded. "Alright."

"Alright, then. That shit's squashed," said Slim G-Zus. He and Murder Worth looked each other in the eye. Neither of them nodded or said anything.

Russell felt like everyone on the yard was staring at him and Slim G-Zus as they walked back to the others. And for good reason. They were. He felt like he'd just dodged a bullet, but he knew better than to exhale. At least for the next year or so.

Slim G-Zus said, "That shit's dead," swiping his hand in front of his neck.

"What'd they say?" asked Sidewinder.

"C-Life's tryna plead his case. Murder Worth ain't tryna hear it."

"Fool's got cell phones and dope coming at all times. I think his mule works this card," said Youngbuck.

Slim G-Zus said, "So he ain't tryna miss a drop 'cause we're on lockdown for some drama. Works for me."

Big Body Slim said, "I'll be over there slangin' the weight pile around if y'all need me." He adjusted his Oakleys as he sauntered off.

"Lemme holler atcha, Ogre," said Slim G-Zus. They stepped away from the pile.

Sidewinder said, "Told ya it'd be awright, li'l dawg," and shook Russell's hand.

"McCann," said Slim G-Zus over his shoulder. "Don't ever let anyone call you a whiteboy again."

Russell paused as Slim G-Zus kept walking. He looked at Sidewinder, "What's the deal with whiteboy?" he asked.

Walker stepped up and said, "Boys take dick in the ass and give up their commissary. You ain't gonna do that are ya?"

"No," said Russell.

"Then you're a White *man*," said Walker, sounding and looking like a drill sergeant with that matter-of-fact tone and flat-top haircut.

Slim G-Zus and Ogre walked about ten paces and stopped. He reached out and shook hands with Ogre. "'Preciate you being out here on this."

"Yeah, well. We cut for the independents 'cause we prospect from the 'woodpile. S'only right I be out here."

"Yeah, that clown, C-Life, came from another unit not too long ago. Most places ain't got it like we do here."

"Nah, they sure don't. Where I came from it was hit or miss. Those of us could take it, you know we made it after a fight or two. Those that didn't..."

"Right. Straight-up gettin' fucked in the butt," said Slim G-Zus.

"Yeah. Or they'd start 'em out just busting store. But it'd never end with commissary. Start out lettin' 'em have your soups and chips," Ogre raised his eyebrows, "gonna end up lettin' 'em call you Iggy or Angelina."

Slim G-Zus said, "Took us awhile to get it like this."

"Bet it did," said Ogre, hooking his thumbs into his waistband.

Slim G-Zus said, "Back in the day? They'd have some motherfucker the size of them fake wrestlers on TV checking a honky that weighed a buck fifty." Ogre nodded and clasped his hands behind his back. Slim G-Zus said, "Me, Sidewinder, the Big Body, and Youngbuck all got on the building about the same time. We were all established, them from other units, I'd had two jolly Black giants try me, one on medium custody, another when I got on this side. Anyway, we decided to worry about our own sections first. Figured we'd set an example. Eventually get enough respect to have it understood, can't no Blacks or Mexicans check Whites." Slim G-Zus squinted. "Well, they weren't feeling that."

Ogre chuckled. "Imagine that," he said.

"We'd tell 'em," Slim G-Zus said, "when they'd try and call out a honky fresh off the bus, 'We're not checkin' Blacks so y'all can't check us.'" Slim G-Zus mimed a reaction of shock. "Sometimes it'd go down right there. Sometimes they'd just burn off like a spoiled brat. Either way, they eventually got tired of the drama. Like this shit here. Even though we didn't do anything to ol' boy, we let 'em all know there's still consequences—or at least potential consequences. Some kinda repercussions."

Ogre nodded. "Right, I gotcha."

Slim G-Zus held his arms out wide. "All us out here on the yard, tension so thick you need a chainsaw to cut it. Nothing actually went down, but they'll remember that something *coulda* went down." Ogre nodded. Slim G-Zus shrugged. "They're not scared of us," he said.

Ogre grinned. "Nah, I don't reckon they are."

"To them it's like, 'Is trying to break this ho-ass whiteboy worth the drama that could turn into a riot and have me stuck on B-side for a year?' Over the last four or five years, they've answered *no* more often than not."

Ogre nodded, "And y'all deserve alotta respect for that. I ain't got but six bros on the unit, one prospect on eight building. Being the district captain, though, I'll make sure they all get with the program."

Slim G-Zus said, "I haven't met but a couple of them. They're scattered out. Heard nothing but good things about 'em, though."

"I gotta legal visit scheduled with Chitwood. They call him Hoosier. You know him?"

"Heard the name," said Slim G-Zus.

"He's the building lieutenant for seven building. I'ma lace him up. Tell him I was out here. Tell him we're gonna back y'all on this checking thing. Surprised they wasn't already doing it."

"Well," said Slim G-Zus, "I talked to German about it years ago and he said he'd have to holler at somebody off the unit—don't know if that was you or somebody else—but he said they'd get out there with us if a riot kicked off, just not the checkin' thing in particular."

"Yeah, well, from now on, all of mine are gonna be obligated to step in the breach if anyone tries to check a White." Slim G-Zus nodded. They shook hands.

The blue racquetball got away from the handball court, rolling between the two of them, all the way to the fence. Ogre said, "I like the way you do your thing, Slim. Real tight ship. You gotta good head on your shoulders. You been independent the whole time you been down?"

"Yeah. Almost fifteen years now."

"You just don't like the family life?"

"I always tell people, if I was good at doing what I was told, I wouldn't be in prison."

"Hell, I don't know about that. You looked like a soldier following a strict set of rules earlier."

Slim G-Zus shook his head. "Nah, there's really just one rule: They can't do to us what we don't do to them. Only thing I'm strict about is making sure they don't violate that rule."

"I like that," said Ogre.

Slim G-Zus smiled. "It's not the rules so much as it is the pecking-order shit. The rank. I'm pretty sure you call good shots, but on some other unit, y'all may have somebody I wouldn't want in that position. And if I need to move, I don't wanna have to holler at somebody above me. Especially if I don't like him."

"Yeah, I hear ya on all that. Family life ain't perfect; I guess I just like a little more organization."

"Yeah," said Slim G-Zus. "I won't say I haven't considered it, but I been independent all this time..."

"Well, if you ever decide you wanna get in a car, National Socialist Reich is the one to roll in. Especially here on this unit. I'd make sure you made rank real quick-like."

Youngbuck stood, feet far apart, punching his left palm with his right fist and telling a funny story about robbing a dope dealer and having to give the money back.

Russell, Squirrel, Sidewinder, and Walker all listened. A pasty White guy wearing tight pants and a tank-top walked up, leaned against Squirrel. "Are y'all done?" he said, in an overtly feminine voice. His brown hair was gelled and swept back in some sort of female pompadour, his eyebrows cartoonishly arched.

Youngbuck said, "Hell nah, we ain't done. And you ain't even got no make-up on, girl." A worried look appeared on the guy/girl's face.

"They were outta cherry *and* strawberry cool-offs when they ran store." He/she looked at the ground.

Youngbuck and Squirrel exchanged looks like they were trying not to laugh.

Youngbuck said, "We ain't talkin' 'bout nothin', Rexy. Know you want your man." Rexy smiled and clasped his/her hands around Squirrel's upper arm, leading him away.

Walker shook his head. "Fuckin' faggot."

Sidewinder clapped Russell on the back, giggling. "You ain't gonna fall off the turnip truck, are ya boy?"

Russell looked at the others. "What's that mean?" he asked.

Youngbuck leaned in, "Means you ain't gonna fuck wit no punks, right?"

"Nah, I..."

Sidewinder said, "Ah don't know, boy. The look you had on your face when you saw sexy Rexy..." Sidewinder straightened up and patted his forehead, right to left, like he was blotting sweat.

"Don't do it, McCann!" shouted Youngbuck. "Don't do it, bro!" Russell forced a half-hearted smile. He knew this was supposed to be great fun, but the events of the last twenty-four hours still had him on edge. Sidewinder gave Youngbuck a conniving grin. "Say, Young, maybe he'd like something a little darker." Sidewinder threw his head toward the fence where three dark Black inmates stood, dressed almost identically like Rexy. Youngbuck hollered: "Lookout, Naomi."

The tall one in the middle waved. "Hey, Youngbuck," he/she hollered back flirtatiously.

Youngbuck held his hand over Russell's head and pointed down at him. "I gotta new homeboy. Say he don't like nothing but blue foots." Russell turned to face Youngbuck. He wasn't sure what a blue foot was, but he had an idea. Sidewinder grabbed him in a playful chokehold. Youngbuck started feigning combinations of body blows to his gut. "She waitin' for ya, dawg," said Sidewinder. "Just know, Naomi's known for pitchin' after she gets done catchin'!" Roaring laughter. "You gonna fade that radiator hose, boy?"

Russell played along as best he could. It was an unsettling acceptance to this tribe. Russell wondered, what's Dell gonna think about these guys when he gets here?

CHAPTER 9

Russell sat at the foot of Adisa's bunk, peering over the top of the *Chronicle's* sports page, reading the titles of the books stacked on the shelf. *The Encyclopedia of Commodity and Financial Spreads, Trading for a Living, Come Into My Trading Room,* and *Create Your Own Hedge Fund Using ETFs and Options* were in one stack. The other stack was *Race and Economics, Conquest and Culture,* and *Black Rednecks and White Liberals.* The last one caused Russell to blink. *Economic Facts and Fallacies,* and on top, *The Meaning of the Holy Koran.*

"Say, Adisa," he was still holding out on using *lookout,* "you read all those books?" Adisa was at the desk making his typewriter sing.

"Oh, yeah. Most of them numerous times. Especially the ones dealing with the markets." It was after rack up, almost 11:00 p.m.

The door rolled. A Nigerian guard stood in the doorway reading from a piece of paper, "Meek-an. Chwenty won twop."

Russell stood. "Yessir."

"Reepwort to wuhk."

Russell looked at Adisa. Adisa said, "They give you a job? He's saying report to work."

"When I saw that major he made me an SSI."

"Oh, snap." Adisa laughed. "Man, you gotta go up to the front desk. SSI's sweep and mop. Clean stuff up."

Russell stepped up to the desk with his hands behind his back. The female guard sitting there, talking on the phone, ignored him. And that was fine with Russell. It gave him more time to gaze. Her mocha skin and glossy black hair made her look Arabian, or Middle Eastern. Egyptian maybe. But her name tag said Salinas, and Russell was pretty sure that was a Spanish name. That skin couldn't have been smoother. Her face looked like it didn't even have pores. *Why would someone who looks that good work in a place like this?* Russell wondered.

A deep but friendly voice brought him out of his trance. "Lookout, youngsta, wussup?" Russell turned around. Carrying what looked like a broomstick in each hand was the biggest convict Russell had seen yet. Dark Black and in the neighborhood of six foot five inches and 280 pounds, somehow broad-shouldered and barrel-chested. *A strong-side defensive end,* Russell thought.

Russell said, "Wussup, man?"

The giant extended his hand with a smile. "They call me Big Ike," he said. Russell reached out and felt his hand get swallowed up, "McCann." He wasn't quite the guy from *The Green Mile,* but damn near.

"Missed ya last night," said Big Ike.

"I didn't know I was supposed to be out here."

"No big deal. If you want, we can take these here scrub brushes and knock out the showers. Be done by breakfast. Or you can sweep and mop with Paco and them. They normally get done around shift change. 'Sup to you."

"When's shift change?"

"'Bout 6:30."

Russell noticed a wooden cross hanging around Big Ike's neck. "Think I'll try the showers."

"Already," said Big Ike, rapping fists with Russell.

Big Ike came out of a doorless closet carrying a yellow plastic mop bucket. "We'll have to get her to give us the chemicals." Ike rolled his eyes and looked at an imaginary watch on his wrist. Officer Salinas was speaking rapidly in a hushed tone; a mixture of mostly Spanish with occasional phrases (*oh, my God*) in English.

Ten minutes passed before Salinas finally hung up the phone. She glanced at Big Ike and Russell, then looked down at a computer printout on the desk. "Donaldson," she said, "I got you, Foxtrot forty-three bottom, right?"

"Yes, ma'am," said Big Ike.

"Where you at, waydo?"

Russell said, "D-Pod, twenty-one cell, top bunk."

"Delta twenty-one top?"

"Yes, ma'am."

"McCann?"

"Yes, ma'am."

Salinas scribbled some notations on the printout.

Big Ike said, "We're gonna clean the showers, miss. Need the chemicals."

Without looking up, Salinas said, "They didn't bring any." Big Ike dropped his head and sighed. "Miss Salinas, we didn't get any last night either. Can you at least call the kitchen and see if they gotta bag of bleach or dishwashing detergent? We need *somethin'.*"

Salinas was flipping through the pages of the printout. "I'll see what I can do. Y'all go get busy. Find something to do."

Ike shook his head. "C'mon youngsta. I got some bleach at the house. We'll use mines to clean the state's showers."

Russell looked at Salinas who was picking up the phone and dialing. He thought about saying something to her, then realized this wasn't a nightclub. She wasn't going anywhere, he thought; he'd have another chance.

It took them a little over an hour to clean all fifteen showers on F-Pod. Russell made a point of cleaning the shower he and C-Life fought in. A way of proving to himself it was no big deal.

Russell was struggling with the mop bucket, pushing it down the hallway using the scrub brushes as a steering wheel. The bearings were shot and the wheels only swiveled when they wanted to. He couldn't push the thing in a straight line if parole depended on it. He plodded forward, head down, almost to the desk, frustrated beyond belief. The bucket banked right, careening into the wall where he continued pushing it, scraping it along, but at least in a straight line.

Other than the scraping noise, it was working quite well. Then—"Lookout, youngsta—"

"Hey!"

Russell stopped and looked up. An obese female guard stood next to the desk about twenty feet in front of him. "What the fuck do you think you're doing scratching up my wall?" Russell looked at Big Ike, both their eyes wide.

Big Ike said, "Hey, captain. That's my bad right there. Youngsta's fresh in the system. Just got here..." Ike was holding his hands up, smiling as sheepishly as someone his size could.

"I don't give a goddamn *fuck*," said the captain, now on the war path towards them. "Did you scratch up your walls when you were out there?"

It'd been a rough couple of days. And Russell knew, from what his lawyer had told him, that it was important not to get any major disciplinary cases if he wanted to make that first parole. But at the moment, he'd had just about enough of this place. He wanted to cuss her out, call her everything but a child of God. But a whuppin' his dad had given him for cussing in front of a woman when he was a child still had power over him, so he bit his tongue.

The captain stood, fists on her hip, scowling. She had red hair and a body shaped like an egg, with legs that looked way too small to support her. Her chinless, asymmetrical face told the story: *Everyone made fun of me—especially the boys. Now I have power, and payback's a redheaded bitch with captain's bars.*

Capt. Johanson pivoted toward Big Ike. "Donaldson, is he deaf *and* dumb?" Big Ike glanced at Russell without turning his head. Russell gripped the shower brush, squeezing his anger into a safe place, teetering on the edge.

Big Ike said, "I'll drive. Lemme have that stick, youngsta," stepping in between the standoff. Russell hesitated letting go. Big Ike took the stick, patting Russell's forearm.

Capt. Johanson smirked, then stormed back to the desk, her backside—the complete opposite of her front—flatter than the unscratchable concrete wall she was so worried about. Ike motioned for Russell to follow him to B-Pod. Russell took a breath and headed that way, reminding himself he wasn't supposed to be here.

Apparently the guard in B-Pod's picket didn't catch the heads-up Salinas had given him when she flashed the overhead lights to warn him the captain was on the building. Because when Russell and Big Ike got to the door, he was still sound asleep; only repeatedly pressing the intercom button woke him. They entered the dark dayroom of one section. Ike leaned the scrub brushes up against the wall and sat down on a table top. "Lemme holla atcha, youngsta," he said. Big Ike smiled, "Iss gon be awright. Don't let that gal steal ya cool. You gotta watch Johanson." He grabbed the cross around his neck. "She's a real piece of shhh," he raised his index finger to his lips. "She dirty. Lord won't let me say what I really think about her." Russell stood nodding, fists still clenched tight. Big Ike looked him over, raised his huge mitts, "I don't want no trouble, youngsta," he said grinning. "I'm tryna help." Russell nodded again, noticing for the first time how hard his heart was beating.

Big Ike said, "You see that rang on her thumb?"

"Nah," said Russell.

Ike lowered his head. "Watch out for them gals that gots that ring on they thumb. They dykin'. Captain Johanson be lookin' out for all of 'em."

Russell frowned inside. The Acirema Unit was full of conspiracy-theorist wackos, and it wasn't just the Whites. *Even this old-school Black Christian cat is out there,* Russell thought. *A gang of lesbian prison guards out to get inmates...*

"Trust me, youngsta. The Big Ike won't steer ya wrong."

CHAPTER 10

OW FUH JAN-HEE, OW FUH JAN-HEE!" Russell looked up from the sports page. "What the hell did he say?"

Adisa laughed. "That's one of those Nigerians. He's saying, 'Out for johnnies.'"

"That's the sack lunch, right?" asked Russell.

"Yeah. Anytime they're short of staff, we don't go to the chow hall. They bring it to us. Meals on wheels." Russell went to the door and looked down into the dayroom. A dark Black guard who needed a haircut—or at least a brush—held two red mesh bags in his hands. Adisa said, "Those Nigerians are something serious. They're mostly on the units around Houston, but they get overtime to come down here. Lotta the people in Bee Ef Eee used to work here went to the oil field. I hear they start 'em out at twenty-five dollars an hour. I know *I'd* rather work there than here." Twenty-five dollars an hour sounded great to Russell. He made a mental note to look into that when he got out.

The door rolled and they went to the dayroom. Russell was handed a bologna sandwich and a peanut butter and jelly sandwich in waxed paper bags. He sat down on the bench against the wall and observed the dayroom: Slim G-Zus had his back and right foot against the wall below the window, like he owned the spot, as he tried to stare a hole through the book in his hand. Big Body Slim stood to his left, Itchy Foot across from them; both were eating and talking with their mouths full. O.T. had a gang of paperwork and several legal books taking up an entire table. Larson and Jew Boy were playing dominoes with two Blacks. The dayroom din was picking up.

The Nigerian guard, who looked a little like Don Cheadle (a homeless Don Cheadle) came back into the dayroom and hollered something. Russell couldn't hear what he said and was pretty sure that, even if he had, he wouldn't have been able to understand it. But it looked like he had the mail in his hands, so Russell headed towards him, hopeful but not expecting to hear his name.

"Feef-tee baw-toom." Russell was pretty sure that was fifteen bottom. Big Body Slim strutted over and said, "Fifteen bottom. Wallace." The guard handed him two letters. Russell noticed one of them had a candy-striped border, which he thought only came from foreign countries.

"Aytee twop." The bald-headed Hispanic guy Russell had seen come in and out of eighteen cell came over. Yeah, Russell thought, the guard's accent was a little tough to deal with. But he knew the benefits of having people of different cultures working together. His English teacher at Football Factory having shown the class a study that found the more diverse a company's management team was, the more successful the company became.

"Tweh-tee wohn twop."

"Twenty-one top? McCann?" asked Russell. The guard wasn't wearing a name tag.

"Wush yah nuhmbah?"

"Seven one three two eight one." He eyed Russell. With what? Skepticism? Recognition? In Nigeria that look probably meant something—or not. *Maybe he recognizes me from the news. It's been a while but me and Dell's pictures were all over the place,* thought Russell.

When the guard finally handed him the letter, Russell didn't recognize the address or the handwriting. But he did recognize the name, Cordell Youngblood.

'Sup, bro,

I'm on Michaels Unit in some place they call Tennessee Colony. My mom's supposed to call the D.A. and find out why we're not on the same unit. You alright over there? This place is crazy. I told the major when I got here that I'm not a criminal. He looked at me like, *nigga, please.* He wasn't trying to hear nothing I had to say. I'm in the exact same spot as murderers and rapists. Ain't nobody

trip with me though. Seems like all these cats are short. Is it the
same way over there? You know I'm barely over six foot, and in my
section of forty-eight there's only one cat taller than me.

These fools out of Dallas wearing shags! I'm going to tell Demetrius
Great Hair-ass that's what he needs to sport. My celly's from east
Dallas projects. He busted out his pictures, and damn near every
car in them has Daytons or McCleans on there. Cadillacs, Corvettes,
it don't matter. Somebody had a clean-ass '84 El dog and it was
sitting on them California wheels, too! LMAO. It makes me love that
city even more. At least in that H we got our own style. Swangers
and Discs, nothing but them Vogues.

You been to commissary yet? It's way better than what they had
in the county. I'm going to get back on the weights. All they have
here is some bullshit machine weights. I haven't worked out since
football, though, so I'm not trippin'. I remember you always telling
me to eat a lot of protein. I got the jack mack off commissary. It
tastes better than it smells, and for the money it's probably the
best deal for protein. Had you ever heard of mackerel before?

These fools call every gal they see a bitch or a ho. They make
me feel like a boy scout. Natasha's supposed to come see me.
Have you heard from Megan? I went to the church service. I was
surprised at how many instruments they had. A couple of them
boys could play and sing. It was alright, I guess. I'm going to start
college next semester. My celly told me the tests are all multiple
choice. I imagine our classes from Northside will transfer. Yours
from Football Factory probably will, too.

One and a half years, bro. Actually only about one. We got this.
Keep your head up.

Ya boy,
Dell

Russell was on a roller coaster. He went in as soon as the doors
rolled again and wrote Cordell back.

Sup Dell,

WTF. I can't believe they put us on different units. I'm going to write my parents and tell them to get ahold of the D.A. It was part of our agreement. The first couple of days I was here were crazy. I had to fight this Crip fool because he wanted to try and break me. He was real quick. I got knocked down, and we stopped. He went and told the other Crips that I gave up and was Crip property. I had to go to the rec yard with these crazy-ass White dudes to get that shit straightened out. Everything's all racial. Is it like that there? My celly's alright. He's from Hiram Clark. He's an older cat that's been locked up nineteen years. We got the same machine weights here. I'm going to gain 25 pounds and try to play linebacker when I get out of here. I'm hoping they'll still have the same coaching staff at F.F. when I get out. I haven't been to church yet. The commissary is way better. Its a lot of drama to get down there though. That D.A.'s got to get his shit together. I am not feeling this.

Ya boy,

Russ

P.S.: I saw the preview for your new flick *Transformers 4: Acting Career Extinction*. Maybe you can do *Baby Boy Part 2*.

Russell took out another piece of paper and started to write his parents about Cordell being on another unit. Then thought better of it. He didn't need his dad thinking he couldn't handle this. And Cordell had already told his mom to call the D.A.

Russell stepped into the "church house," which was actually a gym with a concrete floor, re-tucking his shirt after a rigorous pat search by a loudmouthed female guard. There were about ten rows of twenty or so folding metal chairs, a stage covered in grey carpet with a wooden podium, and three black speakers hung along the walls on each side.

Russell hadn't been able to get anyone to come with him: "What would I look like praying to myself? I'm a Savior, not a narcissist, potna," Slim G-Zus deadpanned. "I'm an Odinist. Christians used to burn us at the stake," said Itchy Foot. O.T. was in the law library. Larson was gambling on the domino table. Jew Boy was Jewish. And Youngbuck was getting some "work" done, which Russell had learned meant he was getting tattooed.

He walked down the center aisle looking side to side. It looked less color-coded than the dayroom or the rec yard, but not by much. Russell spotted Big Ike in the second row with a few empty seats next to him.

"Wassup, coworker," said Russell holding out his fist. Big Ike looked up, a broad smile growing across his face. He rapped Russell's fist. "Sit on down, youngsta," he said. "Glad to see ya."

"Yeah, man. I heard this was the Protestant service. Do you know what the preacher is?"

"Whatcha mean? Like Baptist or whatever?"

"Yeah."

"Nah, they got different ones. One of them's Baptist. 'Nuther one's Pentecostal. Can't remember what the others are." Big Ike tilted his head to the side and said, "Long as they preaching the Word, I ain't trippin."

"Yeah, nah, me neither. I was just curious."

Russell's family had gone to the same Presbyterian church all his life, though only sparingly. He'd been to the Baptist church Cordell's family attended a few times, but that was the extent of his churchgoing experience. He knew his mother felt more strongly about the different denominations than his father did, but neither seemed to be zealous either way. He looked around. There were a few more older guys in here. The vibe was good. So long as the preacher didn't force him to drink strychnine or dance with rattlesnakes, Russell would stay as long as he could.

A small balding Hispanic man wearing khakis and an untucked white button-up shirt stepped to the podium. He leaned in to the microphone, holding a Bible up in his left hand. "*¿Cómo están, mis hermanos?* How are you, my brothers?" came crackling through the speakers. "*¡Dios es bueno!*" he said.

A dozen inmates responded, "*¡Todo el tiempo!*"

"God is great!" the preacher said.

"All the time!" thundered the Black and White inmates.

He went on, back and forth, Spanish first, English second. *Two languages, one Word,* Russell thought.

About ten minutes into the sermon, there was more Spanish than English. Russell enjoyed seeing the Hispanic inmates get into it, raising their hands and shouting their approval, even if he had to wait a bit before he could understand the message himself. When the English did come through the speakers again he heard, "An' so, juss as God led his showsen people out of Egypt and slavery in dee past, today he leads them out of poffertee and eenjustice into dee land uff their forefathers. Remember, dee Bible tells us, dee first chall be last, and dee last chall be first! Dee Egyptians who kept God's people from their better life are still with us today. Dey used to be on the outside looking een. Today dey are on the eenside looking out."

He then launched into a barrage of emotional Spanish that went on for about five minutes. Then the English came back. "You see, hermanos, today's *insiders* are yesterdays *outsiders.* An' today's insiders are *very worried* about today's outsiders. Dey don't want them to come into dee land of their padres, juss like dee Egyptians tried to keep dee Issreelites from *their* destiny. So dey call them 'illegal' an dey make 'laws' to try and deny God's will!" Several Hispanic inmates to Russell's left sprung from their seats, thrusting their open hands into the air with their eyes closed, shouting, "Ahh-min, Ahh-min!" It was the first time they'd done this during the English portion of the sermon. Russell was unsure of the message. Was it about inmates? Immigration? He looked at Big Ike. He had a contemplative look on his face. Spanish again thundered through the speakers, the little preacher's voice rising hysterically.

The English came and went. Throughout the entire sermon, Russell heard very little about the Bible. The verses that were quoted were the ones you heard in everyday life, with a strong emphasis on helping the poor. And the preacher seemed to be angry about something. Russell couldn't quite put his finger on it. The laid back vibe he'd felt was gone. Everybody was wired up. Only it didn't seem like they were wired up for the Lord.

That night at work, when the elderly guard assigned to the desk went to use the restroom, Russell slipped behind the desk and grabbed the building roster. In the doorless SSI closet he jotted down the full names and the numbers of Itchy Foot, Slim G-Zus, Big Body Slim, Youngbuck, and Jew Boy. The roster listed every inmate on the building according to pod and cell number, and gave their height, weight, race, and birthdate. Russell knew their cell numbers and could differentiate between them and their celly's because no one had a White cellmate.

The next night he dropped a letter in the mailbox.

Dear Mom and Dad,

Hope everything is OK there. I made it to the Presbyterian service a few days ago. It was great. Just like going to church out there. Everything's fine. More people recognize me everyday. Has Megan called? If y'all talk to any of my boys make sure they've got the right address. I still haven't heard from anybody. I hate to complain but they serve us food I honestly can't identify. It's usually better than what they had in the county jail but not much. Really makes me appreciate the money y'all send for commissary. THANKS.

Mom, I was wondering if you could check out these inmates on the TDC website. See what they're in here for. I'm trying to get them to go to church with me. Peter Austin Wallace 210770, Nicholas Dumas 409713, Ronny Earl Dehaven 915006, Seth Martin Vexler 281832, and John Robert Lane 713832. My cell mate is Thomas Edward Byars. He is an older guy but we get along real good.

I'm going to try and gain about 20 pounds and try out for linebacker at F.F. Juco. I'm hoping coach Webb is still there. I think he'd give me a tryout. Tell Mitch I'm fine. Thanks.

Love,
Russ

On Friday afternoon, count cleared at 3:15. Russell was at rec hitting the weights hard like he was trying to gain that twenty pounds he needed to be the next Pat Tillman in one workout. None of the other Whites from his section had come out. When he entered the dayroom he saw—and smelled—why.

Itchy Foot rolled up on him, dipping and rolling a thick shoulder with each step. He wore a devilish grin and carried an Ozarka water bottle filled with yellow liquid. "Took it off a day early," Itchy Foot said, holding the bottle up, his breath scorching hot, making Russell wonder if his eyebrows were going to be singed off. Itchy Foot waved the bottle in Russell's face, slowly, so as not to spill any. "Nectar of the gods, broski. Have some."

"Nah, I'm cool," said Russell.

"C'mon, McCann. You wudn't scared in the world." Itchy Foot swigged. "Ahhh—here." He stuck the bottle to Russell's chest. "Peer pressure bro, everybody's doin' it."

Russell couldn't help but laugh. He grabbed the bottle and turned it up. The jet fuel smacked the back of his throat, bitter and warm, probably melting his esophagus. He fought off a reflexive cough. Barely. Eyes watering, face pinching, he handed the bottle back to Itchy Foot.

Big Body Slim and Youngbuck were squaring off in the middle of the dayroom. Youngbuck crouched low, stepping laterally, like he was trying to find the perfect opening. Big Body Slim stayed put, pivoting toward whatever direction Youngbuck went. They both seemed to be focusing on each other's torsos, but had far-off, glassy-eyed stares and maniacal smiles through clenched jaws.

Itchy Foot took notice. "Oop. Gotta go," he said, and tried (unsuccessfully) to make a beeline for the coming bout. O.T. and Larson sat on the back bench raising their bottles to Russell. Jew Boy and Adisa were nowhere in sight. Neither were any of the guys he'd talked sports with, Lonnie Ray and Campos. The only person in the entire dayroom Russell knew that wasn't shit-faced stood in his customary position by the window, mad-dogging a book.

Russell walked over and took the spot usually occupied by Big Body Slim. He leaned back against the wall and reached up behind his head, grabbing a crossbar, not even looking at Slim G-Zus. And Slim G-Zus didn't look at him. Russell leaned forward to look at the cover of the book he was having the staring contest with and read it aloud, "Knowledge and Decisions. Thomas Sowell?" No reaction. Russell looked to the entertainment. Youngbuck had his arms wrapped around Big Body Slim's torso, ramming his ribcage with his shoulder. Big Body Slim had him in a headlock and was trying to grab the waistband of his pants. Itchy Foot was standing too close, egging them on between sips.

Slim G-Zus had fewer tats than any White in the section save for O.T. On his left delt was a scroll that read

THE PECKERWOOD CREED
The cowards caught out
The weak got broke along the way
Only the Peckerwoods survived

Russell stared at it, trying to be obvious enough to get a reaction out of Slim G-Zus. No dice. The *Knowledge and Decisions* must have not been real easy to acquire or make. Russell exhaled and put his right foot up against the wall, mimicking Slim G-Zus' pose.

Russell said, "How'd they make that shit?"

Slim G-Zus said, "Check this out, fella. If I'm standing here reading a book, it's because that's what I wanna do right now. Not because I don't have a conversation to engage in."

Russell felt the heat rise off the back of his neck. "Damn," he said, drawing his head back.

Slim G-Zus said, "You need to holler at me about something important?"

"Yeah. My celly showed me how to write an I-60 to education? About college?"

"Right. And?" said Slim G-Zus, still staring at the page.

"And it hasn't come back yet. I wanna make that next semester. I know registration's coming up. Don't wanna miss it."

"You got anybody out there? Can call?"

"Call up here?"

"Yeah," said Slim G-Zus.

"Probably get my moms to."

"They're never in a hurry to do their jobs in that school house. Which ain't no different from anywhere else on this unit."

"Have you taken any classes here, Slim G-Zus?" Russell felt his stomach turn as the words *Slim G-Zus* left his mouth.

"Yeah. I done took a bunch. A honky'll have an Associates degree at the end of next semester, and then I'll get shipped to a unit where I can get a Bachelors degree."

Russell nodded, trying to think of how many hours he had. "I went to a junior college one semester. I took four classes. Passed all of 'em. I was playing ball, so I had tutors and shit to help."

Slim G-Zus had been holding his place in the book with his index finger. Now he closed it all the way. "What'd you play?"

"Football. I walked on at Football Factory Junior College, made it as a safety but I mostly played special teams. They thought I couldn't cover, but they never really gave me a chance. One coach said I hit like a linebacker but couldn't cover like a D.B."

Slim G-Zus said, "Lotsa cats in the NFL started out there. Far as Jucos go, it's tops in Texas. Helluva shit just to make the team."

"I gotta few letters my senior year but nobody offered me a scholarship. So I tried out there."

Slim G-Zus gave him the once over. "You played there, you oughta be able to do a little damage with your hands." Russell's eyebrows rose as he twisted his head and looked at the ground. "Yeah. I don't guess I fought a whole lot out there, but I don't remember losing too many."

Slim G-Zus said, "They time y'all in the forty? Get your vertical? All that?"

"Yeah."

"What was your vert?"

"Thirty-four."

"Oh, yeah," said Slim G-Zus nodding. "You oughta be pretty explosive. A bevy of the quick twitch. What was your forty?"

"Low four-sixes. My best was 4.61. At the end of practice the whole team runs gassers, end zone to end zone. There weren't but about five guys that'd beat me."

"You weigh what? Two hundred? Two-ten?"

"Somewhere in there. I wanna gain about twenty pounds and try and play linebacker. If I make my first parole I'd be twenty-one with three full years of eligibility left."

Slim G-Zus smiled (really). "Sounds like you gotta goal there to pursue. That's a good way to do your time. Have something to reach for—to occupy your mind. If not," Slim G-Zus held out his hand towards the dayroom. "You'll get caught up in this."

Russell nodded and said, "Itchy Foot's breath smells like turpentine."

"Shots of wood rubbing alcohol chased by a gallon of pineapple hooch'll do that to you." Slim G-Zus started to open his book, then stopped. "Itchy's a good dude, but don't let him crash you out."

"What do you mean?" asked Russell.

"Don't let him get you in a wreck—make you a crash dummy."

"Oh. Nah."

Slim G-Zus said, "He's alright. He'll get out there if we get into it with the Blacks or Mexicans. But he does every drug known to man. Always got some wine on, taking some pills..."

Russell nodded as he watched Big Body Slim pick Youngbuck up off of the floor but fail to do anything with him. Youngbuck had his hands clasped behind Big Body Slim's back in a death grip to keep himself from being thrown.

"Me," said Slim G-Zus, "I go by Mike Taylor's nine-tenths rule: Nine-tenths of the people you meet in life aren't worth your time."

"Who's Mike Taylor?"

"He's a sports jackass on the radio that had some cat from Houston beat his ass, steal his girl, and take his lunch money when he was a kid."

"Oh," said Russell, confused.

Slim G-Zus said, "The fool really hates on Houston. Especially the Texans. So I just figure he got done bad by some H-town cat." Slim G-Zus shrugged.

Russell said, "My mom always told me a stranger is a friend you just haven't met yet."

Slim G-Zus looked like he'd just smelled a dead skunk. "A stranger," he said, "is a con artist looking to meet his next mark."

Russell turned his head to hide the frown. *Guy's a freakin' psycho,* he thought.

Big Body Slim and Youngbuck crashed to the concrete floor. Russell felt a thud travel through the ground. They fought for position, still smiling like madmen.

Russell said, "Are we the only two White guys in here not drunk?"

"Pretty much. Jew Boy's in the house."

"You don't drink, Slim?"

"Nope. I ain't never even drunk a beer."

"For real?" asked Russell, waiting for the punch line.

Slim G-Zus said, "I had a sip of some Mad Dog 20/20 in seventh grade. Never tried alcohol again." Russell watched his face for a clue. Slim G-Zus said, "You wanna drink, I'm sure they got some more. I think they put on four g's."

"Nah. I drink every now and then. Beer or some vodka. I was always worried about my athletic performance.

"Yeah, I was the same way. Basketball was pretty much my life in the world. Plus, I grew up around a lot of losers. Saw how alcohol did them."

"Where you from?"

"Houston," said Slim G-Zus.

"Where about?"

"Northside. Not too far from where you're from. Your celly told me."

"Oh, Adisa?"

"Yep."

"What high school you went to?"

"Same one you went to."

"No shit? When were you at Northside?"

"I was supposed to graduate in '97. Didn't happen."

"Where you stayed at?"

"Off Imperial Valley, Veterans Memorial, Greens Road—lots of different apartment complexes. Half the time I was at Northside, a honky was living outta district. I knew coach Terron from

BCI—Basketball Congress International. Summer league. He knew I lived on my own. Let me play the one 'stead of the two."

Russell said, "How come y'all call each other honkies?" Slim G-Zus grinned and looked away. "Long story," he said. "The short version is, when I first came down, a lotta these White cats knew I had a lotta Black potnas in the world. They'd hear Blacks hollerin' at the picket, 'Why we ain't gettin' no rec? Y'all gotta nigga fucked up. A nigga goin' to rec,' when the guards would claim they were short of staff. So they'd come to me, 'Damn, Lane, why do they call themselves niggers but then get mad if we call 'em that.' So I tried to explain all that hip-hop, term of endearment, and my own personal theory—they like being wild because in the ghetto that's what gets you props. And, anyway, a couple of days later, this older White cat—big cat, like the Big Body but bigger—he's a little throwed off, too, a little crazy, he's playing bones with three Blacks, and he jumps up from the table and slams a domino. Hollers, 'Y'all gotta honky fucked-uuuupp!" Slim G-Zus chuckled. "So that 'honky' shit is, I guess, a little bit making fun of the Blacks and a little bit of flattery. 'Cause that's what imitation is." Slim G-Zus shrugged. "Eventually we all retold that story so much, it got normal."

Russell stared. "So you had Black friends out there?" A pained expression crossed Slim G-Zus's face. "When I got locked up," he said, "both my roommates were Black. My fall partner's Black. My daughter's *mother* is Black. Were you payin' attention when I told you where-all I lived?"

Russell's eyebrows rose and stayed there. "You gotta Black baby's momma?" A total eclipse passed over Slim G-Zus' face. His normal look—like he was about to rob a Seven Eleven—had returned. "I don't play that 'baby momma' shit. That's some Jerry Springer bullshit."

"Oh," said Russell, thinking there was no way he could've known that would offend Slim G-Zus. "And... You don't like him 'cause he's Jewish?"

Slim G-Zus cocked his head, staring, his jaw muscles flexed. He said, "How many prison movies you watch, kid?"

Russell shrugged. He knew he'd hit a nerve, and needed to get off it.

Slim G-Zus frowned. He turned back towards the dayroom. "I'll get out there with Jew Boy as quick as I would Young. He's in the 'woodpile. Messcans and Blacks treat him like he's White. To them, he's just another *gavacho* who stole the land from Mexico or a slave master." Slim G-Zus turned to Russell and pointed. "Just like you."

Russell managed to hold his stare this time but still didn't say anything. A couple minutes passed while they both watched Sportscenter on the far TV. Slim G-Zus started to open his book again. Russell said, "Northside always had some good basketball teams back in the nineties," then immediately wished he could have it back. It sounded like ass-kissing.

Slim G-Zus said, "How much time you got?"

"Three years. Pistol case." Perfectly natural the way that came out, like he was a regular, Russell thought.

"That'll fly right by," Slim G-Zus said. "'Specially if you're goin' to college. Keepin' your nose clean."

"I'm supposed to get a letter from the D.A. to the parole board when I become eligible. You think that'll help?"

Slim G-Zus exhaled. "I couldn't tell ya. I don't really know anything about parole 'cause I don't come up for a long time. From what I've seen though, there ain't no rhyme or reason to who gets it. You should ask your celly. He knows about all that shit."

"You and Adisa are pretty tight, huh?"

"Yep."

"So, he's alright even though he's Black?"

Slim G-Zus lowered his head into his hand, rubbing his eyes and exhaling. "Where's all this shit about Blacks coming from?"

Russell shrugged. "Like, the way everything was on the rec yard that day. I know Walker had some racist tattoos. That 1488 is like the year Whites found Africa and invented slavery. I think some of Squirrel's and Sidewinder's were racial too, right?"

"Racist tattoos, huh?" asked slim G-Zus.

Russell turned his hands up.

Slim G-Zus said, "Speaking of Walker, did you hear what happened to him?"

"Nah. What?"

"He and Squirrel fell outta place to one section to smash that ho Stallion for letting *you* get checked. They caught the shower and went, like, four rounds. Walker gets the better of him and tells Stallion he's gotta go. That he can't live on four building no more. Stallion don't say nothin', so Walker assumes it's understood. Ho's gonna catch out. But Stallion runs and tells these messcans he's been gambling with—that he owes to—that Walker's makin' him catch out. So the messcans get wired up and go holler at Walker. They tell him Stallion's gotta pay off his debts before he goes. Well, Walker don't like that, and him and Squirrel damn near get into it with 'em.

"So Walker tells 'em that ho's gotta be gone by breakfast. And that the messcans can take all his property to cover the debt. Fan, radio, hot pot, all that shit. That he and Squirrel are gonna stand aside. So they take the fools shit, and when Stallion goes to catch out," Slim G-Zus threw up his hands, "he tells on 'em. The extortion pig locks up Walker and the messcans." Slim G-Zus glared disrespectfully.

"So a *good* motherfucker plus a couple messcans are sitting in PHD 'cause some *Blacks* wanted to check you—because you're *White*." Slim G-Zus squinted his eyes and sucked his teeth. "*Issa new ho-ass whiteboy jus come thu da doe, my nigga, we gots ta break dat ho.*" He stared down into Russell's face, dark gray-blue eyes piercing, railroad-tie eyebrows so furrowed they were almost touching. Russell felt himself turning red. He kept his face up but couldn't keep his eyes from falling. Slim G-Zus had to be at least six foot four. He was a good inch or two taller than Cordell. And Russell knew—he could see it—this guy was so full of anger and hate he was capable of anything at any time.

Slim G-Zus raised his hand, index finger and thumb extended in the shape of a gun. "Check this out, potna," he said jabbing at Russell's chest. "Fourteen eighty-eight ain't the year Whites 'invented' slavery. *Fourteen* is for some fourteen-word creed a buncha White separatists came up with. The *88* is *Hail Hitler,* H bein' the eighth letter of the alphabet." The hand-gun striking like a cobra. "And, yeah, that is some racist shit. But you know what?" Slim G-Zus put his hands behind his back and leaned even closer to Russell's face. "Walker ain't have that shit when he got here."

Russell felt a mix of anger and frustration overwhelming him. In a new world, that primary instinct—self preservation—is even more dominant than when you're in your native land. The average newboot has to constantly wrestle with the stressful dilemma, *do I or don't I?* Do I punch this guy in the mouth—because he really just pissed me off. Or can I let it go and avoid risking a major case that could keep me from making parole? And most importantly, if I let it go, is it going to lead to more trouble? Eventually it hits you. The perfect proverb for the penitentiary: Damned if you do, damned if you don't.

Russell said, "Look, man," hoping that made them sound like equals, "my senior year at Northside? I was the only White starter on defense. Most of the White students had late arrival or early release. When you walked down the hallway, you'd hardly even see 'em. I know what it's like to hear all the little comments. 'Whiteboys can't jump, or dance, or whatever.' I know shit gets old. But look at where a lotta Blacks live. You said you lived off of Imperial Valley—Greens Road?" Russell rolled his head in small circles, as if to say *duh*. "Look how messed up it is. Look at all the Blacks in here—every one of 'em from the ghetto. Look how they were treated in the past. You can't expect them to have the same views on race or whatever. 'Cause they've had different experiences."

Slim G-Zus said, "When I lived in North Borough Station off of Greens Road, I never saw the KKK—or any White people—come through there robbin' Black folks or sellin' dope. Not once. The only White cat besides me in the whole apartment complex got his truck broken into so many times he moved out before his lease was up. But fuck all that. Did *you*," the hand-gun striking the air more force-fully than before on the word *you*, "ever oppress C-Life? Put him in chains or refuse to let him move in the house next door? Hell, nah, you ain't. When did any of these," Slim G-Zus gestured to the dayroom, "go through slavery or whatever the fuck? Ain't nar' one a these Black cats on this compound been a slave."

Russell searched his mind anxiously. "See, I was lucky. My generation, we're different. Like in high school we had to take World Cultures. And I know most of y'all that's been down here all this time—y'all didn't have that back in the nineties, right?" Slim G-Zus folded his arms and frowned like a father skeptical of a son's story. "I'm just sayin'," Russell actually had no idea what he was saying, he was just trying to save face by seeming defiant after being dressed down by some psycho who's been in prison half his life. He decided to go for what had to be safe ground. "If we didn't have all this between us, we could come together and force the system to change for the better."

Slim G-Zus rolled his eyes then closed them, dropping his head. He rubbed his eyes, smiling. "Them cats that wanted to break you?" The literal hand-gun was back. "They weren't upset about the parole rate or the menu. Or the fact that we don't get no conjugal visits in Texas. Matter of fact, if you hadn't have fought, they'd have solved the conjugal visit problem for themselves and their homeboys. They wanted your shoes and your butt 'cause you're *White*. But, hey, if you want, you can try and organize a group of multiracial convicts and teach them all the wonderful things you learned in—what'd you call it? World Culture? While you're telling all them they shouldn't try to fuck you in the butt 'cause the world has cultures? Guys like me'll make sure we get our respect by doin' what we been doin.'"

CHAPTER 11

The National Football League is made up of thirty-two teams split into two conferences, American (AFC) and National (NFC). Each conference has four divisions: North, East, South, and West. The Houston Texans are in the AFC South, the Dallas Cowboys fall in the NFC East. Teams from different conferences only play each other every four years, unless, of course, they meet in the preseason or Super Bowl. Over the years, Texas prisons have seen their share of fights and even all-out riots over loyalties to these two cities' football teams. So, as expected, this Sunday, with the Texans in Arlington (their stadium isn't even in Dallas) to play the Cowboys, the usual tension between prisoners had become more pronounced. It had morphed and redirected itself. The traditional fault lines of race and gang were now complicated by allegiances to Jerry Jones's and Bob McNair's football teams. Both of which had fans in every race and gang.

The dayroom had two TVs. One for sports, which normally stayed on ESPN when there wasn't a game on, and one for everything else. On Sundays this changed. One TV would be on Fox, for the NFC game, while the other was on CBS, for the AFC game. This particular Sunday, however, which Slim G-Zus had been billing as "World War III" for quite some time, both TVs were on CBS for the Texans and Cowboys game. All three benches in front of the TVs were packed. The tables behind them were teeming with warm bodies and warmer food. Guys bounced around, roughhousing. The din steadily increasing as kickoff approached. Standing room only.

Russell managed to cop a spot on the edge of a bench on the Houston side of the dayroom. Next to him was an Hispanic inmate from Houston, a young guy like himself, with an Astros logo tatted on the left side of his neck. Slim G-Zus stood next to a table where O.T., Itchy Foot, Youngbuck, and Jew Boy sat. On the table were large tortilla chip bags that had been cut open and laid flat like placemats, only side by side. Piled on top of the plastic were what Big Body Slim called "Super Honky Nachos."

The chili, refried beans, and tortilla chips were all bought from commissary. The cheese, salsa, and jalapeños were stolen and smuggled from the officers' dining hall by Itchy Foot. He first spread the chips out over the plastic. Then Itchy Foot poured a precise mixture of chili and refried beans from a plastic bowl over them. Next came the cheese, which had been made by dropping the slices into a bowl of boiling water. Then another layer of chips, beans and chili, and cheese. Itchy Foot repeated this simple process until he ran out of ingredients.

Big Body Slim came in from a visit. He and Slim G-Zus shook hands as Itchy Foot poured the last of the cheese. The table next to them was occupied by four older Black inmates from Dallas or Fort Worth. All of them wore either a white t-shirt or a skull cap made from a white t-shirt, with the Dallas Cowboys star on it. Slim G-Zus had been giving the biggest one, who he called School or Nipsy, a hard time all week. "Lookout, School, you ain't even from Dallas. You're from Cow Town. Fort Worthless. Why y'all don't get your own team?" To which the old Black convict would reply in his raspy, blues-singer voice, "School ain't nowhere on my birth certificate. And the metroplex is one area. If you'd a left Houston once in your life, you might know that."

Russell had heard Slim G-Zus telling him, "You just mad 'cause you look like Nipsy Russell." One time, the old man replied, "Least Nipsy was in some good movies. They say *Gigli* was the worst movie ever. Then J-Lo burnt off on yo ass." To which Slim G-Zus replied, "Yeah, well, if you consider *The Wiz* a good movie..." Russell didn't know who Nipsy Russell was but he was certain the old man got the better of that one. Slim G-Zus did look a little like a psycho Ben Affleck, and not even J-Lo could make *Gigli* watchable.

Slim G-Zus put some nachos in a bowl and walked over to the old convict and offered him some. He took a chip and pointed at the food on his table. A penitentiary pizza made with a crust of finely ground Ramen noodles, ketchup for tomato sauce, and cheese (purchased from Itchy Foot), with thinly sliced Spam for pepperoni. Slim G-Zus patted his stomach and declined and clapped the old man on his back.

Larson was under the TV trying desperately to get a bet with Lonny Ray, a thirtyish Black inmate from Acres Homes in Houston. Russell had overheard that Lonny Ray's cousin and Youngbuck's brother were fall partners (codefendants) on a string of pawnshop robberies where they'd stolen some tow trucks and rammed them through the storefront. Lonny Ray stood, all arms and shoulders with a flat chest, the Texans logo on his do-rag. "I'm takin' Houston and three," he said.

Larson threw his head back and rolled his eyes. "I ain't *giving* three. It's a straight-up game."

"They playin' in Dallas!"

"Okay," said Larson, "I'll take two and a half and Houston."

"I ain't goin' against my team."

They'd been back and forth like this for awhile now. Both of them bent at the waist, leaning towards each other, arms outstretched, exasperated looks on their faces. Slim G-Zus walked up with his bowl of nachos in one hand and slapped Lonny Ray on the ass with the other. "Good game, bitch," he said.

Lonny Ray and Slim G-Zus played what inmates called "the come-on game." They talked to each other as if one of them were a man and the other was gay or a woman or sometimes both. Sometimes Russell couldn't tell. Lonny Ray spun around and stuck his finger in Slim G-Zus' face. "Bitch, I done told you about interrupting me when I'm talking to another man. Ho-ass gets jealous—"

"Shut cho gay ass up, punk, and eat somma dees nachos, ho. Make that ass fatter," said Slim G-Zus. Some guys on the front bench started laughing.

Lonny Ray turned to them and said, "Only reason I put up wit dis ho 'cause she old-fashioned." He smiled and took a nacho from the bowl. "See, my snow bunny cooks for her man, y'all. Most hoes nowadays can't microwave popcorn."

Now Slim G-Zus turned to the crowd. "On Sundays I let her pretend to be a man till kickoff. Here in a minute, though, she's gotta pick up her pom-poms and earn her keep." Slim G-Zus looked at Lonny Ray. "If we lose to them ho-ass cowgirls, I'ma put you on cell restriction for a week: No whoring with men or daggin' with your girlfriends—"

"Bitch, if we lose I'm tradin' yo ass to a Dallas pimp for a third-round pick. Have yo ass on Harry Hines lookin' crazy than a muthafucka-bitch."

Slim G-Zus smiled and tilted his head. "Oh, you a pimp now, huh?"

"Goddamn right," answered Lonny Ray.

"You know when a pimp ain't got no ass to sell, he sells his own, right?"

"BULLSHIT! BITCH! Where you goin', ho?"

Slim G-Zus strolled away grinning, then blew a kiss over his shoulder. "I love you Loneesha Ray Ray," he sang.

Slim G-Zus backhanded Russell's shoulder. "'Sup fella? Want some?" he asked holding out the bowl before Russell. "Yeah. 'Preciate it," said Russell.

Slim G-Zus handed him the bowl and said, "Rest a that's you, potna."

I hate the way everybody sits around on Sundays watching these forty-million-dollar slaves damn near kill each other for these White folks' entertainment. Nothing but crackers in the stands cheering for niggas like they love them. Knowing that if their daughter brings one home they'll hang his ass and cut his nuts off. White folks got them getting so many concussions they commit suicide after they retire because they done went crazy. If the NFL was all White, they'd have some kind of special helmet or something to stop the concussions, but that's Amerikkka for you. They'll use a nigga up until they can't profit off him no more, then discard his ass. Slavery never ended.

I played tailback in junior high and could have played in high school, but didn't like dealing with the coaches. I was a street nigga. School wasn't never really in my plans no way. Even before

I had knowledge of self, I knew that was bullshit they were trying to teach us.

I liked the Saints when they had Aaron Brooks at quarterback. They couldn't never win nothing, though, because they wouldn't get him any good receivers to go with Joe Horn. Now that they got a whiteboy, they got all kinds of receivers and tight ends. The Texans and Cowboys don't even try having a Black quarterback. They could have both had Vince Young but the NFL didn't want him to succeed. The only reason Dallas drafted Quincy Carter was because they knew he wouldn't make it.

These TVs in the dayroom pacify these niggas. We're steadily getting fucked over by these laws, claiming they ain't got enough of them to run the unit. They feed us johnnies, even though we're not on lockdown. They don't run us to rec. They keep us racked up when we're supposed to be in the dayroom. All because these ho-ass pyahs want to stay home and smash on tortillas all day instead of come to work.

The nachos were good. Not as good as those Russell had eaten at NRG Stadium, but better than anything else he'd eaten since being locked up. The bowl empty, he took out his I.D. and put it where he'd been sitting to save his place. Russell cleaned the bowl out in one row shower and walked it over to the table where everybody was.

Slim G-Zus stood with another bowl in his hand, full of nachos. Big Body Slim held a clear plastic jar full of sliced jalapeños over that bowl, a mischievous grin on his face. Without looking, Slim G-Zus maneuvered his bowl back and forth while carrying on a conversation with O.T. about the Texans quarterback, Ryan Fitzpatrick. Big Body Slim tilted his jar to pour some peppers. Slim G-Zus yanked his bowl out from under it. Big Body Slim tried again, Slim G-Zus moved his bowl again. Laughing, Big Body Slim said, "C'mon Slim. Try some fuckin' peppers. Give that shit some flavor."

Slim G-Zus jerked his bowl again, foiling the Big Body's latest attempt. He turned towards him and raised his index finger like a teacher correcting a student. "Heat creates a rise in temperature, not flavor," he said.

Russell sat the cleaned bowl on the table. "Thanks y'all," he said, "that was good."

Big Body Slim said, "Want some peppers, youngster? Put hair on your nuts."

"Nah, I'm cool," Russell answered.

O.T. looked over the top of his bifocals. "Young man, I hear you played a little Juco football. That right?" The Old Timer had a thick, trapezoidal neck and large but round facial features, including a forehead that Russell was certain wouldn't fit into a regulation helmet.

"Yessir," said Russell. "I made the roster as a safety, but I mostly played special team."

"Yeah? Well, hey, that's still doing something."

Slim G-Zus had his right hand covering his bowl. Big Body Slim grabbed his right upper arm and tried to pull his hand away to dump some peppers into his bowl. "Fuckin' goddamn Slim," said Big Body, wrestling, "wiry sum-bitch!" Slim G-Zus ripped his arm away, successfully defending his bowl again. He raised his free arm and flexed his bicep, another one of those squinty-eyed grins on his face.

Russell shrugged. "I guess," he said, "I wanna try and gain enough weight to play linebacker—the will— weak-side guy?"

"Oh yeah," said O.T., "I follow ya. I's an option quarterback at Marshall High in San Antonio."

Russell nodded, "Oh, yeah."

"Whatta ya think 'bout this ticket?" asked Itchy Foot, as he held a small rectangular strip of paper up to Russell's face. It had each of the day's NFL games with the point spread in between the opposing teams. Itchy Foot had circled Dallas on the line that read HOU +3 DAL, meaning that he was betting Dallas would win by more than a field goal. He also had picked the game to go over 45½ points, Dez Bryant to have over six receptions, and Tony Romo to throw for over two hundred and seventy yards.

Russell nodded, "I could see that working out," he said. "But the Texans are my squad, so I'm hoping it doesn't."

Itchy Foot said, "I don't know nothing about sports. I just gamble on 'em." Russell expected that comment to get a laugh out of everybody but that wasn't the case. Apparently it was nothing new.

"Lookout, Slim G-Zus." It was Nipsy.

"'Sup School?" asked Slim G-Zus.

"You wanna check this out?" said Nipsy, holding up a copy of *Dallas Cowboys Star*, the "official magazine of the Dallas Cowboys."

"Nah. I got plenty of toilet paper, Nipsy, thanks." That brought some laughs.

"You just mad 'cause y'all ain't got no magazine. Maybe y'all win four or five Super Bowls like them 'Boys and y'all get one. How many y'all won anyway?" School looked up and rubbed his chin.

Slim G-Zus said, "What y'all did in the 1600's don't count. It wasn't but three teams back then."

School pointed a long crooked finger at Slim G-Zus. "There were more than three teams in the nineties."

"Before the salary cap, Schooolll," sang Slim G-Zus.

"Just have my scratch ready when them Houston sissies lose," snapped Nipsy. Russell had heard *sissies* a lot that week in reference to the Texans. It was supposed to be a comeback to Slim G-Zus saying *cowgirls*. But it just didn't work well.

"We could always up the ante, School," said Slim G-Zus, power walking around the table towards Nipsy. The old man rose much quicker than Russell thought possible.

"Nah. 'Cause I ain't no big money sonny like you. All 'em stocks and shit."

Now about a foot apart from each other, Slim G-Zus said, "Commodities, School. Not stocks."

"Same thing. And we betta dolla. I got mines right here." Nipsy held up a dark-blue plastic pouch of Spam.

Youngbuck jumped up, punching his fist into his palm. "Whoomp! I see ya, School! School brought that dolla to the dayroom Slim G-Zus! He done showed you the money!"

Slim G-Zus half-frowned, unimpressed. "Those're actually a dollar forty-five now, School. I see ya big money. Let 'em hang."

School pointed again, as he often did before addressing Slim G-Zus. "School ain't nowhere on my birth certificate."

"Would you like for it to be on your death certificate? 'Cause when them 'girls get slaughtered you're liable to go to slicing your wrists."

Everybody seemed to enjoy football Sunday. Almost everybody. There was a group of Hispanic inmates, a gang that kept a table for playing dominos on while everyone else watched the games. They were all from Mexico and only spoke Spanish. Russell figured the games were hard to follow if you'd never seen the sport before and the TV commentators only spoke English. But everybody else interacted. Guys of different races, different generations, all had something to talk about, a common ground.

Adisa walked up wearing a white t-shirt with a Texans logo identical to Lonny Ray's. Russell made a mental note to give Big Body Slim a t-shirt so he could take it to the craft shop and paint the logo on it like he had all the others. He only charged a bag of coffee. School said, "'Disa, do somthin' wit your boy," motioning towards Slim G-Zus.

Adisa put his hand on Slim G-Zus's shoulder and said, "Main event's about to start. Why don't you fighters go to your corners." Slim G-Zus and School stared at each other like prize fighters at a weigh-in. Even with his stooped back, School was only a couple of inches shorter than Slim G-Zus.

The team captains took the field for the coin toss, and the fans went to their sides of the dayroom. Slim G-Zus and Lonny Ray stood right in front of the TV, which hung from the wall about seven feet off of the ground. They stood there, arms folded, like coaches on the sideline. Everybody clapped hard like they were at the game when something good happened for their team. Both sides jeered one another for the slightest of mistakes. When the scores from the other games were shown the gamblers would clap or cuss, depending on how their picks were doing.

Tony Romo, the Cowboys quarterback, threw an interception. The Texans side of the dayroom erupted. Slim G-Zus and Lonny Ray slapped three rapid-fire low fives. Slim G-Zus cupped his hands and hollered at the other side of the dayroom, "Lookout, School! You know Toneesha's like an alcoholic when it comes to picks. Once she's had one, she's gotta have another." School turned and looked, snarling, his eyes tightened.

At halftime Dallas led 3–0. Each side bragged to and taunted the other. School reminded Slim G-Zus of the Cowboys' historic Super Bowl glory and how only San Francisco and Pittsburg could compete with them when it came to titles. Slim G-Zus reminded School of the Texans' historic glory when they became the only expansion team ever to win their first game, and that their opponent was the Dallas "Cowgirls." At which point School hollered, "Only you would know some shit like that. You ain't no real football fan. You only pay attention to them Houston sissies." To which Slim G-Zus replied, "Bullshit. I got two favorite teams: the Texans and whoever's playin' Dallas." Russell had to admit, that was pretty good.

The scoring picked up in the second half. The Texans' All-World running back, Arian Foster, got loose and gashed the Cowboys' defense for several long runs and a couple of touchdowns. The Cowboys got a couple of lucky scores. The game went into overtime. On third and eight, Tony Romo heaved the ball down the sideline to Dez Bryant, who was single-covered by Johnathan Joseph. Bryant held out his right arm, effectively stiff-arming Joseph, then pushed off as the ball came, making an incredible catch for a Cowboy.

But the referee threw a flag, as well he should have, and offensive pass interference was called. When they replayed that third down, J.J. Watt sacked Tony Romo and saluted the many Texans fans in the stands who had been so loud Romo had been forced into a silent snap count—on his home field.

The Texans got a good punt return from Keyshawn Martin. Ryan Fitzpatrick hit Arian Foster on a wheel route, then Andre Johnson on a bubble screen. Deandre Hopkins came free over the middle of a soft Dallas zone. Fitzpatrick threw a strike. The Texans were in field-goal range. Arian Foster ran the ball off right tackle to get it centered. Randy Bullock came on the field and kicked a thirty-seven-yard field goal that split the uprights—and gave Houston the win.

As the ball sailed through the goal posts, the Houston side of the dayroom erupted. Slim G-Zus bear-hugged Lonny Ray, picking him up off of the ground. Russell and the young Hispanic cat next to him slapped hands and forearm-checked each other. Youngbuck jumped nine and a half feet in the air, landed, and pumped his fists. Big Body Slim, not from Houston nor much of a football fan, stood beaming, thumbs tucked in his waistband, eyes squinted, nodding his head approvingly. Russell looked over to the Dallas side: Itchy Foot tearing up his ticket, then throwing it to the ground. Nipsy, sitting with his face in his hands, elbows on his knees. Everybody else on that side was either looking at the ground or staring at the TV in complete silence—some in denial, some in mourning, all of them refusing to acknowledge the triumphant ruckus less than a check-down pass away.

Russell saw Slim G-Zus and Lonny Ray huddled up by the shower. Lonny Ray's head jerked back as he laughed at something Slim G-Zus said. They switched shirts, Lonny Ray taking Slim G-Zus' tattered muscle shirt, and Slim G-Zus putting on Lonny Ray's Texans shirt. Slim G-Zus pulled the Spam he'd collected from School out of his back pocket and threaded a shoelace through the hole in the top of it. Lonny Ray grinned and nodded as Slim G-Zus hung it around his neck, the Spam pouch dangling next to the Texans logo.

Slim G-Zus slung his green nylon jacket over his shoulders but didn't put his arms in the sleeves. He walked to the defeated side of the dayroom and stood under the TV, watching the beginning of the six o'clock news. School was on the front bench, about five feet behind him. He shifted and turned, crossing and uncrossing his legs. Russell noticed several people tapping and elbowing someone else, pointing them in Slim G-Zus' direction.

Slim G-Zus spun around to face School, flinging his arms out to the side, causing the jacket to fly off his shoulders. He stood there, a *don't say nothin'* glare on his face, Spam medallion hanging next to the Texans logo. Slim G-Zus said, "I got one thing to say to you, School—HOW 'BOUT THEM COWGIRLS!"

A chorus of "Daaammmnnn" and "Awww, mannn" inflated the dayroom. Slim G-Zus set off, marching around the dayroom, shaking hands with everyone, preemptively saying, "Oh, this, I'm glad you asked," as he held the Spam out. "School gave me this because the Houston Texans are the best football team in Texas. It's my new piece and chain."

CHAPTER 12

Gabriel Valdez was born in Juárez, Mexico, but grew up in the small West Texas town of Tornillo. As a child he preferred to stay on the outskirts of the playground, mostly keeping to himself—which bothered his mother to no end. She had taken to calling him shy boy in hopes of goading him into becoming more assertive. More like the *fuertes* she grew up with in Mexico. It was the Ladinos, their culture here in America that had made her son the way he was. She chided him constantly with the best intentions of making a *pelado* out of him.

The worst of these episodes was the time Gabriel, then aged fifteen, left his thirteen-year-old baby sister unattended at a convenience store while he played a video game. While Gabriel was trying to break his previous high score and his mother was grabbing several sacks of flour, two *muchachos* had begun hitting on his sister. His mother made a beeline to her daughter and shooed the boys away with some harsh words. She scolded her daughter, who insisted she hadn't asked for the company. But the bulk of her wrath was reserved for Gabriel for neglecting his primary duty of protecting his baby sister's chastity. Gabriel tried to plead his case: That he was playing the game and unaware of the would-be violators. But this only incensed his mother more. He was just like a Ladino with all his words. Talking their talk. She berated him there in the store in front of everybody for not being a *pelado*. Her words that day cut wounds that were never allowed to heal, only fester from similar treatment time and again.

Now, seven years later, those wounds—far from healed—and the memories that caused them, were being used as internal motivation. Gabriel's external motivation was the thin ice he was walking on with his homeboys for having a Rick Ross picture he'd torn from a Vibe magazine on his cell wall. *Pinche moyo* they'd said, before ordering him to take it down. Gabriel was the youngest member of Forasteros Indígenas, and yet to have made his bones. Had he been from a city like Houston or Dallas, he could have been Tango—the hometown—most of whose members were young, listened to rap music, and carried themselves more like urban Americans, like Gabriel himself. Blasting, as they call it, would have suited him much better than being in Forasteros Indígenas, whose members openly despised Tango as wannabe *moyos* and not authentically Mexican. The older *soldados* always told Gabriel he was lucky to have been born in Mexico; if not, he couldn't have been Forastero Indígenas. At the moment, Gabriel felt a lot of things and lucky wasn't one of them.

A large drug deal between Forasteros Indígenas and Hijos De La Reconquista went bad in the free world. The Forasteros Indígenas captain on Acirema, Chief, received a two-word text after rack-up at 11:09: *LUZ VERDE* (green light). He called his lieutenants on the other buildings and told them what to do. Gabriel was Chief's only *soldado* on D-Pod three section where the captain of H.R., El Lobo, was housed. Chief knew if he waited until they ran rec—which would be the first real opportunity for any of his *soldados* to fall out of place to D-3—he could lose the element of surprise and lessen his chances of getting to El Lobo. And getting to El Lobo would almost certainly get him promoted in the Forasteros Indígenas hierarchy.

As he began packing up his property, Gabriel told his celly, a Blood from the east side of San Antonio, that he had to take care of some business at breakfast and that it didn't involve any Blacks. He'd gotten his orders from a kite delivered by the new green-eyed *guero* on the shower crew. Now he was on his knees pulling out a small slab of J. B. Weld concrete filler that concealed his shank in the door frame. The welding rod was fourteen inches with poly–cotton wraps hot-glued to one end for a handle and an ice pick–like tip at the other. Gabriel gripped it tightly and stood, the intoxicating mix of fear and excitement trickling in progressively.

Three thirteen a.m.: The doors are rolling in D-Pod three section. Gabriel Valdez stalks out of sixty-eight cell on three row and heads for the stairwell, his shirt folded and laid over his shoulder, his hands in the front of his pants. El Lobo never goes to breakfast. *Mucho commissaria* from all the ice he sells.

Gabriel hits two row and turns right for sixty-two cell, confident Lobo and his celly are asleep. He's surprised his nerves are in check other than the stretched feeling in his chest. Gabriel forces down a swallow. *Chy boy is dead,* he says to himself. He stops at sixty-two and peers through the door's grate: lights out, a sleeping lump in each bunk.

The doors on two row unlock. Gabriel's stomach turns somersaults as he crosses the threshold and unsheaths his weapon from his pants. It's three good steps to the bunk, and Gabriel extends the last one, planting his left foot in front and plunging the shank into Lobo's back like he was planting a flag. The welding rod glances off of a rib and then, poof, through the meat and into the lung tissue.

Juan Madrid was sleeping on his side, facing the wall, when his door slid open a little too quickly. He didn't feel a burning sensation or a sharp pain. He felt what had to be eight inches of a metal rod stabbing into his back. He rolled towards the door and caught the second blow in his left forearm. The gushing adrenaline helped his eyes focus, allowing him to figure out why this was happening by way of who was doing it.

Another blow came down through his right palm. Juan folded his fingers around the rod with it still stuck in his palm. He grabbed the *chavalon*'s wrist with his left hand.

Gabriel was stuck. He couldn't let go of his shank and he couldn't pull away from El Lobo. He threw a weak punch with his left hand that Lobo ignored as he got to his feet and muscled Gabriel backwards. The stool for the desk, bolted to the floor, tripped him. Gabriel's back slammed into the corner of the steel desk.

Gabriel was on the ground now. Maybe knocked out? *Nah, I can still see,* he thought. *Why can't I move or feel anything?*

Lobo still had the shank sticking through his palm as he stomped his bare heel into the *chavalon*'s face. He didn't move. El Lobo found the handle of the shank and gripped it tight. He knelt down and drove it into Gabriel's chest. He raised it again, but before he could bring it down, a choking cough stopped him. Blood was spilling from his mouth. The cell light came on. A guard stood in the doorway aiming his can of mace. The shank clanged on the floor as Lobo held his hands up. Lobo tilted his head back so he could say "No" without letting more blood pour from his mouth. The guard sprayed a yellow stream of gas. Lobo turned to avoid a direct hit. The last thing he saw was his celly, sitting in the top bunk, squinting his eyes in the bright light, mouth hanging open.

The head warden at the Acirema Unit was informed by his head Gang Intelligence officer that Valdez and Madrid were both on file as suspected members of two security-threat groups. The question then became was this an isolated incident between these two individuals or was it just the opening salvo in a war between their two gangs that would spread unit- and then system-wide. He decided it was the former and ordered the cell doors to roll at six thirty a.m. as usual, except for D-3, which he would keep locked down for twenty-four hours.

When everyone hit their rec yard at 7:10, the first of what would be seventeen stabbings between Forasteros Indígenas and Hijos De La Reconquista began. Chief's *soldados* still had the element of surprise on most buildings but word spread fast. By 9:30 a.m., a total of nineteen people had been stabbed, with four dead, including Gabriel Valdez and Juan Madrid. The warden called Huntsville and was granted a thirty-day lockdown.

"So, how long do lockdowns last?" asked Russell.

"Three to four weeks," answered Adisa. "When it's something like this—two gangs—they normally do it in three weeks. Shake us down for shanks. Let us up."

Russell stood at the door. The dayroom looked a lot bigger with nobody in it. Adisa was on his bunk reading *Investor's Business Daily*. "What's the shakedown like?" Adisa inflated his cheeks like a blowfish then exhaled. "Whew. It's something serious. You gotta pack up all your property and take it to the gym. They're gonna have a bunch of tables set up. Two pigs at each one. Gotta put all your property up there. They go through it piece by piece. They can read all your letters, look at all your pictures—all that."

"Damn," said Russell, turning around.

"Lucky for you though, you don't have much property. Haven't been locked up that long. I gotta typewriter," Adisa pointed at his shelf, "all those books, plus the ones in my locker..."

Russell sat down on the toilet. "Why do you have so many books?"

"Well, a lot of them are legal books. I need 'em to write motions, writs, sue these folks, all that there. The rest are mostly books dealing with the markets. Lane and I have an account with Ira Epstein Futures. Trade commodities and options on commodities. All those books have different strategies, charts, examples of trades, just a whole bunch of information we need. Lane's got just as many. Other than that I have a few Thomas Sowell books. He's gotta PhD in economics. Real smart cat. Found him on the op-ed page of IBD. He's written, like, fifty books."

Russell asked, "How'd y'all get into the stock market?"

"Just trying to make some money from down here. We've tried everything else. Mail-order business, I've done a lot of legal work for people, Lane's done tried every hustle in here. Sold drugs, cell phones, supplements—that creatine stuff? One time he was gonna run off a snitch for two hundred dollars. He's gotta daughter out there. I don't have any living relatives. He wants to support his kid, I wanna be able to keep myself afloat when I do get out."

Russell figured it would be disrespectful to ask how much money they had made, like it was to ask somebody what they were in here for. You could ask how much time they had, and then depending on how that went, maybe indirectly ask what they were in for. So Russell went with, "Have you made enough to support yourself when you get out?"

Adisa grinned. "I'm of the opinion that money's like good luck: You can't never have enough of it. I've got enough to get me some transportation that'll get me to whatever job I scrounge up. Probably find some lawyer to work for."

Russell nodded, thinking maybe he could loan his Oldsmobile to Adisa.

Adisa said, "You need the desk for anything?"

Russell shook his head, "Nah."

"Alright then, I'ma get going." Adisa lifted the clear plastic typewriter from under his bunk and set it on the table. Russell took his customary spot at the foot of Adisa's bunk and began reading the days-old sports pages from the *Houston Chronicle*. The Texans were leading their division. The Rockets were finishing up the preseason, and the World Series was tied two games apiece.

Russell finished reading and jumped into his bunk. "Say Adisa," he said. Russell still thought 'celly' sounded corny. "Mind if I jam your radio?"

"Nah. Go ahead. I told you whenever I'm not on it." Adisa lifted the headphones up to Russell. "Do your thing." Adisa always had his radio on AM. Either sports talk or some station called Biz Radio that talked about "the markets" as Adisa called them. One day, Adisa sat his headphones on the desk and turned the volume up so both of them could hear it. The AM signal wasn't that strong, and the words crackled with static, making it hard for Russell to follow. The guy talking was named Vince Rowe. He was president of a school called Online Trading Academy that taught people how to make money with the markets. Russell could tell Adisa was really into it, so he tried to keep up, but the guy might as well have been speaking Chinese, and Yao Ming was nowhere around.

The sports talk stations were all right, but they didn't talk about the Texans enough. They were too much like ESPN: All they talked about was the Jets' quarterback situation—no matter how terrible the Jets were.

There were three hip-hop stations on FM that Russell could pick up. Two were out of Corpus Christi, the other out of San Antonio. None of them played *real* rap. Even growing up in Houston, which had 97.9 The Box, Russell and his friends hardly listened to the radio. The rappers they liked only had a couple songs on each album that could be played on the radio. Not being able to hear real music was something Russell hadn't worried about while he was out on bond waiting for his sentence to begin. Now he was going through withdrawal. He went back and forth between the three stations. Niki Minaj was in heavy rotation. She had flow, but it was still pop rap with overdone yet watered-down beats. Not to mention she was so fine she made him miss women more than he already did. One of the Corpus stations even played Katy Perry, or was it Miley Cyrus? Same thing. All three stations played a lot of Latin rappers. Nothing against Latinos but the particular songs they played all had the same synthesized female voice singing their hook. And it had to be said: The rhymes were nursery school shit. Besides that, every other song had a rapper trying to sound like Lil Wayne. No Slim Thugga, no Z-Ro, no Mike Jones, and worst of all, no Paul Wall.

The real R&B music he'd listened to on Houston's Magic 102 had no equivalent—or even substitute—in South Texas. At nighttime, one of the hip-hop stations had a weak imitation of Magic's slow jam show, The Quiet Storm, called The Love Hour.

Straight garbage.

They didn't play real slow jams. You might get a Jaheem song here, or an old Jagged Edge song there, but then they'd come with one of those Latin hip-hop songs. And when they did play Jaheem, it was a fast song, some shit you'd dance to.

These problems with radio stations—and every other problem for that matter—were magnified exponentially on lockdown as time began to crawl.

You and your cellmate in a six by nine cage, twenty-four hours a day, except for a five-minute shower on Monday, Wednesday, and Friday. You start to wish, for the first time ever, you and your boy Dell would have stayed in the parking lot... 'Cause the guard is steadily blowing by your cell at mail call... Where are all those people you saved now? What happened to that reporter that wanted to write that book? The judge's gag order had expired. Your daydreams (mostly regrets) don't get interrupted on lockdown. You can go back and relive every mistake you ever made, every opportunity you passed up, and thrash yourself repeatedly for doing so... If you'd lifted for size instead of explosiveness, you'd have been able to play linebacker and would have been the fastest one on the roster. All the playing time. You'd have transferred to a division one school, then got drafted to be an in-the-box safety like Pat Tillman... Pat Tillman... Pat Tillman should've played for the Texans... I should play for the Texans... And wear Pat Tillman's number 41... Unless they retired it... Which they should... Until Pat Tillman's wife comes out publicly and says, "I want Russell McCann to wear Pat's number because he's a warrior and a hero just like Pat." Pat Tillman wouldn't have stayed in the parking lot... Pat Tillman would've whupped C-Life's ass.

Then there were the missed opportunities. Which were mostly chances you missed or passed up with the opposite sex... Too brutal.

CHAPTER 13

A Nigerian guard hollered, "Roostuh cow—katcho eye-deez ow! Roostuh cow—katcho eye-deez ow!" Then came a chorus of "Bitch-ass ho, we ain't got no roosters or cows! This ain't Africa, bitch!" from many of the Black inmates.

Russell sat up in his bunk and looked down at Adisa. "What'd he say?" asked Russell.

Steadily typing, a smile growing across his face, Adisa said, "Roster count, get your I.D.s out." Russell hopped down from his bunk and grabbed their I.D.s off of the shelf, Adisa's typewriter singing away. Russell said, "Why would they do a roster count when we've already been on lockdown two weeks?" This got Adisa to stop typing and turn towards Russell. "I try not to figure out their thought process," he said with a chuckle. "Afraid I'll start thinking like them."

The Nigerian guard's name tag said Abdulallah. Russell knew that was an Arabic name and wondered if the guy was a Muslim like Adisa. He'd been meaning to ask him about his faith and tell him that, even though he was a Christian, he respected all of the world's religions. And with Adisa shutting the typewriter down for the evening, now seemed as good a time as any.

After the guard passed, Russell returned their I.D.s to the shelf and sat on the toilet. Adisa exhaled loudly, like he was glad to be done for the day, and slid the typewriter under his bunk.

Russell asked, "Say Adisa, you're a Muslim, right?"

Adisa sat down on his bunk and faced Russell. "Yep," he said.

"Were your parents Muslims?"

"No. I came into Islam after I got locked up." He pronounced it Iss-lohm. "Oh," said Russell. "I went to high school with a couple of Muslims. Guy I played with. He went to a mosque on the north side, off of Adel Road, I think."

Adisa rubbed his knees, smiling, rocking back and forth. "You interested in Islam?"

Russell said, "Nah—I mean—I know it's good to learn about other places and cultures. I'm a Christian. But I know 90 percent of the world's either Muslim, Jewish, or Christian. Teacher I had, he was an atheist, but he told us that. I don't think my religion's better'n anybody else's."

Adisa nodded and leaned back, saying, "How'd church go? They still got them sodomites making out in the bathroom?"

Geez, Russell thought, *even this guy hates gays.* "Have you talked to any of the Nigerian officers?"

"About what?" asked Adisa, "Islam?"

"About, like, living in a different country, speaking a different language."

"I haven't really talked to any of them. Most of 'em are real by the book. A lotta guys say they don't like American Blacks. I just think they're a little aloof. They see how America is," he rolled his hand, "so many opportunities, and yet so many Blacks locked up. They probably look down their noses a little. We have it so much better here than they do there." Adisa shrugged and folded his hands in his lap.

Russell leaned forward, resting his forearms on his quads. "I know they're the guards and they screw us over, but the way everybody cusses at them and makes fun of the way they talk," Russell shook his head. "I kinda understand why they might look down on inmates."

"Yeah, I hear ya on that," said Adisa, looking down, his eyebrows afloat.

Russell said, "Slim G-Zus doesn't really make fun of them, but he always says he can't understand them. I think he just doesn't like them 'cause they're different."

"Well, I been knowing Lane for a long time. In fact, when I met him he was about your age. And if somebody's being 'different' makes it harder for him to deal with, or in this case communicate with, well, that might be a reason to dislike them, or at least their presence." Russell's brow furrowed. He sat up, unsure of what Adisa meant.

Russell said, "How'd y'all get to know each other anyway? He's gotta nickname that makes fun of Jesus Christ. And don't Muslims believe Jesus was at least a prophet? Messenger or something?"

Adisa cocked his head and looked at the ceiling. "We first got to kicking it when someone told him I knew about the law. I got him to start going to the law library. Helping him with his case. We got to talking about Houston, sports and whatnot."

"Did anybody, like, say y'all couldn't hang out 'cause he's White and you're Black?"

Adisa chuckled, "Nah, or if they did, they didn't say it to our faces. I would've laughed at them, and Lane would've probably went off and slapped 'em."

"Why is he always pissed off?" Russell looked earnestly at Adisa.

Adisa blinked, "You talkin' about 'cause of how he looks? Like he's gotta mask on his face?"

"Yeah. I heard Big Body Slim tell him that once. 'Get that mask off your face.' Slim G-Zus was like, 'knock it off, chump face.'"

Adisa smiled wide, "Yeah, those two are characters."

"Yeah, I guess. I'm just not—don't tell 'em I said this—but I'm just not like them. I don't like all this bullshit. They seem like they like it."

"Like what?" asked Adisa.

Russell waved his arm wide. "All this. The way it is. Like when I fought that Crip? We were out there on the rec yard the next day, and they all looked like they were enjoying it. The Crips and the Whites. And Slim G-Zus was like, 'We gotta smash Stallion. We gotta show this won't be tolerated' or some shit like that. It was sorta like saying a fender bender totaled a car out, you know what I mean?"

Adisa rubbed his bald head. "Well, from my understanding, it was a pretty serious situation. Didn't that Crip say he broke you and you were Crip property?"

Russell looked down. He'd assumed that Adisa didn't know the details. "It was something like that, but... even before C-Life claimed that, Slim G-Zus was all," Russell balled his fists up and stuck his chest out, "like... I don't know."

Adisa was confused. His celly seemed to have a problem with Lane, though nothing specific, even though he'd gotten him out of a jam. "You know, celly, on a lot of units the Whites have a lot more trouble than they do here. I can remember when Lane first got here." Adisa shook his head. "He fought a big ol' cat out of Dallas. Had black eyes for almost a month. Then he got his MI and fought another big ol' cat. Probably 250. He had other fights besides those two, but those cats were just trying to break him. He didn't get into it with them about anything. That was just how it worked. At some point all the Whites got together and decided they weren't gonna let it go down like that no more." Adisa raised his eyebrows, "You benefit from all the drama they went through."

Russell frowned, "I can't tell. Still had to prove myself," he said.

Adisa said, "Yeah, but that was an exception. And the guy didn't outweigh you by a hundred pounds either."

The kid shrugged. Adisa nodded his head knowingly.

Lonny Ray hollered out from his cell, "Look ooout, Slim G-Zus... Look oout, Slim G-Zus! You know you hear your man calling you, ho!"

Slim G-Zus came to the door and hollered back, "Whatchu want, Loneesha-bitch?"

"What's the score on the baseball game, whore?"

"Shut cho gay ass up, punk! You don't care about no baseball. You just want some Louisville sluggers up your butt, bitch! You know you like them 'woods, ho—Peckerwoods!" Laughter broke out from most of the cells. Somebody yelled, "Damn Lonny Ray. You gonna let him handle you like that?" Lonny Ray proceeded to call Slim G-Zus every insulting word ever created for the fairer sex with an F-bomb in front of it for good measure.

Adisa had heard all this before and knew it would now continue for at least an hour. He looked at Russell, "You hear that?"

Russell nodded, "Yeah. Unfortunately."

"Well, I first got locked up, you would've never heard a White and Black inmate playing the come-on."

Russell smirked, "Maybe progress isn't always good."

"Bitch, what's the score on the game, ho?" yelled Lonny Ray.

"I'll tell you what, mama, shit in a sock and send it down here so I can beat myself with it while I jerk off. And then I'll give you the score." More laughter as Lonny Ray erupted again, "Ho-ass bitch!"

Adisa grinned, shaking his head.

"Are you gonna give me the score or not, ho?"

"Not—bitch!"

"Are you still mad?" asked Lonny Ray.

"Mad?" said Slim G-Zus, sounding genuinely confused.

"Yeah, are you gonna file a grievance?"

"About what?"

"'Cause they ain't passed out nary a sausage link on lockdown, you gay-ass faggot!"

Roaring laughter. A few people slapping on their doors, and a lone voice sounding like it belonged to a blues singer, shouting, "I don't play them gay games, but that was pretty good!"

"Check this out, Loneesha Ray Ray bitch, when we come off lockdown, ho? I'ma braid yo booty hairs so you can't get no dick! That's right ho, you heard of commissary and rec restriction? Bitch, I'm puttin' your ass on dick restriction—45/45—no dick in the ass, no dick in the mouth."

Youngbuck hollered out, "Lookout, Lonny Ray, Slim G-Zus said he gonna braid yo asshole shut. How's he gonna keep your mouth shut?"

Slim G-Zus said, "I ain't. I'ma keep it fulla my vanilla gorilla!"

A chorus of laughter rang out among the studio audience.

Russell thought it was funny but refused to laugh. If he laughed he felt like he was giving in.

CHAPTER 14

I get tired of going on lockdown every time the pyah's start stabbing each other. We get three johnnies a day to eat, and that's it, unless you got some commissary in your locker. I catch up on my reading though. My sister just sent me another book by Dr. York. This nigga knows his shit. He talks about all the benefits of having melanin in your skin. White folks ain't got it. Some people even say if you're pure Black, no cut, melanin will keep you from getting HIV. I'm a yella nigga—BAD ASS YELLA BOY—so I ain't properly melaninated. In the streets I used to fuck with all types of hoes. When I get out I probably still will, but when I plant my seed, I'm going to make sure I get a dark-skinned sister. And I'm going to raise my kids to do the same. Malcolm X's mom married a dark nigga because she was trying to get that slave master blood out of her genes. See, the Black gene is dominant. So eventually my African DNA will overtake the European DNA that was forced into it. It'll take several generations, but eventually my genes will be all African again. Just like it was in the beginning, the whole world'll be Black. The colored peoples of the world outnumber the Whites like five to one. And when hoes can choose who they really want, they always pick a nigga. We got Kim Kardashian, Miley Cyrus—any cave bitch we want. We had J-Lo, Tia Tequila, all them Mexican hoes too. Blacks will eventually absorb all the lesser races and the super-masculine Original Man will take his natural place as God in the center of the universe.

I was just about to get some gangstas—that's a weed square—when these hoes locked us down. That nigga Murder Worth gots all the gangstas, thugs (tobacco squares), powder, and cell phones. A few other niggas got nice hustles, too, but not like Murder. On this unit, it's like Mexico. The pyahs got most of the mules and get most of the contraband brought in. Some of these laws are in the same gangs as the inmates: Forasteros Indígenas, Hijos De La Reconquista, all that shit. They try to keep these Mexican hoes all to they self but niggas be pulling them.

I remember when I worked in the laundry. I had this little bitch named Villareal cutting for me. She was choosing. Told me she wanted to be with a Black man. I start fucking with the ho, having her bring me little shit like wave caps and shades. That way, when I tell her to bring the dope and cell phones, she can't say no—because I can threaten to dime her for bringing me that little shit. So I'm staying late, fucking the ho down, and the pyahs get wind of it. One of them Aztlán motherfuckers goes to her and tells her she can't be fucking with me because I ain't Mexican. When she tells me this, I'm thinking she's just getting scared, and all I gotta do is bang that pussy one more time and she'll get over it. But then she tells me who it is, so I confront the fool. Little short, stocky motherfucker named Ortiz. He tries to tell me she's with them, but I know that's some bullshit because she's taking this Black dick like a champ. The bitch likes hip-hop and niggas, y'all dig? So me and my boy, Damn Fool, and some other niggas outta Dallas tell them pyahs they gotta discipline that fool Ortiz. They don't wanna do it, but they also don't want a nigga to beat they ass, so they take the fool in the shower and bang his ass up. You know Mexicans ain't got nothing with they hands but they swole the fool up. Anyway, word got back and the bitch ended up quitting. Just the everyday trials and tribulations of a Black man in America. Whiteboys or pyahs, it don't matter, always got to do some fuck shit to hold a nigga back because they can't compete with us.

Along with catching up on my reading, on lockdown I also like listening to them racist-ass Republicans on the radio. I listen to Rush Limbaugh, Sean Hannity, Glenn Beck—all them hoes. I love hearing how scared they are of niggas. They wet they pants every time Obama steps out the house. They see all their power going away and niggas taking over. I smile. All that shit is *over*. All of it. Getting rich off niggas, building a country on niggas' backs and not giving them anything for they work. Amerikkka is over.

Now, it's going to take a little time. We're going to have to clique up with these pyahs early on to have a majority, but eventually it's gonna be way more than forty acres and a mule for every nigga right here in the good ol' U S of A.

I'll never forget when Obama got reelected, Bush Bimbaugh came on the next day and said he went to bed thinking they lost the country. I was as high as a kite at the time but if I wouldn't have been I'd have cried tears of joy. Hearing White men talk about how they know it's over does something to me. When your enemies have held you down for four hundred years, always told you couldn't be shit, locked you up when you started to have shit. Seeing them crumble in defeat... I can't compare it to anything. 'Pac said revenge is the sweetest joy next to pussy, but I'd probably pass up a shot of coochi for the day when we're finally back where we started. When we've made the White man bow down and pay reparations.

When you're a Black man in Amerikkka, revenge is the best thing you can hope for. All that shit is over. I can't stop smiling.

Adisa turned and looked behind him. His celly was doing push-ups, flying up off the floor and clapping his hands, rapid fire. "How many you do like that, celly?"

"On the first set, I do twenty-five, which is almost to failure. The next three sets, I go a couple reps shy of failure, and on the last I go to failure—normally about thirty. Adisa was impressed. "Man, I can't do 'em clapping like that. Going fast makes it a lot harder."

"Yeah," Russell said, on his feet and shaking his arms out, "it's supposed to make you more explosive, help you disengage from blocks. I was thinking it might make me punch harder, or at least quicker."

Adisa considered this and scratched his freshly shaved head. "You know, I think I read something about fast-twitch muscle, some science magazine, during the last Olympics. Something about doing jumping exercises instead of squats to make you jump higher."

"Yeah, jumping, punching, those are both explosive movements. To get better at 'em, you gotta train explosively. Do like those powerlifting movements: snatches, cleans, jerks. We did all that in the weight room."

Adisa spun around from his typewriter. "You ever had any boxing lessons?" he asked.

"Nah. My dad boxed in the military. He and my older brother were real into it. I always played football and baseball. My dad showed me some stuff when I was real young, but I never really used it in a fight. I took taekwando for like six months, but I never used any of it either."

"Why don't you let me show you a few things when you get done?"

Russell shrugged. "All right."

Adisa reached under his bunk and pulled out a pair of black flip-flops and a pair of socks. He fit the slides' nylon straps in between his middle and ring finger; his palms where the bottom of the feet would be, and held them up to Russell, his fingertips coming over the tops like overgrown toes. "Slide the socks on. Like a mitt." Russell stretched the socks, and Adisa wiggled them on. He clapped the flip-flops twice to make sure they were secure. "Alright," he said, "let me see how you post up." His student lifted loose fists up around his chest, looking like he was unsure of what Adisa meant by *post up*.

Adisa squinted, "That how you started with C-Life?"

"Yeah. I guess."

"Okay. You're righthanded, right?"

"Yeah."

"Step back with your right foot." Adisa demonstrated, staggering his stance. Russell imitated. "Gives your opponent less of a target than when you stand head up. Now hold your hands here." Adisa held his fists out to the sides of his face.

Russell followed suit. He couldn't have looked more uncomfortable. Adisa tapped the outside of Russell's elbows. "Keep ya cage in tighter." Adisa stepped back, eyeing him. "Tuck your chin. Alright," Adisa held up his left mitt. "Lemme see that jab."

Russell threw a right that landed softly.

Adisa said, "Nah, nah. You're right-handed. Jabs oughta come from your left."

Adisa demonstrated, flicking two fluid lefts on time. He held up the mitt, "Step forward with your left foot when you shoot." Adisa demonstrated, expelling compressed air from his mouth with each punch, "Ssst, ssst."

The kid flexed his hands and cracked his neck. He lifted his hands and stepped into the punch, hitting the mitt solidly. "Okay," Adisa said, "try and bend your knees more. When you step," Adisa jabbed his left foot forward and sprung up into the punch, getting power from his legs, "push off your right foot." Russell tried to replicate the move.

Awkward.

Adisa said, "It's like anything else. The more you do it, the easier it gets."

He watched him repeat the move. "Did you box in the world?"

"Nah. But I've worked out with a few guys down here that did. You ever talk to Black Gotti? Eight cell. With the golds in his mouth."

Russell shook his head, "I know who you're talking about, though."

"Yeah, he's from the Clark, too. He used to box at George Foreman's gym. We used to work out all the time. You should holla at him."

Russell kept on stepping and jabbing. Actually getting into a little rhythm.

Adisa watched. "There you go. You wanna work on that a lot. Gotti'll tell you, the jab sets up everything." Adisa clapped the mitts. "Alright, let's see that one-two." Adisa let go a left and right, twisting his body into the right. The kid set up, hands by his jaws. Adisa raised the mitts. Russell fired, one-two. Adisa clapped the pads hard, then turned them forward. "Again."

The youngster bent his knees and fired again, one-two; the thud of his hands hitting the flip-flops growing louder and deeper.

Adisa said, "Widen your stance, it'll help you keep your balance. Keeps you from getting knocked down as easy."

Looking less and less awkward every second, Russell bent his knees and began bouncing on the balls of his feet.

Adisa said, "You know how to throw a hook?"

Russell swung his right arm out wide like he was putting it around a girl's shoulder. Adisa smiled. "Try it like this." Adisa slow-motioned a left that started out like a jab but turned ninety degrees inward towards the end of its trajectory. "You throw hooks with the same hand you jab with." At full speed, Adisa shot a quick jab followed by a hook. "You wanna turn your hip into that hook," he said as he demonstrated. "See how my left foot turns in?"

"Yeah." Russell was seeing it.

Adisa held the left pad sideways. "Alright. Shoot."

Youngster threw the hook. He shook his head in embarrassment at how weak the punch was.

"Loosen yourself up. Breathe. Don't worry about hitting the pad hard. Just try to throw the punch correctly for now."

Youngster continued trying but didn't get enough power behind the punch to do any damage.

"Alright. Let's try out your uppercut."

Over the next couple of weeks they fell into a routine. Russell began to look forward to their daily workouts, gaining confidence with each one. He began to toy with the idea of fighting C-Life again. Playing different versions of a redemptive triumph in his head, all of them ending with C-Life on the ground bloodied and begging for mercy. Adisa typed during the day, only stopping for their workouts. Russell continued reading the sports pages and flipped through *Investor's Business Daily* once in a while, reading a front-page article or one of the op-eds. The lockdown dragged on. The johnny meals were quickly getting old and the guard with the mail kept passing them by. Some idiot ran to his door every time a female officer came on their section yelling, "All hands on dick, all hands on dick, this not a drill, I repeat this is not a drill." Slim G-Zus and Lonny Ray continued using inventive ways to call one another gay and/or female. "How can I be a girl with all this dick?" yelled Lonny Ray.

"'Cause that ain't no dick, bitch, it's a kickstand for high-speed butt-fucking, ho!"

The monotony was growing cumbersome until, finally, Russell heard, "Chwenty wuhn twop. Meek-ahn."

A Nigerian guard slid two letters in between the door and its frame.

Dear Russ,

Hey there. How's it going in that place? Are you and Cordell learning to play golf? I've been working everyday. I'm about to start
school to become a physician's assistant. They make good money.
I'm so tired. I got so drunk last night. Mike told me to tell you hi.
He said he was going to write. Has that reporter contacted you? If
he writes a book and it turns into a movie I think Keira Knightley
should play me. If not her Rachel McAdams. What do you do all
day in there? Must be nice not to have to work. I gotta go. Be good.

Always,
Megan

Russell swallowed. Hard. That was tough. Crushing actually.
Luckily he had another letter to fall back on.

Dear Russ,

Hello, son. I'm sure this letter has found you in the best of health
and spirits. The Doyles came by. We showed them your letter about
how good the church service was. We had a good time. Your dad
really likes it when they visit. Speaking of visits we're coming to
see you again as soon as the lockdown is over!!! I hope to have
heard back from the D.A. by then.

I went to the TDC website and found the people you asked about
awhile back. The one you live with, Thomas Byars, has two aggravated robberies. I guess he was aggravated when he did it. Ha!
Peter Austin Wallace killed a police officer in San Antonio. I did
some math and it looks like he was barely 17 when it happened.
Ronny Earl Dehaven did a bunch of burglaries where some people
got hurt. Nicholas Dumas has 8 counts of aggravated assault with
a deadly weapon. Why does it matter if they were aggravated?
Seth Vexler has aggravated assault and receiving stolen property
crimes. John Robert Lane has a capital murder charge for killing
someone in a robbery.

We haven't heard from Megan. Your dad has been in the garage reloading shotgun shells. Turkey season!!! I know it'll be hard on him and Mitch going to the lease without you.

I'll write more soon. Keep your faith. We're all praying for you everyday.

Love,
Mom & Dad

The info on the psychopaths he was surrounded by was appreciated but the letter hadn't saved him like he'd hoped.

Megan's letter couldn't have stung more. She had no idea what he was going through. She didn't say anything in the slightest to let him know... what? That she understood? That she...

CHAPTER 15

Karl Clarkson dropped his keys into a Tupperware dish and stepped through the metal detector, thinking to himself how, if he wanted to bring some contraband into the Acirema Unit, this certainly wouldn't stop him. The magnetic field projected by the metal detector couldn't be completely blocked but the right material could deaden it enough to where you could convince the machine's operator your contraband was just your pants zipper. You learn these types of things working in the State Department with retired Secret Service agents all around you.

Clarkson passed through a series of steel and plexiglass doors, showing his Virginia driver's license to the appropriate guards. He'd grown up in Austin, the son of the state comptroller, and joined the army for eight years as soon as he graduated high school. When his enlistment ended, he used his connections and Bachelors degree in political science to get a job in President Clinton's State Department. He spent most of his time working in Latin America but had managed to earn a Masters degree in government, which was what Bee Ef Eee Community College required for its prospective teachers.

Clarkson stepped into his classroom and hung his charcoal gray blazer over the back of his chair. His black knit shirt fit tightly around his thick muscular upper body. His Casio G-Shock watch said he had about ten minutes before his students arrived. He got out loose notebook paper he'd been given by the guard working the door and began dividing it up into stacks of ten for each of the twenty-seven students about to arrive.

Slim G-Zus stepped into the classroom—first one there—and took a seat at the front, directly in front of the teacher's desk. He'd heard Clarkson was a good teacher. Everybody who'd taken his class said he looked like an action figure and really knew his stuff. Slim

G-Zus had been looking forward to this. Clarkson did look like an action figure, all right. He had a thick neck and a blocky build with closely cropped, sandy blond hair.

Russell came in and sat down a couple of rows over and several seats back from Slim G-Zus. The classroom was smaller than he'd expected but didn't look much different than any he'd been in in the free world: white brick walls, a large blackboard, posters with quotes from famous people. Russell recognized most of his classmates' faces. Ogre took a seat right behind Slim G-Zus. Russell wondered if the t-shirt he had on under his state shirt was the one with the red suspenders painted on it. The guy who looked like Nelly was in the back corner, slouching down in his seat. Clarkson looked a little like a shorter version of Russell's older brother Mitch. He was checking the numbers on the textbooks as everyone got seated.

Clarkson sat on the front of his desk, fists resting on his thighs, surveying the room full of convicts. "My name is Karl Clarkson. Write this down: *The sky is blue.*" His students did as they were told. "Is there anyone here who thinks that statement is false?" Most everyone shook their heads.

Clarkson said, "This statement is a lie. Like so much else of what you have been taught, this is demonstratively false. The sky is translucent." Clarkson was up and pacing now. "I'm going to force you all to think independently in this class, as we reexamine most of the things you believe to be fact, you'll be challenged to let go of beliefs that, frankly, will be painful to let go of." Clarkson sat back down on his desk, clasping his hands in his lap. "This semester we're going to divide into two groups and explore two issues: inequality and immigration reform—and how the government should deal with these problems." The one with the eyes right in front of him winced. Clarkson knew the White inmate population was rife with Bible-thumpers. Tim McVeigh types. None of his students had ever expressed those sentiments, but he knew they were there. "While government is controlled by political parties, our approach will be apolitical, nonpartisan. We'll be debating the best solutions without regard to where they come from."

"You'll have two outside reading books in addition to your textbook. Has anyone read *A People's History of the United States* by the late Howard Zinn?" Clarkson looked over his class. "Your tests will have essay questions that come from this book. You'll also read *The Power of the Dog* by Don Winslow. It is a work of fiction, but as you'll see over the next few months, sometimes fiction tells the facts better than 'the truth,'" gesturing quotation marks with his hands. "You're going to write a paper on *The Power of the Dog*. It'll be due one week before we take our finals. The instructions for the paper appear at the end of your syllabus, which you'll get here in a minute when I issue you your books. Before we do that, lets go ahead and separate into our two groups." Clarkson stood and held his hand out like he was going to karate chop a board. "We've got twenty-seven, so we'll need thirteen on one side and fourteen on the other."

Russell saw that Slim G-Zus and Ogre were staying to the right of Mr. Clarkson's hand. He got up as inconspicuously as he could and moved to the left. A few other people switched sides but most stayed put. Out of the six Whites there were in the class, only Russell and one other were on the left.

Clarkson said, "Whenever you come in, sit on the side you're on now. I'll throw out the topic, we'll all discuss it, then amongst yourselves, collectively, you'll come up with some solutions and how the government should implement them. Each group will need to find someone with good handwriting to write your proposals down, because at the end of class you're going to turn them in for a participation grade."

Slim G-Zus was disappointed. He had hoped Clarkson's class would be more academically challenging than the others, considering the guy was ex-military. But after that introduction, he was pretty sure that wasn't going to be the case. There weren't going to be hour-long lectures that you had to take detailed notes on. The tests would probably be multiple-choice and true-or-false... *It's a required class, I need the credits,* he reminded himself.

Clarkson called everybody in alphabetical order to his desk to issue them textbooks. Ogre tapped Slim G-Zus on his shoulder. "What's up, man? Y'all alright over there?"

"Yeah. Glad to be off lockdown. What about y'all?" asked Slim G-Zus.

"Yeah, we're good. You make it through the shakedown alright?"

"Oh yeah. All my shit's legit. Or it looks legit."

Ogre shook his head, "Hoes took my radio, said it was altered."

Slim G-Zus sat up and turned around, "What'd you have done to it?"

"I had the AM bar wrapped so I could ground it out. I was charging cell phone batteries off it, too, but they didn't snap to that."

"Yeah," said Slim G-Zus, "I got my AM bar wrapped, but it's behind the sleeve so they can't see it. When I charge, I just run the wire behind the *on* switch."

Clarkson finished issuing the books and stood up. "Warren Buffet, the second richest man in the world, makes hundreds of millions of dollars a year. His secretary makes $30,000." He clasped his hands behind his back. "Is that fair?"

Muffled *nos, nahs,* and *uh-uhs* amid shaking heads.

"Of course it's not fair," said Clarkson.

Slim G-Zus said, "Why's it not fair?"

Clarkson chuckled, "Yeah, right?"

Slim G-Zus stared, looking quizzically at Clarkson.

Clarkson raised an eyebrow, "You're serious," he said.

"Yessir, I am."

Clarkson folded his arms. "In what way is that gross inequity fair?"

Slim G-Zus said, "Warren Buffet gets paid millions because he does something a lotta people can't do, and people are willing to pay him handsomely for it. If his secretary wants to make his kinda money, she shouldn't have been a secretary."

Clarkson looked up at the ceiling. "Hmm. Well, they both work jobs. Why should one make so much more than the other?"

"The same reason you make more money than the cashier at McDonald's. You gotta college degree or two. People are willing to pay you more for what you produce."

Clarkson bounced his head from side to side. "Okay, but I don't make a hundred times more than a minimum wage worker." He looked out to the class for support. "I don't have a problem with someone making good money. But I think at some point, especially in Mr. Buffet's case, you've made enough money. And many people of color never had Buffet's privileges."

Slim G-Zus shook his head, "And who's gonna decide when somebody's made enough? You started off by saying their incomes weren't 'fair.' How is it fair for a third party to determine how much money people pay Warren Buffet for what he does? Why would a third party's opinion be more fair than millions of people's beliefs about what they should pay Buffet for his service?"

Clarkson looked over the class. "How many people think that income is distributed fairly in America?"

Slim G-Zus lowered his forehead into his palm. "Income isn't 'distributed,' it's earned—"

"I'm talking with the other students now."

Slim G-Zus picked up his head and looked behind him. Nobody was talking.

Raising his voice, Mr. Clarkson said, "Even Warren Buffet himself has admitted that the talents and privileges he inherited have given him an unfair advantage."

A middle-aged Hispanic with gold wire-frame glasses said, "Nobody chooses where they're born. So, it's not fair for rich people to know how to make all that money and just give it to their kids."

Clarkson pointed at him. "Right. I mean, why should being born to rich parents—through pure luck—guarantee someone an easy life—"

"It doesn't," said Slim G-Zus.

"Well, it sure increases the chances," said Clarkson, visibly frustrated.

Slim G-Zus sighed heavily, "So, randomness isn't fair, but the personal preference of some third party is? Yeah, I could see that."

I hate this bitch-ass whiteboy. He thinks he's smarter than the teacher. Taking up for some rich motherfucker who got rich making people poor. He just don't know all that shit is over.

Africans are a communal people. Even President Obama has that in his biography, *Dreams from My Father.* He talks to this conscious brother, a high-school counselor. You can tell he's got that knowledge. The fool tells Obama how he tries to teach young Black men about their true identities. How capitalism only helps those with capital. That's why we didn't have it in Africa. It ain't fair. Now here we go with this Nazi motherfucker.

Ogre said, "Mr. Clarkson? I worked hard inna oil fields and offshore, and I never made a million dollars. The system is set up to screw the working man. It's always been like that. Rockefeller didn't pull all that oil out the ground. He got working men to do it for him and took all the profits for hisself. That Buffet boy—he does stocks, right?"

"Right," said Clarkson.

"Okay," said Ogre, gesturing with his hands like a juggler. "That ain't hard. You just gotta have the money to do it. And—"

Slim G-Zus whipped around and looked at Ogre, "You tried it before?"

"Nah, but—"

"Making money in the market ain't easy."

Clarkson slid his hands in his pockets and smiled at Slim G-Zus. "Have you ever traded stocks?" he asked.

"Yes, and I've traded commodities, and I know most mutual fund managers can't beat the market average. I also know Buffet beats that average on the regular."

Most of the class were either shaking their heads or holding a long-term smirk.

Clarkson waved his hand from left to right. "And nobody's saying Warren Buffet shouldn't be rich. I think what most people would say is that we're a *society,* that we're in this *together,* and that Buffet and the rest of the rich have a duty to look out for their countrymen, who helped make them rich, by paying their fair share."

Slim G-Zus nodded his head, looking like he was really considering Clarkson's latest statement. He threw his thumb towards Ogre while looking at Clarkson, "If y'all wanna beg Warren Buffet or Bill Gates for money, y'all can. None of my business. But nobody—Buffet included—owes society anything. Rich people are usually rich because they have something—a whole lotta something—people want. In a vacuum? Maybe it could work. But in realville, telling people you're gonna take more of what they earned has consequences. Most rich cats ain't dumb. If they're smart enough to make all that scratch, they know how to protect that scratch. Look at California. Look at all the people done burnt off to Arizona, Texas, and Florida. California has politicians that think like y'all. Texas and Florida don't."

"Well, I don't doubt that the rich would go to great lengths to keep their wealth, but laws could be passed to make sure they pay their fair share."

"The F-word again," said Slim G-Zus.

Russell was enjoying the back and forth, pulling hard with Clarkson regardless of what he said.

Slim G-Zus said, "Bottom line, y'all think somebody, a third party, can decide for two other individuals better than they can for themselves. How would we pick that individual? How could a process like that be 'fair'? You can think it's unfair that Buffet makes way more than his secretary, but the truth of the matter is, Buffet made that money *very* fairly—in one of the most heavily regulated industries in the country—by having people voluntarily pay him for his services. Period. He worked hard to be who he is. He sacrificed part of his teens and twenties going to college to acquire some of the knowledge he needed to be a successful investor. His secretary probably spent those years dancing in night clubs. And again, if you wanna beg him for money, or give all your own money away, you're free to do so."

Hands back in his pockets now, Clarkson said, "Okay," nodding his head, "everybody else here thinks income inequality is a problem. How do we solve it?"

Among a few *uh-huhs* and head nods, Ogre said, "The government should control the industries 'cause then you wouldn't have them CEOs making all the money and the working man wouldn't get screwed. That's how it is in Germany."

"I served in Germany," said Clarkson. "You certainly don't have the glaring inequality there that you do here. What do y'all think about the current administration and its commitment to reducing inequality?"

Ogre cocked his head, a begrudging look on his face. "Obama's right about a lotta things. He helped GM and some other companies. If he'd just take 'em over and spread the CEOs salary out among the workers? They'd all be a lot better off. In them Viking countries? The government owns the oil industry. They spread the profits around to the people. That's way better than letting the Rockefellers make all that money. Hoardin' it."

"They've gotta population of five million," said Slim G-Zus.

"Good point. What do y'all think about that?" Clarkson said looking the class over.

The Nelly stunt double said, "President Obama knows that to heal this nation—stop the rich from being the only ones doing good—it's gonna take more than just money. That's why he gots his wife out there with that nutrition program. There ain't no organic food in the ghetto—or the chow hall here—"

"That's in *Mein Kampf*," blurted Ogre. "Organic food. It talks bad about tobacco, too." Ogre nodded at Yella Fella. "And Obama quit smoking."

Clarkson was unsure. He was exhilarated by the White and Black student finding common ground, but wondered how many in the class knew where *Mein Kampf* came from. A thirty-something, dark-skinned Black inmate said, "If Obama wouldn't have had to fix all that Bush screwed up, he'd have been done handled that. Alls he's gotta do is make a law that says you can't be sitting on all that dough. That the rich gotta pay taxes, too."

"The Democrats had a majority his first two years..." said Slim G-Zus.

"Yeah, but Bush screwed everything up so bad Obama had to fix all that and make sure everybody could go to a doctor—not just the rich," replied the Black man in a raised pitch.

Slim G-Zus said, "Ever heard of Medicaid? And you can't just pass a bill to make everybody equal in talent and work ethic."

Clarkson said, "No, you can't. But we don't need everybody to be equal in those two areas in order to make society more just. The question should be, what would American society look like today were it not for all the discrimination and privilege? And, since we live in a democracy, how do we convince the people that something must be done?"

Slim G-Zus lowered his head and began massaging his temples with his middle fingers.

Clarkson said, "Also, would the Constitution, as it's written, allow for the types of laws needed to rectify the situation here?" He held his hands out, "After all, the Constitution only tells us what the government can't do. It's a charter of negative values. It actually constrains the government from helping the people in many ways."

Slim G-Zus said, "If you'd ever been under the control of a warden and prison guards—or anybody with power—you'd probably understand why it's a good idea to limit the power of the government."

Clarkson smiled. "Ah, yes. The old 'tyranny is always lurking around the corner' argument."

Slim G-Zus nodded. "The people of Sri Lanka, Nigeria, Czechoslovakia, and lots of other places wouldn't share your sarcasm there."

Clarkson was thrown off. He knew there had been civil wars in these countries, but couldn't connect the dots. He cleared his throat. "If you're hoping to claim these countries had civil wars because they lacked a constitution of negative rights, well, we had quite a Civil War in this country, you know."

"They had civil wars in those countries because people were pitted against each other over 'inequalities.' Politicians got into power by saying that, if elected, they would make things 'fair.' Once in power, they passed laws that ripped the countries apart in the name of fairness. Extreme affirmative action."

Clarkson folded his arms and stood there, almost in shock and trying hard to keep his emotions from manifesting on his face. "Well," he said, "sometimes oppressed peoples have to crack some eggs to make an omelet."

His surly adversary nodded. "They cracked a lotta eggs, but never got any omelets. Most of those countries were turned upside down with violence that lasted generations. Sri Lanka was peaceful for over one hundred years until its majority was told they weren't doing as well as the minority—that things were unequal—"

"So they should've just accepted it," said Clarkson. "Okay. Are you finished?"

His opponent's gaze hardened. He pushed a thumb and index finger into his eyes. "Mr. Clarkson, sir, you oughta try mixin' in a little Thomas Sowell with your Howard Zinn. The *Quest for Cosmic Justice*'ll knock you on your ass. Walter Williams is good, too."

CHAPTER 16

Russell walked through the chain-link corridors a few paces behind Slim G-Zus and Ogre. "I don't think todes are inferior as a race," said Ogre, "I just don't think we should govern them or they should govern us." Russell looked down, his stomach turning.

Slim G-Zus said over his shoulder, "Lookout, McCann. What do you think about that statement?" A shit-eating grin was on his face.

Russell shrugged and said, "You could say my football coaches governed White and Black players on the same team."

Slim G-Zus threw his head back and let loose a crazed belly laugh. "Too-shay, young McCann! Too-fuckin'-shay!" he shouted.

Ogre lowered his head, half frowning, as Slim G-Zus clapped his back wildly.

Russell and Slim G-Zus stepped into the dayroom. Slim G-Zus hollered at Lonny Ray about the Rockets' score on the ESPN Bottom Line. Itchy Foot motioned for Russell to join him, Big Body Slim, and Youngbuck by the back window.

"How'd it go, school boy?" asked Itchy Foot.

"It was all right," said Russell. "Slim G-Zus and the teacher argued the whole time. It was almost like being in the dayroom when the Texans played the Cowgirls."

Youngbuck grinned. "That's my boy. Likes that debate shit."

Big Body Slim hollered, "Lookout, Slim G-Zus," and waved him over.

They formed a loose circle with a gap Slim G-Zus stepped into. He shook hands with Big Body Slim and placed his forearm across his meaty shoulder.

Slim G-Zus said, "Y'all got everything under control?"

Itchy Foot said, "Youngster here says you're in there goin' off on the teacher."

Slim G-Zus frowned and shook his head. "Fuckin' clown's a left-wing bleedin'-heart pinko commie."

"Yeah! Yeah!" said Big Body Slim, doing his best Bevis and Butthead imitation.

Itchy Foot and Youngbuck looked at Russell.

Slim G-Zus said, "Ol' boy wants to teach that social justice nonsense, saying this cat makes way more than that cat and that's unfair."

Youngbuck put his hands behind his back and shifted his weight, listening intently.

Russell looked around the dayroom, doing his best to let everyone know whatever Slim G-Zus had to say was of little consequence to him.

Slim G-Zus must have noticed Russell wasn't paying attention. "Check this out, potna," he said to Russell, who turned his head slowly from the Sportscenter highlights. "You like my haircut?" asked Slim G-Zus.

Russell looked it over. "Yeah, it's all right."

"You see Lonny Ray over there?"

Everybody looked back towards the showers. Lonny Ray had a young Black kid sitting on a metal trash can, giving him a bald fade.

"Lonny Ray came here knowing how to cut hair. He charges about seventy-five cents a cut." Slim G-Zus raised his deep voice, "I personally give her a dollar 'cause she's my punk."

"Shut up, whore!" hollered Lonny Ray without taking his eyes off his customer.

"Now, you see Maestro over there?"

All the heads turned toward the dayroom where an old balding Hispanic man was washing clothes.

"Maestro charges twenty-five cents per piece of clothing. He can't charge what Lonny Ray charges because any of us in here can wash clothes." Raising his voice again, "Yet only MY PUNK LONEESHA RAY RAY can fade like this," pointing at his head. "That's why Lonny's got more commissary in his locker—" looking serious now, "'cause he can fade the best—and give the meanest head. *Not* because he *oppressed* Maestro."

Smiles and nods all around.

Except for Russell. He said, "Yeah, but this isn't like society. Here in prison, all inmates have access to the same stuff. It's not like that in the free world."

Slim G-Zus waved him off. "Check this out, fella: Everybody pulled up to this barbecue with different skills. The Germans know how to make beer, from farming barley, hops, or whatever the hell. The Jews knew how to be middlemen because they weren't allowed to have regular jobs in most places. That's why whether in America, Brazil, or even China, the best-selling beers are all made by Germans. Big time financiers? Bankers? Lotsa Jews. They didn't come here and 'corner the markets' or 'oppress' everybody. They came here *knowing* how to produce a good or service everybody wanted."

Itchy Foot said, "Them Jews hoard all that money."

Slim G-Zus frowned and gave a dismissive wave. "Oughta be trying to figure out how they got so good at getting it instead of hatin' on 'em for havin' it."

Big Body Slim said, "I'd bang Wynnona Ryder."

"She Jewish? What about Jennifer Love Hewitt?" said Youngbuck.

"Goddamn right," said Big Body Slim. "I'd misogynate," his personal slang term for a hook up. Russell had heard this frequently when watching TV with the Big Body. Especially the Tyra Banks Show.

Russell said, "Germans and Jews are both White. They never had to go through what Blacks and Hispanics did."

All heads turned to Slim G-Zus who said, "Blacks have had to come from further back than any other group. But Hispanics of Mexican descent were never enslaved and always had Mexico close by where there were people who spoke their language and observed most of their customs. If the evil gringo's racism ever got to be too much, they could always go south. Blacks were discriminated against but so were Asians. Did you know Asians couldn't testify against

Whites? Yet, since at least the seventies, Asians of Japanese and Chinese descent have had higher incomes than White Americans. So, if discrimination were the main cause of some groups doin' worse than others, then all the White ethnic groups would be at the top income-wise, then Jews, Hispanics, Asians, and Blacks. But in reality Asians and Jews are at the top. Then Whites, then Blacks and Hispanics."

Big Body Slim said, "That's pretty fuckin' great, Slim. Lucy Liu? I'd misogynate."

Slim G-Zus palmed Big Body Slim's bald head. "I bet she digs White convicts."

Big Body Slim squinted his eyes and nodded, sucking his teeth. "You know dey all wants a honky in dey life, fi'zool."

"Ah, yeah, my honky," said Itchy Foot, also squinting his eyes. "Fo' rizeel, my hizeel."

These spontaneous routines where they mocked Blacks were never funny to Russell. He made a point of not laughing or even smiling. He'd once mentioned to Youngbuck that he and Slim G-Zus sometimes talked like the Blacks they were mocking. Youngbuck had looked at him expressionless, either oblivious to the irony or completely unconcerned with it.

Slim G-Zus smacked himself in the forehead. "I almost forgot. Check this shit out. Ogre's in the class. Sat right behind me. Itchy, I know you know what *Mein Kampf* is," Slim G-Zus waved his hand gun at the other three, "do y'all?"

Big Body Slim said, "Yeah. I read that shit a long time ago."

Youngbuck said, "That's some shit Hitler wrote?"

"Yeah," said Slim G-Zus, "so check it out." Slim G-Zus threw his thumb over his shoulder towards the sports TV. "That piece of shit Yella is in the class too, right? And he goes to singing the praises of Obama caring about nutrition, organic food, whatever the hell, right? And Ogre blurts out, 'That's all in *Mein Kampf!*'" Slim G-Zus doubled over with rumbling laughter. Everyone else chuckled. "So maybe Ogre and them can make an exception for Yella. He'll be the first Black prospect for the NSR." Slim G-Zus and Big Body Slim laughed the loudest this time, followed by Youngbuck and Itchy Foot. Russell smiled and looked away to Sportscenter.

Big Body Slim said, "That's fuckin' classic, Slim." Then added his best Jim Rome impersonation. "Huh-larious."

Slim G-Zus was still smiling ear to ear, backhanding everyone in the chest, when the Nigerian guard walked in and cupped his hands around his mouth, "Eee-nan-ow!" Slim G-Zus brought his fist to his mouth and blew in it. Two fingers sprouted into a peace sign. He headed for the stairs, "Peace to the honky nation," he said.

The doors on one row rolled as Russell began climbing the stairs, hoping Adisa would be down for a little conversating.

Adisa was at the table typing away when Russell came in. He came to a stopping place as Russell sat down heavily on his bunk and picked up the sports page. "How'd it go?"

Russell exhaled heavily. "It was all right. Slim G-Zus and the teacher argued, like, the whole time. I just need the credits. Gave us these books to read." Russell held them up.

Adisa's eyes widened. "*A People's History of the United States?*" He shook his head and laughed. "Wow. I can see why Lane was trippin'."

Russell put the other two books down. "You read this?"

"Yep. Thomas Sowell mentioned it. How Zinn conscripts the views of people he never met. It's real popular with college professors."

"So, it's pretty good?"

"Nah. It's pretty terrible. There isn't a single source site in the entire book. Not my style to go after a cat who can't defend himself, but..."

"Well, I gotta read it anyway. Teacher's gonna have us debate problems in society, so..."

Adisa grinned. "If he's got you reading that, you can be sure he comes down on the left politically. Him and Lane are gonna bump heads. What'd they get to arguing about anyway?"

"Slim G-Zus thinks it's okay that rich people keep all the money to themselves. Mr. Clarkson was saying they could share a little more. Slim G-Zus was basically saying everybody gets what they deserve. Which is bullshit. Nobody picks the environment they're born into. Some people don't even have parents. I guess it's 'cause he's been locked up so long. He doesn't understand..." Russell gestured with his hand, searching for the words, "... like, how it is."

Adisa said, "I know Lane real well. He's got a good understanding of a lot of subjects. When he and I've talked about things of that nature, he seems to focus more on the big picture. As in 'okay, things aren't exactly fair—but what are the options?' Guys like Howard Zinn—and probably your teacher as well—they don't consider the consequences of what they teach. They believe it's okay to take from someone who they think has too much and give it to someone they think has too little. Doing that has led to a lot of bloodshed all over the world."

Russell said, "So we should just leave it alone." Russell shook his head, "I can't get with that."

"It's not about leaving it alone, it's about not making it any worse than it already is. The unintended consequences of 'solutions' often screw things up more than they were. And if you think that convincing everybody they need to give up more of what they've earned—or just taking it from them in taxes—neither has a very good track record." Adisa turned and reached for a book, *Black Rednecks and White Liberals,* and handed it to McCann. "I recommend the entire book, particularly the last chapter, History vs. Visions, should help you out with understanding why you don't want to classify groups of people as victims when they're not."

Russell thumbed the pages. "I hate this fuckin' place Adisa. I don't see how y'all do it."

"Yeah, it's rough. Especially when you just starting out. Lucky for you you got Lane and some other guys around here."

"You know he's just like the others? I don't know how y'all got to be tight. He's so stuck on himself. He thinks he's so smart. The way he talks to people..."

Russell was lying in his bunk listening to his new headphones when the door rolled at midnight. He got up and dressed for work. At the front desk, Salinas was on the phone, and Big Ike was pouring a jug of HiLite cleaning solution into their raggedy yellow mop bucket. Russell reached out and rapped fists with Big Ike. "'Sup Ike," he said.

"'Sup youngster?" followed by a smile as wide as his shoulders. "Ready to handle up?"

"Yeah. Let's get after it."

As always, Ike had a copy of the New Testament the size of a deck of cards in his shirt pocket and a wooden cross hanging from his neck.

Russell had come to really like his job. At night they were the only ones out. Everybody else in their cells, mostly asleep. The guards were in the pickets, also mostly asleep, but that wasn't exactly a change from the daytime. Everything was quieter, more laid back. Most of all, Russell enjoyed Big Ike's company. They'd talk about sports or the Bible in between cleaning the showers. Ike was the most even-keeled inmate Russell had met, and their being a quarter of a century apart in age never seemed to matter. Over the last several months they'd worked out together at rec and always sat together at church. Ike was a little intolerant towards homosexuals— "sodomites," he called them, just like Adisa did—but other than that he was gold. He called him Russell instead of McCann, and Russell never heard a bad word about him from anyone. They'd even talked about going to each other's churches when they got out.

Russell finished up his last shower and stepped out of it, dripping sweat. Big Ike had finished his last shower a couple of minutes prior. He sat on a table in the middle of the dayroom wiping off the sweat with his state shirt. Russell put his scrub brush in the mop bucket and picked up his own shirt, wiped his face, and took a deep breath. "Man, Ike, we finish sooner every night."

Ike nodded, "Yeah. When we get the right chemicals it's a lot easier."

"You going to afternoon rec today?"

"Probably not." Big Ike lowered the shirt from his face. "You might not see the Big Ike on the yard no more."

Russell tossed his shirt on the table, a puzzled look on his face. "Why not?"

A smile so broad it threatened to split Ike's face appeared. "Gotta FI-1."

Russell's stomach knotted. "That means you'll be gone by the end of the month, right?" his voice an octave higher than usual.

"Not necessarily, but an FI-1 is the quickest parole they can give you."

Russell knew this was something to be celebrated, and he was managing to keep a convincing look on his face. But inside his chest there was a tourniquet tightening, and it must have been choking off blood from his brain as well, because he was getting light-headed.

Big Ike put his hand around his cross and nodded assuredly. "He'll bless you if you walk with Him. I prayed and prayed for Him to get me out. While my momma's still alive." Ike nodded slowly. "He done it."

Russell sat down.

"I told you my mom done had two heart attacks, right?"

Russell succeeded in making eye contact, "Yeah. Yeah, you told me. Remember we prayed for her at church that day?" *As in, we prayed for your mom together, worked out together, made plans together—and now you're leaving while I've still got a ways to go.*

Big Ike said, "So, just to kinda stay out the way, I probably won't go to the yard too much anymore."

Russell sat hunched forward, forearms across his knees, staring at the ground between them. *He's just some guy you met in prison,* he thought. *He's going home... good for him... no big deal...*

Time crept by.

Ike said, "It's early. Salinas probably won't let us go yet. Let's work out in here."

Russell stood, getting his bearings back, and took his shirt over to the stairwell. He folded it in thirds and laid it upon the highest step he could reach. "Do ladders again?" he asked.

"Bet," said Ike loosening up his arms.

Russell reached up and took as wide a grip as possible. He hung for a second, arms completely extended, before pulling all the way up and bringing his chest to the step. He then lowered himself to Big Ike's count of one, two, and released. Now Ike would do one rep up, then down slowly, one, two. Then Russell did two reps... Then Ike did two... Then Russell did three... Then Ike did three... They kept going in this manner until they couldn't add a rep to the next set. Russell got up to a set of seven, which gave him a total of twenty-eight reps. Ike got up to six for a total of twenty-one. They rested sixty seconds exactly and started another ladder. One for Russell, one for Big Ike. Two for Russell, two for Big Ike. Three for Russell... on and on. After four ladders, they'd each done over one hundred total reps. Done with that, they put their feet up on the bench against the wall and began their push-ups. They lowered to a count of one, two, then paused with their noses a centimeter off the ground—one, two—then pushed up and started over again. The incline and the pause at the bottom held both of them to the high twenties, rep-wise, in each of their five sets. After that Russell did three sets of clapping push-ups while Ike did his "diamonds"— hands so close together his thumbs and index fingers touched one another, making out the gem shape. The clapping style Russell was doing were too hard on the forty-four-year-old's joints when most of his 265 pounds were coming down on them.

They did their leg raises hanging from the same step they had done their pull-ups from. Russell was pumped. His chest and arms full and tight with blood. He finished his second set of twelve and dropped down as he heard the section door opening. Salinas walked in. "What're y'all doing?" she said, eyeing Russell.

"We're done, Miss Salinas," said Big Ike, "so we're just getting in a quick workout before we take it to the house."

Russell kept his body facing Salinas. He flexed his abs hard, but kept looking at Ike so she could take another look without being detected. "Well, I need one of y'all to go to the turn-out and get paperwork." "I'll get it," said Russell.

"Put your shirt on and hurry up."

"Yes ma'am."

Elka Salinas turned towards the door and looked down, using her peripheral vision to do a double take. *Pinche green-eyed gavacho's in shape,* she thought.

Elka had spent almost all of her twenty-two years in Bee Ef Eee, but considered herself Mexican. Her father often reminded her that the gringos moved the border on them. Spanish was the only language spoken in her parents' house, but she could easily flip to sing-songy English when she wanted to. After graduating from Bee Ef Eee High, she moved to Corpus Christi with her boyfriend, against her parents wishes, and worked as a cashier at an HEB grocery store. They had a son, Enrique Maldonado. That life lasted as long as it could; two and a half years of eating mostly Ramen noodles, and she moved back home with her son, but no boyfriend. The Dairy Queen, Post Office, Piggly Wiggly, and Exxon station didn't need any help. The only other game in town was the Acirema prison unit. She had a friend and a cousin who had worked there, each lasting about six months. Her friend quit to join the Navy. Her cousin was forced to quit or face an investigation for having an improper relationship with an inmate. They both warned her not to go work there, but Elka had a mouth to feed and was forced to fill out a TDC job application when she went to the welfare office. She wouldn't get with an inmate like her *pansona* cousin. In fact, after her experience in Corpus Christi, she wasn't exactly sure it was the affection of a man she was seeking.

Russell came back from the turn-out with a stack of count sheets and held them over the desk. Salinas took them without looking at him. Russell checked the clock behind the desk: 5:20. Forty minutes to shift change. Russell put his hand on the desk and tapped his fingers. Salinas looked up. Her expression asking, "What in the hell are you doing still standing there." Russell smiled. "What's up, Miss? You need me to do anything else?"

He couldn't get over her hair. And that was weird. Who cares about hair? It was so dark, yet shiny... like polished onyx. They were completely alone.

"No. Go to the house," she said, looking at the papers in front of her.

Russell looked off, not feeling the sting of rejection, instead warming to the challenge. "You sure?" he said. "You might get lonely."

Salinas glared, equal parts surprise and anger. "Are you trying to establish a relationship with me?" Attempting to establish a relationship was a level-one case, guaranteed to be graded major and get you sent to B-Side. A major case would also get your parole denied. Guaranteed.

Russell shook his head, grinning. "No ma'am. That'd be against TDC policy."

Elka opened her mouth in disbelief. Only a couple of other inmates had attempted to flirt with her, and as soon as she made her patented threat about the level-one case, they either clammed up or accused her of being a *marimacha*. Who does this *guero* think he is, standing there smiling, all cock-sure of himself.

Russell said, "Do you exercise a lot?"

Salinas' mouth opened wider, her face saying *Are you really this crazy?*

Russell ignored it. "I was just curious. You look really healthy. Especially your hair." Russell stared at her face, holding eye contact without blinking. "You look like you're from one of those islands. I bet you could do one of those shampoo commercials with that hair." Russell nodded towards her, "It's so shiny." He hated the word shiny, especially the way it sounded coming out of his mouth, like a kid, but what the hell else could he call it?

Elka stood up... or did she levitate on fury and shock? Somehow she got to her feet. "I don't know if you're high or trying to catch out—" She knew neither of these was the case, but she had to mount some kind of a comeback to what she saw as a challenge to her authority. "But you are *way* over the line, and if you don't—"

The heavy steel front door, about ten feet from their conversation, rattled and opened.

Salinas's face couldn't have made a more drastic change. "Captain J," she said, with an exaggerated smile.

The huge walking egg with fire engine–red hair tied up in a bun lumbered through the door and stopped about three feet from Russell, scowling. "What the fuck are you doing here?" she asked.

Russell said, "I'm an SSI. I clean the showers."

Capt. Johanson jerked her head away and put her arms behind her back. She leaned forward, "I know what you *are*. Do you see any fuckin' showers around here?"

Salinas said, "He just brought me the paperwork, captain," holding up the count sheets. "He's on his way to the house."

Johanson looked at Salinas, then back at Russell. "Then get there," she said.

Russell turned and headed down the hallway. He was probably blushing but it was so dark he doubted either had noticed. His heart rate was up, but so were his spirits. Big Ike was going home, but he might have found someone else to kick it with at night. Salinas didn't put handcuffs on him and send him to pre-hearing detention (solitaire) with a major case. And because she didn't do that, he knew he had a chance.

CHAPTER 17

Randy Leckie was the building lieutenant for the National Socialist Reich on eight building, closed custody. He got locked up for aggravated assault of a peace officer when he was eighteen. He pled guilty and signed for twenty-five years, a sentence he'd now done eleven years on. The trouble started one night when Leckie had a little less than two ounces of ice in his pocket and a sheriff's deputy tried to frisk him after a bar fight. He belted the cop across his nosebridge with a forearm and shoved him to the ground. He ran into the woods and tossed the dope. Randy was already on probation for a DUI.

At times like this, he would often wonder whether or not that dope was still where he'd tossed it. He had made an anxious decision that would have consequences unit-wide, and had to alert his bros. He sat down and wrote Ogre a kite:

Greetings with All Due Respects,

Thor whupped his celly on JPod. Some tode they call Bless One. It was some celly shit but they handled it in the dayroom. Thor was handling up so the other blacks cliqued. A 'wood jumped in and him and Thor got smashed. They took them to the infirmary. Haven't brought them back. You may have heard the 'wood pulled steel but he didn't. Blacks are lying, trying to justify clique action. SSI ran it all down to me. I think they called the 'wood Walker. A tode Bless One fucked with lives two cells down from me. I got 99 and a prospect over here with me plus a 'wood who says he'll roll with us. There's nineteen Blacks in the section but only one on three row with me. I'm gonna hit that ho first thing in the morning with a piece of fence. This is an extraordinary circumstance in which I can't wait for a response. I am proceeding under Article IV of our bylaws. We're too outnumbered to give up the element

of surprise bro. I have no choice. Be on guard. We'll kick it off in
the morning.

Much Love and Respect,
Your Leiu

Ogre took the kite to the rec yard that afternoon. Word had
already spread about the initial incident and Leckie's retaliation,
which resulted in two Blacks and three Whites being stabbed in a
riot on L-Pod that only ended when the guards shot every canister
of tear gas they had into the dayroom.

Slim G-Zus read the kite and passed it to Sidewinder. "It was
Walker," he said. Ogre had two of his soldiers, Jordan and Hot Rod,
flanking him. Forming the rest of the circle were Slim G-Zus, Youngbuck, Big Body Slim, and Sidewinder. Behind them stood Russell,
Itchy Foot, Jew Boy, Squirrel, and the other nine peckerwoods on
four building.

Sidewinder passed the kite to Youngbuck and nodded, "That's
basically the same story ah heard."

Slim G-Zus nodded. "Yeah, well, the ball's in their court now.
Are they acting funny down there on F-Pod?"

Sidewinder said, "Nah, not no funnier than they're always
actin."

Slim G-Zus grabbed the waistband of his pants. "I brought my
sword. Hope everybody else did too."

A dark-haired guy named Jordan with a swastika tattooed
on the left side of his neck said, "I cut up my mirror last night. My
celly's a messcan. He's cool. Ain't gonna say nothing. Got about
seven shanks ready to go."

Russell knew the polished piece of plexiglass that each cell
had on the wall for a mirror could be cut up and made into shanks.
Itchy Foot had told him that. He had also told him that the mirror
could bend, and if it did the shank wouldn't break the skin. He
looked on, oddly impressed with his superior knowledge of shank
manufacturing.

Youngbuck handed the kite to Big Body Slim, who glanced at
it and passed it to Ogre.

Ogre said, "Any y'all know Leckie?"

Everybody nodded.

Slim G-Zus said, "I was on medium custody with him. He's a good dude."

"Yeah, I cut for him," said Youngbuck, "used to tattoo."

Ogre said, "I heard he got one of them real good. Me and Hot Rod's alright where we're at. Ain't nobody actin' crazy in our section." Ogre pointed at Jordan. "He's got one that was roarin' before he went to work this morning."

Jordan said, "A-Mac. Homeboys with the one Leckie got." Jordan shrugged. "I'll have a shank in each hand, it's whatever." Youngbuck smirked. Jordan was always boasting.

Slim G-Zus said, "We're gonna keep an eye on 'em. If they pull steel on him in two section, we're gonna do the same in one section." Slim G-Zus looked at Jordan. "If they were gonna do something they'da probably already done it. A-Mac might wanna do some boxing, but he ain't tryna stab nobody." Heads nodded all around.

Slim G-Zus said, "Wish we could get you moved to one section."

Big Body Slim said, "Y'all know I got some Ginsus in the craft shop. Probably bring a few home tonight. Doubt these hoes are gonna do anything, but just in case."

That night, when Russell and Slim G-Zus returned from school, the dayroom looked as it always did: A couple of domino games over here, a couple of chess matches over there. The Oklahoma City Thunder were playing the Brooklyn Nets on one TV, *The Dark Knight* was on the other. Itchy Foot stood right under the TV, where Slim G-Zus stood when the Texans or Rockets played. The Joker had just given his line about wanting to watch the world burn when Itchy Foot turned around smiling excitedly. "I cut for that muthafucka right there boy," he said.

Russell went upstairs to take a shower before the next in-and-out.

Youngbuck was torn between *The Dark Knight* and his pick'em ticket. If Kevin Durant scored over twenty-seven points, the game went over 205½, OKC won by three or more, and Russell Westbrook had over seven assists, he'd hit for eighteen dollars. Batman was just about to transform his slab into a motorcycle when Youngbuck noticed someone in two section throw a mean combination.

Jordan Cowart was sitting on a bench with Lil Wood when A-Mac came in from his job in the laundry. They had been waiting for this all day because he had went to hollering and cussing when he'd heard about Jordan's bro, Leckie, stabbing his homeboy. They sat with their arms folded, not expecting much, watching A-Mac talk to some other Blacks, trying to get a read on the tone of their conversation.

A-Mac broke away, coming toward Jordan with a full head of steam. A-Mac said, "You one a them Reich mutherfuckers?"

Jordan hesitated, "...Yeah."

A-Mac fired off: Left-right, left-right, left-right—the last one an uppercut as Jordan covered his face and stumbled forward off the bench. He stopped and turned around. "What'd you do that for?" Words that would live in Acirema infamy.

A-Mac said, "Bitch, you's a ho." Jordan looked at Lil Wood, who's mouth was still agape, then back at A-Mac. Two other Blacks approached. Lil Wood stood up.

One of the Blacks said, "Come on, my nigga, that ho don't wanna do nothing," and reached for A-Mac's arm.

A-Mac jerked away. "Fuck that shit." A-Mac stepped towards Jordan. His road dog got in between them. Jordan held up his hands as he backed up, shocked and scared.

Youngbuck couldn't believe what he'd just seen. He blinked and looked around the dayroom to see if anyone else was witness to this penitentiary fraud being exposed. He looked back into two section. A-Mac was being blocked from getting at Jordan by another Black. Jordan was holding his hands up like, *What the hell, dude?*

As shocking as all this was, Youngbuck thought it was more funny than anything else. Jordan—Mr. *I got a shank factory in my cell*—just straight up caught that pussy. The fact that this could very well lead to more violence and possibly even a riot wasn't totally lost on Youngbuck; it just didn't override the hilarity of the ordeal. It's

prison. Violence comes and goes. After it makes so many predict-
able appearances, you stop worrying about it or trying to avoid it.
To quote every professional athlete who's ever done an interview,
"It is what it is." And when you're Youngbuck, the kind of guy who
thrives when shit and fan blade collide, you learn to appreciate the
humor in a self-proclaimed tough guy getting his head used as a
speed bag in front of an entire dayroom—and not defending himself.

"Say, bro," said Youngbuck grinning, "I just seen that tode
A-Mac hit Jordan wit' like a fifty-piece."

Slim G-Zus lowered his book, *Option Volatility,* perpetually
furrowed brow now furrowing more. "C'mon man. You bullshitting."

Youngbuck jutted forward. "Nope. And the fool ain't do
nothing, homeboy—nothing... but catch that cat!"

Slim G-Zus turned his head in disgust, jaw clenched tight. He
walked to the front of the dayroom and looked into two section.
Jordan and Lil Wood were under the stairwell. Lil Wood had his
arms folded, not trying to hear whatever Jordan was saying. Slim
G-Zus got the attention of an older Hispanic inmate and pointed at
Jordan and Lil Wood. The grey-haired cholo got Jordan's attention
and pointed at Slim G-Zus, who waved Jordan towards the crossover
door that connected one and two sections.

Through the door crack Slim G-Zus asked, "What the fuck
just happened?"

"Me and this tode just checked paper. I think it's cool, he don't
want no more."

"How long did y'all go at it?" asked Slim G-Zus.

"Man, I don't know."

"Tell Lil Wood to come here." Slim G-Zus shot Youngbuck a
discouraging look.

Lil Wood said, "Ay bro."

"What happened?"

"Man..." said Lil Wood.

Slim G-Zus listened. He could hear Jordan's voice in the background but couldn't make out what he was saying. Then he heard
Lil Wood say, "I ain't saying that shit."

"What?" said Slim G-Zus.

Lil Wood said, "Man. Say, bro, some fucked-up shit just went down. This tode A-Mac? He just took off on Jordan... and Jordan ain't done nothing... yet."

Slim G-Zus shook his head. "Okay. So ol' boy pieced him up and he ain't bust a grape."

"Right," said Lil Wood.

"You think you're alright over there?"

"Yeah, I reckon so. He asked if he was Reich before he went to chunking. Guess it's that shit that happened on the other side."

"Yeah. Ogre and them's gonna have to run that clown Jordan off. If they clique on him—which I doubt they will—don't get in it."

"Boy... I don't know..."

"Yeah, you do. A peckerwood don't fuck himself off for a broad," said Slim G-Zus.

"Yeah. Okay," said Lil Wood.

"Alright." Slim G-Zus peeled away from the door.

Youngbuck stood there, smashing his fist into his hand. "That ho gots that pussy. That ill na-na."

Lil Wood stood with his thumbs tucked into his waistband, head down. Ogre and Slim G-Zus stood across from him. Jordan stood next to Ogre, his hands on his hips, his mouth opening and closing as he shuffled his feet. Russell was about fifteen feet away. Crouched down next to him was Youngbuck, as serious as Russell'd ever seen him. The rec yard was less crowded than it normally was. Side-winder, Big Body Slim, and the rest had gotten stuck at work.

Everyone's body language pretty much said it all: Lil Wood tried to beat around the bush, biting his thumbnail, spitting what he came away with. Ogre stood, his meaty arms tight across his chest. Slim G-Zus, hands behind his back, head down, like he was at a funeral. Jordan kept talking, saying nothing. Ogre seemed to be listening, though he had to know nothing Jordan said mattered. He had committed an unforgivable sin, and disgraced himself and the entire NSR in the process. "What'd you do that for?" Those words Jordan had uttered were now the punch line to almost every joke on the unit. Yet Jordan was in denial, the man he'd been pretending to be beaten out of him in the blink of an eye. Russell looked at the ground. *This guy's going to get beat half to death for not fighting someone he didn't have a problem with,* thought Russell, *and it all seems normal.*

When they came off the yard, Jordan was walking by himself. Ogre and his bro, Hot Rod, went back to E-Pod; the rest of them lived on D-Pod. Russell heard Slim G-Zus tell Youngbuck under his breath that Ogre had to talk to the rest of his bros to see who was gonna smash Jordan. Youngbuck shook his head. Slim G-Zus walked ahead of everyone into the sally port. Nobody spoke as the door behind them closed and the one in front of them opened. Jordan and Lil Wood headed for two section. Slim G-Zus and Russell for one section. As he crossed the section door's threshold, Russell's peripheral vision caught another White convict heading into two section.

Youngbuck strolled into two section and took off his shirt, folded it methodically into a symmetrical rectangle, a look of focused rage on his face.

Nicholas Dumas grew up being shuttled back and forth between his dad in Beaumont and his mom in Houston, depending on which school district had most recently expelled him. He took his first trip through the Texas Youth Commission when he was thirteen for beating his stepdad, who'd made the near fatal mistake of hitting Nicholas' mother with an Easton aluminum baseball bat. After years of honing his fighting skills against Latin Kings, Folks, Crips, and Bloods, and building a healthy distrust for authority—due to the corruption of the guards, many of whom were in the same gangs as the inmates—he was released at age eighteen.

And momma tried. But by the time his nineteenth birthday rolled around, Nicholas was wanted for an assortment of felony warrants. The most severe, eight counts of aggravated assault with a deadly weapon, came from an incident in which one Martavius Green sold Nicholas what was supposed to be five monkey nuts (forty-dollar rocks of crack cocaine). After Nicholas chopped the dope up into tens and served a few regulars, his PrimeCo phone began blowing up, fiends demanding refunds.

Nicholas loaded two thirty-round banana clips for his SKS and piloted his Cutlass Supreme (tee-tops down) to the dope house where Martavius was normally at that time of night. He left his headlights on as he rounded the front fender. There were a handful of people on the porch. None of them moved. Nicholas later figured his high beams had kept them from spying his "girlfriend." He stood in front of his car and hollered, "Where the fuck is Martavius Green? Oh! Don't nobody know nothin'?" He dropped down to a knee and tore back the bolt action on his girl.

When he was done, all 60 rounds later, the front of the house had no windows, eight people were bleeding—none of whom were Martavius Green—and his Cutlass Supreme needed new tires, windows (the teetops survived) and a lot of Bondo for all the bullet holes.

After being sentenced to eighty years, he hit the French Robertson unit in north Texas, where he had to fight for his manhood almost as soon as he stepped off the chain bus. He fought a Blood they called Big Ag so long and so hard that another Blood actually stopped the fight, telling his dawg, "You ain't gonna break that fool, you gonna kill him." But even after that demonstration of heart, his celly, a Tango Mexican from Austin, allowed one of his homeboys to steal Nicholas's shoes while he was at work. When he came in that night, he had no idea who had stole them, but he knew his celly had let someone in their cell. And that was good enough. He took a boot lace and ran it through his steel Master combination lock.

His celly ended up with his jaw broken in two places, eleven teeth missing, and a right eye that was for cosmetic purposes only. Nicholas was put in administrative segregation for a year and then shipped to the Telford unit in east Texas. He made it from closed custody to medium custody before stabbing someone twelve times in a riot with the Blacks. Then it was back to seg for another year, after which he was shipped to the Acirema unit in South Texas. He met Slim G-Zus, who back then was still known by his last name:

Lane. Along with Big Body Slim and a few other core guys, they made Acirema unlike any other unit. And Jordan was unworthy.

The Black and Hispanic inmates in the dayroom elbowed each other and nodded in Youngbuck's direction. He'd never been over there before. Something was up. Jordan was oblivious to all this as he trudged up the stairs to three row. Youngbuck set his shirt down on the table and started up the stairs two at a time. "Don't take them shoes off! Lace 'em back up tight, bitch!"

Jordan straightened up and managed to put on a brave face. Youngbuck stood in front of him, his broad shoulders and v-tapered torso no doubt intimidating. Jordan must have read *The 48 Laws of Power* (like almost every inmate Youngbuck had ever met) because he decided to "enter action with boldness." If only he had done that with A-Mac the night before.

"Fuck you talkin' about, Young? You lookin' for trouble?" Jordan shuffled his feet and flexed his hands. Nervous tics he must have hoped would seem threatening.

Youngbuck pointed a hand-gun with a two-finger barrel, "You run around this motherfucker talkin' all that mad-dog-killer shit, and now you done got your card pulled—"

"That's between me and my bros—"

"Fuck you and your bros, bitch! Getcher ho-ass in that shower!"

"—and you ain't one of 'em, so you can get the fuck out my face!"

Youngbuck had never been accused of being patient or prudent. In the shower, a fight had a good chance of not being seen by the guard in the picket. On the walkway in front of the shower, where they now stood, the odds went up. Get caught fighting and you were guaranteed a level-one major case that would get you at least six months on B-side, where The National Socialist Reich had plenty of soldiers who'd gladly accept the orders to retaliate against you. Even though their bro was to be smashed and dropped from the family, he was still their bro, and you'd better not touch him... But Youngbuck didn't give a fuck about all that.

They were about five feet apart. Youngbuck closed some of that distance when he stepped his left foot forward and lifted his hands up. Jordan bit down hard and hurled two punches. Youngbuck raised his forearms into an X and blocked the first punch. He then bent at the knees and ducked the second, rising up with an uppercut that landed square on Jordan's chin. Jordan stumbled backward and then came toward him swinging wildly. Youngbuck kept his chin tucked in close to his chest and his shoulders shrugged up. He'd give Jordan the top of his head in order to land his own punches, because he knew that after blocking Jordan's, his punches would do far more damage.

Youngbuck slipped a punch and landed one of his own below Jordan's right eye. A left glanced off Youngbuck's forehead. They were in the phone booth now. Rock-'em Sock-'em Robots. Both men punching as hard and as fast as they could. Jordan's head popped back repeatedly from the punches. Youngbuck's occasionally jerked left or right. Jordan started to fade. His body becoming more upright, his punches softer. The second rush of adrenaline Youngbuck always got at this moment was flowing nicely. Victory close at hand. Jordan's arms stopped swinging. He tried to cover his face, his legs giving slowly as his eyes rolled back. "Bitch-ass ho!" cried Youngbuck as Jordan crumpled to the concrete floor. Youngbuck turned, gasping for air, checking the picket and the dayroom. The guard in the picket had a sandwich in one hand and the phone in the other. Most everyone in the dayroom was glancing up at him carefully so as not to alert the guard in the picket. The actual fight lasted less than a minute.

Jordan was out cold on his back, mouth slightly open, wearing a blood goatee from his busted nose and lip. Youngbuck reached down and grabbed him under his shoulders to drag him into the shower in case one of the laws decided to do a walk-through before he woke up. Jordan stirred and jerked his arms up like he was trying to catch something. Youngbuck let go and stepped aside. Jordan lay again on his back blinking, trying to get his eyes to focus. Youngbuck said, "You shoulda fought that tode as hard as you just fought me, you color-scared bitch!" Jordan looked in his general direction, still trying to get his eyes to focus.

damn sure ain't gonna let 'em do nothin' to Youngbuck, dawg," drawled Sidewinder, his Popeye forearms folded across his chest.

"Yeah, I'm just letting you know. I know Young was in the wrong but he's my road dog, and if they're talkin' about discipline, I ain't tryna hear it. Call it what you want," said Slim G-Zus, "that's the hypocrisy I allow."

"Nah, I'm with ya. Ho shoulda handled his business when ol' boy busted him in the mouth. 'What'd you do that for?'" Sidewinder shook his head. "Whether he's family or an independent, he's got this." Sidewinder ran his hand over his forearm indicating his white skin. "Shit reflects on us all."

"Ball! Ball!" yelled someone from the handball court. The blue racquetball had gotten away from whoever was holding the line. Slim G-Zus reached down and grabbed the swiftly moving rubber ball and threw it back to the courts a little harder than was necessary. "Yeah. I just know Ogre and them are gonna be fucked up about it. Him and Young not having no beef. He just beat his ass on G.P. Know what I mean?"

"Yeah."

"So, I imagine most are gonna think he deserves some kind of discipline. Alls I'm saying is anyone tries to put their hands on Young, they're gonna have to deal with me, too."

"You know ain't nobody gonna go against you."

"You never know, Sidewinder. Like I said, Young's in the wrong. But maybe since we told Ogre we had their backs... I mean, if we're willing to get out there with them when they get into it with somebody, it ain't that much of a stretch..."

Sidewinder said, "They ain't got that many over here anyway. I can't see 'em gettin' frisky."

Slim G-Zus, Youngbuck, Sidewinder, and Big Body Slim all stood shoulder to shoulder. Ogre had one of his guys next to him, and two more behind them. Jordan was in his cell healing up, trying to avoid the guards and the "code 33: fighting with an unknown inmate" case they could write him. Ogre looked at Youngbuck. "You and Jordan had some words after rec yesterday?"

Youngbuck stood with his hands behind his back, lats flared out like a cobra's head. "Nah, we ain't."

Ogre looked off, then back. "Then what the fuck happened?"

Youngbuck brought his hands around to his front. "I smashed your homeboy," he said.

Ogre's eyes narrowed, his face flushed. He glanced at Slim G-Zus, then back at Youngbuck. "And who the fuck said you could do that?"

One thing I've learned in life is that whiteboys can only go so long without starting a war or stealing something from somebody. They're not satisfied unless they're conquering and controlling shit. I've always known this, but this book by Howard Zinn, *A People's History of The United States,* just cosigned it. In Africa we had everything we needed. We shared and worked together instead of enslaving people to do the work for us. Like I told you before, we were a communal people. I wish these ho-ass whiteboys would just kill each other. Them Reich motherfuckers got away with some shit on B-side. These niggas on this side don't really want to do nothin', except my boy A-Mac. He put them hands on that ho and he ain't even fight back. That's how most of them are. They can't fight. They can't jump. They can't dance. They ain't got shit 'cept what they stole. Now these hoes is mad at each other because the one that tries to be fly whupped the one that A-Mac exposed. I been tryin' to think of some way to give them all shanks and hooch so they'll go to stabbing each other. That's how they do us in the world. Only they use guns and drugs pushed by the NRA and the CIA. When Jason Whitlock—he's a brother that writes for ESPN— said that the NRA is the new KKK, he said some real shit. I ain't agree with him when he was dissing hip-hop and blaming rappers for what that slave ship owner, that hook-nosed diamond merchant, Don Imus, said about those sisters at Rutgers. But he has to say that kind of shit if he wants to keep his job. Massa ain't gonna let him tell the truth all the time.

The NRA and the CIA been pushing guns and drugs into our communities for decades. They know they had to do something because discrimination had been outlawed and if we were allowed to compete with whiteboys, we'd dominate them in everything. They only let us compete with them in sports because they're all flabby and weak. They'd rather watch us play than play themselves. They all sit around and watch us on TV, or pretend to be us on video games. When it comes to every other profession, they keep us out. My nigga Jamie Foxx said Black people are the most talented people on earth, and he's still makin' movies because everybody knows he's just speaking the truth. Think about it. Did you ever watch the news when Bush was in office fuckin' everything up? Even them White reporters was going off on him. Then Obama gets in there and you never heard nothin' bad about him. That shit with the healthcare website wasn't his fault. He don't build websites. And them Republicans made him let all the pyahs stay. But that was really game. Once you get them here they have kids that will vote, and they will remember who let Mommy and Poppy stay. It's a majority-rule country, White folks. God Bless Amerikkka! The wannabe fly whiteboy and the big Nazi might be gettin' into it. That would be some cool-ass shit if they killed each other.

Youngbuck cocked his head to the side, "Lemme tell you somethin', man. The day I ask for your permission to whup somebody's ass is the same day I suck yo' dick!"

Ogre looked at Slim G-Zus, "Oh, that's how we doin' it?"

Slim G-Zus said, "If we're gonna back y'all, we can't have one of yours getting done like that. Makes us all look bad."

"We're all White, dawg," added Sidewinder.

Ogre said, "Jordan was gonna have to catch out. If he didn't, we'd have smashed him off the farm. That was NSR business—nobody else's."

"I did that. I can't take it back," said Youngbuck.

"You gotta real smart fuckin' mouth—"

"You gotta problem with my mouth, why don't you punch me in the muthafucka."

"I sure the fuck can!"

Slim G-Zus stepped in front of Youngbuck. "Y'all wanna box y'all can handle that in the shower. Nobody's gotta go to jail."

Russell could tell the farthest thing from Ogre and Young-buck's minds were the consequences of getting caught. Ogre's two flankers stepped up. Itchy foot and Jew Boy started forward. Russell followed. Sidewinder and Big Body Slim fanned out. Ogre had to notice the number disadvantage. They'd get beaten down and look even worse than they already did. He needed to protect the Reich, but fighting a losing battle was almost never a good proposition. Rec ended and they all headed for D-pod one section.

Youngbuck gave up about thirty pounds and five inches to Ogre, but seeing them standing with their shirts off in front of the showers on three row, a betting man would have wagered on the smaller fighter.

They fought in rounds, stopping for less than a minute periodically to catch their breath. Youngbuck would dip or weave on occasion while Ogre stood tall, absorbing more punches than he was landing. When Slim G-Zus finally stopped it, Youngbuck had a couple of red marks on his forehead that looked like hickeys. Ogre had the same on his cheek, plus a busted lip. Russell watched as they stepped out of the shower, heaving and gulping air. They shook hands. Ogre and his went downstairs to the dayroom to wait for chow. After eating, they would all go back to where they were housed, undetected.

Russell had just finished running all of this down to Adisa when his door rolled for him to go to work. Adisa said, "We'll finish that up tomorrow," as they rapped fists.

CHAPTER 19

When Russell arrived at the front desk, Salinas was speaking Spanish into the phone at a frenzied pace. Russell thought to himself, *Man, I gotta buy that Spanish-English Dictionary they sell on commissary.* He went to the closet for the mop bucket and heard the phone hang-up. It had been a few days since he had made his pass at her, and there hadn't been a chance for him to follow up. He carried the mop bucket to the desk. "Say, miss, you got the chemicals back there?"

Elka looked up and stared at the *guero.* He smiled without showing his teeth. Nodding, she looked down each hallway to make sure they were alone. She stood, her lips curling in anger, "I hope you've come to your senses. Because if you ever come at me like that again, I'm gonna write you a major case and you're gonna be on B-side with a bunch of *moyos* who'll love those green eyes."

"What's a *moyo*?"

Salinas rolled her eyes and exhaled, her cheeks puffing out cutely.

McCann asked, "Is that how you say *Hispanic* in Spanish?"

"What? *No!* How long have you been locked up?"

"About four months."

Elka folded her arms and set her jaw. "*Moyos* are Blacks," she said.

"Oh, well, I'm not into guys. Black or otherwise. What about you? Do you like green eyes?" He smiled again.

Elka unfolded her arms and leaned forward, exasperated... but she couldn't figure out why she wasn't angrier than she actually was...

She raised her hand and pointed at him, "I swear to God—" But his cocky smile only widened.

Russell knew that if she was going to make good on her threat, she'd have already handcuffed him and escorted him to PHD. He still didn't want to push his luck too much, but he wanted to keep the conversation going, there was no telling when Ike or one of the guards would show up. It could be days before he'd have another chance. "Miss Salinas? Sorry if I upset you. Not my intention. I know you think all inmates are trying to get guards to smuggle stuff in, but that ain't me. I don't want anything from you. I just wanted to talk to you. I wouldn't do anything to get you in trouble."

Elka had folded her arms again. She took the *guero*'s measure. He wasn't bad looking. In fact, if you liked *gavachos,* he was kind of cute. But that wasn't why she let him talk. It was the way he stayed so calm when she threatened him. He wasn't scared. He was confident. Maybe a little *too* sure of himself. "Well, I don't wanna talk to you. Got it?" she said. His face cinched up. "Coulda fooled me," he said, and smiled like he could read her mind.

CHAPTER 20

"My name is Sharon Sontag. Everybody here for Cultural Anthropology?"

Russell nodded his head with everyone else. Ms. Sontag went on to ask everyone to state their name and why they were taking the class. She wore a cream-colored heavy-gauge sweater and brown pants. After giving a bleached-white smile to every student for accomplishing the feat of saying their name and, "It's a required course," Ms. Sontag said, "I'm here because, in my family, when you finished high school, you went to college." Another exaggerated smile before she lifted her arms out to the side, "That's just what you did. So I know how privileged I was growing up in the household that I did, in a society where, gosh, pretty much everybody on TV and everybody in my textbooks looked like me." She looked around the class. Russell followed her eyes. They paused on Yella Fella, who was grinning and nodding his head. "Teaching this class," she raised her eyebrows, "here in this prison, is my way of giving back." She cleared her throat. "Looking out over this class, the diversity I see is heartwarming. The college I went to had very few Latinos or African-Americans. I'm thankful for my education, but I know it would have been much better if the student body had been more reflective of society. So, with that in mind," she turned and reached for two piles of books on the desk, "I went out of my way to get these two outside reading books approved for this class." She held the books out in front of her, shaking the one in her right hand. "This is by Deidre Barrett. It's called *Supernormal Stimuli*. This..." she shook her left hand, "is *White Teeth*. It's a novel by Zadie Smith. *Supernormal Stimuli* explains how evolution has programmed our brains to engage in unhealthy behavior. The reason I'm assigning it in Cultural Anthro is because, as we'll see, some of the principles it explains are responsible for many of society's problems. And the reason we study humans—anthropoids—is to learn from our mistakes, so we can better solve our problems going forward."

Russell didn't like the sound of this—*evolution has programmed us...*—but that's what he got for letting an atheist named Slim G-Zus tell him what classes to take. Now, this woman was going to try and tell him he came from a monkey.

"*White Teeth* was written by Zadie Smith. She was born in England to a Jamaican mother and English father. The book is basically about her family's history, but it does such a great job of illustrating the benefits of diversity and the many problems we face today in regards to the dominant culture imposing its will upon and destroying the cultures of minorities."

Slim G-Zus tilted his head and sighed audibly. Ms. Sontag looked at him, but he did not acknowledge her.

"Smith is a really talented writer. The cast of characters is so diverse and their goals and problems so lifelike. Well, I don't want to give it away so I'll stop there, but it's a good read."

Russell walked a good ten feet behind Slim G-Zus. A cold wind from the north bottlenecking through the spaces between the buildings was hitting them hard from a different direction each time they turned a corner. Russell cussed himself for not bringing his jacket. Slim G-Zus had his hood pulled over his head, books in one oversized hand, his other jammed in a pocket. Russell held his arms tight against the sides of his body, looking down at the sidewalk and shivering.

Slim G-Zus hollered, "LOOK OOOOOUT, ADISA!" Russell looked up.

"Hey!" said Adisa. He was walking alongside a cart with an officer and three other inmates on the sidewalk that led to 18 and 19 buildings.

"Wassup?" asked Slim G-Zus.

"Man, they're moving me to the dorms!"

Slim G-Zus cocked his head back then dropped it to his chest.

Adisa hollered, "Say, Lane, holler at Big Body!"

"Alright!" answered Slim G-Zus.

The door rolled and Russell stepped inside. One of the local imitations of a hip-hop station blared through a homemade speaker. The *Investor's Business Daily's Ten Rules for Success* was gone, replaced by pictures of Beyonce and Miley Cyrus. His new celly was brown-skinned with a bunch of individual tats, not the kind that ran together to cover entire areas like most everybody else had. He was about Russell's size, though less muscular.

"'Sup, man?" asked Russell.

"'Sup?" he answered, giving Russell the once-over, trillion-cut diamonds in his mouth blinging through a crooked smile. A pause that lasted too long ended with, "You look like you fresh in the system," and another alligator smile.

Russell purposefully tried not to reply too quickly. He said, "Yeah, I just got here a few months ago." More bling from his new celly's dental artwork.

Russell said, "What do they call you?"

"Oak Cliff."

Russell nodded. "Outta Dallas, huh?"

"Yeah."

"I'm McCann." Russell nodded at the radio on the desk. "They play some weak-ass shit down here, huh? I imagine Dallas is like Houston. Y'all probably got some real rap stations, right?"

Oak Cliff sat down on his bunk and started tying off his wave cap. Russell waited for a reply. "C'mon, whiteboy, you don't know nothin' about that."

Whiteboy. Why did that word all of a sudden bother him? He'd never thought anything of it until... Slim G-Zus... That day on the yard... That deep voice telling him, "Don't ever again let anyone call you whiteboy." So, the arrogant, verbally challenged psycho was now in his head. Great.

Russell forced a smile. "Shi-it. In that H, we got The Box. They play the most real rap. Then a few other stations that play some hip-hop shit, plus Magic. That's a real R&B station."

Oak Cliff reached over to the desk and took a copy of the *Dallas Morning News* off of a large white spread bowl and stirred its contents, ignoring Russell.

"Mee-Khan?" asked the chubby guard through the grate in the door. Russell turned around to see a letter slide through the side of the door.

Russell grabbed it and said, "Say, Morales, what time y'all calling me out tonight?"

"S'up to the desk boss, Salinas," which Russell already knew; he just wanted his celly to know he'd be leaving before too long. Russell sat down on the toilet and opened the letter from Cordell.

Sup Bro?

Just got a visit from my Mom and Natasha. They're good. Natasha had on some jeans... DAMN!!! I almost had to leave visitation bent at the waist. College is all right. I got a good sociology teacher. She's got us reading books called *Makes Me Wanna Holler* and *Stupid White Men*. They are saying some real shit. I know you would understand them. These White boys in my class don't get it. One of them dropped the class because of it. I didn't think he was like that. He didn't have all them racial ass tattoos like some of them do. I know you ain't fallin' for none of that bullshit. I think half of these redneck guards are in that shit, too. Most of the Black guards here are from the country, too. A bunch of slo-motion fools. Half of them think they're still slaves. It's a trip how some things never change. The D.A.'s, lawyers, and even most of the cops that put us here were all White. It's no wonder why, when you look around the dayroom, it's packed with Blacks. It's fucked-up how much time they gave us. But I'm glad that I got to see how it is. It has opened my eyes to a lot of shit I'd have never seen otherwise. I went to the Muslim service the other day and it was live. They had bros up on the stage speaking on all kinds of things. You should try checking it out. I asked this one brotha if Whites could go, and he said, "Yeah." Looks like the Texans aren't going to do anything this year. The Rockets need a couple more pieces. Keep yo' head up. I'm cutting the string on this one and putting it in the wind.

Much Love Bro,
Cordell

P.S. The rap station 95 The Beat out of Dallas played your old jam *Expensive Tastes*. Time for you to do something new.

Dear Wannabe Tyreese,

'Sup, Dell? I know Natasha came in there and shut visitation down! That's good her and your Mom came. I haven't heard from Megan lately, but I'm sure she's coming pretty soon. College is pretty good here. One of my teachers looks like G.I. Joe. I like him because he argues with this one White cat I can't stand. This fool thinks he knows everything and he talks real raw to people. He's about your height, real cut up but not that big. I think I could take him if it came down to it. You said you were reading a book called *Stupid White Men*. Is that really what it's called? I've never heard of it. All the guards here are either Hispanic or Nigerian. There's only a few Whites. Everybody makes fun of the Nigerians. They are a little hard to understand sometimes, but I know they bring a lot to the table coming from another country. I don't think all of the Whites here are racists. Most of them just don't have any education. A lot of them come from messed-up backgrounds. Our families weren't rich but we were lucky compared to these folks. Did you tell your Mom you went to that Muslim service? I know you didn't. She'd flip out. My last celly was a Muslim. We got along real good. I wish they wouldn't have moved him. Anyway, I hope you don't start thinking I'm the devil. LMAO. Yeah, the Texans are out of it, but they're still our Texans. I'm thinking the Rockets may need to work a deal for Rondo. He's not working out in Dallas. I still like Beverly but Rondo has won a championship already. That's all I got. Lemme hear back from you.

Peace Out My Brotha,
Russ

Russell stepped out of his cell at 11:30 p.m. wondering why he was being called out thirty minutes early. He shut the door behind him and started for the stairwell when he heard, "McCann." in the husky voice of Slim G-Zus. "Come holler at me 'fore you go." Russell sighed quietly and headed for Slim G-Zus's cell.

"'Sup Slim?"

"Check this out, potna. You probably need to have the jackin' conversation with your celly." The jackin' conversation was where you pulled your celly aside and told him you weren't down with him masturbating on the female guards when y'all are in the cell together. It was the ultimate disrespect. Russell had learned about this from Jew Boy, who'd fought with one of his cellies over the issue. Slim G-Zus said, "Cat's prob'ly a jackmonster. Looks like a real piece of shit."

Russell asked, "you know him?"

"Nah. Don't have to. I'm a commodities trader. I play the percentages."

Russell nodded. "Yeah, well, I gotta get to work. Thanks." He walked off, thinking to himself how racist Slim G-Zus and his "percentages" were. Assuming his new celly was going to do something like that just because of the way he looks—mainly because of his skin color. Russell shook his head at the stereotyping as he stepped into the sally port and saw Salinas sitting behind the desk.

Elka looked down the hallway to D-pod when she heard the humming of the electronic sally port door. The green-eyed gringo was on his way. He stepped up to the desk and laid his right forearm across it, as if the whole building belonged to him. She looked the opposite direction toward F-Pod. All Clear. She took a deep breath, digging her short unpolished fingernails into her palms as she stood, looking him in the eye. "I looked your crime up. You're in here for having a gun on a school campus. Then I Googled your name and..." she shook her head slowly, "...You and some Black guy killed the gunman at that college in Houston..."

Her words blasted a charge through his limbs. "Uh..." was all he could manage.

Salinas said, "Why did you have a gun?"

Russell shrugged, turned his palms up. This was an odd question to him. Like asking someone why they had toilet paper. His Dad carried a gun. His brother carried a gun. Even his mother carried a gun. Russell said, "Pretty much everybody I know—"

"Were you in a gang?" asked Salinas.

"No"

"You weren't in a *moyo* gang with your friend?"

"Nah. I ain't."

"Are you in one of those White gangs in here?"

"Hell, no!"

She folded her arms and studied his face, "You got a three-year sentence. When do you come up for parole?"

"Less than six months from now. They're giving me credit for the time I was out on bond waiting to be sentenced."

"Six Months..." she said like she was considering it. She looked off, "That's not that long."

Russell noticed her lips. She wasn't wearing lipstick but those full lips looked fuller than usual with the gloss she had on. Her hair wasn't in a tight bun either. It was swept up with a pencil sticking out in back.

She unfolded her arms and pointed at him like a mother scolding a child, "If you ever tell anyone we had this conversation..."

Russell compressed his lips, thinking, *If it ends now it wasn't much of a conversation.*

Salinas put her hands on her hips and looked around again, "Do you do drugs?"

"No." It was beginning to seem like an interrogation.

Her facial expression changed from deadly serious to slightly angry. "If you think Mexican women are just for fucking and cooking, you're wrong."

"No, I don't think like that." A look of *Where the hell did that come from?* on his face, Russell said, "I'm from Houston. I've dated Hispanic girls before—"

"Hispanic? That's a Black. I'm Mexican," which sounded like *Mettsi-can* when she said it.

"Oh. Right," said Russell nodding.

"What do you mean you 'dated' them? You mean you fucked 'em?"

"No. I mean, like, when we all went out some of the girls were..." he gestured toward her in a circular motion with an open hand, afraid to use the words Hispanic or Mexican. "...you know, and..."

Salinas raised her perfectly arched eyebrows waiting.

Russell was trapped. Come to think of it, he'd never really been on a "date" with anyone. He and his friends all went out together, and at the end of the night everybody just paired up with someone, and you were pretty much guaranteed second base or better. The two Hispanic girls he'd been with, Crystal and Maria, weren't any different than any of the White girls Russell had ever messed around with. "....I don't care what color someone is. I'm not like the rest of these idiots running around here. Okay?" Russell jerked forward at *okay*, thinking a little aggression would help his cause.

Elka liked the way his neck seemed to flare when he said *okay*. She folded her arms. "All I know," she said looking away, "is when I was in high school the *gueros* only wanted to screw Mexican girls—" which was bullshit. Bee Ef Eee High only had a handful of White students and neither she nor any of her friends had ever talked to them. In fact they used to make fun of them on a regular basis. "What's the difference between marrying a *gavacho* and a broom? At least you can dance with the broom."

Elka turned back and looked into his emerald eyes, "So, are you gonna stay out of trouble and make parole?"

He inhaled deeply. "Yes. I'm getting a letter from the D.A., so it's pretty much guaranteed."

Elka smirked. "Alright, get to work," she said and turned her back dismissively.

"Not yet," said the green-eyed gringo.

Her eyes bugged, "What?"

"Let your hair down so I can see how long it is."

¡Vaya que atrevido! What does he think this is? She sat down behind the U-shaped desk. The *guero* just stood there smiling. She would do it just to make him leave.

Salinas lowered her head and took the pencil out. Long, thick cords of black silk spilled past her shoulders, glistening in the lone light of the darkened area. She looked up, almost sad, like she was revealing a part of herself she wanted to keep private, and held his gaze. She was gorgeous. A movie star face and a body so curvy not even the bulky uniform could hide it. And she seemed so serious. So smart. She was perfect.

Russell and Ike finished cleaning the last shower of the night and took a seat on the back bench in the dayroom. Russell said, "So, have you thought about what you're gonna eat first when you get out?"

Ike leaned back, smiling wide at the thought. "Well," he said, "Momma's gonna want to cook, but I don't want her to go to all that trouble. I been thinking about some Popeyes. I had some of that when I was on Cofield. Lawman used to eat that Popeyes and he'd leave me a piece when he throwed the box away. Maybe I can get Momma to fry some okra." Ike turned to Russell, "Eat that chicken and that okra? Whew!"

Russell nodded knowingly. "Popeyes has them cajun fries and that red drank. Man, that red drank's goin' down."

Big Ike said, "It's not gonna be much longer for you, li'l brah. Lord gonna bless you when you come up. Watch what I tell you."

"Yeah, you know... I leave it all in his hands," said Russell, "Coming down here really gave me some time to think. To get my priorities straight. If I'd have had my head on straight when I was at Football Factory—like I do now—" Russell shook his head, "no way I'd have washed out."

Big Ike dropped his hands in his lap, "You said awhile back you were gonna try to pick up some weight, play when you got out." Ike grabbed Russell's right biceps, "You've done got a little bigger."

"Yeah, I gotta be about 215 now. If I had creatine or some nitric oxide, I could get to 225 easy."

"Think that's all you lacked?"

"Nah, problem was coverage. When you're a D.B., they want you to be able to turn and run. I didn't get that many chances, and when I did, I got beat a few times. Devon Hamilton—you know, at LSU?—had like a hundred yards against Ol' Miss last week? He was one of the receivers when I was there." Russell shook his head, "You wouldn't believe how quick he is to be so big... If I can play linebacker, I'll have to cover tight ends and running backs. Once in awhile a receiver in the slot, but it'd be mostly about making tackles. Which is what I'm best at."

Ike nodded his head. "My Mom wouldn't let me play football. Scared I'd get hurt."

Russell laughed, "C'mon man. You'd have been the biggest kid on the field."

Big Ike shrugged, "My Momma wasn't tryna hear it."

"I knocked a guy's helmet off once. They ran some kind of misdirection. I stayed home. The back came up the middle, and he was looking off in the direction everybody else went. I unloaded on that fool. His helmet went, like, five feet up in the air. I got the video sitting at the house right now." A small shadow on the ground by the trash can caught Russell's eye. He looked over and saw a rat scurry into a hole in the wall.

"Anyway, I overheard a couple of coaches—I was outside their offices but they didn't know that—they were saying shit like, 'Number 34 has stiff hips. He can't flip his hips and run,' some ol' nonsense." Russell held his hands up, "You ever hear men talk about other men's hips?"

Ike shook his head, "Nah, can't say that I have."

"NFL linebackers are like six four, maybe 250, at least 240. I can't put on that much weight without juicing. Pat Tillman played linebacker in college, then got drafted and switched to safety. That's what I'd like to do. Even guys on the practice squad make, like, eighty grand a year. You can live fat on eighty g's a year."

Ike whistled then said, "You sure can."

"That's a big part of my motivation when I hit the weights. That and proving everybody wrong."

"Yeah, I can dig it, li'l bro," Ike stood, "Ain't nothin' to it but to do it," he said as they rapped fists. "What they got in that chow hall, anyway?"

"I don't know. I'm thinking about hittin' the shower and going to sleep. Gotta work out tomorrow—er, today. Later today, I mean."

"Yeah, I think I'ma make an appearance out there on that court here in a couple days."

"Oh yeah? Thought you were layin' low?

"I was. But I gotta get some fresh air. Ain't no drama goin' on right now anyway. I just wanna play me a li'l ball. Run up and down that court." Ike mimed a jump shot.

Elka was sitting behind the desk scarfing Tostitos and talking on the phone when McCann and Donaldson turned in their mop bucket and scrub brushes. She placed her hand over the mouthpiece and said, "McCann, go to A-turnout and get the count sheets." When he returned, she was still on the phone. He placed the paper in front of her and stroked the back of her hand with his fingertips. Sparks. Her mouth went dry. "*Uno momento,*" she said into the phone, her neck on fire. She was only slightly more angry than aroused. She pointed at D-pod, "If you don't get to the house right now..." He half frowned and the twinkle went out of his eye. She couldn't take that. Softly she said, "Please go before you get me in trouble."

CHAPTER 21

Karl Clarkson had spent several classes on inequality and social justice. He had acquitted himself nicely, getting his points across to all of his students save for John Lane, who Karl had figured out pretty quickly was a White supremacist. In this environment, however, he had to keep it veiled because he wasn't a member of the majority. And not being a member of the majority was a difficult adjustment for someone so used to that privilege. To cope, he'd obviously resorted to the mainstream ideology of the political right, a bunch of closet racists themselves, in hopes of hanging on to the comforting feeling of security one gets when they know theirs is the dominant culture. *It all fit so well.*

Clarkson was pondering all of this and how he would use it to his advantage when Lane marched in and sat down right in front of him. They locked eyes. Exchanged terse nods. "Mr. Clarkson, we start debating immigration today?" His chin was up, his eyes a perpetual dare.

Clarkson sat back in his chair and clasped his hands on top of his head, nodding slowly. "Yessir, we do." They had both taken to being overly formal with one another, as if not to do so would've given the other an opportunity to slip through and deliver a decisive blow in their ongoing debate.

Russell was one of the last to take his seat. Mr. Clarkson stood up and walked around to the front of his desk. "America is a nation of immigrants," he said. Slim G-Zus shifted in his seat, causing Russell to roll his eyes. If Clarkson said it was nighttime outside, Slim G-Zus would disagree. "One of the main reasons America has had so much economic success, albeit mostly for those at the top, is because of the diversity that immigrants have brought here. Diversity brings respect and tolerance where before it could not have existed. It gives us new insights and new ways of doing things. Better ways of doing things. When a company has, say, an African-American, Asian-American, and a gay Latino on their board of directors, it has a built-in advantage over other companies that don't have such diversity." Clarkson paused. "A government and its nation are no different. As crazy as it sounds to some people, there are actually things we can learn from the rest of the world." Russell knew that was a shot at Slim G-Zus. Clarkson sat down on his desk and folded his arms. "Knowing these facts about diversity, why do we have so many people opposed to immigration? And, how do we reach out to these people and educate them so they won't fall for the disinformation that... well, scares a lot of them." Clarkson scanned the classroom and pointed, "Yes?"

A bald Black inmate cleared his throat, "When I took sociology in Ms. Estrada's class, we learned about conflict theory and some other theories that explained why American society is so... unfair. Basically, it's the group in power trying to stay in power, and I think those people are the ones scared of immigration because," he gestured, "they want to keep what they got."

"Oh, I don't doubt that at all," said Clarkson. "But what do we do to change their minds?" Yella Fella raised his hand and Clarkson pointed.

"People need to be taught the truth about this country. How it was stolen. How it was built by people—my people—who were stolen from Africa because they were Black. How their culture was stolen. How the gold and diamonds were stolen from Africa... Stolen people and stolen goods—both from Africa—plus stolen land from the Indians. If everybody knew the good ol' U S of A was sitting on stolen land—which means it ain't theirs," he shrugged, "maybe they wouldn't be tryna keep everybody out."

Clarkson looked down and tapped his chin with his fingertips. "So, what you're saying is, the people who are against immigration have a faulty understanding of how America came to be, of what America really is, and if that weren't the case they'd be more likely to embrace immigration and the diversity it brings."

"Yeah," said Yella Fella.

"Okay," said Clarkson nodding his head.

An Hispanic—check that—a Mexican raised his hand. Clarkson nodded at him, "Yes?"

"My grandfather came here from Oaxaca. He thought he could make a better life for himself and for his family." He leaned forward and placed his forearms on the desktop, "The same reason the pilgrims came here. But now it's like, all of a sudden, no one else can come." He shook his head. "Everybody needs to learn what you said, Mr. Clarkson. We are a nation of immigrants. Unless you're a Native American, you're an immigrant."

Clarkson jabbed a finger towards him, "Right! So, it's hypocritical—not just coldhearted. Excellent point. Because," he lifted his arms out wide, "nobody wants to be a hypocrite." Clarkson slid his hands into his pockets and looked at the floor. "One of the more effective ways to bring about social change is to find your target, in this case, those opposed to immigration, and show society the error of their ways through ridicule. Eventually, shaming them into changing." Clarkson smiled, "The pilgrims did not have passports or some 'official' paperwork giving them permission to immigrate here. They were undocumented. In fact, their ancestors hadn't even lived here like a lot of today's immigrants from Latin America. Yet, the natives welcomed them and showed them how to survive." Clarkson looked over the class, "Not exactly the same kind of treatment immigrants receive today. It's no wonder our neighbors and trade partners in Mexico look at us with disgust. Instead of reaching out to today's immigrants and helping them get ahead like they did us, we marginalize them and force them into ghettos and barrios and tell them to stay there unless they speak English and give up their culture." Clarkson looked down again and ran his tongue between his bottom lip and teeth.

I know it's getting bad when even one of their All-American whiteboys, like this teacher here, is admitting it. I'll never trust a White man but there's a few who at least get it. Michael Moore gets it. Maybe a few others. John Brown.

I ain't real big on letting all these pyahs come across the border, but if it makes them Rush Limbaugh faggots scared, it can't be that bad. Letting the people who originally had this land have it back is technically right, but what about the people who truly built this country? What about my people? We were brought here in chains, built the whole thing and made all them White folks rich—and ain't got nothing to show for it. Why are we so worried about all these pyahs in Mexico when all the ghettos and prisons are packed with Blacks? I get it that they'll vote for Obama, but when they get the majority they may not be much better than these ho-ass White folks. I have a cousin out in Cali, he done lived in L.A., Sacramento, and the Bay. He says them pyahs done got so bad, trying to run everything, some nigga spraypainted *Bloods and Crips unite* on an overpass.

I had an old-school nigga down here tell me that, back in the day, the Mexicans and whiteboys would ride together against the Blacks because there was so few of them. But once the Mexicans got enough numbers, they kicked the whiteboys to the curb. They'll try to do my boy Obama the same way. It's all these White folks' fault anyway. They wasn't ready for the teachings they stole from Africa. I respect the Brown man. They have a right to their land. But this land wouldn't be what it is without Africans building everything for free! Africans and Indians had everything they needed till these White folks crawled out of their caves and stole it all.

Slim G-Zus raised his hand.

"Mr. Lane."

"When you say we're a nation of immigrants, don't you mean we're a nation of *descendants* of immigrants?"

Clarkson sighed and looked up. "Everyone who came here that looks like you or me came from somewhere else. Most would take that to mean we're a nation of immigrants."

"Well, sir, I believe the definition of an immigrant is—"

"We know what an immigrant is, Mr. Lane. We're not that stupid."

"I was born here, Mr. Clarkson. I'm not an immigrant. If you wanna say some of my *ancestors* were immigrants, well, I guess you could, but this land wasn't a country with established borders when they came here."

Clarkson frowned. "And what do you recommend we do with these gems of information you've bestowed upon us, Mr. Lane?"

Slim G-Zus frowned. "My point is, Mr. Clarkson, sir, that your premise about us all being immigrants—and therefore, we can't object to immigration—is false."

"We're not here to get into semantics, Mr. Lane. America was founded by immigrants; therefore, it's a nation of immigrants. Period."

"Then every nation outside the Olduvai Gorge is a nation of immigrants."

Clarkson closed his eyes and took a deep breath. "Anything else, Mr. Lane?"

Slim G-Zus cleared his throat, "Yes, sir. You present diversity as a guaranteed strength instead of a concept to be tested or debated."

"Right. I do. You see, Mr. Lane, for some of us, some things are beyond debate: water is wet, the Earth is round..."

Slim G-Zus smiled. "Diversity is our strength?"

"You disagree?"

"Personally?... I think different races or skin colors can coexist inside a country. I don't think different cultures—even if their skin is the same color—can. In my never humble opinion, a nation is a group of people who speak the same language, study the same history, live on the same soil, et cetera, et cetera. You need those things to make a country stick together. To make it willing to defend itself. As for diversity being responsible for America's economy, well, Japan has practically no immigration, and its workforce is as productive as any in the world. Germany's was just as productive before they allowed mass immigration."

Clarkson said, "Have you ever been to Germany?"

"No," said Slim G-Zus, "I haven't."

"I have."

Slim G-Zus squinted his eyes, then nodded. *Amazing what passes for an argument with this guy,* he thought.

"Mr. Clarkson, have you ever read any of Robert Putnam's stuff? He's a professor at Harvard, wrote that book *Bowling Alone?*"

"Doesn't ring a bell."

"He says social capital—how much people trust each other and whatnot—has been in decline since the 1950's. He found Los Angeles—the most diverse city in the US—had the least amount of trust amongst its citizens." Slim G-Zus interlocked his fingers on his desktop, hoping to appear more like a learned gentleman than a working-class johnny-come-lately intellectual who'd been locked up since he was nineteen. "Does that give you any pause, sir?"

"No," said Clarkson flatly.

Slim G-Zus sat up straight and folded his arms. He leaned back, the top of the small chair barely reaching the middle of his long torso. "He interviewed like thirty thousand people."

"Well, he's one guy. The Supreme Court has said diversity is a compelling state interest. So, it's practically the law of the land."

"So, damn the evidence, full speed ahead with the emotionally satisfying theory?"

"Albert Einstein's contributions as an immigrant aren't a theory, Mr. Lane, emotionally satisfying or otherwise. We brought WWII to an end because of him and other immigrant engineers."

"Albert Einstein didn't come from a Third-World country like eighty-five percent of America's immigrants have since 1965. And immigrants with college degrees or some kinda skills? They actually put more into the treasury than they take out. Unskilled immigrants do the opposite. The country is already broke, Mr. Clarkson." Slim G-Zus raised his hands and shook his head, as if to say, *Don't blame me.* "And you said we need to embrace immigrants instead of making them choose between giving up their culture or being poor. Well, I think that's a... whatta ya call it? False dichotomy—wait. Not that. Like a false proposition. Because poverty in America is middle-class living to most of them." Clarkson's eyebrows catapulted up. "More importantly," said Slim G-Zus, "you seem to think people can act and think the same way they did before and get the results

Americans get. And as for Mexico being 'disgusted' with us because we supposedly treat illegal aliens harshly... well, Mexicans have a fence across their southern border and they beat and rape Guatemalans and everybody else they catch comin' across... wouldn't that make them hypocrites worthy of your ridicule? I mean, if our border patrol did that, President Obama would bring Eric Holder out of retirement and send him down here in a heartbeat."

Clarkson let out an exaggerated sigh. "What are you scared of, Mr. Lane?"

Slim G-Zus flexed his jaw muscles as his eyes narrowed. "Do I look like I'm scared of anything?" he asked.

The silence in the classroom was deafening. Clarkson smirked. "What do you think will happen if America keeps getting eighty-five percent of its immigrants from the Third World, as you claim?"

"It'll cease to be America. People bring their culture with them. If you keep importing the Third World, you become the Third World."

Clarkson looked at the other faces in the class, hoping they felt his outrage. Most of them just looked on, except for one Black man in the corner who was visibly upset. "So, helping the poor, the tired, the sick, by letting them immigrate here—as the sign says—is gonna fill the country with people who don't look like you, which means the country is no longer America. Right?"

Slim G-Zus grinned and chuckled. "The looks are immaterial. I haven't mentioned appearance once. You're bringing it up to try and paint me as a racist because, in your mind, once you've done that, nothing I say matters. To better prove my point, sir, what would your home town, Austin—which has about a million people—be if we imported a million Scottish people and swapped them with all the Austinites? There'd still be a place on a map called Austin, but would you feel at home walking down sixth street?"

"Horrible attempt at analogy, Mr. Lane. America welcomes less than a million immigrants each year. We are a nation of 350 million people. At that rate you'd be almost 400 years old when America became a Third World nation, teeming with undesirables."

"Ever heard of Dearbornistan? It's how people refer to Dearborn, Michigan, now. The whole country doesn't have to be replaced. Who lives in the whole country at once? Maybe some of your friends in D.C. have multiple houses in multiple cities, but most of us live in one spot. Think about it. If you only wanted to live in Austin and its population was completely replaced by Norwegians, would you say 'oh, no big deal, I'll just move to Houston?' I doubt it."

Clarkson raised his eyebrows mockingly, as if to say, *Deep thinking indeed.* "I'm curious, Mr. Lane, what makes you think it's such a travesty to have one group of people replace another? After all, the pilgrims—yesterdays outsiders—came here without passports and replaced the country's natives by committing genocide. I would much rather be free to move if I choose than to have the US Army bash my head in with a boot heel so they could save bullets."

Slim G-Zus cocked his head sideways. "That sounded a lot better when ol' boy said it in *Young Guns.*" They stared at one another. Slim G-Zus continued, "Ninety-five percent of the natives who died after contact with Europeans did so from germs. The Europeans didn't commit genocide against the Indians. Try reading *Guns, Germs, and Steel*; the author is a lefty just like you. You know, one of the good guys." Slim G-Zus smiled and raised a Power to the People fist in the air. "But to answer your question, I think you should ask the people in whatever country is about to get hit by a tsunami or earthquake why it's a *travesty* if America ceases to be America." Slim G-Zus leaned forward, raising his voice, "They'll tell you, because those imperialistic, racist, genocidal yankees are the only ones gonna send an aircraft carrier fulla food and water when our own country is in shambles."

Clarkson thrust an open hand towards Slim G-Zus as if he were offering it to be shaken. "So, you believe only current Americans are capable of acts of good will?"

"No, I—"

"The problem with that, Mr. Lane—"

"—didn't say—"

"—is that Americans have committed some of the greatest atrocities in the history of *mankind.* Many argue—rather convincingly, I might add—that this country's unjust founding precludes its citizens from ever taking pride in who they are. Slavery, lynchings, Jim Crow—have you not been reading the book I assigned you by the late Howard Zinn? You must not be if you think America is somehow 'exceptional' and better than any other country."

"I think it's the best country ever—"

"When it's lagging in education, health care, income equality, and a host of other measurables." Clarkson placed his hands on his hips and shook his head., "Do you think the Arawaks or free persons of color who were sold into slavery believe America's the best country ever?"

"I don't know what they thought. But I do know that every evil that has ever gone on in America has gone on everywhere else."

Clarkson's eyes bugged as he jerked back. "So your argument, Mr. Lane, is, essentially, 'But, Mom, everybody else was doing it.'"

"Not quite—if you'll let me finish—people don't say America's exceptional because they think nothing bad ever happened here. They say tyranny has been the rule; America's freedom and democracy, the exception. *And,*" Slim G-Zus raised his voice in anticipation of an interruption that didn't come, "that when it comes to evils like slavery, America and most of the West has gone to hell and back to stop these evils—even though they existed way before America or England were even countries. Believing in the greatness of America, Mr. Clarkson, also helps with patriotism, which is real important to a country's survival. If you believe your country's evil, why would you fight for it? Why would you try to preserve it?" Slim G-Zus lifted his hands palms up, "I don't know, sir, maybe you're not a patriot, and that's just a difference between me and you."

Clarkson cut his eyes hard at Slim G-Zus and pointed at him. "Don't you ever question my patriotism." He pointed at himself, "I served in this nation's military."

Slim G-Zus nodded his head, "So did Timothy McVeigh and Jeremiah Wright."

ussell came through the dayroom door a little after nine p.m. The guard everybody called Porn Star—fake platinum-blonde hair, fake fingernails, a face more sexy than pretty—was passing out the mail and flirting with everybody she could. Russell listened to her Kim Kardashian voice call out the cell numbers. He was expecting—make that hoping—to get a letter from Megan... or Cordell, or Mike, or Demetrius...

No dice. She went from fourteen to twenty-three. By now, though, Russell had perfected his striking out at mail call pokerface. He'd stand watching the sports TV, just far enough away from it to hear the officer's voice, yet close enough to look like his main concern was Sportscenter, not the mail. He'd stare intently at the TV, keeping his breathing steady.

Russell lay awake in his top bunk, fingers laced behind his head, listening to the last watered-down slow jam of the night. He was off that night, no showers to clean for another twenty-four hours. He was dividing his thoughts among three things: Why he hadn't heard back from Megan, whether or not he should make a bolder move on Salinas, and, though he wished it weren't the case, the artillery between Slim G-Zus and Mr. Clarkson. On the first two questions, he'd answered, *She's probably just busy,* and *Hell yeah,* respectively, though he knew that *Hell yeah* could peter out once he was outside the riskless confines of his cell. On the third, he just wished Clarkson and Slim G-Zus could fight, because he was sure the action-figure teacher would win.

He glanced at the digital clock on his radio: 11:57. It was about to be count time. Russell figured he'd better take a leak before Porn Star came around with her flashlight and count sheet. Although, half the section would probably be standing at the door jacking-off on her as she passed by, his accidently exposing himself to her while taking a piss wouldn't exactly be a traumatic event for her. At least from what he'd heard. He still didn't believe half the stories about the female officers who were considered "good"—meaning that if they liked what you were working with they'd stare at it and sometimes egg you on... And why would a fully clothed woman make you want to pull your shit out anyway... Like a lot of things in prison, Russell didn't understand the "jack game."

Russell stepped down from his bunk and walked to the door to make sure she hadn't started early; Porn Star or not, you just don't expose yourself to a woman. "Don't be on the flo' when that ho come through to count," said Oak Cliff.

Russell looked back, over his shoulder, "Yeah, I know, she might think I'm jacking on her. Damn sure don't need a code twenty. That's guaranteed to go platinum."

"I ain't worried about all that—"

Russell hit the button to flush the toilet, drowning out the end of his celly's sentence. He washed his hands and jumped back in the bunk, a little concerned where Oak Cliff was going with that statement... Russell put his headphones back on while his celly stood up and tied a string from the clothesline to the shelf, and hung his sheet up like they did when they had to shit and were both stuck in the cell. Russell rolled towards his window and cracked it open so the incoming air would push the smell out the door.

A couple of minutes passed and he hadn't heard the toilet flush. Russell pulled his headphones down and heard his celly's bare feet pattering across the concrete floor. He rolled over slowly and saw the sheet between them still up with Oak Cliff's silhouette pacing back and forth. Russell started to make a crack about constipation but kept it to himself.

He heard the mechanical whir of the section door opening, then the low thud of each step the officer took up the stairs to three row. Oak Cliff dropped his boxers. Russell's heartbeat picked up, drumming the fight-or-flight chemicals into his veins. Even though it was the ultimate disrespect, Russell knew he had to wait for the officer to leave the section so she couldn't hear the ruckus. He prayed silently: for God to keep him from getting caught. A fighting case would undoubtedly go major and fuck off his chance for parole, but he had no choice. Oak Cliff finished, washed his hands and took down the sheet. Russell stared at the ceiling but could tell his celly was looking at him as he folded his sheet. He wouldn't have time to put on his shoes when he hit the floor, so with Oak Cliff back in his bunk, Russell brought his knees to his chest and stripped off his socks; sitting up to do so would've made too much noise and alerted his celly.

Russell knew he had to get to the front of the cell to hit the light and try to cover the grate on the door with a towel so the guard in the picket couldn't see them. Russell closed his eyes. *Please, God,* he prayed.

As soon as his foot hit the ground he heard his celly suck his teeth. "Bitch-ass whiteboy."

Russell yanked his towel off the clothesline and stuffed it in the grate. He heard his celly sitting up. Russell lunged for the light switch. He missed. Oak Cliff didn't. He landed a right above Russell's left temple and staggered him. Russell could barely see him, the towel blocking what little light there was from the dayroom. Russell sprung forward, like he was trying to make a tackle. Oak Cliff slammed the bottom of his fist on the back of Russell's head. "Why you tryna wrestle, whiteboy?" Russell managed to clasp his hands around Oak Cliff's back and drive his shoulder into his rib cage, moving him backwards toward the bunks. Oak Cliff hammered Russell's back but didn't generate enough force to do any damage. Confident he had pushed him back far enough, Russell turned him loose and shoved him in the chest before spinning around to go for the light again.

This time he got it.

Russell turned back around with his left foot out in front and his hands up in front of his face. The large fluorescent light was too bright. They both squinted, their eyes nearly shut. Russell's eyes teared up and went blurry as the thought to turn the light back off crossed his mind. They stood about five feet apart blinking rapidly and exchanging feints, anxiously waiting for their eyes to stop burning.

Oak Cliff came at him. He swung lefts and rights hard and fast, but Russell's hands deflected most of them.

The short time that had passed while they wrestled and then waited for their eyes to adjust had allowed Russell's initial surge of adrenaline to rise and plateau. Now, with mental faculties in tune with the changes in his body's chemistry, the stress butterflies were being netted and his tunnel vision was widening and the thousands of combinations he'd delivered to Adisa's shower slides were ready to be unleashed.

In one motion, Russell bound forward off his back foot and landed a stiff left on the right side of Oak Cliff's face. He followed that with a right uppercut that missed, then a left hook that didn't, landing right above the jaw and turning Oak Cliff sideways. Thinking he had him almost knocked out, Russell abandoned all technique and stood up straight, launching a haymaker right, trying to win the fight in one punch.

He missed. Completely. His momentum carried him into Oak Cliff who threw a backhanded right elbow that failed to hit directly because Russell was too close. Instead of the hard bone of the elbow Russell took a triceps muscle across the ear.

Russell pushed off and stepped back into a staggered stance, fists by his temples. The look on his celly's face couldn't have been more condescending. "Bitch-ass whiteboy," he said. But even in that moment, Russell didn't give in to the prevailing prison mentality. He didn't call his celly a nigger or even think to. He breathed and waited for his opponent to make a move.

Oak Cliff tried to mirror Russell's stance and hand position, but it looked awkward, unnatural. A confidence-builder for Russell.

Oak Cliff's resentment seemed to catapult him forward. Russell waited, bobbing slightly on his toes. Oak Cliff came into range and Russell fired off a left jab. This one landed square on the mouth. It was like hitting the start button. Oak Cliff came alive, swinging wildly in frustration. Russell parried his punches like they were playing patty-cake and shot two more lefts—pop pop—before getting all his weight behind a right that connected above his opponent's left eye, splitting it deep, slinging blood against the wall as Oak Cliff recoiled.

Daquan Moten removed his hand from his eye, looked at the blood on it. "Ho-ass whiteboy just mad 'cause a nigga jackin' this Black cock on a White hoe!" Because at this point, what else could he say? Growing up in Dallas he'd seen a steady stream of Blacks on TV with the words *community leader* or *activist* after their names, and every time they appeared, they were accusing White people, or even a term like *black hole,* of being racist.

Russell was bothered by the accusation, but his brain filed it away to be reflected upon at some later date.

Oak Cliff rushed him again, dipping his shoulder and ramming it into a solid wall of abdominal muscle. Russell absorbed the blow and grabbed his celly in a headlock. He leaned forward, lowering them both before grabbing the waistband of Oak Cliff's boxers and trying to throw him into the wall. When he jerked, Oak Cliff managed to keep his hands locked behind Russell's back, causing them to rotate in a circle. Oak Cliff tried to grab his legs but Russell backed up, making his torso almost parallel to the floor.

Russell released him and threw a right uppercut followed by a left hook. Neither had much behind them but they both landed. Oak Cliff rose up. The blood was flowing and so were the tears. Again, Russell recognized this and made a mental note of it, but stayed in the moment. He threw a combination: left, right, left hook, then dipping a right cross to the sternum. Oak Cliff was punching all the while but without any accuracy. They stood there, punching until they ran out of breath. Russell backed up to the bunks, his celly to the door.

Oak Cliff's blood was on the floor and the wall, but most of it was on him and Russell. They stared at each other, chests heaving.

Daquan went into damage-control mode. He was about to be in one of the worst places any Black inmate could ever find himself, and the shame and stigma of losing a fight to a ho-ass whiteboy was more than he could bare. He needed an excuse... *The ho stole me from behind 'cause I was jackin' on that White bitch... And he said can't no niggas jack on White hoes...* Yeah. He hoped that making Russell out to be a racist would get one of the other Blacks to jump on him, because he certainly didn't want any more himself.

Russell was ready to go when his celly, holding his hand over his eye and gasping for air said, "Yeah, you won that."

Between breaths Russell said, "I may not be finished."

It's a strange position to find yourself in: Nowhere to retreat to, and not enough oxygen in your lungs to keep fighting. Neither side is defeated because that requires annihilation or surrender of one side. Russell's breathing was evening-out and he was wondering if he should call this halftime or if the final whistle had already blown. Oak Cliff decided it for him. He stepped toward Russell, determined, with a look of pure menace on his face. Russell raised his fists again and set his bare feet.

They went three more rounds after that. They quit only after Porn Star hollered, "Out for chow." That was at two thirty a.m. By that time the unmistakable sound of fists pounding flesh had woken up most of the section. Those hollering "Who is that?" and "Y'all alright up there?" woke up those that the actual fight itself did not.

Slim G-Zus's celly, Gordo, woke him up. "Flacco Christo," he said standing at the door. He pointed at 18 cell, "*Chavalon es* fighting his *cellaco.*" Gordo shadow boxed and said, "The *moyo.*"

Slim G-Zus rolled over and pulled his ear plugs out, "What?"

The guard came through rolling the doors for breakfast at three a.m. Slim G-Zus stepped out of his cell in long white cotton gym shorts, no shirt, and his black brogan boots laced up tight with no intention of going to chow. McCann came out of his cell looking the opposite way of the guard, trying to hide the marks on his face. He and Slim G-Zus met in front of the shower. "What happened?" Slim G-Zus asked, inspecting the kid's war wounds.

Russell said, "Fool jacked off on Porn Star." Slim G-Zus could tell from the way the kid kept his eyes down that this was hard for him to admit, so he spared the youngster an 'I told you so.'

"Don't look too bad," Slim G-Zus said. "S'it over with?"

Russell shrugged. "Guess so. I dunno. We went at it several times..

Big Body Slim, Itchy Foot, Youngbuck, Jew Boy, and Larson all walked up. Slim G-Zus looked down in the dayroom and saw Oak Cliff grouped up with some other Black inmates, most of them from Dallas. "What was y'all squabblin' about?" asked Youngbuck.

Slim G-Zus said, "Oak Cliff was killin' on that freak."

Youngbuck smiled and said, "Seen that fool's face coming up the stairs. Looks like you got on his ass." He bobbed his head and widened his smile, "A honky got on that ass!"

"Yeah," said Russell, "I don't think he wants any more. I didn't drop him or nothin' but I bet I hit him more than he hit me."

"That'll work," said the Big Body.

"I don't care if my celly is jackin'. I kill on them hoes too," said Larson while looking down into the dayroom, arms folded across his chest.

As usual, Slim G-Zus didn't acknowledge Larson. Turning to Russell he said, "We may need to get you moved. Anybody in good with the night shift captain?" Everyone shook their head no. "We'll have to see what these clowns are talkin' about. Prob'ly give you my piece."

Russell looked up, a strawberry on his cheek and two on his forehead. Slim G-Zus said, "McCann, I'm guessing you ain't never stabbed nobody, right?"

The kid shook his head, "Nah."

"Here's the problem. They don't like losing to us. I don't know if they're gonna wire your celly up to try and fight you again or what." Slim G-Zus barged through their little circle, headed towards the stairwell.

Russell turned as Slim G-Zus brushed by him. He saw South Dallas and Damn Fool coming down the run towards them. Youngbuck followed behind Slim G-Zus, cutting off Big Body Slim, who also had started in that direction.

Slim G-Zus said, "'Sup South D?" Slim G-Zus and South Dallas had worked together in the kitchen years ago. One was Black and one was White. One was from Dallas, the other from Houston. But scrubbing pots and pans for hours on end in the sauna that is a TDC kitchen can be like bootcamp for soldiers—a bonding experience regardless of how different those involved may be. It was the two of them in a pot room that seemed to have an endless supply of dirty pots, pans, and utensils.

Everyone in the kitchen was required to wear a shirt at all times, but the heat and lack of ventilation in the pot room moved South Dallas and Slim G-Zus to take a stand. When the food service manager made her rounds and told them to put their shirts on, Slim G-Zus said, "If y'all ain't gonna bring us a fan, we ain't wearing shirts."

South Dallas added, "Y'all lucky we doing this shit. All these ho-ass jobs pay the same." The FSM, of course, then went and got the security officer, who threatened to write them both disciplinary cases, to which they replied, "You ain't wrote it yet? You better spell our names right!"

"So, why ain't ya boy say he wasn't down with his celly killin' while they in there?" asked South Dallas.

"Not sure he didn't," said Slim G-Zus.

South Dallas was a good six inches shorter than Slim G-Zus, but stocky, with a build that said when he worked out he only did shrugs and curls. "O.C. say ya boy stole him while he was jackin'. Tode him he can't jack on no White hoes."

Slim G-Zus turned around and looked at Russell and thought, *No way Mr. World Culture said some shit like that... Christ! Don't let me bust out laughing.* Before he could contest that, South Dallas said, "It's really some celly shit. We ain't trippin' 'cause O.C. say he dropped the fool and he's through with it."

Slim G-Zus winced internally then nodded, "Yeah, okay. Oak Cliff whupped him so let's just leave it in the cell."

"Good news, kid," said Slim G-Zus, "you're not gonna get a crash course in Knife Fighting 101."

Russell asked, "What's the deal?"

Slim G-Zus pointed down to the dayroom, "Clown's down there telling them fools you stole him and that he dropped you, making it sound like he won the fight."

Russell's head jutted forward, "What!"

Smiles and chuckles all around.

Slim G-Zus said, "I told you they don't like losing to us. Best of all," Slim G-Zus fought to keep from laughing, "he said you told him Blacks can't jack on the White pigs—" Slim G-Zus clapped his hands and jerked backwards laughing. "You of all people. We're gonna have to start calling you Lil Hitler."

Young leaned in close to Russell, ready to run with this. "Say, uh, Grand Dragon is it? Alright if us honkies jack on these fat-in-the-back messcan hoes?"

"Hell, no!" said Big Body, pointing. "When you skeet in the toilet, it better be while looking at a blue-eyed Aryan princess. Or David Duke here is gonna put them hands on ya!"

Everybody laughed. Itchy Foot clapped Russell on the back, "I knew you'd come around eventually, youngster." A Cheshire cat smile on his face.

Russell said, "So, now I gotta go back in the cell with this fool?"

"Maybe not," said Big Body Slim, "We might be able to get y'all switched out with somebody else. Gotta see who the captain is."

Fortunately for Russell (and especially for Oak Cliff), the captain on duty that night was Daniel Fernandez, who Big Body slim had already made a name tag and a keychain for in the craft shop. Fernandez was late on the payment for the second item, so the Big Body told him, "Got a kid havin' problems with his celly. If you can switch him out for me that key chain is on the house."

To which Fernandez replied, "Go tell him to pack his shit."

To play along with Oak Cliff's fantasy, Russell agreed to move to another cell, as if he had been the actual loser of their fight.

CHAPTER 23

Russell sat in the dayroom, watching Mel Kiper Jr. on ESPN rant and rave about the prospects for this spring's NFL Draft. O.T. was at his usual table, legal books and documents sprawled about. A conversation that Shameekwa and her man, South West, were having, played in the background: "So, you back in there?"

'Hell, yeah, I'm back in there," said Shameekwa, waving a plump finger.

"I told that chaplain when he kicked me out, my alternative lifestyle wasn't no grounds," her artificially effeminate voice rising and falling for effect. "You know Warden Jackson wasn't tryna hear that."

Russell wished it didn't upset Big Ike so much when he/she sang, seeing as how he/she was apparently now back in the choir. Ike had thrown his hands up in celebration when he heard chaplain Villareal had kicked him/her out for missing practice. But Ike was going home, to a real church and real food, so Russell wasn't too worried about him.

Things were still tense from his fight with Oak Cliff, and Russell hadn't heard from anyone other than his mom in over a month now. He was being propped up as some sort of a mascot by these White guys. Why did it matter so much that he'd won a fight against someone who was Black? He and Salinas had barely been able to talk with captain Johanson and another SSI, Paco, always hanging around the desk. The frustration was mounting.

Mel Kiper Jr. was praising Darnell Wescott, a defensive back from Virginia Tech: "...has the ability to turn and throw his hips in coverage. Also tackles well. Played against good competition in the ACC. Had a standout week at Senior Bowl—"

"And I'm still gonna sue that messcan. Is two things you don't fuck wit' a woman about: her family, and her job. Is my job to sing in the church and bring the spirit into this penitentiary—"

Russell imagined Mel Kiper Jr. giving a scouting report on him: "A tough, in-the-box striker type in the Pat Tillman mold with a motor like J. J. Watt. Also excels in coverage, with elite ball skills and the ability to mirror receivers. Some scouts have said he's stiff in the hips. I say, who cares? Have you seen him tackle? McCann's a bonafide first-rounder—"

"Look oouuut, McCann," hollered Itchy Foot from his cell. Russell turned and looked, held his hands up. "Come holler at me."

Russell jogged up the steps and stopped in front of thirteen cell. Something similar to the smell of burning tires punched him in the nose. He waved in front of his face, "The hell is that?"

"You can still smell it?" asked Itchy Foot.

Russell frowned, "Hell, yeah, I can smell it. What is that?"

Itchy foot held up a plastic bottle, "Burned some ink earlier. Need you to run this up to Slim G-Zus."

Russell pressed his face to the grate on the door and looked in. Itchy Foot was down on a knee reaching under the toilet. He pulled out what looked like a short, fat candle that, after further inspection, was actually hair grease in its container with a paper wick as thick as a pencil. Itchy Foot stood up and grinned, "Green motherfucker, you don't even know how to burn ink." He shook his head and slid the bottle full of ink under the door. "Run that up there to Slim G-Zus and tell him to get an ounce or whatever he needs. I think he's sending some to his homeboy on seven building." A gopher boy for Slim G-Zus. Winning a fight against a Black guy obviously hadn't boosted his social standing like he'd expected. "Look," said Itchy Foot, "check it out." He held up the clear hair grease container. "Make your wick outta toilet paper—wrap it around a paperclip. Then put it in your locker or under the toilet. Let that bitch burn for about four hours, then you scrape all this soot," Itchy Foot knelt down and ran his index finger under the toilet. He stuck his finger through the grate. "Take this and mix it with baby shampoo and a little water. It's a good hustle. Sell an ounce for eight bucks."

Russell raised his eyebrows and compressed his lips, "Yeah. Good to know. I'ma take this upstairs." Russell turned and headed toward the stairwell. Itchy Foot yelled out, "Look ouuut, SlimG-Zus."

Russell rapped on Slim G-Zus's door and slid the bottle underneath it. "Itchy Foot said for you to get what you need and I'm supposed to take the rest back to him."

Slim G-Zus said, "'Sup, Lil Hitler," and held the bottle up like he was examining a test tube. He grabbed a small white eye-drop bottle from the shelf and sat it down on the sink next to the ink. "Looks like ol' boy's still a little bruised up, huh?"

"Yeah?" asked Russell. "Guess so. I haven't really been paying attention."

Slim G-Zus grinned and nodded his head, "Make one of 'em bruise like that, you done a li'l something."

Russell shrugged, "Ain't shit to me."

"Nah. To you it ain't. But to your old celly it is. That was damn near the worst day of his life. See," Slim G-Zus stopped transferring the ink, "to you, it's just a fight. To him it's... an affront to his manhood, 'cause you're a ho-ass whiteboy. He probably felt like he was doing you a favor just letting you live there."

Russell didn't like the sound of that. He wanted Slim G-Zus to finish getting his ink so he could get Itchy Foot's bottle and be on his way. Russell tried to cut it short by saying, "I don't care about all that shit."

"Yeah. I guess if I only had three years and I was on a unit like this," Slim G-Zus bounced his head from side to side, "I probably wouldn't know any better."

Russell stepped closer to the door and stuck his finger tips through the grate, "I know plenty," he said.

Slim G-Zus turned and stepped toward the door, "Nah, kid, you don't. You got a lot to learn."

Russell stared up at him, forcing himself not to blink. Slim G-Zus stared back until a smirk cruised across his face, and he went back to filling the ink bottle.

Slim G-Zus finished and slid Itchy Foot's bottle back under the door. "Tell Itchy I said 'preciate that."

Russell reached down and grabbed the bottle, "Right," he said.

Slim G-Zus said, "Adisa hollered at me before he got moved. Said you was having a hard time dealing with this place."

Russell stopped.

"You know most of us here got a lotta time under our belts. You can holla at one of us if you need to."

"Nah, I'm all right."

Slim G-Zus stuck his hands down the front of his pants and pulled out a small Nokia 5380. "You wanna call somebody? Got Internet on it too, might do you some good."

Russell had heard there were cell phones on the unit but this was the first time he'd actually seen one. "Uh... man. I really don't have anybody to call... I wouldn't mind using the Internet though."

"Alright, bet. How much time you need?"

"Oh, man, whatever you can spare, I guess."

"Well, you can take it in the shower if you don't need too much time. I can watch the door from here. Or, if you're gonna be awhile, wait till the doors roll again and I'll bring it to you—your celly's at work, right?"

"Yeah. Yeah, he won't be back till after shift change."

"'Sup to you," said Slim G-Zus.

Russell looked towards the shower. Possession of a cell phone was a level-one offense that would get you put in administrative segregation, making you ineligible for parole. And since it was a felony, it would also get you another sentence—anywhere from five to ninety-nine years—stacked on top of the one you were already serving. Russell said, "Lemme just run down here to the shower right quick."

Slim G-Zus dropped the phone in an empty black coffee bag that Russell recognized. It was the same bag he'd seen Adisa, Big Body Slim, and Youngbuck with, plenty of times. Slim G-Zus said, "Take that back to Itchy Foot, then go in the shower on the right, here on three row. If I holler, 'who's got some hot water' that means the laws fiddin' to come through the door."

Russell took off his shirt and laid it over the shower door. He sat down on the small stainless steel bench that ran along the left wall. The 5380 was slow compared to what Russell was used to, and the fact that it was a felony made the wait for the connection even more excruciating. Finally Russell got his Instagram account to pop up. The picture of him and Cordell with Megan and Natasha was still there. He stared, holding his breath... Maybe this was a bad idea. Russell flipped through his other pictures: he and Cordell after they were released on bond; Megan sitting in his lap; Mike and Demetrius with Russell in between them, shirts off, trying to look tough. After that it was mostly pictures from Football Factory Juco. He logged out and stood up to check the walkway. The coast was clear. Russell sat back down. He could call Megan... But she never answered her phone anyway, she only used it to text, and she wouldn't recognize the number... Right now she was probably at work. He decided to leave a message on her voice mail. He smiled, thinking, she'd probably start crying at the sound of his voice. Russell dialed the number and listened. "Hey, it's Megan, you know what to do."

Russell lowered his head in hopes of making his voice sound deeper, "Hey, girl. It's Russ. I'm on a cell phone. I was just calling to see how you're doing. I miss you. Hope you got my last letter. This place is crazy. Was hoping you could come see me some time. Just check with my parents to make sure y'all don't come on the same weekend. We only get one visit a weekend... I really miss you Megan... Bye."

For no particular reason, Russell logged on to his Facebook account. He hadn't used the thing in years, yet he still had eighty-nine friends. The wall photo was him sitting in the Olds', pointing at the new touchscreen head unit he'd just had installed at Cartronics, off Highway 6, on the southwest side. He ran through the messages: Every last one of them were girls he didn't know telling him he was "looking pretty good," and that they had pictures to sell him. He flipped through his own pictures and stopped at one of him and Cordell. It was their freshman year and they were Tebowing in earnest at midfield after a win over Eisenhower. Russell gripped the phone with both hands and stared at the picture... That was who he was. Not Lil Hitler the White convict mascot. Russell looked up. The beige paint chips that were constantly littering the shower floor stood out against the grey concrete wall. Even though he and Ike scrubbed the showers vigorously almost every night, they still looked like mini-dungeons... I'm sitting in a shower on a cell phone... How in the hell did I get here? And where in the hell are my eighty-nine friends?

He dropped his head, rocking back and forth with the phone pressed against his forehead, smudging the screen with the oil from his skin. He thought about calling home but was afraid he'd spook his parents. A cell phone in prison! They might have heart attacks.

"Here ya go," said Russell, sliding the coffee bag back under the door. "Thanks."

Slim G-Zus pulled the phone out, "Anybody call while you were on it?"

"Nah."

"Damn." Slim G-Zus screwed his face up. "What's this greasy shit on the screen? You in there on some porn site jackin' on my shit?"

Russell forced a laugh, "Nah. Nah, I tried calling somebody and I guess my ears rubbed across the screen. My bad. I wasn't—"

"Lemme find out you were in there on Aryan tripleX goddesses pulling on yourself." Slim G-Zus smiled, wiping the screen on his white cotton shorts.

Russell leaned forward on the door, his fingers through the grates, shaking his head and smiling.

Slim G-Zus said, "We gotta Droid. Adisa left it with Big Body Slim when they moved him. I sent it out there to him once he got settled. We use it to trade commodities—kinda like the stock market but it's tangible shit, like corn or gold, instead of shares of a company." Slim G-Zus lifted the 5380 towards Russell, "S'gotta MP3 player on it. You check it out?"

"Nah," said Russell. "I just went to Instagram. Left somebody a voice mail."

"Yeah, man. I got some old shit on here. Before your time. Some real rap. Not that bullshit y'all listen to nowadays."

Russell smirked, "Like what?"

"Real rap. Geto Boys, Mobb Deep, ESG, buncha ol' Suave House, Gangstarr, Pete Rock, and CL Smooth—I used to jam a lotta East Coast shit—Nas and WuTang."

Russell nodded his head. He knew who the Geto Boys, Mobb Deep, and Nas were. The rest he'd never heard of. "You don't like nothing new? Like that Lil Ron Ron's *Up in da Club*?"

"Pretty much anything with 'club' in the tittle I ain't trying to hear." Slim G-Zus lifted the phone and started pushing buttons. "What'd you say it's called?"

"*Up in da Club,* by Lil Ron Ron."

"Get it off Vuclip. See what you talkin' about."

Slim G-Zus downloaded the song and stepped to the door. He pressed play and held the phone up to the grate.

I pull's up to da club
Shawty say what up
Shawty gettin' drunk
Shawty smokin' bud
Shawty wanna fuck...

Russell had started bobbing his head when Slim G-Zus killed it. Russell looked in. "You don't like that?! Not even the beat?"

Slim G-Zus laughed, "Mannn—hell, nah! Whack-ass shit."

Russell folded his arms and leaned back.

Slim G-Zus said, "Any a that 'this is what we doin' at the club' type shit is whack. When I was coming up, you had to have some MC skills. Some wordsmithing ability. Rap was something serious. You had to do more than just come up with a new way to describe a girl shakin' her ass, or what kind of car you drove to the club, or what you drunk while you were there—and, of course, how many 'haters' was out to get you..." Slim G-Zus shook his head, "That type a shit wouldn't a got no respect."

Russell took the jeers a little personally but didn't let it show. "What about Slim Thugga, or Paul Wall? You used to jam them?"

"They came out after I got locked up. I've only heard their radio shit. What's something good they got?"

"Try *Don't Blame Us,* that's Wall, and *No friends Just Associates.* That's my favorite Slim Thugga. It's got Z-Ro on there, too."

Slim G-Zus typed the Paul Wall song into the Vuclip search engine and said, "I like that Z-Ro cat. He don't have one of them li'l kid voices like everybody else nowadays. I heard him on something else awhile back. He got somethin'."

"Those two songs are real old but you'll probably like them."

Slim G-Zus looked up, "What's real old?"

"Like, early 2000's."

Slim G-Zus laughed and shook his head.

Russell said, "You ever had any problems with that Droid?"

"Nah, we haven't." Slim G-Zus rapped on his chest where the *Blue-Eyed Devil* tat was, "Knock on peckerwood. We had the guy who bought it for us go through all the features, 'cause it's refurbished and unlocked. Didn't want a contract where you gotta get yer credit checked."

"Why didn't y'all get an iPhone? Less problems."

"Adisa read somewhere that Steve Jobs said he wouldn't hire a convict. So, my boy ain't going for nothing by Apple."

"I think he's dead," said Russell.

"Yeah."

Slim G-Zus held the phone up to the grate. The beat to the Paul Wall song started. Slim G-Zus bobbed his head, "Yeah, that's alright."

Russell leaned against the door and tapped his thumb to the beat. "Yeah," he said smiling. "That's that old shit."

CHAPTER 24

My pops always said me and him was the last of a dying breed. I'm sitting here watchin' this H-town nigga, Black Gotti, teach this ho-ass whiteboy how to box. This same whiteboy that done had two fights with two different niggas since he hit the unit. The last one, about a week ago was some bitch-ass shit. This little young-ass nigga, Oak Cliff, he like getting out there on them hoes—and you know how these White bitches love niggas. So, he's killing on the ho and his celly steals him from behind because he's jackin' on a White bitch. Tells Oak Cliff he can't jack on no White hoes. Now, I already know how these whiteboys think. So for me, I didn't need to hear anything else. We shoulda cliqued on that ho for stealing Oak Cliff. But two or three of these other niggas want to say shit like, "Man, you know Oak Cliff be stuntin'," or "Man, that whiteboy don't fuck with nobody." So I say, "Oak Cliff done called his celly a whiteboy and he ain't do nothing—so he's a ho. And a ho got to stay in a ho's place. See, I know that ho caught that pussy when that Crip nigga beat his ass on F-Pod. And since he's a ho, Oak Cliff can do whatever he wants in there. If he wants to jack, he can jack. But these niggas go tell Slim-Bitchus they don't believe Oak Cliff and that it's some celly shit.

So they let a perfect opportunity to get these whiteboys slip away. It don't even matter if the whiteboy said it or not. They been killing niggas for hundreds of years for giving these White hoes what they want. Which brings me back to my pops. I remember when I was a kid, this Black girl said she got raped by some cops and Klansmen. My pops was telling my uncle how it didn't matter whether or not it really happened. He was basically saying it was representative of shit that happened everyday all over America, and that it could be used to help us. See, my pops understood that

196

when you're dealing with White folks, the most treacherous people on the planet, you have to use every tool in the box, ya dig? Even them White attorneys Kunsler and them was saying it didn't matter if this girl was really raped or not. What matters is that Black women have been, and continue to be, raped and brutalized by White men, and that when you have a chance to handle the people who put us in chains, stole our culture, and forced us to build this country for free, you're supposed to take it. Period. Point blank. My pops and I understand this. All these off-brand-ass niggas running around here don't.

So, here we are, this Black Gotti nigga, who's supposed to have some helluva boxing game, giving away the game to this Whiteboy. I'm chillin', looking back through this book, *The Power of the Dog,* my government teacher gave us. It's written by a whiteboy, but it's a lotta truth to it. He shows how the CIA put all the dope in the ghetto, how they brought it on the planes. It's a bunch of shit everyone in the ghetto already knows but it's a whiteboy writing it, so it's like, "Damn, finally even these ho-ass White folks is admitting what they did to us." I showed this shit to my boy, Damn Fool. He's like a lotta niggas though, he buys into the propaganda they put out there. Always showing us going to jail, us on the corner selling the dope, smoking the dope. But Blacks don't own any planes or boats to bring that shit over here, and we don't use or sell drugs no more than Whites. All you gotta do is read that Michelle Alexander book, *The New Jim Crow.* She proves the whole war on drugs was created by Republicans after the Jim Crow laws were done away with so they could keep Blacks down. The CIA pumped the dope into the hood and then Congress passed a bunch of laws to lock all the niggas up and throw away the key. And remember, this is a sister, and she's a professor of law at Ohio State University. So you *know* she knows her shit.

The problem with this *Power of the Dog* book is that it doesn't have any Black characters getting locked up for having some of that CIA dope on them. He mentions that the powder was going to be turned into crack, but he don't show how many lives that whole play destroyed.

They started with slavery, then Jim Crow, now they just lock a nigga up. And we got niggas trying to teach this bitch-ass Whiteboy how to box—knowing he done already got into it with two niggas. Anyway, this book is good. I hope it'll wake up some of these niggas that's just sitting around watching them forty-million-dollar slaves on TV. Yeah, niggas like me and my pops is the last of a dying breed.

CHAPTER 25

Russell stepped backward, lowering himself by squatting with each step before bobbing back up and then down again. Black Gotti was throwing lefts and rights over his head. They worked from one side of the dayroom to the other, everybody staying out of their way and trying to watch without making it obvious.

Russell had gotten really comfortable with their routine. The footwork and combinations were now second nature, just like the drills he'd done all his life in football practice. Black Gotti had learned the sweet science at George Foreman's gym in Houston. Foreman, the former World Champ, one of Fifth Ward's most beloved sons, was now a preacher at a large nondenominational church. Back in the nineties, he'd worked with Black Gotti personally when he was trying to make the US Olympic team. Fighting as a middleweight, Black Gotti had won Golden Gloves three years in a row before getting convicted of his second felony, aggravated robbery. Teaching boxing was now his hustle, like cutting hair or washing clothes.

Black Gotti nodded and smiled a gold and baguette grill he'd had since the nineties. "I see ya youngsta. You got it. Needa keep your hands up." Gotti raised his hands to his jaw and parried two imaginary punches, "Block them counters that's gon' come when you swing. But you pretty much got it."

Russell clasped his hands behind his head and breathed in deeply through his nose.

Black Gotti said, "Don't forget ya jumpin' jacks."

Russell nodded, "I gotcha."

After five sets of one hundred jumping jacks and a cold shower, thanks to the broken hot-water heater, Russell sat down at the table where the Old Timer had his legal work spread out. "Whatcha always working on?" he asked.

O.T. looked up over the top of his reading glasses. "Lawsuit I got on these people." O.T.'s trapezoidal neck was wider than his head. Along with the large features of his face and grey crew-cut hair, it gave him the appearance of an old-school football coach. O.T. added, "Looks like you had a good workout."

Russell's eyebrows rose as he nodded, "Oh, yeah. Gotti'll try and kill you."

O.T. grinned and looked down at the documents in front of him.

Russell poured some powdered milk, stolen from the kitchen by Itchy Foot, into a cup of water and stirred it. It was the closest he could come to the Mega Muscle protein powder he drank after workouts in the free world. Russell said, "Can I ask what your lawsuit's about?"

"Sure. You know who Captain Johanson is, right?"

"Yeah. Works at night."

"Yeah. Big ol' fat bitch with red hair? Muff diver?"

Russell looked away, trying not to laugh. "Yeah, I know who you're talking about."

"She used to be the property officer back in '07." O.T. took off his glasses and rubbed his eyes. "I went on a medical chain for my knee, down to John Sealy in Galveston. Had my property inventoried and put in the property room—you can only take hygiene on medical chain—I get back, half my commissary's missing. All my cookies and 'tater chips gone. So I go to the inmate who works property, messcan I know from Rockin' D—that's what they called Darrington back in the eighties—and he swears up and down he and the other cat didn't take anything. He also says that fat bitch is always eatin', and that they never seen her bring nothing in, or buy anything out the commissary. So I write a grievance."

Russell chugged half of his cup and wiped his mouth.

"The grievance comes back saying, 'there's no evidence to substantiate your allegations,' standard bullshit answer. So I file a Step 2. It goes to Huntsville and comes back saying I'll be compensated. So they call me out to one building and try to give me some rice and soap they confiscated from another inmate. It's the same amount, dollar wise, but I want that bitch to go down to that commissary and buy me exactly what she took. So I refuse that shit."

Russell slammed the rest of the milk and wiped his mouth again. "Yeah. I would have, too." Which actually wasn't true. It just sounded like the thing to say. To Russell being a grown man and making a stink over some chips and cookies was ridiculous. But over the past few months, he'd noticed that even the most laid-back inmates would trip out if they thought they were going to be denied something they considered theirs.

O.T. placed his elbows on the table and propped himself up. "I tell her I'll take her to small claims court. She starts caterwauling about how I'm threatening her. Big ol' bitch huffin' and puffin'. Next morning I get served a major case: threatening an officer." O.T. straightened up and folded his arms, "Now I'm hotter'n fish grease. Case says I told her I was gonna stab her if she didn't bring me some dope."

"Whoa," Russell said, shocked.

O.T. nodded, "Yeah."

Russell shook his head.

"Be right back," O.T. said. He got up and headed for the toilet.

Russell turned to the sports TV. Tod McShay and Mel Kiper Jr. were debating the quarterbacks in the upcoming draft. Out of the corner of his eye, Russell saw Slim G-Zus come off the wall, walking away from the window near the toilet area. He looked like he'd just smelled something awful. Russell looked back and saw O.T. standing in front of the toilet, his shirt pulled halfway up his back, bending at the waist. He was dumping something brown in the toilet from what looked like a bag under his shirt. Russell looked at Slim G-Zus who'd taken a seat at one of the tables.

O.T. walked back to the table shaking his hands dry from their washing. "So, anyway, I go to court and Captain Hang-'em-High slams me. Rolls me to B-Side. Threatening an officer case. Total Bullshit." O.T. patted the backs of his hands dry on his pants. "Soon as I get over there they put me in a cell on one row. Fuckin' todes slammin' dominoes nonstop, every time we get dayroom." O.T. pointed at his ear, "I got ear drum problems." He shook his head. "I can't be on one row with them dominoes slamming." Russell noticed Slim G-Zus had returned to his customary spot by the window. "So I jam up the sergeant at chow, tell him about my ears, to try and get off one row, and he ain't trying to hear nothing. I write medical and they tell me to holler at an officer about the noise—dominoes ain't supposed to be slammed." O.T. rocked back and threw his hands up. "Basically tellin' me to be a snitch."

Russell shook his head. "Rock and a hard place."

"Yeah. So I'd had all I could take. Ear drums about to bust. It ain't but three other Whites in the section." O.T. leaned forward, "You know it's darker over there than it is over here—but I gotta let 'em know—I can't take this anymore. I go to holler at one'a these todes, and I know they're not trying to hear nothing. So I holler at the oldest one, he's maybe thirty-five, hoping he's got some under-standing. He's some kinda O.G. or whatever for the Folks?" O.T. waved off his own question. "Some shit. So, this tode, he's all masked up when I run it down to him, like he's got the best boxing game in the penitentiary. Tells me I need to get moved. I tell him, 'I'm trying,' and that I'd really appreciate it if they'd hold off on slamming them bones until I get moved. He tells me," O.T. twisted his face up, mockingly, "'I wish we was back in the nineties. Whiteboys didn't stud up then.' I took my glasses off and slid 'em under my door. Told him, 'Your momma used to suck my dick in the nineties.'"

Russell's jaw dropped.

"So we catch up under the TV, and that sum-bitch is just too fast. I got some licks in," O.T. leaned toward Russell, "I first come down in '62, when the penitentiary was the penitentiary—but he got the better of me." O.T. touched the orbital bone above his left eye with his index finger. "Sum-bitch split me open there." Russell spotted a scar under the old man's eyebrow. "So we went at it. Somewhere in there he breaks his hand. Couple days later he goes to the infirmary, finds out he's gonna need some pins in it, so it'll heal right." O.T. made a fist and held it up to Russell, "I had 'em once. Fight in the fields on Rockin' D." Russell looked: there were all sorts of scars on the leathery, liver-spotted fist.

"So he catches the medical chain to get the pins put in and when he gets back, well," O.T. held his hands out, "of course his bunk's been filled, and he gets put somewhere else."

Russell was beginning to wonder where this was going.

"Few days after he gets back, one of his homeboys comes and tells me I owe some money 'cause I got their homeboy moved." O.T. rolled his eyes, "So I tell him, 'I don't owe you a goddamned thing.' Crazy—a 'wood that was over there, good kid—comes over and asks me if everything is alright. Tode tells Crazy to get outta his bidness. Another one that was outta place comes over, now it's four of us. I says to him, 'If ol' boy wanted to stay in this section he shouldn't've forced me to fight him by disrespecting me. He broke his hand on *my* head.' See, they thought I was some old ding they could do a bit on." O.T. grinned and shook his head. "But I done called their bluff. Now, they're tryna save face. We're all standin' there, lookin' at each other. One in front of me says, 'You gon' pay to have my homeboy moved back over here.' 'I ain't payin' nothing,' I tell 'em. He jumps up in my face, 'I ain't playin' with you, old man.' I shove him and it kicks off."

"A riot?" Russell asked.

"Yep. It was four of them and three of us, but once all the other Blacks saw we were holdin' our ground, most of them jumped in. Somebody had a shank in the dayroom, pretty sure it was a piece of plexiglass. That's how I got this," O.T. patted the right side of his abdomen. "Shank went through my intestines. Tore me up pretty good"

Russell looked confused. "Got what?" he asked.

"This shit bag." O.T. lifted his shirt. There was a clear plastic bag like the kind they store blood in hanging from his body. "You ain't never seen me empty it out like I just did yonder?" O.T. thumbed towards the toilet area.

Russell shook his head; he was at a complete loss.

"Yeah, it's a pain in the ass. I done got used to it though." He shrugged. "But I shoulda never been over there. That bull dagger,

Johanson, lied on me. So I filed a 1983 claim on her. I've been wrestling with it ever since. Waiting to go back to court now."

"Man, that's fucked up," Said Russell.

"Yeah, but I'm gonna get that bitch. Most people don't push the issue. I got her, though. I don't care how long it takes. She can't get around this." O.T. held a yellowed piece of paper that read "Offender Property Inventory." Every item he'd had in his possession when he went on medical chain was cataloged by the officer who's signature was at the bottom of the page. Johanson, of course, knew this, but, like most unelected people in positions of power, she felt untouchable—and, for the most part, she was.

Russell didn't know what to say. He felt beyond sorry for the guy, whatever that was. O.T. cleaned his glasses with his t-shirt.

Russell said, "I guess that's why you call Blacks toads, huh? 'Cause you consider 'em to be, like, low to the ground, like frogs or whatever?"

O.T. put his glasses back on, a look of amusement on his face. "Hell, nah. Where'd you hear that?"

"I just..." Russell shrugged.

"They call 'em todes 'cause they say," O.T. squinted his eyes, 'Dat nigga went and tode it.' They can't say *told*. Like they can't pronounce the letter *L*. Ain't got nothin' to do with toads."

CHAPTER 26

Russell had struggled through his reading of *Supernormal Stimuli,* one of the books Ms. Sontag had assigned in cultural anthropology. He understood the book's claims—that evolution programed us to do things like eat all we possibly could when food was available because it wouldn't always be so—but he knew we couldn't have come from monkeys, so he refused to agree with anything the author said, no matter how much sense it made.

Ms. Sontag had now spent the first twenty minutes of the hour-and-a-half-long class elaborating on how the book's thesis explained our eating habits, and how large food corporations took advantage of them. "For most of our history as a species, we never had refined sugar or fried foods. These things overstimulate certain parts of our brains, leading us to overconsume—" blah, blah, blah. She then went into aggregate behavior and how human beings were primed for "tribalism" and "proliferation" of our genes by "excluding and marginalizing those who did not look like us." Russell couldn't remember anything in the book like this.

"Along with communities of color," Ms. Sontag said, "the LGBTQ community is also seen as a threat to our gene reproduction because same sex and transgender couples often don't produce offspring."

Russell saw Slim G-Zus to his right and two seats over close his eyes and drop his face into his palm.

"And this illustrates the point I'm trying to make. Our brains are irrational, and programed with only one goal in mind: to reproduce our genes." She looked around, apparently proud of how she was tying all this together. "Think about it. We *know* communities of color have been held back by the dominant group's desire to see its own genes spread and that, were it not for this, we would see a world with virtually no inequality." Russell recalled how often he'd heard that word, *inequality,* in his government class. "Yet," Ms. Sontag continued, "we've seen very little progress the world over when it comes to righting these historic wrongs. Why?" She looked the class over. "Because most of the people in power intend to stay there. Their genes command them to do so. Also, we *know* we've over-populated the planet and that it can't sustain our decadent western lifestyle. Yet, we want to keep members of the LGBTQ community from getting married! Even though these marriages are unlikely to add to the population problem!" She had the ultimate look of *How dumb can we be?* on her face. "It's the marriage of *hetero*sexuals, and the offspring they produce, that has taken us past carrying capacity."

Russell felt the shock and anger mushrooming inside. He and Big Ike had just read something about being fruitful and mul-tiplying... But he didn't hate gays. And he certainly didn't want to "marginalize" non-Whites... He searched for the words to voice his displeasure, but... What could he say? Ms. Sontag believes we came from monkeys... She probably doesn't even believe the Bible is God's word... And I don't wanna sound like Slim G-Zus, like I think I'm smarter than the teacher...

An older White inmate raised his hand, "Ma'am, are you saying Adam and *Steve* should be able to get married because they're better for the environment than Adam and *Eve*?"

Ms. Sontag crossed her arms, "Excuse me?"

"You're making it sound like you want punks to be able to get married because, I guess, you think kids ruin the planet."

Ms. Sontag pointed at him, "I take issue with your choice of words. There is no place for that in my classroom."

The old man stared, blinking. Finally he snapped to, "Oh. I'm sorry ma'am. That's what we call 'em in here. Hell, they call themselves that."

Ms. Sontag's thin eyebrows drew together as she jutted her jaw forward, making it look like she had a severe underbite.

Nelly's incarcerated twin raised his hand.

"Yes," said Ms. Sontag nodding at Yella Fella, still with a look of disgust on her face.

"I understand what you're saying about people tryin' to stay in power."

Ms. Sontag nodded thoughtfully. She always seemed to look that way when one of the Black or Mexican—don't call them Hispanic—students spoke, regardless of what they were saying. Russell shook that thought off as quickly as it had materialized. Sounds like something Slim G-Zus would say.

"Have you ever read *White Man's Burden* by William Easterly?" asked Yella Fella.

Ms. Sontag smiled, her eyes in full participation. "Why, yes, I have."

Yella Fella lowered his head slightly, returning a knowing smile. "Okay... you know how he says," he shifted in his chair, "that when Europeans found the Indians they didn't enslave them, but when they found Africans they put us in chains?"

"Right. But they certainly didn't leave the Native Americans to live in peace—"

"Yeah, I know that. I'm just sayin'... They didn't steal one hundred million of them and keep them enslaved for four hundred years like they did us."

Ms. Sontag put her hands behind her back and bowed her head slightly.

Yella Fella sat up. "See, they knew they couldn't compete with Africans from jump... 'cause, you know...'" Another knowing smile, "You said you read it, right?"

"Yes, yes."

"So, you know, they saw the difference..."

"Right."

"And see, it's a whole lotta them Rush Limbaugh faggots today that know they can't compete with us, so they keep us locked up. This here," Yella Fella held his arms out, "is the new Jim Crow. Look at this class: it's almost all Black." He thumbed behind him. "Back on the pod? It's even more Blacker."

Ms. Sontag was looking up and to her left, eyes slightly squinted. "And when you say, 'Rush Limbaugh faggots', you don't mean to slur the LGBTQ community, you're just trying to voice your disapproval of the establishment from, frankly, a position devoid of power... Right?"

"Nah, I hate punks."

Ms. Sontag looked down. "Mr. Dumashay, where you grew up, was that the prevailing attitude toward gays and lesbians?"

Yella Fella shrugged.

Russell considered saying, "You can't hate all of them or else you and Shameekwa wouldn't have been coming out the shower the other morning when I came in from work—" but thought better of it.

Russell noticed Slim G-Zus and the old convict Ms. Sontag had just went off on exchanging looks that said, "Yeah, that really just happened."

"I bet it was," said Ms. Sontag. "Often class, marginalized groups are pitted against one another by the dominant culture in order to keep them from uniting for justice."

Russell scanned the class. It didn't look like those words were going down smoothly.

Yella raised his hand again. Ms. Sontag nodded. "Being different colors made it okay in the Europeans' minds to enslave us. They have never done that to Whites. You know how you was sayin' tribalism and whatnot? Yeah, that makes it a lot easier to brutalize a people and then hold them back. Never give us that forty acres and a mule? Nome sayin'?"

"Good point," said Ms. Sontag. "Class, do you remember the part where Ms. Barret says they were able to get a robin to sit on an object that wasn't her egg by painting it a brighter blue? Apparently, the color of the egg has something to do with the health or potential of the chick inside, and since the momma robin can only sit on so many eggs, she picked the ones she thought gave her the best chance of reproducing her genes—even though it wasn't even an egg." Her mood was entering Katie Couric territory again after its derailment from old-school saying punks. "In regards to brutalizing what the dominant culture sees as another tribe, I've often wondered if the reason so many slaves were raped by their masters was because of physical traits and how evolution has caused us to view them. For example, scientific studies have proven that Caucasian women with larger lips, like, say, Scarlet Johanson, usually have higher levels of estrogen. And we know the higher a woman's estrogen level, the more likely she is to reproduce a man's genes successfully." Again, she looked over the class, probably for praise, before continuing, "African-American women, on average, have larger lips than Caucasian women. This, along with Whites seeing Black slaves as less than human, is probably why so many African-American women have been raped by White men." The twinkle in her eye couldn't have been brighter.

Slim G-Zus had had enough. He exhaled audibly, then made a production of scratching the back of his head. He took a breath and told himself to be careful, Yella would love to start a riot in the school house, especially with it being just him, the youngster, and a couple of older White cats. He drummed his fingers on the desk and inhaled sharply, then lifted his hand.

Ms. Sontag looked at him. "Yes," she said.

"I notice you use the term community a lot. African-American *community*, LGB-whatever *community*, et cetera, et cetera. Then, in like, the same paragraph, you talk about the problems with tribalism." Ms. Sontag looked slightly more irritated than confused.

"Okay..." said Ms. Sontag.

"If you think tribalism leads to—oppression, I guess?—don't you think you might want to *not* put everybody in these separate 'communities,' as you call them? Maybe focus on the common ground more than the differences?"

Ms. Sontag laced her fingers in front, just below her waist and stared at Slim G-Zus like a zombie. "Sir," she said, "the larger society has forced these people into these groupings by not tolerating their differences. And because of this marginalization, they lag behind in almost every measurable quantity of life."

"Well, Americans of Chinese, Japanese, and Jewish descent were certainly marginalized, and, nowadays, they're more likely to have a college degree or be self-employed than any of the White ethnic groups. Their average incomes are higher, too."

"That's because them White folks ain't scared of Asians," said Yella Fella from the back of the classroom. "They wasn't scared of the Indians."

"I ain't scared of no one," said Slim G-Zus, his head turned back but not directly at Yella Fella.

"Ain't nobody talking about you. I'm talkin' 'bout the government—"

"Shoulda said government then—"

"They all White, ain't they?"

"Not the President. He's only half White."

"The President is a Black man."

Slim G-Zus smirked. "Ms. Sontag, you're the 'expert' here. Is it true that the President—like every other Homo Sapiens on the planet—got twenty-three chromosomes from his Black father and twenty-three chromosomes from his White mother?"

Ms. Sontag pancaked her lips. "You've gotten us off task," she said.

"Oh... well, then I apologize. One other thing about 'communities.' Do you think the Lettuce, Guacamole, Bacon, Tomato... what's one that starts with Q... Oh, yeah, from *White Men Can't Jump*, Quince. Is that community all united as one?" Ms. Sontag looked outraged. Slim G-Zus was smiling. "'Cause I imagine a gay woman and a gay man, if you put 'em together, probably a lot of jealousy there, dontcha think?"

Ms. Sontag said, "Are we supposed to be amused by that?"

"It was an attempt at humor. Something I don't do all that often. But seriously, Ms., a lot of the 'communities' you refer to are anything but. Like last week, you kept saying Latin America was 'one *nación*.'" He kicked the Spanish accent hard to mock Ms. Sontag's pronunciation. "But I've met Mexicans and Cubans, Puerto Ricans and Salvadorans, and they don't consider themselves 'one *nación*.'" Again with the exaggerated accent. "Mexicans consider they're one nation, Mexico; Puerto Ricans, Puerto Rico."

"Uh huh," said Ms. Sontag. "Is there a point to all this?"

"Absolutely. Your vision? That White heterosexual males oppress everyone not like them because of their 'selfish genes'—to borrow from Sir Richard Dawkins—he and I are part of the atheist community—lacks perspective." Ms. Sontag pursed her lips and looked deridingly at Slim G-Zus. He continued, "There was tribalism—just like there was slavery—way before Whites became 'the man' through colonization and oppression. I agree with you that we should try and help the less fortunate. But I think telling people they're members of oppressed groups and that they're not doing as well as some abstract White group because of racism just makes the situation worse. Kinda like giving someone with the flu chemotherapy."

Ms. Sontag folded her arms.

Slim G-Zus went on, "Think about the war on poverty and Great Society programs. The majority of that money went to Appalachian Whites and non-Whites; something like thirteen trillion has been spent on those programs since the sixties. Yet the poverty rate for Appalachia and Blacks and Hispanics hasn't changed. So, to say our genes force us to put our own first may be a true statement. But the people who voted for the politicians that passed all those 'help the oppressed' bills, bills that spent most of that money on non-Whites, were White themselves... In other words, our genes and programming can be overcome—which brings us back to my original point: putting people in groups when we're *supposed* to be one nation undivided. Makes the whole 'us' versus 'them' problem worse. We should see ourselves as Americans. Period. Not African-Americans or Mexican-Americans." Slim G-Zus nodded, seconding himself before adding, "You oughta mix in a little Thomas Sowell and *National Review* with your Noam Chomsky and *Mother Jones*."

I hate this bitch-ass Whiteboy. If I didn't think this teacher was going to put a nigga in the pussy, I'd be whuppin' his ho-ass right now. I swear to God, on my dead pops, my kids, everything I love, this ho ever cuts outta line again I'm gonna take him off the count.

All this bullshit about groups when it was these bitch-ass White folks that put us in chains from jump. They wasn't trying to include niggas. Just using us to build their country 'cause they couldn't work as hard as we could. Our bodies are superior to theirs.

Look at pro sports and all the White hoes niggas got. Bullshit about 'we all Americans.' What Americans you know got hung from trees and had they dicks cut off other than niggas? What Americans got pumped fulla syphilis and left to die other than niggas? Who fills these prisons? Matter of fact...

Russell didn't know if Slim G-Zus was being genuine when he talked about everyone being Americans instead of hyphenated Americans... Yella Fella raised his hand. "Ms. Sontag," he said.

"Yes," she replied.

"Don't you think it's hard for a group of people who've been brutalized like *no other group* on the earth by Americans to see themselves as Americans? I mean—"

"Oh, certainly I do."

"Who else's been shot up with syphilis by the government?"

Slim G-Zus said, "Nobody at Tuskegee was shot up with anything. The patients already had syphilis. The doctors there—some of whom were Black—just observed the effects. Some scholars say they could've treated them. Others say they couldn't have."

Russell looked at Yella Fella who was on the edge of his seat. Ms. Sontag stood stock still, a look of concern on her face.

CHAPTER 27

MeeKhan, what iss yo numbah?"

"281832," Russell replied. The letter slid through the side of the door. It was from Dell.

'Sup Bro,

I saw my Mom and Natasha Saturday. Mom said she still hasn't heard from the D.A. "Wannabe Tyreese," huh? I bet Tyreese bangs more bad hoes than Paul Wall. Speaking of you, I was thinking about showing your picture to a couple of these fools and tellin' 'em you're the real Wall instead of some imitator. You wouldn't believe how these fools dick-ride anybody that claims to be a rapper. They got some underground nigga just pulled up. He's nice, but half the dayroom is nice. Everybody's got flow. And I ain't never heard of this fool. They call him Lil Lil. And they cater to this nigga. Extra food in the chow hall, new clothes out the laundry, all kinda shit. So, I'm wondering what I can get for knowing you since you're actually famous and shit. If you had a grill in these pics of us, I'd really try it.

College is easy. I finished one of those books I told you about. It says Whites should only marry Blacks to take their genes out of society. And the fool who wrote it is White. I guess I'd let you be with a sister. His name is Michael Moore. He made that movie about how all them bankers fucked everybody out they houses. I don't think Whites are all bad, but if there were no Whites at least there'd be no racism. No Black judge or D.A. would've screwed us over like this. I go to Taleem every Thursday. Have you gone yet? They say Whites can go. You should check it out. They expose so much of this bullshit. I keep thinking about my pops—he lost his life for a country that didn't even want him. Mom keeps sending me all this scripture to read. Telling me Pops is watching over me. I want to tell her that the Bible is the same one they used to convince us we should be happy slaves, and that my Pops died fighting against people who practiced the Black man's original religion, Islam. She wouldn't understand, though. She's my Mom and I love her, but she's a part of the masses sleepwalking through all this. I haven't told her much, but it's hard once your eyes have been opened to close them again. Eventually, I'll have to tell her how the view from down here in the belly of the beast can change a man.

Much Love,
Dell

Russell sat down and placed his elbows on the desk, then dropped his head into his hands. He stared blankly at the wall. He closed his eyes and prayed. When he was finished he took out a pen and some paper.

'Sup Dell,

I know this shit is rough, but you can't let this place get to you. We've got to get on that D.A.'s ass so we can be on the same unit. That was part of the deal. Look, bro, I know some of these White cats down here are Klan members or whatever, but Whites are not the only ones who are racist. I'd be willing to bet some of the people at those services you're going to think White people are the devil. As for me being with a Black girl, I guess you forgot about that time me and Erika had been talking and that fool Marcus started to trip with me. ALL that was behind me being White. And I hate to say it Dell, but when we got in each other's face, you were damn near standing on his side. So, I don't know if Whites only getting with Blacks is gonna work. It was working for me and Erika, but not for certain Black guys. That whole shit damn near got me kicked off the team. And you think only White people are racist? Your Dad died working for a country he loved. He fought for America, Dell. And he was a Christian. I'm not saying there's anything wrong with Islam, but I know when we went into that cafeteria we weren't asking Allah to protect us. You need to get moved over here. I'm starting to worry about you. The church

service over there prob'ly sucks and that's why you went to that
Muslim shit. I'll admit the service here isn't great. We got this one
cat who speaks more Spanish than English, and it's hard to follow,
but I still go. I don't have anything against Muslims. I respect everybody's faith, but Dell, we're Christians. Hurry up and write me back.

I love ya Bro,

Russ

P.S. Are you upset because you can't get any acting jobs now that
Fast and Furious and *Transformers* is over?

"But you known him all your life, right?" Big Ike looked at Russell
carefully.

"Pretty much," said Russell. "Since fifth grade, anyway."

It was crazy how peaceful the dayroom was at three a.m. The
square tables made of solid steel currently had no dominoes being
slammed on them. Both of the TVs were off, and no shower or cell
doors were slamming. No one was screaming or hollering in an
argument, "A go-rilla can't whup no lion!" Russell's time at work had
become his time to recharge and unwind from the nonstop stress
of a day in prison. Big Ike had become more than a friend. He was
more like a big brother. Like Adisa had been.

"Well, you know this place is rough, Russ," Big Ike folded his
hands in his lap and leaned back against the bench. "I didn't read
the letter, but what you're telling me sounds pretty bad."

Russell nodded and looked at the floor. Ike leaned to the right
and slid his Bible from his back pocket. He turned a few pages and
searched with his fingertips before finding what he was looking
for. "Tell him to read Psalms 143:8 and Romans 5:3-6." Ike pulled
a pen from his pocket. "Here." Russell took the pen and wrote the
scripture down on his left forearm. "Give those to him when you
write back. I'll keep y'all in my prayers."

"'Preciate it," mumbled Russell, distracted.

The night's work was over. Russell gathered up the scrub
brushes and jugs they kept the chemicals in and put them in the
mop bucket and steered it into the sally port. He looked through

the cloudy plexiglass windows to the front desk for Salinas and saw Capt. Johanson. *Damn.* He heard Ike tell the guard to have a good night and step into the sally port. "Uh-oh, Russ," he said.

"Yeah," Russell sighed, "I see her." He looked at Big Ike, then back up to the front desk as the door began to close behind them. Even at this distance he could see folds of fat hanging like saddlebags from Johanson's sides. She stood behind the horseshoe desk, hands behind her back as Salinas slid back and forth in her chair. Russell inhaled deep. Salinas stood to grab something off of the countertop. Johanson reached out and grabbed Salinas's ass. Russell stopped in his tracks. His stomach tightened. Before he could even think about how Salinas could file a sexual harassment claim, he saw her turn and smile. Johanson smiled back. *No!* He wondered if Ike had seen this... what had he said about the thumb ring?

The front door to the sally port opened. Ike headed out towards the desk. Finally, Russell started moving, now acutely aware of his pounding heart and the sweat on the back of his neck. Johanson looked in their direction, a scowl on her chalky face. The uneasiness Russell usually felt whenever he saw her was now extinct. Replaced by a deep, smoldering hostility. At the desk Russell and Ike rapped fists. "I got it from here, Ike."

"Alrighty then, see ya, brother."

Russell opened the door to take the chemical jugs back to A-turnout. He held his head high and didn't avoid Johanson's stare like he normally would have. He took his time turning in the equipment, hoping the captain would leave so he could talk to Salinas alone. When he walked through the door, Salinas was at the desk by herself talking on the phone. Just as he was about to speak, he saw Johanson and one of the other SSI's, Paco, standing very close to one another. The captain looked like she was pleading her case. Strange. He stared, hoping he looked defiant, and then headed toward D-pod, calling it a night. Russell's mind laid it out for him... Cordell's losing his mind 'cause the D.A. fucked us over and my girl's having to pretend she likes this fat ass dyke because I'm still in here.

CHAPTER 28

Slim G-Zus was alone in his cell. He sat at the desk with several newspaper pages of options and futures prices from IBD laid out before him. He held the 5380 down beside his left thigh, flipping through weekly and daily charts of corn futures. His right hand punched the keys on a calculator to determine the premium prices for May and September options on corn. He was in the middle of looking for their next trade. He stopped with the calculator and grabbed *The Encyclopedia of Commodity and Financial Spreads* from the shelf, his arms so long he didn't even have to stand to do it. He flipped to the 15-year composite chart of corn prices. The bias was obvious: prices were normally high right before harvest and low during the planting season. His left thumb worked the phone until it showed the weekly chart for May 2016 corn. At the bottom of the chart were his two favorite indicators: a MACD—A Momentum and Convergence/Divergence—and a relative strength index. Both measured market movement and intensity by averaging the high, low, and closing prices of a given market over a predetermined number of trading days. The MACD was sort of like a bar graph. Normally, the higher the market rose, the higher the bar for that trading day. The RSI was like a line snaking left to right and moving in concert with the market charted above. Most traders looked at these indicators to determine when a market was oversold or overbought. When they were high, you sell. When they're low, you would buy. Not Slim G-Zus. He only paid them any attention when they *diverged* from price. If corn reached a new high but both of the indicators failed to, this was a divergence between indicator and market, and for Slim G-Zus, an opportunity for a honky to get paid. September corn had made a low back in January of 4.17. Both indicators traced lower, mirroring the new low in the price in corn. Now, a month later, with the seasonal rise due to begin any day, September corn had dropped to 4.13, with *neither* indicator tracing down as low as they had back in January.

Slim G-Zus knew what this meant. As the famed trader Alexander Elder, a defector from the Soviet Union, would say: *The bears could no longer push down this market. And when a market can no longer go down, it must go up.* Slim G-Zus really dug Elder. The cat had run into a US embassy, barely escaping his Soviet comrades, and been granted asylum. Slim G-Zus thought it would do Mr. Clarkson some good to learn about Elder and all the others who'd risked their lives to get to this country. He inhaled deeply and smiled. *I'ma buy my daughter a house and put her through college...* Super honky Dad to the rescue! He texted Adisa:

> Sept crn divrg so confdnt thnkin we
> shld go lng fts cntrct instd of optns
> sprd. if u still wanna sprd a bull put
> wid be best.

Adisa texted back:

> Hit me.

Slim G-Zus was just about to speed dial Adisa when somebody knocked on his door.

Russell was standing next to Jew Boy by the window in the back of the dayroom, across from Itchy Foot and Larson. "I been knowing Paco for some years," said Larson. Itchy Foot stood with his arms folded, white state shirt stretched tight across his wide back. Larson waved his hand, "He ain't about to make some shit up."

Russell looked at Itchy Foot. Surely he wasn't going to go for this. He looked at Jew Boy who was frowning and shaking his head. *Somebody's gonna say something,* he thought. He looked across the dayroom to the stairwell. Paco, who was out of place from F-Pod, stood in a circle with his homeboys. Most of them had their heads down, looking at the floor, waiting for an answer to the question they had put to Larson.

Itchy Foot said, "We're not giving them a green light right now. It'll make us look scared. We—"

"Now you sound like Slim G-Zus," interrupted Larson.

"Need to run this down to the Big Body, Young—"

"And Slim G-Zus," said Larson, shaking his head.

Big Body Slim was in the craft shop and Youngbuck was at work. Russell had to do something, but he'd only been on the unit about six months, so nobody was going to listen to him. The last person he wanted to turn to was Slim G-Zus.

"Yeah, what's up?" asked Slim G-Zus. It was McCann, the confused youngster, which to Slim G-Zus was like saying *poisonous cobra.*"

"Say Slim.., man..."

Slim G-Zus stood up and walked to the door with the phone behind his back. "I'm right in the middle of something, youngster, what's up? You wanna use the horn again?"

The kid slipped his fingers through the grate on the door and put his face so close his nose almost slipped through too. "You know Paco?"

"Messcan? From Mexico?"

"Yeah. Works at night with me."

"What about him?"

"He's in the dayroom, he and a bunch of his homeboys over here outta place. He told Larson that O.T.'s a snitch." Slim G-Zus cussed and turned off the phone. "Larson's down there telling Itchy he's gonna give them a green light to smash him and—"

"Where's O.T.?" asked Slim G-Zus.

"He's at the Law Library, but he oughta be back any time now."

Slim G-Zus put his hand high on the door frame and pressed his forehead into his bicep. *Not what I need right now,* he thought.

McCann said., "Larson's like, 'we don't need to think about it.' Paco said he heard O.T. talking to the Internal Affairs people. And I'm like, where's the evidence? Coulda been talkin' 'bout his lawsuit—"

"Is Nelson still in the picket?"

"Which one's—"

"The messcan lady with the uneven hair." Slim G-Zus dipped down and strained his eyes, trying to determine who was in the picket. "McCann, go down there and tell whoever's in the picket I gotta medical lay-in." The kid stared and blinked a couple of times. Slim G-Zus stepped closer to the door. "O.T. ain't no snitch. I got you. Just get my door rolled. McCann nodded once and headed for the stairwell.

Slim G-Zus removed the already loose screws from the handle on the inside of his door and put the 5380 in its hiding spot. He turned the screws back in with some modified fingernail clippers, courtesy of Big Body Slim and the grinder in the craft shop.

Russell wished there was a way to get Slim G-Zus's door open without everybody in the dayroom knowing he had done it. But there wasn't. And O.T. could walk through the door any minute. What if he *had* snitched... He shook that thought off and picked up his pace, jogging down the stairs, not liking the fact he was trying to talk himself out of this.

He hit the dayroom and felt everyone looking at him. They knew whose door he'd just been in front of. *Jesus Christ,* he thought, *what if this law girl won't open the door?*

Russell banged a plexiglass window with the heel of his fist and then looked to his right. Over his shoulder he saw the circle with Paco opening up towards him. He looked up at the picket, no sign of the guard. He banged the window again and looked to his left. Larson put his hands on his hips and stared at him. Itchy Foot stood next to him, his thumbs jammed in his waistband. Jew Boy was walking toward him. Russell waved both hands at the picket like someone signaling a rescue helicopter. Nelson, the Latina guard who looked like she combed her hair with a brick, stood up and raised a hand, palm up, making a *WTF* face. Russell used his hand to communicate Slim G-Zus's cell number, then made an *L* with his thumb and index finger. Nelson frowned. She shook her head but hit the button anyway. Russell turned and looked up to Slim G-Zus' cell. It rolled.

Jew Boy asked, "What'd Slim G-Zus say?"

"Said O.T. ain't no snitch." Russell turned 180 degrees. Larson and Itchy Foot were at his 2:00, Paco and his homies at his 11:00. Slim G-Zus was coming down the stairs, black brogans laced tight, abs flexing with each step, his face an overconfident scowl.

Slim G-Zus stepped into the dayroom and headed for Larson, with McCann and Jew Boy headed in the same direction. "Fuck's going on?" asked Slim G-Zus.

Larson dropped his shoulders and turned his head, sighing. Itchy Foot said, "Paco overheard O.T. talking to the I.A. chick. Snitching on one of his homeboys who worked the dog kennel."

"Oh, yeah?" said Slim G-Zus.

Larson said, "Yeah, and I been knowing Paco for awhile. He's always been straight up. Ain't the type to lie."

Larson claimed Phoenix, Arizona. He got his time, twenty-five years, for a daisy chain of burglaries he'd committed in Odessa. That eighteen dollars an hour he made driving a water truck in the oil field wasn't enough to support him and his girlfriend's habit. At least that was what he told everybody. Slim G-Zus knew otherwise. Dope wasn't that expensive, there being so many cooks nowadays. If a guy was making eighteen dollars an hour and living in a paid-for trailer, he could've stayed high 'round the clock and still had three-fourths of his salary left over. O.T. had pointed this out to Larson's face awhile back. Larson got hot, tried to sell a wolf ticket that O.T. wouldn't buy. When the old man stuck a finger in his face and told him, "You better lower your voice talkin' to me, boy," Larson had backed away, rambling about how O.T. was lucky he was old. Itchy Foot, as usual, was just along for the ride. It didn't matter where the train was going, so long as it left the station.

"He's not?" asked Slim G-Zus. Russell and Jew Boy now stood next to him.

"No, he's not," said Larson. Slim G-Zus stared. Larson looked like a California surfer type. Curly blonde hair and a cleft chin, and tats covering his arms. He was about eight inches shorter than Slim G-Zus, but maybe twenty pounds heavier. He had muscle tone but looked soft standing next to Slim G-Zus. *Maybe a wide receiver,*

Russell thought. Russell looked over his shoulder. Paco and his homies were still by the stairwell, looking in their direction.

Slim G-Zus said, "So, just how would O.T. know about some hustle the dog boy has? They all stay in the dorms. I ain't never seen O.T. even go out to the dorms."

"Dude, that motherfucker's always up at one building. Paco and his homeboys ain't dumb. Dude just got busted. too. Right after—"

"So, Paco heard this fool snitchin' and then waited till his homeboy got busted to mention it?" Slim G-Zus turned to look at Paco. Larson tried to say something, but it trailed off as Slim G-Zus walked away. Russell didn't know if he should stay put or follow Slim G-Zus...

Larson said, "So, you wanna be a shit starter, huh, McCann?"

Russell felt the heat wave passing through, something he should've gotten used to by now. He said, "That's not enough evidence, Larson. They wouldn't accept that from us." He surprised himself. *That actually didn't sound too bad,* he thought... except the "us." He'd like to have that back.

"Oh," said Larson, "Mr. 'I been locked up a hot year,' knows how all this is supposed to work, huh?"

"I haven't been locked up a whole year." Russell liked that one, too. Liked the way it came out. Like even in this moment, where violence was certainly possible, he was so unfazed he could crack a joke.

Russell stared at Larson. His nose was perfectly straight, and he didn't have nary a scar around his mouth or eyes. Slim G-Zus, Big Body Slim, and definitely Youngbuck had their share. He looked at Itchy Foot. His right eyebrow, dark and thick, had a horizontal scar beginning in the middle and going all the way to his temple.

Russell turned and saw Slim G-Zus talking to Paco. He felt a bit of... Déjà vu?... Then it hit him. Last night. He'd seen someone else standing close to Paco, discussing something with him. That someone was being sued by O.T.

Russell shuffled his feet. He turned to Jew Boy, lowering his head and voice while eyeing Larson, making sure the out-of-stater knew he was keeping something from him. "Last night," whispered

Russell, "I seen Paco talking to Captain Johanson. It didn't look good, but I couldn't tell what they were saying."

Jew Boy's eyes widened. "That's the one O.T.'s suing, right?"

"Yeah," said Russell.

Jew Boy shook his head, "Did you tell Slim G-Zus?"

"Nah, I just now snapped."

"Better go tell him," said Jew Boy.

"Yeah, guess I'd better."

Russell knew you weren't supposed to interrupt two people talking, especially when they were discussing something important. In prison they call that jumping in someone else's car, and it is considered disrespectful. But, in the exchange with Larson, along with the Eureka moment he'd just had, his inhibitions were being overridden. As he stepped towards them, one of Paco's homeboys, a short and stocky guy with the Mexican flag tattooed on the side of his bald head, stepped out of ranks to intercept him. And, just like that, the rest of the convicts in the dayroom were now paying more attention to their little circle.

Paco put his hands behind his back and watched Russell closely as he stepped up to them. Russell spoke quietly and respectfully to Slim G-Zus, "I need to holler at you. Right now."

Slim G-Zus's eyebrows managed to draw even closer together before he said to Paco, "'Scuse me, potna," and stepped away from the group with Russell.

Russell started in a low voice, "I saw Paco talkin' to Captain Johanson last night. Like right up on each other." Slim G-Zus looked over at Paco then back to Russell who went on, "I couldn't hear 'em, but it looked bad. Suspicious." Russell motioned with his hands like a traffic cop, "They were like down towards F-Pod too, I guess so Salinas couldn't hear 'em either."

Slim G-Zus nodded. "Right. And if he was just complaining about his toilet not flushin'..."

Russell nodded in agreement with Slim G-Zus' unspoken thought.

Slim G-Zus said, "I'm not gettin' anywhere with this cat. O.T. oughta be here any minute..." He said it not to Russell, but as if he were simply thinking out loud. Then, "Let me tell 'em they ain't got no green light until I—until *we* get done investigating." Slim G-Zus turned and headed straight for Paco. Russell looked across the now quiet dayroom at Jew Boy and then followed after Slim G-Zus.

Slim G-Zus said, "Paco, I need to holla at all your homeboys." One of them was still there, and Paco said something in Spanish and motioned for the rest to join them.

Every one of them was covered in tattoos. Even with their shirts on you could see the numerous naked women in sombreros, marijuana leaves, and Mexican flags alongside the Virgin Mary and Jesus Himself. Several even had their necks and heads tattooed.

Slim G-Zus thumbed over his shoulder, "Larson should not have given y'all a green light. He had no business doing that." His deep voice sounded irritated, and he was over-enunciating his words like you do when you're talking to someone who doesn't speak English. "I am going to talk to O.T. when he comes in. We will do an investigation. If I find out O.T. is snitchin'? I'll run him off myself."

Russell heard the whir of the section door opening, something you couldn't normally hear during the day. O.T. came through carrying several legal folders and books like always. A couple of Paco's homeboys mumbled something in Spanish under their breath. In heavily accented English, Paco said, "Alls I can tell you, *guerro*, eez y'all needa get chor sheet togetter." An involuntary thought ran through Russell's mind: *Why can they make the* ch *sound when they say* shoes *(choos) but then call the chow hall "the shou hall."* But, he batted that thought away quicker than it had come.

Slim G-Zus folded his arms and frowned. "We got our shit together, potna." He thumbed towards Larson again, "Somebody made a mistake—and it's about to be corrected."

"Do yo investee-gashun, *guerro*. But he's a snitch, and he goss to go."

Slim G-Zus said, "Talkin' to the law doesn't make you a snitch," he leaned in, "right Paco?"

Paco looked confused. He looked at Russell. They stared at one another before the corners of Paco's mouth turned down.

Slim G-Zus said, "Like I said, if I find out he's a snitch, I'll run him off myself. But nobody has a green light!" Again he over-enunciated, "NO BOD EEE"

"What the fuck were you thinkin'?" Slim G-Zus could barely hold his temper. Larson was trying not to squirm. The artificial anger on his face had Slim G-Zus smelling blood. Larson said, "So, you wanna protect a snitch because he's White?"

"How many times you seen the Blacks or messcans give us a green light on some 'I heard him say this' type a shit?"

"So, we're lowering our standard to theirs?" Larson said, emboldened by what he must have thought was a great comeback.

Slim G-Zus shook his head, eyes closed, jaw muscles tight. He looked up and locked eyes with Larson. "We're raising our standards. We're saying we can do whatever they can do, even though we're the minority. Anything less and we look weak. How we gonna be respected and we're doin' shit they'll never do?"

Larson tilted his head back and rolled his eyes. Slim G-Zus went on, "Even if he was snitchin'—which he ain't—just giving them a green light..." he shook his head, "what kind of precedent would that set? There'd be motherfuckers comin' out the wood-work sayin' some honky's a snitch, just so they could run him off. A 'wood couldn't have nothin'. Soon as you get in position, some Black or messcan's gonna say you a snitch—if that's all it takes to get you run off."

Russell didn't know about all that. It sounded dangerously close to the slippery-slope argument so many of his teachers had warned him about. He was, however, glad that O.T. was safe. At least for the moment. No one had spoken to the ol'-timer since he had come in. Paco and his homies had all left when they called out for rec.

Russell now stood on the left side of Slim G-Zus. Jew Boy on the right and Larson directly across from Slim G-Zus. ItchyFoot stood off to one side, unsure of which side he was on. Through the window Russell saw a gray, humid, melancholy day. *Fitting*, he thought. Even though the day's events had his heart rate up, he felt like the weather looked: tired and frustrated. He wondered if he'd ever get used to this.

Slim G-Zus walked over to the water fountain, bent down, and got a drink. *I can't believe this guy,* he thought. *I really can't believe this clown is still arguing, trying to justify what he did.* He called Larson over to him so it would just be the two of them. He said, "Check this out, fella," he stared Larson in the eyes disrespectfully. "That was some dumb-ass shit you just did, and a motherfucker oughta run court on your ass."

"For tryin' to get a snitch smashed?" Larson's voice was a couple of octaves higher than normal. "Where I'm from in Arizona? We don't cut for snitches no matter—"

"This ain't where you're from, and if you keep this shit up you might not make it back."

Larson straightened up with a defiant look on his face. He unwisely leaned into Slim G-Zus's space.

Slim G-Zus slammed his forehead into Larson's nose. He felt the cartilage flatten. Larson spun away holding his face with both hands as blood ran between his fingers. Slim G-Zus threw open the door to the one-row shower and stepped in.

Unlike the showers on three row, a guard in the picket can easily see into the shower. But he was pretty sure the officer was sitting down and stuffing her face with Cheetos, as usual. He felt pretty confident he didn't have anything to worry about. He rubbed his forehead and looked at his fingertips. No blood. Larson's hand grabbed the shower door. Slim G-Zus pulled his right foot back and set it, pinched his long white shorts up over his bent knees and waited. Larson's face dripped blood and tears. His eyes said he was comin' in for certain revenge, as if Slim G-Zus had finally fucked with the wrong guy.

Slim G-Zus raised his right hand in front of his chin, leaving it open, his palm facing Larson. His left hand tightened into a fist, hung by his side. Larson exhaled through clenched teeth. *Straight Hollywood,* thought Slim G-Zus

Larson lifted his hands mechanically, almost Irish style like the mascot for Notre Dame. Slim G-Zus bent his knees a little more and inched his left foot forward.

Russell stood outside the shower next to Jew Boy and Itchy Foot. Slim G-Zus looked like he was posing for the cover of a fitness magazine. He was ripped up with thick veins in his long arms, his muscles short and blocky despite the length of his limbs.

Slim G-Zus's left hand sprung from his waist like someone cracking a whip, and nailed the side of Larson's jaw. Larson's head snapped backwards as if someone had shoved him from behind. When it came forward again, another left jab struck like a cobra with an identical result. Larson, face down now, threw an overhand right that missed. Slim G-Zus extended his left hand like a stiff arm to Larson's collarbone and launched a right uppercut that connected.

Larson's head popped up but he stayed bent at the waist, swimming wildly. Two or three of his punches glanced off Slim G-Zus' forehead, but, with his chin tucked, never landed solidly.

Slim G-Zus rolled to his right and down, bending at the waist. He came up throwing rapid-fire uppercuts: right-left-right-left, like a juggler on fast-forward. Real fights were nothing like what you saw on TV. Punches landing undeflected, spinning a guy ninety degrees before he turns back and tags his opponent—who had his hands down, as if the last thing he was expecting was a punch in the face. In a real fight, your opponent doesn't let you hit him and is constantly trying to hit you. If two guys were close to even in skills, then the one who could keep his cool in the moment—the one with the bigger balls—who can stand there and throw his punches without panicking usually won. This much Russell had figured out during his stay at Acirema, and, as much as he hated to admit it, Slim G-Zus had these characteristics in spades. Not to mention an edge in hand speed and arm length.

Several of the uppercuts had landed. Larson was no longer swinging his fists. He was using them to cover his face. Slim G-Zus switched from juggling uppercuts to Larson's chin, to burrowing hooks into his ears and temples. Larson popped up and threw a telegraphed right that Slim G-Zus weaved. Almost upright now, Larson caught two more stiff jabs with his face. Slim G-Zus bound forward and landed a hard right. Larson crumpled forward into Slim G-Zus on his way to the ground.

Slim G-Zus backed up and stood still, catching his breath, Larson's blood on his six-pack and white shorts. He turned his head and spat on the wall. "Had enough?"

So Slim Bitchus beat up that beach-volleyball lookin' ho. That ain't shit. And it just goes to show you, ho-ass whiteboys can't fight, 'cause that ho had to outweigh Slim Bitchus by thirty pounds. I wish one a them ho-ass whiteboys would get out of line with me.

The pyahs are saying the old one's snitching. He probably is. Look at them Italians. They created snitching. Most of them are White. Whites, the ice people, are material-focused, and that makes them self-centered, more likely to snitch. The sun people, Blacks, are spirit-focused and communal. We don't just think about ourselves. Melanin does that. Blacks have it, Whites don't. You gotta read Karanja Keita Carrol and Dr. York. All that shit is scientific. Proven.

I seen little Captain America run his scared ass up there and get that fool out of his cell. The rest of them were just gonna go along with what the pyahs were saying. They didn't know what to do. If that old motherfucker would've come through the door just a little sooner... Man, that would've been perfect. They'd have smashed that ho. Probably life-flighted his ass, and then Slim Bitchus would've told them whiteboys to kick it off. It would've been Whiteboys and pyahs bleeding all over this bitch.

Them whiteboys showed a lot right there. If a nigga really puts it to most of them, they're going to catch that pussy. If they'd have let them Mexicans smash that old fool, I'd have told them the one that gots that punk Rexy was snitchin', and then scooped that punk up for myself, after they ran her man off. It ain't but a couple more whiteboys that fuck around, and I know I can whip both of them. That sweet white ass'd be in my cell right now... They also gotta couple of whiteboys with mules. They get tobacco, weed, phones.

A nigga could get them out the way too. Tell my boy Damn Fool to say he heard them snitching. Then slide up to they mule and tell that ho, "Bitch, you better keep bringing that shit. Bring it to me." If them hoes is scared of them pyahs, I know they'd be scared of Fool. Whiteboys been scared of niggas down through the years.

Two days after the fight between Slim G-Zus and Larson, Russell was still trying to figure out why he hadn't done what Slim G-Zus did. He knew Larson and Itchy Foot were in the wrong, but he'd just stood there, then ran and got Slim G-Zus. Slim G-Zus... The racist atheist who knew everything and walked around with his chest stuck out, looking all flexed up. Russell shook his head. Slim G-Zus did what Russell had wanted to do, and everybody followed him. When Youngbuck and Big Body Slim had come in later, they'd both threatened to whup Larson's ass without even hearing his side of the story, strictly on the strength of what Slim G-Zus had told them.

"Meekahn?" asked the Nigerian guard at Russell's door.

"Yessir."

"Whoht eez yo numbah?"

Russell got up from the desk and rattled off his number. A letter from Megan slid through the side of the door.

Dear Russ,

Yes, I've been getting all your letters. I've been really busy. Some of us have to work, okay? I don't get to lay around and play golf. Yes, I remember the first time we kissed. It was right before we had sex for the first time. I think you need a little perspective here. We hung out at parties and slept together, Russ. That was basically it. It's not like you were picking me up with flowers and taking me to dinner, nor did I want you to. Yes, I know we've known each other a long time. I'd like to see you too, but you said Texas doesn't allow conjugal visits. I have needs, Russ. When you were out, we could satisfy each other's needs. Why do you want me to drive four hours so we can sit and talk for two hours? We never sat and talked for two hours when you were out here. Why now?

I'm sorry you're there, but I didn't put you there. I'm not the one
who told you to keep a gun in your car. Why did you have a gun
at school anyway?

Megan

Russell sat down and leaned his back against the desk. He
glanced at the letter in his hands... It was real. He'd read it right. He
was glad his celly was at work and he had the cell to himself. He
leaned forward, resting his forearms on his knees. He scanned the
words on the paper then folded it up. Shock and anger were battling
hard for his undivided attention... But he really shouldn't have been
surprised either, because when a relationship is built on sex and the
sex is taken away...

CHAPTER 29

Isaiah Donaldson grew up in the east Dallas projects never knowing who his father was. The youngest of four boys, he'd learned how to steal cars before he was old enough to legally drive. At age thirteen he was sent to boot camp for his second unauthorized use of a motor vehicle charge. At fifteen he went into the Texas Youth Commission for aggravated robbery after sticking up a Kroger's convenience booth with an air pistol that didn't work.

Released from TYC at age seventeen, he managed to stay on the streets all of seven months before joining two of his three brothers in TDC, sentenced to ninety-nine years for an aggravated robbery of a pawn shop in which one of the employees was pistol whipped by one of his accomplices.

Under the seventy-seventh legislature, an aggravated sentence of ninety-nine years required the convict to pull fifteen years before he became eligible for parole. Big Ike hadn't been eligible for parole after his first fifteen years because he was on B-side for assaulting a corrections officer who improperly confiscated his hot pot. Two years later, when he was eligible again, he was given a two-year set-off for "nature of the offense." After that two-year period, he lost track of all the one-, two-, and three-year set-offs he'd gotten for "nature of the offense"—even though TDC's *own policy* explicitly prohibits the parole board from setting off an inmate for the same thing twice. The victim's family also protested his parole, but hey, he didn't blame them. He'd committed a horrible crime.

It'd now been twenty-six years. Counting the time he'd done in TYC, he'd been locked up twelve years longer than he'd been in the free world. But it really doesn't matter. Why? Because He has a plan, and it's great to be washed in His blood. Nothing better than being forgiven. God is good—ALL THE TIME!

It had all started to turn after his mother's first heart attack. Ike knew she was the only person ever truly in his corner. So when she wrote that all she could think about when she was lying on the floor, taking what she thought were her last breaths, was that she couldn't die with her youngest baby still in prison, Ike got his stuff together. He got on his knees and told God that no matter how angry one of the guards made him, he wouldn't lift a hand against them. And that, in order to keep his promise, God would have to walk with him. He couldn't do it on his own.

Next came the Tony Dungy book *Uncommon*. It was the first book Ike had ever read cover to cover. He'd heard about it listening to the Rush Limbaugh show while stuck in his cell twenty hours a day on closed custody. (Those same five songs the FM stations play every hour will make you explore all your options). Ike had never payed any attention to politics, but his grandfather, the only male figure he and his brothers had ever known, once told him that you vote for Republicans because they freed the slaves and the Democrats want to give somebody something for nothing. Rush liked the Republicans and Tony Dungy said he was honored to be on his show. *Must be good people,* Ike deduced.

After *Uncommon*, Ike got the other Tony Dungy books, the daily devotionals and Bible studies. And after several years of walking with the Lord, He blessed him with parole. Ike was going to show her the composition notebook he'd kept with every verse of scripture she'd ever told him copied down in it. He would take care of her, make her proud. She was the only one who never gave up on him.

Big Ike gave his housing assignment to the guard taking count as he stepped onto the rec yard. Typical spring day in South Texas. Heat, humidity, and sun turned the concrete farm into a sauna. It'd been a while since he'd come out here. Laying low, staying out the way. He would be on the chain headed home in less than a week now. He walked over to the weight pile. Shook hands with the youngster. His White brother in Christ and coworker, Young Russ. "'Sup, Lil bro?" asked Big Ike.

"'Sup, Ike?" said the youngster. "Been a while, huh?"

Big Ike grinned, "Yeah. Had to come out here and get some fresh air. Tell a couple of these brothers goodbye."

"You gonna lift?"

"Nah, I'ma try that court one time, though. See if I still got it. Nome sayin'?"

Russell raised a fist and said, "Already," and rapped Big Ike's fist. Ike walked over to the court, "Who got next?"

About fifteen Black inmates stood around, shooting wild shots, jumping for rebounds. Longview said, "I got next."

"I got after you," said Big Ike.

"You can run with us. It's me, Four-Five, West Dino, and Scrapp—" Longview pointed, "the Lil Ese."

"Bet," said Ike.

Big Ike chilled on the sideline while the first game played out. He shook lots of hands and slapped lots of backs. He told every one of them, "He blessed me."

Longview said, "You ready, Big?"

As a kid, Big Ike played power forward. Emphasis on the power. He idolized Dallas's Roy Tarply and Boston's Kevin McHale. Tarply was his hometown Maverick. McHale had low-post moves like no one else he'd ever seen. Ike had a good combination of speed and strength. He could take one step and dunk the ball with two hands, not needing a running start. He liked to catch the ball mid-post, just outside of the lane, fake inside, then drop-step towards the baseline, dunking and letting his momentum carry him around in a circle as he hung from the rim.

At around the age of thirty-two, finishing this move with a dunk became less of a sure thing. He could still throw it down, but it took longer to gather his feet, and he didn't always get high enough to grab the rim and swing around. Eventually, Father Time forced him to lay it up.

The rims on the yard didn't have spring boxes, so they were bent down in the front from guys dunking on them. The concrete was smooth and a little sandy. Sometimes you'd slide when you tried to stop, like them tennis players on TV, or stay put when you tried to take off fast, like a car spinning its tires. The nets were gone too, causing the ball to sail through and roll all the way to the handball court when you swished it.

None of this bothered Ike at age forty-five. In fact, the dirt helped slow those youngsters down. Nowadays, his game was banging in the paint. He'd back his opponent down, down, down, and spin either left or right for a jump hook. The dunks were long gone, but two points were two points. And he had the up and under, a gang of shoulder takes, and plenty of other cagey veteran moves that woulda made McHale proud. The Mavericks shoulda got McHale for a coach. He coulda put Dirk down with a mean low-post game.

Longview, a slim slasher-type cat, shot the die and hit it. He took the ball out at the top of the key. Ike walked down to the paint, saw Fleetwood, a dark bald-headed cat about three inches shorter than him, coming over to pick him up. Three-second lane violations don't get called in prison, so Ike camped out in the paint, walled off Fleetwood, and raised his right hand to call for the hail. Longview passed to Four-Five who caught the ball on the wing, just behind the three-point line, and squared up to the basket. He was quick and could get to the hole, but he couldn't hit a jumper for a conjugal visit. Everybody knew this. The cat checking him played off, sagging in the lane in between Four-Five and Ike.

Ike tried to back Fleetwood further down, all the way under the goal, to create a little more space. But Fleetwood held his ground. He dug his left forearm into Ike's lower back and leaned all of his weight into him.

Four-Five faked right and drove left to the baseline. His man played so far off of him, he easily caught up and cut him off. Four-Five stopped, dribbled behind his back, then hit Lil Scrappy up top. Ike pivoted hard and extended his left arm to keep Fleetwood from jumping the passing lane. Scrappy faked a lob, then looped a slick bounce pass with a lot of English on it into the lane. Ike's right hand collected the ball, his left hand slapped it secure.

Fleetwood was on the left side of his back, so Ike leaned in to create some space and dropped his right foot back. He took one dribble and pivoted away on his right foot down the lane. Four-Five's man came under and swiped at the ball. He was too late. Ike was already laying the ball up off the metal backboard. One–zero.

Russell smiled as Big Ike made a nice lefthanded lay-up for the first point of the game. He lowered the pin on the military press two plates to 180 pounds as Big Ike jogged down the court. On defense, Big Ike was handling this other tall dude they called Fleetwood. Pushing him out of the lane and reaching in front of him to deny the ball. Russell liked that. Guy should've been a defensive end. Mrs. Donaldson tripped out, should've let her boy play football.

Russell was almost done working out. He sat down on the leg press, his last exercise. He'd watched Ike's team win four games in a row and it looked like they were about to win their fifth. Russell grabbed the handles by his sides and braced himself. He pushed forward with his heels and moved the 535 pounds on the horizontal sled.

Quad muscles get used everyday, so in order to stimulate them you have to do higher reps. Instead of a few sets of ten or twelve, Russell always did sets of twenty. Same thing with his calves.

The first set of twenty at 535 went fine. It was basically a warm-up set. The next set of 570 pounds would have him breathing hard the last few reps, and the third and fourth set of 605 would damn near cause him to hurl.

Russ lowered the pin to 605. He walked around the machine, shaking out some of the tightness in his legs. Big Body Slim said, "I see ya, boy. Gettin' up there with the Big Body," and kissed his biceps. Russell laughed.

Big Ike snapped a rebound away from an opponent and hurled a Kevin Love outlet pass right on the money to Four-Five, who took two steps and laid the ball in, slapping the backboard as he floated by.

Russell lifted his arms and folded his hands behind his head to expand his lungs, sucking air. He heard somebody call out the score: 10–9. Ike's team was up by one and they were going to eleven, win by two. Russell counted sixty seconds, the amount of time he rested in between sets. Both teams went up and down, missing shots. Russell sat back down in the sled, that sixty seconds ending way too fast. He pushed the 605 up and held it, his seventeenth rep, and paused, legs locked out. His muscles and lungs a four-alarm blaze. He inhaled and glanced up at the court. Ike tipped a pass away. Lil Scrappy scooped it up and started a fast break the other way. Longview filled the right side, West Dino the left. They had the numbers, three on two. Scrappy no-looked it to his left. West Dino caught it in stride, took one dribble and spun inside, right into the teeth of the defense.

Bodies collided. West Dino passed off to Longview, who dribbled across the free-throw line right to left. Big Ike was trailing the play. Longview flipped an over-the-shoulder pass. Ike came barreling over the three-point line and caught the ball. He dribbled twice and took off. Only he didn't. He stumbled forward through the bodies and off the court skidding onto the uncovered concrete, face first.

Boseko Lokombo grew up in the Democratic Republic of the Congo. The third of seven children, he'd come to America through the country's immigration lottery system. He managed to get a student visa and complete a degree in sociology at the University of Houston. With his visa about to run out, he'd been desperate to find a way to stay in America. A paper shuffler at Immigrations and Customs told him there were certain jobs that, if he would take them, would allow him to stay in America on a work visa. The only one at the moment that was a guarantee was with the Texas Department of Corrections. While at U of H, he'd met others from the DRC and Nigeria that had relatives or friends working for TDC. They complained about the Black American inmates the most. Boseko had the same problems with the Blacks in his apartment complex on the southwest side of Houston. They had no respect or integrity, but he could deal with them if it would keep him in America.

The last six months hadn't been easy, but he was set to make over forty-thousand this year because of all the overtime he was getting. And he had all the medical and dental benefits you could ever imagine. The inmates were as bad as he'd heard. They had no shame. America, as a whole, didn't. Kids would tell their parents *"F" you!*

The inmates liked to say he lived in the jungle with lions and tigers. Boseko thought this was funny because the area in South Texas where the Acirema unit sat was much less developed than his town in the DRC. When he saw pictures of America on TV, they had led him to believe the entire country looked like Manhattan or Beverly Hills. Bee Ef Eee had deer and varmints—especially skunks—all over the place. And Houston was big, but some of it looked like River Oaks, and some of it looked like Third Ward where U of H was. He'd once seen a White man running down Scott Street at 8:00 a.m. screaming about how he'd just been carjacked.

Worst of all was the way they talked to women. They were all bitches and hoes, the most disrespectful terms they could be called. The American women guards would curse back at them and try to be even more insulting and vile. Most of them had children and weren't married. Boseko couldn't help but think their children were neglected. The female guards from the DRC or Nigeria normally wouldn't stoop to their level. They would follow procedure and write the scoundrel a disciplinary case or tell him he was acting like an animal. Boseko had tried talking to them. Tried leveling with them. But they'd just mock him, pretending like they couldn't understand what he was saying. "Speak English, you Black-ass African nigga!" To which Boseko would reply proudly, "I am speaking English. I speak the Queen's English—what do you speak?"

Today he was in the rec tower, about twenty feet off the ground, in between three building and four building rec yards. The sun and humidity were brutal, especially with his long-sleeve, dark-gray uniform on. The inmates mingled on the grass and concrete in white cotton shorts. So proud of their muscles and tattoos. To his right, in between the handball court and basketball court, a large Black inmate stumbled to the ground. He must be unconscious because he didn't use his hands to break his fall... other inmates were gathering around him...

Russell struggled up from the leg press, holding the steel frame to
steady himself. Ike wasn't moving. Russell shook his legs, tried to
catch his breath, and headed towards Ike.

Ernesto Vasquez, the on-duty medical assistant handling the radio
in the Acirema infirmary, grew up in Blanco, the same South Texas
town famous for passing a bill to make Spanish its official language.
Like everyone else in his school district, he'd been taught about the
glory of old Mexico and how Santa Anna, unduly elected, signed that
bogus treaty with the gringos. English as a second language classes
were more like *English is an evil language* classes. Nobody in Blanco
spoke it. Nor did any of his instructors at the school where he got
his medical training. And why should they? America is supposed
to be a free country, no?

Ernesto never planned to work outside of Blanco, but a DUI
and misdemeanor marijuana possession got him fired from his job
at the clinic. The administrators told him he could come back after
he completed his probation and community service the judge in
drug court had sentenced him to. The only place that would hire
him in the meantime was the Texas Department of Corrections.

It was almost 2:00 pm when the radio on the desk in front of
him squawked a little louder than usual. Ernesto grabbed it and
brought the radio to his ear.

Inmates were yelling up at Boseko as he stood in the tower, "Bitch,
call an ICS, he need medical. Bitch, he having a heart attack." He
spoke into the radio, "Officer Lokombo initiating ICS, ICS. Four
building rec yard. Inmate down, complaining of chest pain, possible
heart condition, bring defibrillator. Officer Lokombo initiating..."

Ernesto listened, "Aw-feesuh Lwowmbwoko, eeneesheeting eye-see-
ess. Fwor beelding wek yahd. Eenmatah dwown, cwomplaneeng uh
chess pen. Poss-ee-bull hwaht cone-dee-shawn. Breen Dee-fiboo-
layture. Aw-feesuh Lwowmbwoko initiating..." Ernesto hesitated.
Maybe one of the *moyos* stole a radio from the officer and is playing

games... He hoped that was the case. He certainly couldn't understand what the problem was. Pretty sure it was on four building
but that was about it... He pushed the button. "You must repeat
ICS, over..."

Boseko listened for a response... choo muss weepee uh-see-ess,
ovir..." Boseko's eyebrows furrowed. He looked at the radio. *Maybe
he said repeat... I already repeated it.*

Russell's legs, lungs, and stomach were revolting. He finally made it
over to the crowd surrounding Big Ike. A couple guys came jogging
back from the guard tower. One of them said, "We told that nigga.
He got on the radio..."

Somebody else said, "They need to hurry the fuck up—he
ain't talkin' no more."

Russell stared. Ike was still face-down on the concrete. An
odor hit him... something burning... Russell knelt down near Ike's
head, his legs barely cooperating, still sucking air. "Ike?" said Russell
between breaths. The smell got stronger. Russell's hands were on
the concrete... his lips parted... Ike's skin was burning. "Lookout,
y'all," said Russell, "this concrete's hotter than a motherfucka, we
gotta move him back there." Russell thumbed towards the shaded
area of the court.

"Sheeet—that's a lawsuit. You don't know what's wrong with
that nigga," said someone from the crowd.

Russell saw Ike fall. He was pretty sure he hadn't broke his
neck, and someone had said he was talking, saying his chest was
cramping.

Russell looked at the horseshoe-shaped crowd and said, "His
skin's burning. I can't move 'im myself." He rose up, still bent at the
waist, and reached under Ike's shoulders. "Help me turn him over."
A couple of convicts came up beside Russell. They turned him over
slowly, awkwardly. Russell and an older guy grabbed an arm and a
shoulder. Two others each grabbed a leg. They lifted what Russell
was sure was close to 300 pounds. Russell prayed his legs wouldn't

cramp as they struggled to get under the awning. Ike's forehead, shoulders, chest, and stomach had charred patches embedded with sand.

Russell kneeled down beside Ike's head. He lowered his head to Ike's nose and mouth... "He's still breathing. Ike, can you hear me?"

Two guards appeared. "What happened?" asked a young Latino.

Russell looked up. Someone from the crowd said, "Shit—he fell out. Talkin' 'bout his chest crampin'."

Minutes passed. Russell lowered his head again... "I don't think he's breathing.

A guard straddled Big Ike and began performing CPR. Jesus Christ... not good...

Russell looked away, then back... *God, please...* he felt the tears begin to well in his eyes. He looked up to keep them from pouring out. The guard was pumping Ike's chest violently. Russell didn't think a human rib cage could move like that. He turned towards the handball court, hands on his head. *Jesus, please...* He tried to think of some prayer but couldn't get his mind to focus. An overweight female nurse reeking of cigarette smoke brushed past him, pulling a gurney. No defibrillator in sight. The guards and nurses struggled to get Ike strapped to some kind of board. Finally, Russell and some other inmates got him on the gurney.

Russell felt a tap on his shoulder. "You okay little dawg?" Big Body Slim's voice was surprisingly gentle. Russell stared at a pair of lifeless brown eyes, afraid to speak because he thought he'd break down.

Big Body Slim bit on his upper lip, "He dead?"

Russell looked up at him, breathing through his mouth, almost past the point of no return.

"It's fucked up," said Big Body, "he was one of the decent ones. Y'all were pretty tight, huh?"

Guards busied themselves setting up an empty water cooler on a bench by the weight pile. They then took a picture of it as if it had been there all along.

Russell couldn't get the image out of his head. He tried to picture Ike pushing the ragged mop bucket or quoting from his pocket Bible, but the image that kept popping up was the one of Ike's chest heaving as the guard performed CPR. A human's chest wasn't supposed to bend like that... and why the *fuck* was that the image he was stuck with? Why not when Ike began to fall or when he made that first basket? All he could see was that mountain of muscle and bone being crushed repeatedly. Everywhere he looked, eyes open or closed.

They said it was a heart attack. They said it was a heat stroke. They said it was a whole bunch of shit. Worst of all, Russell had no way of finding out for sure. His parents weren't the most computer-savvy people on the planet, to put it mildly. He wasn't going to ask Megan to try and find something. And Cordell was in the same predicament he was. Slim G-Zus had a phone, but he didn't want to ask him for any favors. Plus one of the rumors flying around was that the guard in the picket and the nurse in the infirmary couldn't understand each other, and that was why they took so long and didn't bring a defibrillator. Supposedly, neither one could speak or understand English very well. The guard was an African and the nurse was Hispanic, *er*, Mexican. Russell thought that one probably came courtesy of Slim G-Zus himself.

Russell sat on the stool, his back against the desk, alone in his cell. He held with both hands the Tony Dungy book Ike had loaned him. He remembered Ike telling him about the title... "comes from a speech Chuck Knoll gave when Dungy was a rookie. Talkin' about what characteristics he wanted in his football players. I looked up every one of those words in the dictionary. Wrote 'em all down."

Russell looked at the yellowed notebook paper with Ike's tiny handwriting on it. Words like *integrity*, along with their definitions. He wanted to find a way to get the book sent to Ike's mother. Had to find an address. Maybe the chaplain.

Just before midnight, Russell walked up to the front desk. Salinas held the phone in one hand while she dipped a tortilla chip with the other. Russell stood there a long time before she noticed him.

She hung up the phone giggling, saying something in Spanish. "Hey," she said when she saw him.

"'Sup, you all right?" he asked.

"Yeah."

It had been weeks since he'd seen Captain Johanson grab her ass, but he still hadn't had an opportunity to bring it up. Big Ike, one of the other SSI's, or another guard had always been around. He looked down the hall to Spod's sally port, then E-Pod's. There was no sign of Paco or any of the other SSI's.

"You sure you're all right?" he asked again.

Salinas looked him in the eye, "Yeah, why?"

Russell shrugged. "Captain Johanson hasn't been giving you any trouble?"

Salinas looked confused. "Captain Johanson? No. Why?"

Russell shrugged again. *Screw it,* he thought. *This is as good a time as any.* "I know she's been harassing you, Elka. I saw her..." he gestured awkwardly, fumbling for the right words, "...grope you."

Salinas' eyes widened. She turned her head and looked down at the desk. She covered her face with the hand she'd been eating the chips with, then pulled it away, leaving grains of salt in her eyebrows. She reached back and adjusted the bun her hair was in and stood up, exhaling hard. "She and I play around like that sometimes. You know how y'all play the 'come on,' the grab-ass? She's just playing."

Now it was Russell's turn to look confused, his eyebrows rising up. *Okay,* he thought. He checked the hallway again, then stepped closer to the desk, resting his fists on top of it. "I get out, I'll make sure all this goes away. You can move to Houston and get away from this place."

Elka closed her eyes, "You know how many times I've heard that?" Actually, it was never. She felt the need for sympathy, and it sure sounded good. The *guero* was cute and sweet, and he had *juevos.* That was a hard-to-find combination. Moving to Houston, though... That would take her away from her job and Jamie. She'd done that before when she had nothing to lose and thought she was in love. Now, she had a steady job that, with the overtime, paid great! Then there was Jamie. Who was always there for her. She could tell by the way that he was acting that he wouldn't understand what she and Jamie had. There were days she didn't understand herself.

One day she only wanted the affection of a man. The next she'd be with Jamie and swear men off for good. She never felt like a stud. That was Jamie. Jamie knew how to initiate things. Men didn't. But, she wasn't with Jamie because there were no good men. As early as age six, she'd known that she was attracted to girls. And not like a guy. She could sit in the locker room and quietly admire the other girls without letting them know. Her volleyball teammate, Sara, who was also a pitcher on the softball team, really did it for her. Elka had fantasized about her for years. All through junior high and high school. The way her legs looked in those volleyball shorts, the way she looked washing her hair in the shower. The way her naked body looked so strong and athletic, yet oh so feminine. Jamie didn't look anything like Sara. She was white. Pale white. She had red hair and a crooked face. There was nothing athletic about her body. And she acted too much like a man. Like she wanted to be a man. But she didn't love like a man. She knew what to do and to do it slow.

Elka wasn't visually attracted to her like she was other women. She was attracted to Jamie because she knew what to do. Kind of like when a young woman likes an older man. And like all women, she was safe in the sense that she couldn't cheat on you and leave proof like a man when he cheats on you and gets another woman pregnant.

But all was not well. Elka had barely patched things up with her parents when she and Jamie started sleeping together. Moving to Houston with a gringo would not go over well. What she had with Jamie, however, if they ever found out would get her disowned. Her parents weren't religious at all, but her grandparents on both sides were devout Catholics. And they had raised her parents to believe homosexuality was a mortal sin.

The *guero* had mentioned the Bible a few times... she'd heard him and the big *moyo* he cleaned the showers with quote some of that scripture crap. Her favorite response to being asked if she was Catholic was, "No, I'm a heathen." Especially on Ash Wednesday when the other Catholic guards showed up to work with a palm-ash cross on their foreheads.

She had time, though. From her calculations on the computer, Russell didn't become eligible for parole for a few more months. Which was another thing that made him so very appealing—she knew where he was at all times. He couldn't cheat on her. But... once he was out... She still had time. She wanted to be with him. She loved the protective feeling he made her feel from the very first time they ever spoke. He made her feel... safe. And, she'd take those green eyes, too.

Russell looked away and then back, "You never heard it from me before."

Salinas frowned the left side of her mouth. Russell pressed down on the desktop, searching for something that would convince her. He checked the hallway again, "Come here," he said.

Elka followed him to the SSI closet. She'd been ready for this for some time now. He stepped in first and turned around. She looked down the hallway to D-pod, then the other way towards F-Pod. She crossed the threshold. Their eyes locked. Russell hit the light switch. *Why did he do that?* she thought, *now I can't see.* He embraced her. She stood very still. *We don't have much time,* she thought. Then she felt his lips kiss the top of her head, pausing, squeezing together. She pressed her head into his chest.

"When I get out, you have to let me hold you like this every night."

She felt a warmth she had not felt in, like, forever. Tears filled her eyes. She opened her mouth, thrust her jaw forward and exhaled silently. She rubbed her hands up and down his back, feeling the muscles bow out in a V-shape as she went up. He squeezed tighter. She had to hold her breath.

He said, "I don't just want you for sex like those White guys you went to school with." It took her a second to remember her fictitious gringo classmates. She was certain he wasn't about to go in her pants. He stood back and took her face in his hands, like they do on soap operas, and kissed her. A peck. Both of his lips covering her top lip. Then another covering her bottom lip. Another on both lips. Again, both lips, a little tongue. She looked into those emerald eyes still shimmering in the dark.

They'd been in here, completely alone for a couple of minutes now, and he hadn't tried to get her pants off. She stared into his eyes one last second and wrapped her arms around as much of his shoulders as she could, pressing her body into his. They kissed again. She couldn't get close enough to him. He took it slow. So sure of himself. Her body might have levitated off the floor. He just held her close... *Houston, here I come,* she thought.

For Russell there was no celebration. His best day in prison had also been his worst. Elka was great. She was the old-fashioned small-town girl with morals that Megan would never be. And she was prettier. He knew she was too scared of Johanson to say what she really thought about the harassment. Ike, bless his soul, had been partially right about Johanson: She was indeed a dyke, but she wasn't the leader of a gang of dykes out to get inmates. She was a bully, and Russell was sure she was trying to force herself on his woman. The way they kissed and held each other, he knew she was his. He'd shown her he didn't just want her for sex. The closet was the perfect opportunity, and he didn't even grab her ass.

He'd have her waiting for him when he got out. He'd hug his parents, then, with Megan standing right there, he'd wrap his new linebacker arms around Elka and pick her up and spin her around a couple of times before planting a kiss on her like the one they'd just shared. All of this was great.

But Big Ike was dead.

The rest of the night, Russell couldn't get excited about Elka, and had to fight not to break down. His job had been a sanctuary because of Ike. Russell recharged every night with the old convict's wisdom and friendship. Prison stopped feeling like prison for those few hours. He tried to remind himself that Ike had been on his way out the door anyway, but it didn't stop his chest from feeling like it was going to implode. It went away when he was with Elka, but they couldn't stay in the closet for more than a couple of minutes.

He couldn't talk to anyone about it because, of course, you're not supposed to feel anything when somebody dies. That's being weak. Bringing it up would only get the bullshit-ass conspiracy stories flying again.

When Russell finished cleaning the last shower, it was almost six a.m. Him and Ike together would have been done hours ago. He looked down into the dayroom where Ike should have been waiting and paused, deciding to sit down on the bench in the shower. He leaned forward, rested his forearms on his knees, and bowed his head. He closed his eyes, holding the shower brush handle with both hands against his head. He squeezed the wooden handle as hard as he could, flexing every muscle in his body. Then he released it. He'd been told by a coach that this would help with pregame tension. It wasn't helping with whatever the hell he had now. He wanted to ask God, "Why me?" But a better question was, "Why Ike?" Yes, Russell was in prison for stopping a maniac, but Ike had just *died* in prison— right when he was about to get out. *If nothing else, didn't his mother deserve to see him before she died? What purpose did his dying serve? And if You're the all-knowing, all-seeing, all-everything—why not accomplish Your purpose without killing Ike? But, I'm not supposed to question Your plan...* Russell straightened up and held the shower brush across his knees. He closed his eyes and took a deep breath.

CHAPTER 30

Slim G-Zus stood under the window in the back of the dayroom, his back and the sole of his right boot against the wall, reading *Options as a Strategic Investment* by Larry McMillan. He'd already read it straight through, but wanted to go back over the section on futures spreads. He and Adisa were considering several spreads with soybeans that involved shorting a near-month contract and going long a month farther off. The trick was figuring out where to place your stops on each contract. You had to leave enough wiggle room to allow the trade enough time to develop. Very few trades ever take off immediately in the direction you're expecting. But, too much wiggle and you'd get stopped out for a loss that was more than three percent of your total bankroll.

He'd have to bust out the calculator when he got back in the cell. Crunch the numbers with McMillan's version of the Kelly formula from his other book. Which was basically a given trade's edge divided by its odds with a couple of added variables.

Youngbuck dropped a ticket onto the page. Slim G-Zus grimaced at the interruption as he looked up. Young, smiling ear to ear as if to say: "Yeah, motherfucker, I can do that 'cause we boys." Slim G-Zus pursed his lips as he looked at the slip of paper. Youngbuck had a four-pick. He took Dwight Howard to go over thirteen rebounds. James Harden to go over twenty-six points. Trevor Ariza to go over twelve points, and the Rockets to win by more than four points against the Mavericks.

"Whatcha think, homeboy?" asked Youngbuck.

Slim G-Zus nodded and handed the ticket back. "Looks like a sure thing. They're in Houston, too? You should knock that down."

"Yeah. Right."

Itchy Foot came in from work and walked over to where they were standing. Slim G-Zus could tell Itchy Foot was strapped up, his mesomorphic frame even more blocky than usual.

"Somebody help me unwrap," Itchy Foot said, as he stepped into one-row shower.

"Whatcha got, Itchy Foot?" asked Youngbuck as he followed him into the shower.

"Burgers. Cheese, onions, pickles, and Super Honky Sauce on toasted bread."

Slim G-Zus watched the picket. The Nigerian guard wasn't paying attention. If she had seen two inmates walk into the same shower, she might have been curious about what they were doing.

Slim G-Zus had visibility from their shoulders up. Itchy Foot took off his shirt. Youngbuck found the end of the heavy-duty saran wrap and grabbed it. Itchy lifted his arms above his head and began turning, unspooling himself like a kite string. Youngbuck caught the individually wrapped burgers as they dropped from Itchy Foot's cellophaned torso. The usual suspects arrived with stamps in hand, ready to eat.

Itchy Foot served his loyal customers and came back over to the window. He tossed Slim G-Zus a freebie. Youngbuck already had his. The toasted bread made the sandwich. The kitchen commissary didn't have hamburger buns, not even for officers, so the generic white bread got heavily treated with butter and toasted to golden perfection. The condiments were all stolen from the officers dining room refrigerator that stayed under lock and key. Itchy Foot could kick the inmates who worked the ODR a few stamps for all the fixings he needed. They were too scared to "strap up" and walk the food out of the ODR and back to their pods like Itchy Foot. But they weren't too scared to wrap up his order and throw it in a trash can that would find its way to the dishroom, where Itchy Foot and all the other guys trying to hustle worked.

The Super Honky Sauce was a proprietary blend of mustard, ketchup, and mayonnaise with lots of relish.

"Where's the youngster at?" Itchy Foot asked holding up his last burger.

Youngbuck chewed and smacked, then he wiped the corners of his mouth and said, "Dunno."

Itchy Foot said, "I got a kite from Walker," as he kicked off his left boot. Itchy Foot handed his sandwich to Youngbuck and knelt down. He pulled the insole out of the boot and fished for the kite.

Slim G-Zus took the damp piece of paper and unrolled it to the size of a PostIt. The print was microscopic.

Greetings and Respects,

Runner here. Just wanted to let y'all know that there's about to be a 'wood on A-side who none of us were really able to check out. He says he came from the Neal unit and talks all kinds of mad-dog-killer shit. Neal is all dorms. It's mostly trustees. He claims he smashed some tode and that's why they shipped him. None of us knows anyone on Neal to holler at and check his story. Nobody over here has ever been on a trustee camp. The dude's a monster with his hands. He says he did that MMA shit in the world. Anyway, he claims he was down here back in the nineties, and when I told him we don't allow nobody to check Whites he acted like he wasn't trying to hear it. I heard him on the yard talking to some todes about how everybody got checked back in the day. It didn't sound good. He was sorta kissing their ass and wiring them up. He talks about organizing the pile like a family. No new boot Whites ever moved into his section, but if they would've he'd have banged them up. I basically told him that wouldn't be tolerated, and we had some words. He smashed a Mexican from the Valley and some tode. Did them both real bad. But when this 'wood, Hughes, got stole and knocked out by a tode, he didn't do shit. Just giving you boys a heads up. Dude's got a boxing game.

Much love and respect,
Runner

Slim G-Zus raised his eyebrows as he passed the kite to Youngbuck. "Walker says some clown is getting his M.I.," then went back to devouring his burger.

Youngbuck scanned the kite. "I don't get it," he shrugged, "gives a fuck?"

Itchy Foot said, "Dude's supposed to have a helluva boxing game," and shrugged.

Slim G-Zus said, "Y'all know how Walker is. Cat was in the military and shit. He's just giving us some... Slim G-Zus flexed his hand out. "You know—some intel shit."

Youngbuck chewed with his mouth open and said, "Hell, yeah. I like that. Some intel shit."

Slim G-Zus looked at Youngbuck and chewed with his mouth open, mockingly, hoping Youngbuck would catch his drift. No luck. Youngbuck kept right on, entirely missing the point. Slim G-Zus grinned inside. *Goddamn Young,* Slim thought. *That's my dog.*

Itchy Foot said, "They say he likes checking dudes when they roll up. That's the way it is a whole lotta places..."

Slim G-Zus swallowed hard and wiped his mouth. "Cats get fucked in the butt a whole lotta places, too—but not here. Not on our watch."

Itchy Foot tilted his head to the side and stared at the ground. *A wide body, built like an empty Bradley tank,* thought Slim G-Zus.

"I'm just sayin'," said Itchy Foot, "s'kinda boring around here sometimes."

Slim G-Zus squinted his eyes and nodded in mock agreement. "Well, Itchy," he said in his best Jay Mohr imitating David Caruso voice, "we could always start carrying steel everywhere we go, like we had to back in the nineties when all the weak motherfuckas were getting *bored* in their *butts.*"

Youngbuck shook his head. "I ain't packing heat 'less I got to. Them hoes gave me five years for that one I got caught with on Robinson."

It was a funny story, and it would cool off the heat beginning to rise in Slim G-Zus. Itchy Foot grinned. "That the time you was stabbing that tode, and the laws hemmed you up?"

"Yup," said Youngbuck. "Had the shank tied to my wrist. Hoes went to bendin' my ass up," he leaned forward, held his arms out to the side, and lifted a leg up behind him, "had my leg in some kinda submission hold, talkin' bout 'Drop it! Submit! Drop it!'" Youngbuck straightened up, then slumped into himself, shrugging and smiling wide at the memory. "I'm steadily hollerin', 'I can't, I can't.' Goddamn shank's dangling, tied to my wrist tight as a motherfucker." He shook his head, his eyes sparkling in amusement.

Slim G-Zus had heard this one a thousand times but he couldn't help but grin. The shank tied and dangling, unable to drop, some redneck tyrant guard thinking Young was refusing his order. It was too much. "Anybody know this clown's name?" asked Slim G-Zus.

"Think it's Orton. Somebody said Orton," said Itchy Foot.

"Orton, repeated Slim G-Zus. "And he came from where?"

"Neal Unit."

"Never heard of it."

"Me neither," said Youngbuck.

Itchy Foot turned his hands palms out and shrugged. "Say he's gotta helluva boxing game."

CHAPTER 31

Russell was glad to be done with *Supernormal Stimuli,* the first of the outside reading books Ms. Sontag had assigned. But now they were on this Zadie Smith novel, *White Teeth,* and it wasn't much easier to get through. It was about some people in London. There was this English guy married to a Jamaican woman, and it didn't really seem like they loved each other.

They had some friends, but Russell couldn't exactly say if they were Pakistani, Indian, or Bengali... He knew they were one of the three, but multiple choice questions would still be a problem... Anyway, the book was basically about their everyday lives in London, the differences between the English and immigrants, and how things you did in the past can come back to haunt you.

Ms. Sontag had opened the discussion with, "Our goal is to preserve cultures and help them coexist."

To which Slim G-Zus had responded, "I didn't know we had a goal other than to learn cultural anthropology." Russell was sure there was more of that to come. Slim G-Zus and her had been really going at it since Ms. Sontag had made her comments about White men raping Black women because of their lips and something about estrogen. Slim G-Zus never addressed that theory in particular, but Russell could tell it had gotten under his skin.

Ms. Sontag sat behind her desk turning the pages of *White Teeth.* "Okay. Before we get into what's going to be on the test, I want to talk a little bit about cultural imperialism and assimilation." She looked up at the ceiling. "Do you all get to watch the news in here very often?"

Several heads nodded yes.

"You do? Okay, good. I'm sure you've seen the struggles in Washington over the last decade with immigration reform, right?"

A couple heads nodded. Slim G-Zus leaned his head into the cradle of his palm and stared at the ceiling. *Here we go.*

Ms. Sontag continued, "One of the things Zadie Smith explores in her novel is the other side of the immigration coin—the troubles of the immigrants.

"Whenever we see or hear the nativist elements—the Tea Party types—complaining about immigration, we only hear about the perceived fears of the nativists, we never hear about the often tragic consequences for the immigrants' culture." She looked as if she were talking about children with terminal cancer and not people who chose to leave their country. But that sounded very familiar... Russell shook it off, afraid to explore the thought anymore, even inside his own head.

"On page 272, Smith writes that the 'fears of the nativists scared of infection, penetration, miscegenation' make the immigrant laugh." She looked up, smiling, "Because, obviously, the immigrant stands to lose so much more! Their entire culture can vanish because of—especially in America—the tyranny of assimilation." Slim G-Zus lowered his head and rubbed the back of his neck.

"And think about the character Mohammed Hussein-Ishmael, aka Mo the butcher? All the beatings and robberies he endured at the hands of Whites because he comes from a culture different than theirs." She shook her head in disbelief. "The average immigrant's culture doesn't stand a chance. 'It's our way or the highway' is basically what society is telling them. So, this whole notion that immigrants come to America over anywhere else in the anglosphere and just have it 'their way' is ludicrous. Their troubles are so much greater than those of the people who are complaining about them..."

Russell looked around the classroom. A few heads were nodding. Yella Fella was in the back corner, slumped down in his seat, arms folded. Slim G-Zus was thumbing through his copy of *White Teeth*. He stopped and placed the book on his desktop, flattening it with both hands. *Gametime,* thought Russell.

Slim G-Zus looked around the class to see if anyone else had their hand raised. He waved his long arm back and forth. Ms. Sontag continued scanning the class without seeing him.

"Mr. Jimenez?" said Ms. Sontag. "I know English isn't your first language, and you've had trouble with some of the technical terms in this class, but were you able to *comprende* most of White Teeth?"

Mr. Jimenez nodded, "*Sí.*"

"And did you find the stories of the immigrant characters somewhat similar to yours?"

Jimenez looked off, then down at his desk. A younger Mexican next to him leaned in and whispered something in Spanish. Jimenez looked up at Miss Sontag, "I likey book," he said in his heavily accented, secondary language.

Ms. Sontag smiled wide, her brown eyes lit up, "Good— *bueno!* I thought you'd like it." She kept up the intensity of the smile throughout the exchange, like a parent watching their child win a spelling bee.

Slim G-Zus waved again, more of a salute this time. Ms. Sontag kept smiling, "Mr. Dumashay?"

Yella Fella cleared his throat and shifted to his right. "I thought it was alright. I read alotta books by sistas, Toni Morrison, Zora Neale Hurston. It was alright. It's a trip how even in London they know about hip-hop and the struggle." He shrugged.

Ms. Sontag said, "What did you think of the immigrants and their struggle to preserve their culture?"

Yella Fella looked down at his desktop and shrugged again. "I mean, that's how it is here in America. They brought us here in chains and tortured our culture out of us. Nowadays, they try to shame it out of us by calling us thugs for actin' Black. Like we supposed to act like White folks when they don't even want us around. They wanna watch us play football, but a couple years ago when that brother, Richard Sherman, went to goin' off after he broke up that pass in the endzone, they went to crying about sportsmanship and calling him a thug. But that's Black culture. We're naturally alpha. We speak our mind. We don't wanna be put in their White box."

Nodding with her eyebrows arched up, Ms. Sontag said, "So you could identify with many of the book's characters." More nodding.

Yella shrugged. "I guess. But I believe my people don't need to learn about other people's problems. 'Cause it'll water down our experience. We need to be focused in on what's been done to *us*—not somebody else."

Ms. Sontag lifted her fingertips to her lips and made a face like she was hearing something profound. She called on several other students who didn't have their hands raised. From their responses, Russell could tell they hadn't enjoyed the book very much. Slim G-Zus waited for each of them to finish, then raised his hand again.

Ms. Sontag finished prying comments from several students and looked down at her desk. She shuffled some papers. She was completely ignoring Slim G-Zus. This bothered Russell a little, but he still didn't want to hear whatever it was Slim G-Zus had to say.

Slim G-Zus cleared his throat. He leaned forward in his seat, waving his arm exaggeratedly. "Ms. Sontag? Ma'am?" His guttural voice a little higher than usual, his pronunciation a little more proper. Ms. Sontag kept her head facing down. She looked at Slim G-Zus with her eyes only at first, as if that look would keep his mouth from opening. She finally raised her head but still didn't say anything. Slim G-Zus started anyway. "You mentioned the beatings of Mo the Butcher." Ms. Sontag inhaled and folded her hands in her lap. "In the book," Slim G-Zus continued, "she says his attackers had one thing in common, that they were all White." Russell knew something like this was coming. He watched Yella Fella out the corner of his eye.

Slim G-Zus said, "Now, this book takes place in London. But then you said Tea Party types, so I'm guessing you think Whites here are also running around beating up people from other cultures or whatever, right?"

Ms. Sontag sighed. "For your information, Mr. Lane? People of color, immigrant or otherwise, have been brutalized and marginalized in America more than in Great Britain."

"Well, ma'am, not in the last sixty years. Since they've been keeping reliable crime statistics, when crimes occurred between Whites and Blacks, eighty-nine percent of them were Black on White. You know those paper shufflers compiling those statistics think like you and the President, so there's probably some severe underreporting."

Ms. Sontag screwed her face up and unfolded her hands, "Excuse me? What are you..." She shook her head slowly.

"Over the last sixty years, when crimes occurred between Whites and Blacks? Eighty-nine percent of them were committed by Blacks against Whites. The numbers for crimes involving Hispanics and Whites aren't much different. The bureaucrats who put out those statistics are mostly left wing—like yourself. They believe things like 'non-Whites can't be racist because they don't have any power,' et cetera, et cetera. So, I wouldn't doubt it if they underreported the Black- or Hispanic-on-White crime rate. You should read the book *White Girls Bleed a Lot*. It's about how the media doesn't report Black-on-White crime. There's a girl in there who was assaulted and robbed at a fair in Milwaukee by some Blacks. When the cops came? They wouldn't take her statement or anybody else's. The mayor or police chief, I forget which, said something like, 'Crime has no color'—even though the only people beaten and robbed were White, and their attackers were heard saying racist things."

Russell could tell Ms. Sontag wanted to mount a comeback but was so angry she couldn't think straight.

"Anyway," said Slim G-Zus, "my point is Tea Party people can't be going around beating up people from other cultures too often or else the crime stats wouldn't be what they are. Also, don't you think there's more examples of immigrants who assimilated and got ahead versus those who worried about keeping their culture at the expense of advancement?"

Ms. Sontag sat up and said, "Assimilation is cultural genocide."

Slim G-Zus lowered his head... it looked like he was fighting off a smile. He looked up, fully composed, and said, "Well, ma'am, where some of these people come from? They have *actual* genocide, and their culture is often responsible."

Ms. Sontag's lips parted, and her hand went to her chest. She was good for at least one of these when she and Slim G-Zus went at it.

"And, I imagine that's part of the reason they left in the first place—where there's a lot more of their culture."

Ms. Sontag said, "Well, in that case, I guess we need to do away with American culture first, since it's produced slavery and gross inequality in income, education, healthcare..." She held her hands out palms up, twisting her head with a *duh* look on her face.

"Slavery was around way before America came into existence and incomes have never been equal, ma'am. However, America and Britain did use their militaries to *end* slavery when no one else in the world was even talking about doing so..." Slim G-Zus tilted his head and gave his own *duh* look. Ms. Sontag looked the class over. No one was coming to her defense. They probably shared her anger but didn't have a legitimate rebuttal. Slim G-Zus continued, "I noticed on page 272 that Ms. Smith said there are 'young White men' angry about immigration. I couldn't help but wonder if she considers the non-White immigrants, who rant and rave about how horrible the West is, as angry."

Ms. Sontag said, "She's giving the perspective a young woman of color would most likely have in that environment."

"Right," said Slim G-Zus. "That's the problem, ma'am. She doesn't seem to see—or maybe she thinks it's justified—the anger among the non-White immigrants. She says: 'There are still young White men who are angry about that,' and that they go after non-Whites with kitchen knives."

"Nativism and racism are real problems, Mr. Lane. I'm sorry if they make you uncomfortable."

Slim G-Zus frowned at that. "My point is that she says these angry White guys are still out there—as if their rage should've expired. But, then she says that the immigrant laughs at Whites' fears because the immigrant has to worry about..." Slim G-Zus scanned the page with his finger, "'...dissolution, or disappearance.'" He looked up, "If they're so worried about preserving their culture, why not just stay where they were born? And why is *their* anger not questioned? Maybe the people in those countries that everyone is immigrating to don't want a culture that condones killing women because they got raped. Their genes aren't better or worse. But their culture may not be compatible with the culture of the place they're immigrating to. Why encourage immigrants to bring a culture that's at least partly responsible for the mess they're trying to leave behind?" He breathed in a deep breath. The rest of the room did not. "You being a good social-justice feminist, Ms. Sontag, ought to know that a lot of those countries are backward because the women aren't able to contribute to society. Why allow so many people in from so many basket-case countries?"

"How about because it's those countries whose bad fortunes are the direct result of imperialism from the West?" A look of *DUH!* mixed with exasperation on her thin face.

"How about those countries were no strangers to conquest and subjugation and their consequences way before White men built boats and left Europe."

Ms. Sontag's eyes narrowed sharply, although no other part of her being even came close to moving. "So, you're going to blame the victim, of course."

"How is somebody who gets to go from the Second or Third World to the First a victim? And if, once they get there, the racism from the kitchen-knife-packing, blue-eyed devils is too much to bear, they can always go back. It just seems to me like she's biased and sees the immigrants as victims when I'd be willing to bet that in real life there are very few Mo the Butcher–like immigrants who get beaten up all the time by Whites. It wouldn't surprise me if Europe's interracial crime stats were similar to America's. Especially in France, where they specifically target White women for rape."

"Okay, Mr. Lane, you're oversimplifying the subject matter and trying to draw a moral equivalent between common crimes and hate crimes, but whatever. You've had your say." She pulled open a drawer and glanced inside before shutting it without retrieving anything.

Slim G-Zus said, "Labeling something simple doesn't disprove it."

She glared at him. She'd clearly had enough. Her clenched jaw and slit-narrowed eyes a stop sign. Unfortunately, Slim G-Zus obeyed traffic signs about as well as he obeyed anything else. On he went, "One more thing, ma'am," he said as he loudly turned the page of his book, "Part of the reason I think these characters and a lot of people in real life like seeing themselves as victims—even when they're not—check out page 364. Alsana, the mother in the Muslim family, says that England is a 'godawful' country. Why stay then? Is she a masochist?" He thumbed through more pages. "Now look back at page 272. Here she says Alsana cries whenever her son brings home a White girl, because if they have kids, her grandchildren could also marry White people and then she wouldn't recognize them. Hortense Boudin? The half-Black, half-White grandmother of Irie quit talking to Irie's mother—her own daughter—because she married a White guy. Hortense says she went out of her way to marry a Black man so she could 'drag her genes back from the brink'. But, if she's half White and half Black, then she got 23 chromosomes from her White parent and 23 from her Black parent. Why does she think marrying a Black guy pulled her genes back? The genes she got from her Black parent are distinct to that individual person. They're not the genes of the entire Black population. And why does she not want to marry a White guy to pull her White genes back from the brink? To me, it seems like she's doing the Elizabeth Warren/President Obama selective-gene-acceptance bit. You know, like, Whites are all oppressors and the one Native American I got in my family, well, I'll identify with them because it makes all of my accomplishments that much greater. You know, seeing as how I overcame the odds—and gets me chosen for jobs over Whites. Or the President's Black father who never had anything to do with him, and his White mother whose White parents actually raised him. Yet he calls himself Black because, supposedly, cab drivers won't pick him up."

Slim G-Zus squinted his eyes and pursed his lips, "Nah, I think he likes the fringe benefits you get when you convince people that you're a victim. Mo the Butcher? That cat is a victim. He actually had some things done to *him*. The rest of the characters trying to keep their kids from marrying White people? I don't feel sorry for them, and it bothers me that their version of 'keep the race pure' is treated as some funny or understandable tragicomedy, or whatever they call it. Let a honky say he doesn't want Whites mixing with non-Whites and he'll get Donald Sterlinged. As well he should. But Jay Z can wear a hub-cap sized 'five percenter' medallion while he's sittin' courtside—on national TV, no less—and nobody wants to boycott his sports agency. Jordan and Lebron didn't tweet their displeasure over that. Common and Jill Scott can both say publicly that they don't believe in interracial marriage, and not only do they not get Paula Deened, Common gets invited to the Whitehouse by the first lady to read his poetry." Slim G-Zus made a fist over his chin and squinted his eyes again, "I wonder if it ever dawned on the first lady that the man she married is a product of the type of union Common doesn't approve of."

Ms. Sontag was resting her chin on the back of her hand, her elbow on the desk, looking like she was listening to the harmless rant of a child. She said calmly, "Did you find any redeeming qualities at all in Ms. Smith's bestselling, award-winning book?"

"Oh, yeah, it's a great book by a great writer. The way she worked all that scientific stuff in there was crazy. She made fun of the Bible, too. The book got really good when she got to Irie, who I'm guessing is Zadie herself, who's only a few years older than me so a lot of those hip-hop and movie references she made brought back some memories. And when it slowed down, being the privileged oppressor that I am, I'd just glance at her picture on the back and instantly get back to reading. She's gorgeous. Like if Lisa Bonet—Denise on the Cosby show?—had a thick sister? She'd look like Zadie Smith. Those lips. Man... Although, come to think of it, I never did get the urge to *rape* her." The last few words came out harshly, in stark contrast to everything else up to that point.

Russell saw Yella Fella fold his arms. His bi's and tri's flexing his shirtsleeves tight. Ms. Sontag gave a delayed frown. Slim G-Zus gave back a squinty-eyed half smile that said, "You like that one?"

With everything that had been going on, Russell had almost forgotten about the last letter he'd written to Cordell. The words were
coming back to him now as he opened the letter that had just been
slid through the side of his door. There was no greeting of any sort.
It began:

> You almost got in one bitch-ass fight fuckin' with Erica. We been
> gettin' killed for four hundred years for just lookin' at White hoes.
> And they was lookin' at us first. Akhi told me White men were
> not ready. I didn't want to believe him, but you've put a stamp
> on everything he said. You think Islam is responsible for 9/11?
> America trying to hog the world for its oil is responsible. They
> declared Jihad on the US back in the nineties for having troops in
> the Holy Land. If y'all didn't want 9/11, y'all should have gotten
> out of there. And you can miss me with that bullshit about how
> you don't think Christianity is better than Islam. If you didn't think
> it was better, why defend it? You got a lot to learn. You're living in
> the bubble with the 85%. It may not be possible for you to ever
> get out. Have you looked around the dayroom? Do most of the
> people in it look like you or me? What color was the judge and the
> D.A.? Who makes the guns and the alcohol? What color are they?
> If we weren't boys I'd have cut you off. Don't ever come at me like
> that again. You've never been a Black man in a White man's world.

Russell dropped the letter on the desk and stood staring at it.
He snatched it up into his fist. He inhaled deeply and leaned forward,
planting his hands on the desk. He exhaled it all as his head dropped
and his chin found his chest.

CHAPTER 32

Slim G-Zus and Big Body Slim stood in their normal positions under the window. Two shirtless convicts in white cotton shorts extending past their knees. Slim G-Zus, a walking diagram of every muscle in the human body, with a handful of tats. Big Body Slim, a barrel-chested side of beef with tats covering everything but his hands and head. Slim G-Zus leaned back against the wall, a white plastic bowl in his left hand, a tan plastic spoon in his right, shoveling the last of the summer sausage and tuna spread The Big Body had put together. This was practically a ritual between these two that took place every Friday night. Big Body Slim had already put away his half.

The summer sausage was only sold on commissary around Christmas time. So, every year Big Body Slim stockpiled them. If there was a limit, he'd find other people who were not buying any and trade them some other item, even if it was a little less than an even swap. He cut the sausages into half-inch cubes and threw them in a bowl with the tuna. In a separate bowl were three bricks of Ramen noodles crushed into tiny pieces. No one in prison put their Ramen noodles into a bowl and poured water on them like you would cook spaghetti. While the noodles were still in the package, most guys would slam them onto the concrete floor like they were spiking a football, while others would pound them with their fists like tenderizing a slab of meat. Big Body Slim put a small hole in one end of the package, held it over the bowl, and slowly crushed the enriched white flour noodles until they were about the size of grains of rice and therefore small enough to fall through the hole.

After the crushed noodles sat in a bowl of hot water for four minutes—not five, not three—he dumped the sausage and tuna on top of them. Then came about half a jar of sandwich spread. After he mixed it all up, he would throw some corn chips on top. Simple ingredients that all had the same thing in common: salt. If it were up to the Big Body, he and Slim G-Zus would eat this exact same dish every Friday, year-round.

Their conversations over this weekly meal varied about as much as the grub. The Big Body would talk about some girl he'd met on a pen-pal website, his latest creation in the craft shop, or which female guard he thought was flirting with him that he was scared to talk to. Slim G-Zus would talk about his and Adisa's latest options strategy, and how much money it would make for his daughter, or his latest scheme to get dope and cellphones smuggled in, and how much that would make for his daughter, or some piece of information dealing with race or politics that would go into the book he was going to write, in order to make some money for his daughter.

Their free-world lives had next to nothing in common. Peter Austin Wallace was from Alamo Heights, one of the toniest neighborhoods in San Antonio. John Robert Lane was from an assortment of economy apartments in and around Greenspoint on the north side of Houston, where crime got so out of control in the nineties, the Houston police department built their very first-ever substation there. But, on the inside, they had both been White teenagers cast into the ghetto of ghettos. A Black and Brown world full of inhabitants who more or less blamed every problem in their lives on anyone who was White. They had both been through the fights, the riots, and the tense moments that don't necessarily lead to violence but are often worse because that righteous release of stress doesn't come to pass. All those episodes eventually get converted into stories, that when told, tend to evoke laughter.

"'Member that time your tooth came through your lip and it stuck while you were still talkin' shit, Slim?" Big Body smiled at the memory.

"What about that time you had to keester that shank 'cause they strip searched us comin' off the rec yard?" Slim G-Zus chuckled.

"I ain't keestered it! I cheeked it!"

"Bullshit!"

"Fuck's for dessert, anyway?" asked Big Body Slim.

Slim G-Zus pointed, "Loneesha Ray Ray's butt."

The Big Body screwed up his face, "I ain't never had no Black girl, and Lonny Ray's not even a girl."

Slim G-Zus grinned, "So, you're not trippin' about the actual dish. You're just hung up on the flavor?"

"I got alotta time, Slim. Tyra Banks? I'd misogynate."

"She don't date honkies," said Slim G-Zus.

"That's cool, I ain't into datin'," Big Body squinted his eyes and sucked his teeth, "just misogynatin', my nigga."

Slim G-Zus said, "You done gave up on Nellarosa already?"

"No, but I got enough to go around."

"I could see that. You with Nellarosa on one arm and Tyra on the other. If only you'd learn to talk."

Big Body Slim frowned, "Maybe an expert conversationalist like yourself could learn me up."

Slim G-Zus had to smile. He'd been voted most antisocial 'wood several times by the pile. (Yes, they actually voted on things like that.)

"Just tell her she looks like she's losing weight," said Slim G-Zus.

"Nellarosa don't need to lose no weight. And I ain't taking no advice from someone who's a penitentiary virgin just like me."

"Well, I may not have slid into home plate, but at least I've had some contact. If ol' girl wouldn't have gotten transferred..."

Big Body put his hand on Slim G-Zus' shoulder. "But she did Slim, and now she's on Darrington, and there's prob'ly a whole lotta convicts sliding head first into that home plate."

Slim G-Zus scraped the bowl and spooned the last bite into his mouth. Chewing, he said, "Yeah, well, have you even managed to hold Nellarosa's hand yet?"

"Not quite. But this chick I'm writing in Australia wrote me a badass freak letter. She was going off. Had a honky stiffen up. Then at the end she said, '...And you come in my face like gangbusters.'"

Slim G-Zus laughed, then rapped on his chest as he choked.

"And I'm like: the fuck?" Gangbusters? The hell is that?"

Slim G-Zus was getting a hold of himself, coughing and laughing, "Aw, geez, man, that's great. Classic. That's a new reason to question our immigration policy." He coughed hard. "Mixing cultures has a bad enough track record. Now this. Foreigners ruining perfectly good freak letters." Slim G-Zus shook his head, "Shit's gotta stop."

"Ol' girl's kinda fat anyway... I'd still misogynate."

"Honky with a life sentence can't be too picky, huh?"

"Nope."

"I hear ya."

Big Body Slim backhanded Slim G-Zus in the chest right where the *Blue-Eyed Devil* tattoo was. "Check this shit out. You remember ol' boy who used to work the turnout at night? Messcan with the glasses?"

"From Ft. Worth?"

"Yeah. You know, he had Villareal dropping off, right?"

"Uh, I knew he always had some for sale, but I didn't know who the mule was."

"Yeah, that fat ho with the glasses and the 69 tattooed behind her ear. They say she's a dyke, but I heard he was fuckin' that ho. Anyway, long story shorter—"

"Lookout, y'all!" Itchy Foot shouted as he came through the door. "Saw your boy Sidewinder out on the streets. Told me to give you this."

Slim G-Zus reached out and took the kite.

Slim G-Zus,

Greetings and respects. Sidewinder here. Next time they call rec I need y'all to fall out there. We got a real winner down here. He just moved into two section from B-side. He's in a soft section. There's only three Whites over there and only one is a 'wood. A youngster named Maclin. This new dude over there is talkin' some mad-dog-killer shit about checking Whites. The youngster hollered at me, and I hollered at the dude through the door. He said he came from the Neal Unit. I don't know anyone from there or how they do things, but this dude is making it sound like he's the Head Honky

in Charge. I told him we'd bring it to the yard, and he said yeah,
get everybody out there so I can get them on point. Dude's about
my size, but a little taller and real cut up. Squirrel and them are
saying he's got a helluva boxing game. We may have to find out.

Slim G-Zus handed the kite to Big Body Slim. "Let Itchy read
it when you're through."

Slim G-Zus scanned the dayroom. "Where's the youngster?"
He spotted him. "Lookout, McCann!" and waived him over.

Slim G-Zus let all of them read the kite. Itchy Foot went to take
a shower, and Russell went back to watching ESPN. Slim G-Zus and
Big Body Slim stayed by the window holding empty bowls.

"Did I tell you my daughter wrote a poem?"

Big Body smiled. Even though Sidewinder's kite had blown
in a bit of cloud cover, news about Janice—li'l half-a-honky, they
called her—always lifted the Big Body's spirits. When she was little,
he had made her a jewelry box in the craft shop that played a tune
when you opened it. Janice liked it so much her mother had to put
it away so she wouldn't break it by showing it to everyone who came
by. Out of everything the brute had made in over a decade in the
shop, that particular jewelry box was his most prized creation. Slim
G-Zus was his most trusted comrade, and he thought of Janice like
she was his own.

"A poem?"

"Yup."

"What's it about?"

Slim G-Zus smiled. "Fried chicken."

"Fried chicken?"

Slim G-Zus nodded proudly. "She's a chip off the ol' block,
man."

"You gonna make her drive a Cadillac like you, too?"

"Nah. G.M. took that bailout money. Hopin' Lincoln will start
making the Mark VIII again. I want her in a luxury car. American-
made too, so..."

"Kinda limits the options, Slim."

"Yeah, well... we got principles in my family."

"I hear ya. I need to make her something else 'fore you burn off. Can't believe you wanna leave all this for college." Big Body Slim shook his head.

Slim G-Zus said, "Gotta have that degree. At least before li'l half-a-honky gets hers. I'ma do it like Webb's dad did him. Remember that part? *Born Fighting*?"

"Nah."

"When Webb's dad graduated college, he walked off the stage and shook the diploma in his son's face. Told him: 'In this country, you can do anything.' I'ma do that to Janice 'cause that's how we roll."

Big Body Slim was half-ass watching a rerun of *Bones* on one TV and Slim G-Zus was watching the Astros highlights—make that lowlights—on the other.

The Big Body said, "I wonder if that Black broad would mess around with a honky? She's fuckin' gorgeous!"

Slim G-Zus shook his head, "I bet we ain't got three players hittin' over .250." Thoughts of the clown down on F-Pod two section came and went from his mind. None of them ever really getting a toe-hold. He'd seen and dealt with numerous similar situations over the years, and he'd learned not to worry about a problem until you were in position to do something about it.

Russell stepped onto the yard and took off his shirt, a warm, humid breeze cooling the sweat on his back. He walked past the weight pile towards the handball court. D-pod had been let out last and there were already four or five convicts on the bench press and on the pulldown bar. E- and F-Pods must have been on the yard for awhile. He spotted Ogre and his boys and then Sidewinder and the guys from F-Pod. Russell was pretty sure the guy in between all of them, with his thumbs jammed close together in his waistband, was the person in question. *Definitely a tailback. A White Adrian Peterson. A jaw straight from central casting.* He was about Russell's height, maybe an inch taller. The scowl on his face didn't change during the thirty or so paces Russell took to reach the pile. Sidewinder, Squirrel, and some other independents were grouped up to his right. Ogre and his NSR bros were on his left.

Sidewinder greeted Russell, "Hey, boy!" They shook hands.

"'Sup, y'all?" Russell said as he shook hands with Squirrel and the others. Nobody was talking. Russell looked around. Everybody else was in their usual places doing their usual things. Slim G-Zus, Youngbuck, Big Body Slim, and Itchy Foot were heading their way. Jew Boy and O.T. were at the door being pat-searched.

Russell looked at Orton, about fifteen feet away. He had several standalone tattoos on his forearms. Vikings maybe. Plus some kind of tribal art on his neck. Nothing on his chest, back, or shoulders that Russell could see. His dark-brown hair slicked back. All in all, he looked pretty tough.

Slim G-Zus was almost on the scene. Youngbuck worked to keep up with his longer strides. Big Body Slim kept up but looked like he was strolling through a park. The hot wind suddenly kicked up and everybody squinted to protect their eyes from the dust.

These ho-ass whiteboys got them a new great White hope. This nigga I know on B-side said this fool's actually got something. For a white-boy. He supposedly knocked out a nigga over there. They saying he wants to check these pink hoes when they come through the door. So, here comes the Klan. They got the short, stocky, redneck motherfucker from F-Pod and them Reich motherfuckers, too. All standin' around. And here comes Slim Bitchus. Walkin' with his head up high and them other fools following him. He better watch out. This new whiteboy looks like he ain't tryna hear nothin'. The fool's got a little size to him, and he's cut up. You don't see too many whiteboys built like that. They're a lesser breed of us. I wasn't never really around White folks in the world, but once I came down here and got that knowledge, it all made sense. The melanin was bred out of 'em. That's why they're wicked and weak. Their men can't compete with us because they're not as manly. Their women aren't built like women. No hips, no lips, no ass... Once in awhile you find one like CoCo, or Kim Kardashian. Now that's some ass! And them hoes? They *always* fuck with niggas. Which is only natural. If you're a woman, you want the most man you can get. Black men make up only about six percent of Amerikkka's population. If we were half? They'd put us back into slavery 'cause we'd be takin' all their women. We're damn near doing it now. Some niggas say 'If it ain't snowin', I ain't hoein', 'cause they like them cave bitches so much. I done fucked some snow bunnies. They're freakier than a motherfucker. I'll give them that.

Slim G-Zus kept his eyes on the one guy he didn't recognize. Sidewinder and Squirrel were approaching on his right, Ogre and a Reich soldier on the left. He purposely ignored them and walked right up to ol' boy with Youngbuck and Big Body Slim beside him. Slim G-Zus said, "You Orton?"

The convict unhooked his thumbs from his waistband and stepped forward. "That's me," he said. The cat had a lantern jaw and some kinda tribal art on his chin that Slim G-Zus didn't recognize.

Slim G-Zus said, "You knew Walker over there on eight building?"

"Walker? Sounds familiar."

"Yeah, he's a good dude. Shot me a kite about you. Said you handled your business over there." Which of course was bullshit.

"Yeah. I'm gonna always handle mine."

Slim G-Zus looked at him for a second trying to get a read off his square face. Neither man blinked.

"What unit you come from?"

Orton's eyes lowered, "I came from the Neal unit," he said.

Slim G-Zus gave a deliberate look of surprise, "Where's that at?"

"It's up in the panhandle—"

"I never heard of it—"

"It's got motherfuckers getting raped and killed every day. It's nothin' but *solid* fuckin' 'woods. *Solid fuckin' 'woods!* Real organized. Every section has got a shot-caller."

Slim G-Zus looked him over again. The guy had a voice like a Hollywood biker. *This cat might be throwed off,* he thought. "Yeah, well," he said, "we don't have guys getting raped and killed *every* day, but this place used to be a lot worse. Especially before we stopped the Blacks from checking Whites."

Orton shook that off. "Don't matter who's checking them, as long as they're getting checked. Gotta know whose solid and who ain't." Orton looked the yard over, "I guarantee you a bunch of these motherfuckers runnin' around here ain't solid—"

"Who do you think ain't solid?" sniped Youngbuck as he stepped forward.

Slim G-Zus extended his arm out in front of Youngbuck and said, "We don't check around here for a lot of reasons. Mainly because all it proves is what two Whites will do when fighting each other. Doesn't prove nothin' about what they'll do when another honky's gettin' cliqued on or a riot kicks off."

Orton bobbed his head and raised his voice, "It separates the weak motherfuckers from the solid motherfuckers. That's what it does."

Slim G-Zus decided there was no reasoning with him. He could go on and explain how, from his experience, when Whites checked Whites, the Mexicans and Blacks often claimed the penitentiary version of equal opportunity and did the same. And that these fights often turned into much more because the Blacks and Mexicans are 5A schools, and the Whites are 2A. That is, the non-Whites have much more to choose from and can almost always find one of theirs who's got more than the White that just pulled up. He could also explain how he'd seen plenty of Whites be color scared. They'd stand up to being checked by another White, but then catch that pussy when they got into it with a Black or Mexican. Take Jordan, for example.

But he'd been here before with other Ortons, and he knew that appeals to reason were not only a waste of time but they'd give the appearance of weakness and further embolden the guy. The problem couldn't be avoided. Hopefully a fist fight would be enough to solve it. And yet... something was wrong. For one thing, the guy only had tats on his face, forearms, and neck; places that were visible when you had your uniform on. He had noticed over the years that the guys who got their first tats on their forearms, neck, or head as soon as they hit the unit were normally doing so out of fear. They wanted the rest of the inmates to see the ink in hopes of giving the impression that they'd been locked up awhile. That they were a regular. So, instead of getting their torsos done first, working from the inside out, they started from the outside and worked in.

Slim G-Zus said, "Check this out, potna, we're not down with the checking thing here."

"Who are you, the speaker?"

"I'm speaking right now."

"'Cause I done talked to some people—"

"And I'm telling you—"

"And they said—"

"And I'm telling you," Slim G-Zus was jabbing the air between them with his hand-gun, "nobody's checking Whites around here. And one other thing: If you're claiming 'wood, you don't let nobody get away with stealing off on another 'wood, like you did on the other side."

Orton stepped forward, slapped himself on the chest, and said, "I'm gonna check whoever I want. And this man right here," Orton gestured to Ogre, "said he and his wanna check, so they know who to prospect."

"I wish somebody would check me," said Youngbuck.

Slim G-Zus was looking at Ogre, pretty sure he was keeping the shock from showing on his face. "Fuck's he talkin' about, Ogre?"

Ogre stared at Slim G-Zus. He shrugged and said "We prospect from the 'woodpile, so the checkin' will help us narrow down our list of who we want."

Slim G-Zus shook his head, "If either one of y'all—"

Squirrel's punk Rexy hollered in his/her high-pitched voice, "Y'all chill, the captain is coming with the G.I.'s, and they got the camera."

Everybody dispersed. Anytime more than ten White inmates grouped up for more than five minutes, you could bet the gang intelligence officers would be en route with the camera. If you got caught on tape among other White inmates that were on gang file—as most of the NSR were—you could get confirmed yourself. And the G.I.'s were Mexican, which meant if you claimed as your defense "guilt by association or stereotyping," they'd laugh at you. Once confirmed, you could be placed in administrative segregation, where you'd be locked in your cell for 23 hours a day. That was if the administration in Huntsville ever labeled your gang a Security Threat Group.

The captain and G.I.'s camped out, clutching the fence like it was the backstop of a baseball diamond their kids were playing on. Slim G-Zus kept moving around. He noticed Orton was practically following Ogre. The clown doesn't know what he's doing... is he trying to get on gang file ... something ain't right. Slim G-Zus just couldn't put his finger on it. Yet.

Part Three

I give you opinions which have been accepted
amongst us, from very early times to this moment,
with a continued and general approbation, and
which indeed are so worked into my mind, that I am
unable to distinguish what I have learned from others
from the results of my own meditation.

—Edmund Burke

CHAPTER 33

Eleven White convicts stood together by the back window in the dayroom on D-pod, one section. Sidewinder and Squirrel were outta place. Itchy Foot, Jew Boy, O.T., Youngbuck, and Big Body Slim all stood in a semicircle facing Slim G-Zus, whose back was to the wall. Russell was in between O.T. and Jew Boy. Larson was behind them, close enough to claim he was in the group, and far enough away to claim he wasn't, whatever the situation may call for.

Everybody had been going back and forth for a while about Orton and the brief conversation he and Slim G-Zus had on the yard. Slim G-Zus said, "The rank will probably have their snitches report to them tomorrow, so I'ma let it die down and chill for a couple of days, then fall over there. See what ol' boy's talkin' about."

Sidewinder said, "Lemme know when so I can be over there."

"Yeah, I'm gonna be down there too," said Youngbuck.

Slim G-Zus nodded, "Probably Thursday. After count." He leaned back against the wall and lifted his right foot to it, rested his fist on his right quad. "Check this out fellas. I don't know where this is gonna end up. Especially with Ogre and these Reich cats acting like they're backing this clown. But me and him checking paper probably won't be the end of it."

Youngbuck said, "After you smash that fool, we'll tell Ogre and them they can get it, too."

Russell studied Slim G-Zus's face, trying to discern whether or not he was as confident in himself as Youngbuck was. Slim G-Zus should have played in that dumb George Clooney movie where they tried to whack the goats by staring at them.

Itchy Foot said, "Maybe tell them NSR dudes they can check the guys they're gonna prospect. You know, like, if somebody wants to get in the car with them, then..." Itchy Foot gestured.

Slim G-Zus shook his head. "Right. Then the Blacks and messcans will say, 'Why can't we check them ho-ass whiteboys who enslaved us and stole our land. That ain't gonna work, Itchy."

Sidewinder gestured towards Squirrel, "We got our section. Y'all got this one." He shrugged.

Slim G-Zus looked at Sidewinder, "That's two outta the nine on the building..."

Sidewinder sighed. His barrel chest rose and fell. "I'm just tired of it all, dawg. I can't see us..." he gestured at the group, "kickin' it off with some other Whites over the checkin' issue."

Slim G-Zus looked away, then back, "The checkin' issue is the least of it. This clown let another 'wood get stole and didn't do nothin' about it." He came off the wall. All six foot four inches looking down at Sidewinder. "What the fuck is that? He's telling you that he wants everyone on the same page. Some kinda top-down gang type of shit? Every pod needs a speaker?" He pointed at himself. "If I wanted some motherfucker telling me what to do I'd have joined one of these gangs a long time ago."

Sidewinder lifted his hands out wide and dropped them, looking out the window. Russell wondered why somebody Side-winder's size, or Big Body Slim's size, seemed to bend to the will of Slim G-Zus. He had seen the fight with Larson. Slim G-Zus was quick, and he had long arms. But Sidewinder, and especially the Big Body, oughta be able to ragdoll him. Just grab him and wrestle him down.

Slim G-Zus clapped the scroll tat on his delt. "This is what it's all about for me right here: *The cowards caught out. The weak got broke along the way.*" he gestured to everyone there, "*Only the peckerwoods survived.* For me? That means commanding respect. Not living like a second-class citizen. Although we are. If the Blacks and messcans aren't checking theirs? What the fuck do we look like checking ours? And if one of us steals off on one of them? What do y'all think's gonna happen?" He looked them all over. "They'd rat-pack us. Mop the dayrooms with our asses. I don't know how they were doing it on Neal unit. But if they were having motherfuckers getting raped and killed everyday? They weren't doing it as good as we are here."

Youngbuck said, "I bet that fool won't check me."

"Hell, nah, he ain't gonna check you," said Slim G-Zus. "He's gonna want to check all the wormy little White dudes he feels like he can whup. Me and Big Body Slim were here when the Blacks and messcans got away with checkin'. We remember walking to chow and seeing little White cats—*who didn't disrespect nobody*—with their eyes black. Lips swole up. Noses broke. All that. And the Blacks and messcans clowning, pointing at 'em, cracking jokes and shit."

Russell said, "Well, they checked me, so—"

"And what happened?"

Russell frowned, shrugged, and looked away. He wasn't scared of Slim G-Zus, but the guy was hard to look at. Especially when he was amped up.

"What happened, McCann?" asked Slim G-Zus, his railroad-tie eyebrows drawing together. "I'll tell you what happened," the hand-gun jabbing at Russell now. "Every fuckin' 'wood on the building fell out to rec, and them fools got reminded we don't play that shit."

"Well, yeah," said Russell, "but it still happened, so..."

"So?"

"So, I mean," the heat on the back of his neck was intense. Russell hoped he wasn't turning red. "Apparently, even when you do things—the way you've been doin' 'em for so long—shit like that still happens." Russell could see Itchy Foot nodding slightly, then cutting his eyes at Slim G-Zus.

Slim G-Zus pushed his thumb and index finger into his closed eyes. "McCann," he said, "have you even been locked up a hot year yet?"

Russell inhaled and exhaled through his nose.

"No, you haven't. Sit back and learn how to do time, okay, kid?"

It was true, but it stung none the less. Russell wanted to mount a comeback. Maybe just blurt out, "You've been locked up all your adult life. You can't be all that smart." But he was having trouble finding his bearings. The mix of anger and embarrassment instinctively keeping his mouth shut.

Slim G-Zus looked at Itchy Foot but spoke to everyone. "Nobody decided to make things the way they are. Me and the Big Body never said, 'Okay let's do it this way.' This isn't my 'system.' We do things the way we do because we've learnt from *experience*. This is what works best—don't mean it's perfect," his voice was louder as he looked at Russell. "There's gonna be some drama, but why do y'all think that when everybody pulls up to this barbecue, they say, 'damn, it's laid back here,' or that it's better than where they come from? Have y'all ever wondered what made it this good? Or how do we keep what we've got?" Slim G-Zus frowned and shook his head. "Again, *forget* the checkin' issue. The question oughta be whether or not we smash this clown for lettin' another honky get stolen. Big Body, what'd we always say after Sherman Texas?"

Big Body Slim nodded once, "Retaliation is mandatory."

"God damn right," said Slim G-Zus, punching his hand. "Rule number 1: somebody disrespects you, you retaliate." Slim G-Zus looked at Sidewinder, who stood with his arms folded, then at Youngbuck. "Before y'all got here, back in, like, 2000, 2001, there was a kid here. 'Bout the same age as me and Big Body. His name was Kenny, from Sherman, Texas. Was on medium custody with us. Stay down peckerwood. Had to fight this big ol' cat over there just like I did. And he got out there. Got his scratch. Anytime there was a 'wood call on the yard, or whatever? Sherman Texas was there." Big Body Slim was looking down, nodding his head slowly.

Slim G-Zus continued, "So we all get to minimum custody, and I had to prove myself again. Can't remember if Sherman did or not. 'Course nobody fucked with Slim here." Slim G-Zus grinned and thumbed towards the Big Body. "Must be nice, huh? Anyway, ol' Sherman Texas done got cool with this Black cat from some other small town, I forget where. But they play Moon or Knock or whatever the hell, like, everyday, right? They like playing partners and they're gambling on the knock table. One day they lose some money and ol' boy thinks it's Sherman's fault. He throws down a domino, says somethin' to Sherman, Sherman says something back.

Then the Black cat raises his voice." Slim G-Zus shook his head,
"Not cussing 'em out, just some, 'You shoulda played the ace-trey
instead of the ace-deuce,' or whatever the hell. But he says it loudly,"
Slim G-Zus held his hands out palms up. "And Sherman don't say
nothing back. Probably thinking, 'Hey, me and this cat's potnas,' or
whatever." Slim G-Zus cut his eyes at Itchy Foot. "So, up jumps this
Vice Lord from Indiana, forgot his name, but he's about the same
size as Sherman Texas. He says, 'You call yourself a 'wood? Let's see
if you gonna stay down.' So they catch three row shower. Apparently,
this Vice Lord cat had something 'cause ol' boy came out with his
head the size of a basketball. About ten minutes later his head was
the size of a beach ball and he couldn't walk." Slim G-Zus paused,
shot Sidewinder, then Itchy Foot, then Russell, a look. "They took
him to the emergency room, but it didn't matter. His brain swelled
faster than his skull. He died. From a one-on-one fist fight. Before
he was old enough to buy a *beer*."

Everybody was stone-faced.

Coming down somewhat now, Slim G-Zus said, "And the fool
he played dominoes with probably couldn't have whupped him. If
he'd have just took flight on that fool as soon as he got loud with
him, or at least verbally checked 'im..." He cocked his head to the
side, "So, kids, the moral to the story is, if you ever get disrespected,
retaliation is mandatory."

He looked at Russell, then everybody else. "How many of y'all
had somebody try to rape you? Better yet, how many of y'all know
somebody that's been raped? You don't. Most of y'all ain't even been
in a riot! Rapes, riots, Blacks and messcans cliqued on us? That's...
basically the rule for most units. This place here is the exception.
And it ain't gotta stay that way. This Orton cat don't wanna do things
the way we do. He wasn't here ten years ago when some of us bled,
fighting in the showers so we'd have the respect we've got now." Slim
G-Zus leaned forward, "He's not one of us. Let a 'wood get stole off
on!" his voice rising above the din of the dayroom. "And ain't do
shit?" Slim G-Zus shook his head. "Our ways of doin' things? I know
it ain't easy. Ask Walker. Lotta times it gets us stuck on B-side, or
worse. And hell, nah, it ain't perfect, but it's kept a whole lotta 'woods

from getting beat down, having their shit stole, or fucked in the ass. And until we find something better, retaliation is mandatory."

And there it was, Russell thought, in a speech worse than any he'd ever heard from his little league coaches: The Gospel According to Slim G-Zus, which was, basically, do it my way 'cause we been doin' it this way for awhile—and I said so. He wanted to feel sorry for them. Some had been in prison longer than they'd been in the free world. But they were grown men. And if they wanted to follow Slim G-Zus and his experience off a cliff, he wasn't going to stop them.

CHAPTER 34

The Thursday afternoon count cleared late, as usual. Inmates of every race were complaining that no matter who counted, they never cleared it on time. "Nigerians, messcans, it don't matter," said an old Black convict.

Slim G-Zus came off the rec yard and headed towards F-Pod. Sidewinder, Youngbuck, and Big Body Slim followed close behind him. It was about the easiest time to fall out of place because there was so much traffic in the hallways. Convicts leaving the laundry, kitchen, or school house, and returning to the buildings they were housed in. Last chow was ran between 3:30 and 6:00 p.m. on most days and was how you left and got back to your assigned wing without getting caught.

Slim G-Zus stepped into two section and reached behind his head, grabbing his shirt and yanking it off. He spotted Orton sitting at a table with three Blacks, staring at the dominoes in his hands. Slim G-Zus handed his shirt to Youngbuck. The dayroom din lowered as Black and Mexican inmates elbowed each other. Slim G-Zus stared at Orton.

Youngbuck methodically folded the shirt and slung it over his shoulder. Orton must've noticed the dayroom getting quieter. He looked up and around, and spotted Slim G-Zus. Their eyes locked. No questions needed. The talking part was done. Slim G-Zus headed for the stairwell. Orton laid his dominoes face down and took off his shirt. Youngbuck and the others backed up to the far wall so they could see the area in front of three row showers. The dayroom was almost silent.

Slim G-Zus stood in front of the showers, balling and unballing his fists. Orton turned from the stairwell and stalked his way. Slim

G-Zus stepped his right foot back, lifted his right fist in front of his chin.

Sidewinder leaned back against the wall, looking up at three row. He didn't like what he saw: That Orton fella had to go about 230. He was at least thirty pounds heavier than Slim G-Zus. Sidewinder swallowed, felt the familiar dragonflies taking flight in his chest. Orton stopped and raised his fists. Slim G-Zus bent his knees a little. They paused for a beat or two...

Slim G-Zus pushed off his back foot and bound forward, landing a left jab. Sidewinder had seen that first jab hit its target several times over the years. That boy's arms were so long you couldn't get too close to him. Orton's head shot back. Slim G-Zus threw a hard right. Orton weaved to the side and made him miss. Sidewinder didn't like that. Orton threw a left and a right, one-two, that landed solidly, while a left hook from Slim G-Zus missed over the top of his head. Slim G-Zus shuffled his feet and threw a right. Orton dipped his chin, causing the punch to glance off his cheek. He and Slim G-Zus then threw several lefts and rights. Sidewinder couldn't tell who got the better of that exchange, but he didn't like the idea of them trading punches. Youngbuck was pacing in front of him. Big Body Slim stared, feet wide apart, arms folded.

Slim G-Zus dipped once, then twice, while stepping backward. He fired off two quick lefts. The first landed, the second Orton weaved. Orton stepped towards him. Slim G-Zus stepped to his left without crossing feet, away from the showers. He and Orton catching their breath, tracking in a circle. Sidewinder ran his fingers through his hair, exhaling nervously.

Slim G-Zus had been here before: You get through that initial flurry of adrenaline-spiked, superhuman punches without getting knocked out, and then you use your reach and endurance to wear the guy out. Just avoid his homerun punches and slip that low-risk jab in there when the opportunities present themselves, and you're good. It's like knife fighting: You're trying to bleed the guy. You don't go hog-wild and try to stab him in the heart right off the bat. You keep your shank in the hand you jab with, and cut whatever he makes available. Fingers, forearms, anything you can make bleed.

Because you took a couple of good shots from this clown and you know if he lands a few more, he could knock you out. So, you fight your fight. You stay light on your feet and you don't give him a still target to load up on. It may not be the Rock-em Sock-em Robots fight everyone in the dayroom wants to see, but it's your best shot to win.

Sidewinder watched. He didn't like seeing two White men fight. He and Slim G-Zus went back a ways, so he was pullin' hard for the ol' boy. He didn't like the situation, though. He was so tired of it all. Coming up on age 47, he could still fight with the best of them; it just seemed more and more that there was less he was willing to fight for.

Orton shouldn't have let that tode steal off on that White guy over on the other side. That shit was over with, though. And, yeah, he wants to check some Whites. Slim G-Zus and them went through a lotta shit to stop all that ... But that was a long time ago. And the rules they came up with were for back then. I should be fishing with my two boys right now. I get outta here again, I gotta leave that dope alone. Come on Slim G-Zus. Come on, boy.

Slim G-Zus kept stepping sideways to his left. Orton did the same. They dropped their hands, catching their breath. Slim G-Zus bounced his head from side to side, like someone trying to crack their neck, lifted his right hand up in front of his chin. Orton tucked his head and started in. Slim G-Zus feigned a left. Orton paused, raised his right forearm to block the punch. Slim G-Zus uncorked a left hook that caught Orton's right temple. Sidewinder came off the wall, anticipating a happy ending. *Come on, boy,* he thought. Slim G-Zus stepped in and hurled a right, but Orton's forearms deflected most of it. He then shot a left and a right that caught Slim G-Zus squarely. His knees visibly buckled. *Fuck.* Sidewinder bit down, looked at Big Body Slim. Youngbuck stopped pacing.

Slim G-Zus lifted his forearms in front of his face, stumbling to his right. Orton stepped and punched, stepped and punched. Slim G-Zus had his feet under him again, but didn't move quick enough. Sidewinder could see blood coming from either his nose or his mouth. Maybe both.

Slim G-Zus bent forward at the waist and landed a body blow, but Orton kept coming, lefts and rights unfazed. Sidewinder lowered his head. Big Body Slim unfolded his arms. Sidewinder looked back up to three row. Slim G-Zus was backed up against the wall now, jabbing and trying to weave. Orton's punches were doing damage. Slim G-Zus tried frantically to weave and block and punch his way out, but it wasn't working. Slim G-Zus was going down.

I was sittin' in my cell when Damn Fool came and told me Slim-Bitchus got his ass beat. Everybody knows bitch-ass whiteboys can't fight. So, now, they're all discombobulated. The whiteboy on F-Pod says he is going to check all the Whites who pull up, which is how it's supposed to be. But Slim-Bitchus told him after they fought that every time he checks one of them, they'd fight again.

I wish I could have seen that! I beat your ass and then you tell me we're gonna check paper again if I do something you don't like. What kind of shit is that? And then he told him he couldn't claim that 'wood bullshit because he'd let some other whiteboy get stole off on. They supposedly started to fight again because that whiteboy wasn't tryna hear it, but them other hoes wouldn't let them. Oh, I wish I could have seen it. Slim-Bitchus has a couple of marks on his face, and it looked like his lip was cut up, but he ain't that bad. I would've maxed that ho out. I seen the other whiteboy going to chow. He had a couple of strawberries on him but that was about it. Them hoes bruise easy anyway. They don't have no melanin in their skin.

So, now I hear Ogre and them Hitler hoes are only dealing with this whiteboy on F-Pod. They don't got no respect for Slim-Bitchus no more. Yet, most of these other whiteboys still roll with him. I know he finished his associates degree and should be getting shipped pretty soon. Between now and then, though, I'm hoping something jumps off and they go to fighting each other. Maybe a new whiteboy pulls up and ol' boy looks at his ass one time. Then Slim-Bitchus goes down there and gets his ass beat again. If not, at least we know his ho-ass is leaving.

CHAPTER 35

Russell sat on the front bench watching NFL Live on ESPN. Slim G-Zus rounded the bench and sat down next to him. "Check this out, youngster," he said as he handed Russell a newspaper article with the heading *When Is Racial Motive Newsworthy?* Russell read:

Apparently, a perp's racial bias only matters when he is White and biased towards a minority group. According to reports coming out of Houston, the man authorities believe to have shot 25 students before two students shot him, Jon Loc Tran, was filled with hatred towards Whites in particular and America in general. The website insidenewsbusters.com has obtained an internal email from the Houston Police Department showing that their czar of community relations and outreach, Ms. Julisa Washington Kenyetta, advised the HPD to conceal the racist writings that were found on Tran's person and at his home. Kenyetta also advised HPD to keep private the anti-American comments that Tran made to other students.

Records show that one of Tran's classmates told investigators that when Tran was asked if liked Houston's NFL team, the Texans, Tran replied, "No. I hate that team! They suck! Texas sucks! America sucks!" Another classmate said Tran often claimed America was "fake" and "rigged" so only White people could succeed. And that he understood why terrorists wanted to destroy the US.

So much for Tran being a misunderstood youth whose motives were "mysterious" and "unknown." They were known all along, just suppressed, because, as Kenyetta recently said during a telephone interview, "It's important not to subject entire communities of color to suspicion and vigilantism." Yet, when the perp is White, and the victim is a non-White, as was the case when Peter Debroccio killed Roland Martin on New York's Coney Island several months ago, the NYPD thinks it's important to mention to the press that witnesses said they heard Debroccio using racial slurs during his confrontation with Martin.

One could argue that the NYPD and the HPD are two separate entities, but does anyone really believe Kenyetta would have been concerned about subjecting Whites to "suspicion" or "vigilantism"?

The two young men who stopped Tran's murderous rampage, Russell McCann and Cordell Youngblood, are serving three-year sentences for possessing firearms on a school campus. They, and certainly all of the victims families and friends, deserve to know the truth.

Russell stared at the article. His blood had long ago turned to ice water, even though his skin was blood red. Slim G-Zus said, "Adisa sent me that. Why didn't you tell anyone?"

Russell shrugged, "I dunno."

"Thought somebody would mess with you or something?"

"No." Russell frowned. "Let somebody try to mess with me."

Slim G-Zus grinned. "Slow down, killer. I'm just curious. I won't show it to nobody else if you don't want me to. Adisa's probably the only cat on the compound that gets *Investor's Business Daily*. I doubt any of the liberal rags everybody else gets will mention ol' girl at HPD covering that shit up. Don't worry about it. Speaking of your old celly, he got an FI-1. He's going home."

Russell shifted, unable to hide his discomfort. He didn't know what angered him more: his cover being blown or Slim G-Zus having an article that he thought proved his conspiracy theories about diversity or the media.

Slim G-Zus said, "The law is the law. But it sure don't seem right for you to get locked up. You and your homeboy got fucked over. You didn't have no prior felonies?"

"Nah. I had a minor in possession of alcohol, but I wasn't even drinking. I was just at a party where there was alcohol."

Slim G-Zus shook his head. "And they still gave y'all that trey-piece?"

Russell nodded his head. "Said it was a mandatory minimum. The D.A. said he'd get me and Dell on the same unit." Russell turned up his hands. "That was like, part of the deal. But, he's on Michaels and I'm on Acirema."

Slim G-Zus said, "Yeah, D.A.'s, lawyers in general have a tendency to make promises they don't keep."

"My mom called the office. They kept saying he wasn't there. Then she called Huntsville. TDC's main office, or whatever, and she hasn't heard back from them either."

"Yeah, that's messed up. No accountability. You can't fire them by taking your business somewhere else. It's like getting a driver's license. Gotta grin and bear it."

Russell flattened his lips and looked away. Slim G-Zus said, "Must've been a helluva day. Took nuts for y'all to do that."

Russell didn't acknowledge the compliment. He was thinking about whether or not he wanted to discuss any of this. He looked back down at the article before handing it back to Slim G-Zus. He said, "So, what do you think that means? So what if she told HPD to keep that stuff from the public? She probably went to college and got some degree in public relations, or whatever the hell, and she learned it's better to keep that kind of stuff under wraps. You don't want some fools going around doing stuff to Asians that didn't have anything to do with Tran." Russell liked the feeling rising in his chest.

Slim G-Zus said, "Don't you think people have the right to know why the guy did what he did?"

"What difference does it make? At this point, with all those people dead..."

"I think it makes all the difference in the world. Haven't you ever wondered why? Don't you think the parents of those kids who died wanna know why it happened? And maybe to look for the same signals from somebody in the future who might try the same thing? Maybe try to explain to others America doesn't suck."

Russell waved that off as quickly as he could.

This was the first time he and Slim G-Zus had talked directly since the fight with Orton, and Russell—never impressed with the convict to begin with—desperately wanted to let him know he knew the results of the fight. And that the sheen had worn off.

Slim G-Zus looked at McCann. The hostility from the kid had always been there. It reminded him of himself when he'd first come down. Before he was able to read an entire book, cover to cover, and educate himself. Before he'd learned, specifically, that teenage hormones combined with the culture and blood of the Scots-Irish, made for a combative, combustible mix. And that his temper—no matter how good it felt to loose it—had to be controlled. That natural urge to argue and be confrontational had to be tamed. He'd given the kid a few of the books that'd helped him arrive at what he considered his present enlightened state.

"Been reading them books I gave you?" asked Slim G-Zus.

McCann held his gaze on Sportscenter. "Yeah. They're kinda slow."

"Which one you on?'

"I've read a little bit of all of 'em."

Slim G-Zus nodded. "Yeah? Whaddya think about *Born Fighting?*" Slim G-Zus lifted his chin, "The Jim Webb book."

"It started off okay. Kinda reminded me of my family. I'm a little ways past the Braveheart chapter. It's slowing down. It's sorta like a history book."

Slim G-Zus said, "You see all that about why the Scots like their weapons so much? Why they're so warlike?"

"Yeah, pretty much."

"You and your homeboy both had guns but y'all weren't in the jack game, right? Y'all were both squared up?"

"Yeah. Everybody in my family carries. Even my mom. Dell's dad was in the army. He was over in Iraq during Desert Storm. That pistol Dell had was given to him by his dad before he died in Afghanistan. He was working as some kinda civilian contractor."

Slim G-Zus nodded his head. "You read all that about the weapons and military service being like a privilege and honor? About top-down rule? Like how the English and Romans were trying to conquer them for—" Slim G-Zus gestured, "—a thousand years, or whatever it was?"

"Yeah. It was like they thought they could tame 'em, or whatever."

"Right." Slim G-Zus shook his head. "I forgot to tell that to Clarkson. He was always makin' it sound like the only people Europeans ever conquered or enslaved were Black or Brown. They did that shit to anybody who couldn't stop them. Just like the Mongols, Zulus, and Aztecs smashed whoever they could."

McCann folded his arms and flexed his jaw muscles.

Slim G-Zus recognized the resistance and smiled on the inside, deciding to switch gears a little. He said, "Have you got to the part where Webb says that Blacks and Americans of Scots-Irish descent have more in common than any other two ethnic groups?"

"I think he mentioned something like that."

"You having a last name like McCann, your family being Presbyterian, all y'all packing heat, lawfully, I'd be willing to bet you're of Scots-Irish descent... Y'all do a lotta huntin' and fishin'?"

"Yeah. Mostly when I was younger."

"Your fall partner—what'd you call 'im?"

"Name's Cordell. I call 'im Dell."

"Yeah, he sounds Scots-Irish, too, just Black. Webb said somewhere his two best friends are Scots-Irish. They just happen to be Russian and Filipino. You said his dad was in the military?"

"Yeah."

"Y'all write each other, right?"

McCann looked down. "Yeah, something like that."

Slim G-Zus noticed a change, the defiance ebbing some. The kid's face looked like he'd just remembered something he wished he hadn't. Slim G-Zus said, "Y'all gotta be pretty tight, right? Going through some shit like that?"

McCann nodded, still looking at the ground. Slim G-Zus looked at his face, trying to figure out what brought on the sudden change. McCann unfolded his arms and rubbed his knees.

Slim G-Zus said, "My fall partner was Black, too. But he lied on me, said I shot somebody he shot."

McCann shrugged. "They messed us up by putting us on different units."

"Yeah, that ain't cool. Least y'all can write. You oughta tell him about what you've been reading. See if you can get him to check those books out, too."

McCann said, "I don't think too many Black folks wanna hear that stuff in *Black Rednecks and White Liberals*. Some of that shit might be true, but it's offensive. It's like, 'Y'all Blacks aren't doing that well 'cause a y'all's culture—which really ain't y'all's but actually the rednecks'—and until you change that—who you are—you're gonna be stuck in the ghetto.' And that dude in *Born Fighting*? Tryna say ninety percent of the people lynched in the south before the civil war were White?" McCann shook his head, "I ain't never seen a picture of a White person lynched. When you read a history book? Like in school? Everybody in there lynched is Black."

"Right. But that's the problem. The textbooks are written by people who think like Clarkson. They think if they can make White people feel guilty enough, they'll agree to reparations, or higher taxes, or some type of shit that'll redistribute the wealth to its 'rightful owners,' as our President said. If you thought lynching was invented for Blacks because of White racism, well, you'd feel a lot worse for the victims, right? I mean, being lynched is bad enough, but it's even worse if lynching was created for you simply because of your skin color. And that's the effect they're going for."

McCann folded his arms again. "Well," he said, "whatever. Doesn't matter."

"Sure it does," said Slim G-Zus. "Why do you think you had to fight that Crip when you first pulled up? You'd never seen that cat before in your life."

McCann shrugged. "I dunno. Probably 'cause alla y'all got swastikas and all that racist shit tattooed on you. He probably thought I was like you."

Slim G-Zus turned towards McCann and set his forearm behind him on the bench and calmly said, "I don't have any swazis on me. Neither does Youngbuck. Neither does—"

"Okay, but you got *Blue-Eyed Devil* on your chest. That's like, tryna rub their face in it, makin' fun of their beliefs—"

"—Neither does Sidewinder or most of the White cats around here. And the ones that do—as I told you when you first got here—got them after they'd been here. And, yes, I know, McCann, your generation's all about that glorious, majestic T-word: Tolerance. But if you tolerate everything—especially in here—you might as well sign your death certificate yourself. Just because somebody labels something a 'belief,' doesn't mean we're all required to tolerate it. And a lotta times you're gonna have to tell someone their belief is wrong. Their 'belief' is the inch they need in order to try and take a mile."

"Ah, yes," said McCann. "The philosophy of Slim G-Zus. Or is that a proverb? Sorta like 'retaliation is mandatory.' Which you've always said, even though it obviously doesn't work."

Slim G-Zus laughed. McCann said, "That's never worked."

Slim G-Zus said, "Well, I'm glad you've got it all figured out, potna. I shouldn't be here much longer." Slim G-Zus clapped McCann on the back and stood.

CHAPTER 36

I just re-read my boy Ta-Nehisi Coate's article "The Case for Reparations." It was in *The Atlantic,* a White-folks' magazine. I found it laying on a bench in the dayroom about a year ago. That all-black cover caught my attention. He points out how important slavery was to the American economy. How all the slave owners became millionaires and we got nothing for it. He explains the red-lining, how they kept us in the ghettoes. He mentions how the Japanese got reparations, even though they weren't done nearly as bad as we were.

It's an article every White person needs to read because this stolen land, Amerikkka, is majority rule. And they won't be the majority much longer. They ought to go on and do something now while they've still got the numbers. Because the longer they wait, the more we're going to take. And it's not just the four hundred years of labor they owe us for. They owe us restitution for all the crimes they committed against us. They also owe us for all the opportunities we've been denied. Because even after slavery, they kept us from getting most of the jobs worth having. They made the laws so that they'd gain while we stayed at the bottom. All they got after slavery wasn't earned fairly because we weren't allowed to compete with them. And we built everything up till that point. We're the foundation. Without us, this place could be just as poor as Mexico, or anywhere else they didn't have slavery.

Then there's the racism that, even though we had access to certain professions, from a legal standpoint, kept us out anyway. Think about Warren Moon. He'd have been the NFL's all-time passing leader if he'd gotten drafted coming out of college. But them White folks didn't want to see a Black quarterback because we already dominate every other position.

Whether it's money, property, or any other asset White people have, they owe Blacks a piece of it. In some cases, they owe us all of it. Those neighborhoods we couldn't buy houses in? Those jobs we couldn't have?

Bottom line: They owe us.

CHAPTER 37

Russell watched the guard carry the red mesh chain bags up to Slim G-Zus's cell shortly after shift change. Big Body Slim, Youngbuck, Itchy Foot, and Lonnie Ray all went to his door. Russell opened his locker and gathered up all the books Slim G-Zus had given to him: *Race and Culture* and *The Quest for Cosmic Justice* by Thomas Sowell, neither of which he'd finished; *Born Fighting*, by Jim Webb, which he did finish; and what Slim G-Zus had called the "unholy trinity of atheism," *The God Delusion* by Richard Dawkins, *God is Not Great* by Christopher Hitchens, and *The End of Faith* by Sam Harris, all of which he'd barely skimmed.

The Thomas Sowell books were more difficult than the one Adisa had, *Black Rednecks and White Liberals*. Especially *Race and Culture*. *The Quest for Cosmic Justice* was easier to understand but still a little too intellectual or whatever. *Born Fighting* was basically saying "All us rednecks ain't that bad." It made Russell think about his cousins and grandparents. All of them lived out in the sticks. He never saw any of them with a rebel flag, though. For some reason that Webb guy didn't understand how most people viewed that flag. How it represented the army fighting to keep slavery. The atheist books were all saying religion was bad because Catholic priests molested kids and Muslims blew people up. Russell didn't bother with them too much. Religion had its problems, but there was obviously a God and the majority of religious people weren't child molesters or suicide bombers.

When Russell left out for work at rack up, Big Body Slim and Youngbuck were standing by the window in the dayroom with Slim G-Zus. Russell slid the books under Slim G-Zus's cell door without being seen, then slipped out the section door to the front desk.

Salinas and another young female officer were sitting there talking and sharing a Little Caesars pizza. Russell was pretty sure Salinas would hand him the box to throw away later that night, with a few slices left in it, of course. They'd been stealing away a few minutes in the SSI closet most nights she worked.

Russell walked down to the E- and F-pod sally ports to see who was working the pickets. He recognized both of the guards and his mood began improving. He knew those two especially would soon be taking a siesta, giving him and Salinas plenty of time to tongue wrestle.

Russell grabbed the mop bucket and scrub brush from the closet and approached the desk. "They bring the chemicals, Miss Salinas?" he asked.

Salinas chewed. "No. Hold on. Lemme call the turn out." She dropped a half-eaten slice back into the box and grabbed a napkin. Her partner in crime, Delgado—young and plump with a cute face—mumbled something in Spanish. Salinas laughed and replied in Spanish. Russell grinned, figuring they were talking about him. Salinas spoke Spanish into the phone. Couple of sentences, and then she hung up. She looked at Russell, "They're gonna bring 'em later. Go wait on a pod, and I'll call for you when they get here."

Which was not what he wanted to hear. He needed to get started now, since he was by himself—not to mention he was counting on two giggling girls to want him around. Russell turned and headed back down the hallway to D-pod. He decided he would find somebody with some contraband bleach and get started cleaning the showers. That's how Big Ike would do it.

Slim G-Zus lay in his bunk, lights on, under a green wool blanket, the Corpus Christi rock station, C101, playing loudly. He had the S380 pressed to an ear, Adisa on the other end. "If you go with that ratio spread on the Euro, you gotta be sure ol' boy can offset and reestablish the spread when it gets to runnin'."

Adisa said, "Right. That's understood."

"And I'm afraid if the market's movin' too fast, he's gonna get a bad fill. Whereas with them soybeans..."

"Right. I hear ya. I just don't like the volatility in beans this time of year. One limit move and we're blown up."

Slim G-Zus reached from under the cover for his radio, *The Devil in I* by Slipknot rocking just a little too loud. He turned it down some, to where it would still cover his voice if a guard passed by. "Well, hey. I ain't trippin'. If ol' boy can do that, jump out there."

"You can rest assured we'll get that understood before I place the order."

"Yeah. Alright. Well, I guess that's that... Ol' girl you met on MocoSpace still gonna pick you up at the Walls?"

"Yeah," said Adisa, "that's the plan. I tell you she tried to make me take my page down?"

"What? Hell, nah, you ain't tell me that."

"Yeah. She's gettin' out there. Thinking I better not get a pet bunny rabbit. Might end up in a pot."

Slim G-Zus said, "Yeah, well, she's gotta crib with a computer and Internet access. Nothin' wrong with a little rabbit stew. Hell, they say it's hard to find a woman who can cook nowadays."

"Yeah, but Bugs in a hot tub could be the tip of the iceberg. Like, if I forgot to take out the trash. What if I come home late? She might try and perform a nocturnal chopadickotomy. I ain't tryna be the Black John Wayne Bobbit."

"Actually, I think that fool became a porn star—"

"After they sewed it back on—"

"And porn stars make a lotta scratch."

Adisa laughed. "Yeah. I think I'll pass."

"Hey. Alls I'm sayin' is you ain't got a job, transportation, or place to stay. Ol' girl's got all that... might have to take one for the team."

"That's what that is? Takin' one for the team?"

"Yep." They both chuckled. Then silence. There wasn't really anything else to say. In the morning Slim G-Zus would be hand-cuffed to another inmate and put on a chain bus that would take him to the Richards Unit, where he'd begin work on his bachelor's degree in Humanities (imagine the arguments). In a couple weeks Adisa would do the same, only he'd be headed to the Walls Unit in

Huntsville for release, after almost twenty years on the inside, ten of which he'd done on Acirema with Slim G-Zus.

Adisa getting out was like both of them getting out. Like Tommy getting made in *GoodFellas*. He'd be in position to manage their trading account, no longer having to pay the exorbitant broker-assisted commissions that'd been a drain on their profits. And they had big plans for those profits. Adisa's and Janice's wellbeing were the short-term goals; the long-term goals were college tuition for Janice and a lawyer that could get Slim G-Zus's case overturned.

Adisa said, "You ever show my old celly that article?"

"Oh, yeah. Man. He wasn't trying to hear it."

'Whaaat?"

"Ah, yeah. He's worse than I was when I pulled up. He's got it in his head that all us honkies are dumb racists."

"That's crazy," said Adisa in mock seriousness, "Y'all aren't *all* racists."

Slim G-Zus paused, waiting for something about them not being dumb either... It wasn't coming. "Well, you know how it is."

"Yeah. That's just crazy, though. Ol' girl at HPD tripped out. And Lane, she didn't even try to clean it up—"

"I know—"

"She was like, 'I did that and I'm an expert so y'all shut up—'"

"Right. No shame in her game."

"Right," said Adisa. "Exactly."

"Yeah, man. Just don't tell anyone else you think she was in the wrong. You're already a borderline sellout for reading Thomas Sowell."

Adisa laughed.

"Well," said Slim G-Zus, "guess I'll holla at ya soon as I find a horn over there."

"Do that."

"If they're hard to come by I'll write."

"Yeah. If I have to I'll bring one through visit," said Adisa.

"Yeah, we'll figure something out."

It was past time to go, but neither of them was hanging up. Moments passed. Adisa said, "Say Lane? Pigs comin' through to count."

"Alright, homey... here we go."

"Alright, brah. Peace," said Adisa.

"Peace out."

Slim G-Zus hung up the phone and lay still. They'd been counting down the days to when Adisa'd be able to better manage their account. Now it was finally here. Slim G-Zus got up and went to the door. The dayroom was empty, all the lights off. McCann was coming through the door. Perfect timing.

Russell stepped through the door, heard Slim G-Zus call for him, and headed to his cell.

"Check this out, potna. I need you to take this horn to Big Body Slim for me. You wanna use it, go ahead. Battery's almost full."

Russell said, "Nah, I'm good. I'll take it to him." Russell heard the crinkle of the trusty foil coffee bag rolling up as Slim G-Zus placed the phone inside of it and slid it under the door.

Russell glanced at the picket before bending down to pick it up, then said, "You get your books?"

"Yeah. I got 'em. Hope you read all of 'em."

"Read most of 'em."

"You at least finish *Born Fighting*?"

"Yeah, I finished it."

Slim G-Zus nodded approvingly, slipped his fingers through the grate, and leaned into the door. "Yeah," he said, "reading that book helped me understand a lot of shit. I always thought all White people were the same, culture-wise, I guess. I didn't know hunting and fishing, learning to take care of guns, not liking unions—all that's mostly just us of Scots-Irish descent. Others have picked it up, like with NASCAR, but it started with our ancestors." Slim G-Zus gripped the grate tighter and said, "Here, I've always tried to do things from the bottom up. Though I never called it that. Families are all top down. Guess that's why I stayed independent all these years. Anyway, I never wondered where I got that from, but after I read *Born Fighting*, I understood why we did things the way we did."

The last thing Russell wanted was a conversation with Slim G-Zus, or anything else that might ruin the high he was on from knowing the psycho was on the chain in the morning.

Russell said, "Yeah, Slim, I'll take this on down to the Big Body—"

"Hold up, kid," said Slim G-Zus, "I'm tryna run something down to you."

Russell stood, exhaling slowly through his nose, tightening his abs. Slim G-Zus grinned but his brow stayed furrowed. "You don't have much more to go till you come up, right? With back time from the county and whatnot?"

Russell said, "I dunno. I wrote classification about that when Adisa was still my celly. Still ain't heard back from 'em."

Slim G-Zus said, "I don't know how all that parole shit works 'cause I don't come up till I'm fifty-nine—that'll be forty flat—but I think it goes from the day you get arrested. You'll probably be up in a few months."

Russell started to say, "Thanks for the info," and walk off, but before he could, Slim G-Zus said, "Yeah, man, you were real lucky to come here. 'Specially this section." *Here we go,* thought Russell. Slim G-Zus said, "When I started out," shaking his head and smiling as if to say, *You just don't know.* "It was a totally different ballgame. Soon as you came through that door? Especially if you were White, the baddest cat in the dayroom was gonna jam you up. It was, 'Watcha gonna do, whiteboy?' You could fight, fuck, or bust a sixty-five. Lotta cats couldn't make it."

Russell turned away and rolled his eyes. "Say, Slim, I gotta roll, bro. Gotta drop off this felony downstairs and get to cleaning these showers," he blasted out. He turned for the stairwell but stopped when he heard... silence. Slim G-Zus wasn't saying anything... Russell turned to look... Slim G-Zus hadn't moved. He stood there, his face behind the grate, looking concerned. Russell felt the heat that always came with stress. A feeling prison was teaching him to deal with through repetition. They stared at each other. Slim G-Zus took a deep breath and exhaled a stream of frustration. The look of concern was gone, replaced with a half-ass frown, like he was dealing with a child.

Russell rapped the steel door. "I'ma take this downstairs," he said as he turned and made for the stairwell.

CHAPTER 37

A few weeks after Slim G-Zus caught the chain, Russell had an interview with a Mr. Daniel Salazar, the regional parole representative assigned to the Acirema unit. The meeting wasn't what he expected. Salazar never once asked if he'd learned his lesson, changed his ways, or seen the light—all of the things Russell had been imagining he'd ask. All he wanted to know was the address Russell planned on paroling to, and whether or not he'd have employment waiting on him when he got out. From the way their brief conversation went, Russell was pretty sure his parole file had nothing about him and Cordell stopping one of the worst school shootings in history. As far as TDC was concerned, he was just another inmate. A criminal because he carried a firearm unlawfully... And, in a sense, that's exactly who he was. He and Cordell had been carrying guns on a school campus, which was against the law. The nightmare that forced them to reveal that ongoing transgression was completely separate. He knew this was right in his head, but in his heart he hoped the parole board would have some sympathy.

He'd written home right after the interview, telling his parents how it went, and asking them if the D.A. had written his letter to the parole board yet. They came for a visit the following Saturday with an answer from the D.A.'s secretary: "He's working on it." Which Russell of course didn't like the sound of. How long does it take to write a letter? His mother also said that the writer who'd been interested in doing a book on Russell and Cordell couldn't find a publishing company to give him an advance, something about the publishers not wanting to do a book that might be used by Republicans or gun lobbies. The visit ended without Russell asking about him and Cordell being on the same unit, a first.

Things were good at work. There'd been plenty of time in the closet and plenty of leftover free-world food. The former had barely stayed PG13, and the latter was limited to Little Caesars pizza and homemade tacos, but Russell wasn't complaining. He'd gone so far as to have Salinas call his mother a couple of times, to show he was serious about being with her when he got out. She still put on her tough prison-guard routine from time to time, ordering him around like he was just another inmate, but Russell liked it. He interpreted her random bouts of by-the-bookness as a product of being a good, wholesome, small-town *chica*. Something Megan, and the other girls he'd had, could never be.

Russell was up to 220 pounds now. Concentrating on bench and military presses, pull-ups, and leg presses was paying off. He'd worry about the single-jointed movements—bicep curls, pec flies, et cetera—once he got out. If only he could get some Creatine... Cell-Tech by MuscleTech. He'd thought about asking Salinas, but he could tell she had some trust issues, and he didn't want her to think he had ulterior motives. Plus, he already had her doing Internet searches for Big Ike's mother. With Cell-Tech or a nitric oxide supplement, he knew he'd be able to put on another ten pounds, easy.

All the boxing work with Black Gotti had paid off as well. His hands were quicker, and his lungs were stronger. He'd even been thinking about challenging Mitch to a few rounds when he got out. His dad and older brother had always been big boxing fans. Russell had imagined himself catching Mitch after a seven-day shift out in the Gulf. He'd be worn out and still underestimating his little brother. Exactly what Russell wanted. He played that imaginary triumph out like so many scenes from a movie, always dropping the curtain with surprised looks on the faces of Mitch and his dad.

Things were moving along. He had a daily routine down, and he was sticking to it. With Slim G-Zus gone, no longer able to wire up some drama that could get him a major case for fighting or participating in a riot, Russell could see light at the end of the tunnel.

There'd been some TPS (Typical Prison Shit), as O.T. called it, but nothing too severe. The guy on F-Pod—Orton, who whupped Slim G-Zus's ass—checked some new guy. He was a real young, real small, pasty White dude. The next day on the yard, Big Body Slim and Youngbuck channeled a little ghost of Slim G-Zus, telling Orton he should've checked the big White guy that hit the pod a week before. Youngbuck got animated as usual: "You gon' check one, you gotta check 'em all," and, "I wish a motherfucker'd check me." Big Body Slim wrapped him up and kept him from getting at Orton, who smiled the whole time. Ogre told Big Body Slim to let Youngbuck go. To which Big Body Slim replied, "Get you some business, Ogre."

If Slim G-Zus had still been here, things would've been much worse. There'd have been a speech full of his dumb-ass slippery slope arguments, bullshit about how great it was on Acirema, and, of course, some violence. Because *Retaliation Is Mandatory* or whatever the hell that ten-cent slogan was he had. It was amazing to Russell that so many of these guys had bought into all that nonsense.

But now the forbidden had come and gone. A White guy had been checked, and there was no retaliation as a result. Yet, no Blacks or Mexicans were running around checking Whites and raping and pillaging. In fact, days after Orton beat the kid up, the sun still rose. Little birdies still came out singing and chirping. Big Body Slim tried to say that if the kid Orton checked had folded up, and become Orton's property, things might've changed. As if somehow that would've been the chum in the water that set off a feeding frenzy of Great Black Sharks. But weeks passed and, shock of all shocks, nothing happened.

Russell lowered the pin on the bench press to 340 and started his fourth set. He knew the 340 pounds he was about to rep on the machine wouldn't translate to a barbell in the world, but it still felt good to get under that 340 and hit it six times. Doing a lower number of reps, four to six, allowed him to lift a heavier weight for a longer period of time, increasing the overall tonnage he did in a given workout. This led to, on average, about ten sets of four to six reps on the bench press and lat pull-downs. Russell had been increasing the weight gradually, every third or fourth workout, always setting a weight that still allowed him to do at least four reps.

It was Russell, Big Body Slim, and, making one of his sporadic appearances on the weight pile, Itchy Foot. Every station on the pile was occupied except the leg press. The curl bar and bench press had close to ten convicts on each, illustrating why so many guys had the top-heavy "penitentiary build."

Almost an hour after rec began, the crowd at the weight pile had thinned out. Russell and Big Body Slim had finished up on the bench and moved on. Russell had banged out sets of twenty on the leg press, then went to the pull-down bar. He'd do about ten sets, using between 160 and 180 pounds. Big Body Slim went to the curl bar and put the pin at eighty pounds. The couple of times Russell watched him do a set, it was always at least ten reps, and he never once looked like he was straining. Guy should've played football instead of murdering cops.

Yella Fella and Damn Fool swaggered around the weight pile to the pull-down bar. Yella said, "How many's over here?"

Russell looked back, "Just us three," and gestured at the two others.

"Who last?"

Russell pointed, "*Ese* right there."

An older Mexican raised his hand, "I'm last," he said.

"Got after you," said Yella Fella.

Russell figured he'd get about four more sets done before he couldn't do his minimum of four reps per. Big Body Slim finished doing curls and strutted over to a deserted steel bench. He put his feet up on the seat and started a set of diamond push-ups that looked like it could go on forever.

Yella Fella grasped the bar wide and pulled it down to his chest, just above the *Bad Ass Yella Boy* tat. Damn Fool stool behind him, loosening up his arms.

Russell looked around the yard. Most everybody was in their usual color-coded groupings. The volleyball court on the small patch of grass was full of White players with one or two token Mexicans or Blacks. The basketball court was all Black except for Youngbuck. The handball court was a little different. It was almost equal parts White and Mexican. Everyone who wasn't playing their preferred sport loitered in groups that had no exceptions. Ogre and the rest of the Reich had a group. Itchy Foot, Sidewinder, and the rest of the independents had their group, which Russell now noticed Big Body Slim was headed towards. Peeling away from Ogre's group, and heading for the weight pile, was Orton.

About a week before, Russell had overheard Youngbuck saying that Orton would only get on the weights when Big Body Slim wasn't there. Russell acknowledged that it did seem that way, but knew it wasn't because Orton was scared. He looked like the guy from *300*, more ripped than Russell himself. Big Body Slim, Ogre, Sidewinder—they were all bigger than Orton, but Russell was willing to bet if they lowered their body-fat percentage to whatever Orton's was, Orton would be bigger.

Orton stepped up to the military press, lowered the pin, and started a set. Russell couldn't see the amount from where he was, but it had to be close to 180, which was a lot of weight, especially considering the speed at which Orton was hoisting it up.

Orton set the weight down and caught Russell looking at him. Russell had talked weights and nutrition with him a few times before, but nothing important. Orton lifted his tribal-art-tattooed chin and said, "'Sup, youngster?"

"'Sup, man?" replied Russell.

"I see you over there getting your paper."

Russell said, "Tryin' to. Gotta few more to go. Probably do some abs next and be done with it."

Orton nodded, looked down, and fingered his abs, "Yeah, always get them abs in."

Out of the corner of his eye, Russell saw Yella smirking, probably at Orton's voice. He couldn't help but wonder what would happen if Yella and Orton locked up. They were the same size and looked to be about the same age. Both had been locked up awhile. Russell didn't have anything against either one of them, just figured it'd be a good fight.

Russell did three more sets of pull-downs, then walked over to the pull-up bar to do some hanging leg raises. After his second set Orton came over and said, "Lemme get in here witcha."

Russell stepped aside as Orton grabbed the bar with an underhand grip and pulled himself up until his arms locked at a ninety-degree angle. He jerked his legs up quickly but in a controlled manner, keeping his body rigid, not using any momentum whatsoever. He knocked out a set of twelve like it was just a warm-up. Russell said, "Say, Orton, you play any football when you were in the world?"

Orton stood with his hands on his hips bending backward at the waist, stretching his abs. "Hell, yeah, I played football, boy," he said grinning.

Russell asked, "What position?"

"Linebacker."

"Oh, yeah?" Russell nodded and smiled like he'd just been surprised with some good news. "I was a safety. I'm trying to gain enough weight to get outta here and try and play the Will."

"Weak side," said Orton. "I played the Mike."

"Yeah. Middle," said Russell.

Orton looked Russell over, "Hell, you put on about fifteen pounds, you'll be all right."

Russell looked down at his own torso. "Yeah, I'm up to about 220 now."

"Get you some free weights and blow that shit up."

Russell nodded. "Hell, yeah," he said and went for a set of ten. This was the third or fourth time he'd spoken to Orton. They probably didn't have much in common (Russell wasn't in the market for a chin tat), but the guy didn't seem that bad. He just didn't want to do things the way Slim G-Zus had. And because everybody was scared of change, even inmates, they'd turned Orton into a boogie man.

Russell dropped down from the bar and glanced at Yella Fella. He and Damn Fool were still at the pull-down bar, doing tricep press-downs. Yella was one of the few inmates Russell'd seen do them correctly. Most guys would hunch over the bar and press it down using their pecs and delts, like when you do a dip. Not Yella. He stood upright and kept his elbows locked at his sides, allowing only his triceps to do the work. And those horseshoes were pushing eighty pounds with ease.

Orton began his second set of leg-raises, whipping his legs up and down at a breakneck pace. Russell was impressed but kept it to himself. From what he'd seen over the last ten months, there were only two things worse than a suck-ass: a cho-mo or a snitch.

Orton finished and took some deep breaths. Russell wanted to wait ninety seconds in between sets but had a feeling Orton would think that was soft. He decided on a diversion. Russell cleared his throat. "Say Orton," he said, "you been gone awhile, right?" Orton nodded, his eyes thinning. "Most units you been on pretty much like this?"

"Fuck, no. Place is trash."

So much for all that nonsense Slim G-Zus was always talking about. Acirema wasn't anything special. Slim G-Zus just wanted everyone to believe it was because it helped him get his way. Guys like Youngbuck and Big Body Slim couldn't be blamed for going along with him because they'd been locked up all their lives and probably came from broken homes.

"I haven't been locked up that long, but a bunch of guys here said it's better—" Russell shrugged.

Orton started counting off on his fingers, "There ain't no organization. There ain't no checking—so you don't know who's who. There ain't no respect for us, Blacks and messcans do whatever they want—" Orton snorted. "And it's boring than a motherfucicer around here. Ain't shit happening."

Russell nodded, a sincere look on his face, contradicting thoughts in his mind. He'd only started the conversation to get a longer break in between sets. Now having gotten that break, he grabbed the bar, pulled himself up, and tried to run through a set as quick as Orton had. He noticed Yella looking at Orton. The expression on his face was hard to read. There was a glint in his eye, and he was almost smiling. Russell continued through his set.

CHAPTER 38

Russell came down the stairs wrapping his hands and wrists with strips of poly-cotton he'd cut from a bed sheet. When he hit the dayroom, every Black inmate was under one TV staring at what looked like a cable news program. It was the first time Russell had ever seen a dayroom TV on MSNBC. Yella Fella was front and center, his arms folded, scowling. Russell looked for Black Gotti... saw him in the pile to the left of Yella and Damn Fool. *Guess the workout's gonna have to wait.* Itchy Foot and Youngbuck were back by the window, looking distant but irritated. A few Mexicans were scattered around the edges of the crowd; most were watching from the tables, where the domino games and chess matches had stopped.

Russell eased up to the left of the pile and cupped his ears. It was the Raquel Matthews Show, and the host was talking energetically with her hands to a guest: "... and we know, according to the timeline we've constructed here, that if Lashonda died when doctors estimated she did, it absolutely coincides with the time at which witnesses say they saw the pickup truck heading east on FM 3120, does it not?"

"Sure it does, Raquel," replied her guest, reporter Nancy Garza, as she gazed into the host's eyes.

Raquel leaned forward in her chair, gesturing with her hands in a circular motion and slowly nodding her head, "And so all of this blowback about how those of us who fear this might be a hate crime are supposedly jumping to conclusions..." Raquel leaned back, shaking her head.

"... Right, right. I mean," said Nancy, "I know it's considered unpatriotic to bring up America's brutal treatment of African-Americans throughout history, but we know the history of South Carolina and—"

Mathews pointed at Garza, "Exactly. And the description of the vehicle fleeing the scene—I mean, my God, in that area?"

"Right. I mean, we know that driving a pickup is code for—at least in particular regions—certain beliefs."

They nodded at each other, *You go girl.*

Mathews said, "The other bits of evidence, the uh... looks like a triangle? A metal triangle that was hanging from a tree. Right by the house she was found in?"

"Yes," said Garza.

"So, all these AM radio talkers are saying that's not a hangman's noose or whatever."

"Right."

"And, again, probably because of their ignorance of history, certain people are screaming that the news organizations shouldn't be showing this."

"You know, as if the only thing African-Americans were ever hung from were nooses, as if we're somehow crying wolf, basically."

"Right. Great point, Raquel. In reality," Nancy tucked her hair behind her ears, "African-Americans were hung from all sorts of devices—and dismembered with impunity—not just hangman's nooses."

A picture of a triangular device was shown hanging from a tree next to a cabin in a wooded area. Russell recognized it immediately. It was what you used to hang a deer or a hog from by its hind legs so you could gut and skin the thing. Russell tried to put the pieces together.

A girl named Lashonda. A pickup truck. A device for hanging game. The "history" of South Carolina... A hate crime? Russell looked the crowd over. About thirty Black convicts, most of them arms folded, shaking their heads.

Mathews said, "Okay, at this time we're going to bring on one of the smartest people you can talk to when it comes to these types of issues, my personal friend, Vance Michael Smith. Vance, I didn't hear back from you when I last texted, glad you could join us. How are you?"

A shot of Smith from some other location was now on the screen. He half-assed a smile and said, "I'm fine." The screen split showing Mathews on the right and Smith on the left.

Mathews said, "Vance, I know you've been following this case very closely, as we have been here. I'd like to get your thoughts on this heinous crime, and, especially, the latest developments. Witnesses are now saying they saw a pickup truck fleeing the scene—or at least the area where Lashonda Lawson was apparently raped and beaten to death."

Smith pursed his lips and nodded his head. "Well, it's a heinous crime indeed, Raquel, and I'm hopeful the authorities are getting some useful information that will assist them in bringing those responsible to justice. As an African-American, I can say this is a very troubling matter. In the African-American community we're wondering, will this brutality ever stop?"

Mathews was nodding thoughtfully, hyper-focused, as if she'd just heard something profound. "Vance, there seems to be a lot of backlash in the talk radio world towards this network—and especially this show—for supposedly jumping to conclusions—just because we've discussed the possibility that this might have been a hate crime. Now, you've known me a long time. You know I have always been outspoken on issues of racial justice. I'm not going to apologize for that. Do you see the fingerprints of a hate crime here, considering the circumstances?"

Smith tilted his head, pondering. "Well, from what we know—a young, mentally challenged Black girl was raped and beaten to death in rural South Carolina, found in a cabin that's only used by White hunters, on some land owned by a White man... And now there's this about a pickup truck—"

"Vance, I have here, in the studio with me, Nancy Garza. Before you came on, she and I were discussing the problem of historical ignorance as it pertains to the triangular apparatus we saw hanging from the tree where young Lashonda was found. Nancy pointed out that, while obviously, this wasn't an actual hangman's noose, in the South, African-Americans were hung by lynch mobs and other assorted White supremacists with all sorts of devices—not just hangman's nooses."

Smith closed his eyes and nodded slowly.

"Yet," continued Mathews, "we're supposedly 'crying wolf' or jumping to conclusions." Mathews raised her hands in exasperation. *She's more worried about what someone said about her show than the actual crime,* thought Russell.

Smith unfolded his hands. "And it's that reluctance to talk about that part of America's past, about race in general, that makes it so hard to talk about these types of issues when they happen today. Ergo, you're getting this 'crying wolf' accusation."

"Vance Michael Smith, you are dead-on, and that is why I love having you on this show. Nobody had a problem with speculation about Osama Bin Laden being responsible for 9/11—way before Al-Qaeda claimed responsibility. That wasn't 'crying wolf.'" Mathews shook her head dismissively. "People have to check their privilege."

Russell peeled away from the crowd, to the back window. He stood there unwrapping his hands, taking in the scene.

Itchy Foot said, "Fuckin' todes gettin' wired up." Youngbuck nodded his head slightly.

Russell smirked. "Probably just tryna figure out what happened." Itchy Foot looked at Russell for a beat and frowned.

They stole our culture, diamonds, gold, and people. And that wasn't enough. We built their country and made them rich from our free labor. And it still wasn't enough. When they finally gave us our freedom, it was game. They knew all along they'd keep us in some form of bondage—either Jim Crow or prison. Four hundred years of fixing the rules to keep us out. And yet, they still have to rape and murder our beautiful little girls.

I just got word some ho-ass whiteboy down there on F-Pod got stomped out for bumpin' his gums. The dumb-ass whiteboy got to arguing with a nigga in the dayroom that it wasn't no proof Whites killed that little girl. So the nigga—I think he's out of Waco—went to getting on his ass, and the whiteboy must have gotten a couple of lucky punches in because this other nigga jumped in—which is what we should do every time we fight one of them hoes, anyway—and dropped his ass. When he went down, this Waco nigga stomped on his head a couple of times—I'm guessing the pyah in the picket was takin' a siesta—and them other whiteboys ain't do shit. The Great White Hope was there. My boy said he didn't even get up from the domino table. Just sat there.

I've been around that fool a few times, on the yard mostly. He's cock-strong and ripped up, especially for a whiteboy. But a couple weeks ago, they had some new whiteboys hit F-Pod and he only tried the small one, he didn't do shit to the bigger one. Straight coward. Regardless, he's checking whiteboys, and I ain't fixing to go through them slave days or the original Jim Crow (I currently live the new Jim Crow) again, where whiteboys get to do shit we don't. Especially, when these hoes are still raping our women, beating them to death, getting away with it, and then trying to argue with us in the dayroom.

How long are we supposed to put up with this shit? Ain't four hundred years enough? Them hoes on AM radio saying wait for the DNA. Black folks done did enough waitin'. And White people know this shit. At least the ones that aren't sitting around drinking their Pabst Blue Ribbon, or whatever shitty-ass beer they drink. Or Bill Ayers. That whiteboy was trying to blow up a judge, and all them Rush Limbaugh motherfuckers hate his ass. Even that teacher I just had, Mr. Clarkson, he's actually worked for the government, and still knows what's up. So, if some of them know what's up, they all know what's up. It's just that this is what they do. They're the ice people, material focused, always have been, always will be. They can't compete with us, the sun people, because we're a spirit-focused people. And because they can't compete with us, they imprison us and rape and kill our women. Even when we get down to their level, using their bullshit-ass academic style like that brother Ta-Nehisi Coates did, they reject it. No justice, not even reparations unless you're them friendly-ass Japs—not even a thank you to the people mostly responsible for all you've got.

Enough.

Russell stepped up to the desk, curious as to why Salinas had called him out early. She hung up the phone and smiled at him, then checked the hallways.

"*¿Cóma estás, mi vida?*" said Russell, not exactly nailing the accent.

"I talked to your mom before I came to work. She got that letter from the D.A." Russell was afraid he'd heard her wrong. He felt himself turning red, his pulse quickening. *Thank you, Jesus.*

He put his hands on the desktop to steady himself and exhaled. "'Bout time," he said.

"Your mom said that should help with parole."

"Yeah," said Russell, nodding his head and looking around at nothing in particular. "Yeah, they say the parole board gets that..." He knew there were no guarantees, yet he still wanted to jump over the desk and tackle her. All of this was about to be over. The long, loud, violent nightmare was about to end. Salinas must've sensed his euphoria. She pulled the ribbon from her hair and shook it out. She gazed at him, running her fingers through her hair and then laying it on her left shoulder where she stroked it. She arched an eyebrow. "*Vamos a nuestro lugar especial.*"

Russell headed for the closet.

Salinas crossed the threshold and put her arms around his neck. He squeezed her into his body and plucked her up off the ground, inhaling her scent as she wrapped her legs around his waist. They grinded into each other, Russell trying to envelop her body, his chin pressed into her shoulder, every inch of his arms occupied... *can't get close enough.* He squeezed... until she gasped. Salinas pulled back and took his head in her hands. They looked into each other's eyes. Russell turned and stepped, gently placing her back against the wall. Her fingertips glided from the back of his head to his face. Her full lips were parted, their lower bodies trying to compress the air between them into a diamond.

Part Four

No peace keeps itself.

—Donald Kagan

Russell stepped onto the yard after being pat-searched by a young Mexican guard with a seal of Texas star tattoo behind her ear and the inside of her wrist. It was sweltering on the yard and stifling inside the building. The feeble breeze the only difference between the two. Russell took in the scene. All the usual suspects in their usual groups, taking up their usual places... except for three people: Itchy Foot, Orton, and Yella Fella. Russell's curiosity got the better of him.

Big Body Slim lowered the pin to the bottom of the stack, 225 pounds. He turned to the short, slightly built Mexican to his left, gestured toward the stack of weights. "You wanna jump on that to make it interesting?"

The young cholo grinned and said, "I tole my homeboy you could do the stack about chwenny times. I try to bet him, but he say no."

Big Body Slim looked at Jew Boy with his Mickey Rourke in *Bullet* Star of David tat on his chest, and smiled knowingly. The opaque lenses of his all-black Oakleys, which he'd basically extorted from a guard who was late paying his craft shop bill, gleamed with the cholo's reflection. Big Body Slim said, "Tell your homeboy I can do it twenty-five times." He sat down and pulled the bar to his collar bone, the first of twelve reps.

Peter Austin Wallace grew up in Alamo Heights, one of San Antonio's most exclusive neighborhoods. His parents were both school teachers. Mom taught English and Social Studies in intermediate school. Dad coached varsity football and taught P.E. or Driver's Ed. But it was a couple of successful commercial real estate investments in their hometown of Austin that they made their money on.

Peter grew up an only child, wanting for nothing. Even though he had his dad's size—the old man was a three-year starter on the defensive line for the Southern Methodist University Mustangs—Peter never played a down of football. There were plenty of lackluster swim meets and soccer matches until he got to junior high and discovered wrestling. Unfortunately, about this time, he also discovered alcohol, marijuana, and acid. Much more unfortunately, he and his buddies—all grunge, punk-rocking, rage-against-the-machine rich kids trying desperately to be "different"—also discovered the thrill of breaking into houses. But despite the drugs and being a borderline alcoholic, there were top-five finishes in citywide wrestling competitions. A bevy of fast-twitch muscle fiber, inherited from his father, was mostly responsible, but an ever-present disregard for life helped. By age twelve, he'd forgotten how many pet cats he'd tortured to death for entertainment.

In Peter's case, momma and daddy tried. But during his junior year of high school, the wild ride that had to end did so tragically. On a spring night when they knew the home's occupants would be at their son's tennis match, Peter and three boys broke into a two-story home in a cul-de-sac. Everything went fine—for the burglars, that is—until they exited the home with their loot. Victor Reyes, the off-duty Bexar County Sheriff's Deputy who lived three houses down, had seen the four boys and didn't recognize them. He grabbed his Browning Hi Power 9 mm and headed down the sidewalk in street clothes.

Christopher Hinrich, the oldest of the four boys, had found a loaded Colt .38 Special in a nightstand. He had it in the front pocket of his baggy cargo pants when he got to the end of the driveway and heard, "What do you think you're doing?" Christopher looked up, saw a man pointing a pistol at him, and froze. Peter and the others then stepped out of the house and fanned out around them. The man with the gun was pointing it at Peter, who was taunting him with lines from *A Clockwork Orange*. Christopher reached into his pocket, pulled out the gun, and shot straight.

Peter and his codefendants were all seventeen and eighteen years old. They sat in the Bexar County Jail for sixteen months before going to trial, where they were all convicted of capital murder of a peace officer. Christopher was sentenced to death by lethal injection, the rest to capital life, a sentence requiring the inmate to do forty calendar years before becoming eligible for parole.

Before he was Big Body Slim, Peter Austin Wallace was just another ho-ass whiteboy with a pair of black Chuck Taylors every 'inmate of color' wanted to try him for. He lost a few fights early on, never said uncle. Eventually, a late growth spurt, coupled with improved boxing skills, made him unattractive prey, Chuck Taylors notwithstanding.

When he hit Acirema, after being shipped from Telford for a riot with the Blacks, he met this dude Lane. A lotta people called him Slim, even though he was ripped up. He was kinda weird but funny, especially when he wasn't trying to be. Lane liked giving everybody nicknames and they always stuck. All of them had the word Slim in there somewhere. Why? Because, as Lane said, "You treat people the way you wanna be treated... So, if everybody's calling me Slim, they must want me to call them that—" which he said with a straight face. Dude was a character. He was a fly honky in the world. Better check out his pictures. He had some pretty-ass Black chicks out there. Lane was always talking about big-body Cadillacs and shit. He could talk about all that shit with the Blacks like he was one of the crew. One day, after being back to back in the dayroom surrounded by six unfriendlies, six very restless natives, because those honkies drug that tode behind their truck, Lane started calling Peter Big Body Slim. Other than a few fist fights over the checking issue, Acirema had been a piece of cake compared to the other units he'd been on. He'd gotten in the craft shop, where he was basically unsupervised, making contraband all day long, and able to flirt with numerous female guards... Though he got a lot more contraband done than he did flirting. He was somehow, even at six one, 240 pounds, wholly incapable of starting a conversation from scratch with the fairer sex. Which was different from his boy Slim G-Zus, who could start a conversation with any female, if there was a purpose behind it. Even though conversing was dead last on his list of things he enjoyed doing. He missed that dude, Slim G-Zus.

The "'wood from the hood," they used to call him, before he got the hoe squad to lay it down (and refuse to work) and became Slim G-Zus. Big Body Slim wished he was still there.

Big Body Slim stood up and rolled his shoulders, trying to work out the lactic-acid in his back muscles. He flung his arms wide, then flexed his lats (he called it the cobra) as he surveyed the yard. Everything looked normal... except the grouping between the grass and the handball court. Big Body Slim sighed. He wasn't about to fuck off his workout for some politickin', but this didn't look right. He said to Jew Boy, "Lookout, Goldenkikestein."

Jew Boy paused at the top of his rep on the bench press, "'Sup, Adolph? Forgot what comes after three again?"

"Walk with me," said Big Body Slim.

Russell knew what he was hearing wasn't right. There'd been some sort of misunderstanding. But nobody was saying anything, including Russell, as Big Body Slim and Jew Boy rolled up. Russell looked around and saw Damn Fool and two other Blacks coming up behind Yella and Itchy. Sidewinder, Youngbuck, and a few others were leaving the handball court and heading their way. Squirrel left Rexy on the wall. Everybody on the yard had now stopped dribbling, lifting, running, or whatever the case was, and was staring at them. Orton had walked away and was now talking to Ogre and four Reich members about ten yards away.

Yella Fella said, "I just talked to ya boy," he gestured toward Orton and the NSR. "He's gonna fill y'all in on most of it. But shit's done changed."

Itchy Foot stood with his arms folded, staring ahead at no one in particular. Big Body Slim said, "Why don't you fill us in on what's done changed." He smacked the word *done* sarcastically.

Russell knew that wouldn't go over well.

Yella Fella's brow creased, and he raised his voice, "All this shit."

Big Body Slim unfolded his arms, frowning.

Yella Fella said, "There's a bunch a weak motherfuckas 'round here actin' like men." Russell thought that sounded like Orton talking. Yella continued, "And that shit ain't happenin' no more. This gonna be a real unit." He punched his hand. "Mothafuckas is gonna get checked in—and it don't matter if they whiteboys—"

"I ain't no boy," said Youngbuck.

"—Messcans, or niggas," said Yella Fella.

Big Body Slim shook his head. "So, when your homeboy from da hood—Lil Deuce Trey—comes through the door, weighing a buck-oh-five soaking wet in his brogans, and I twist his fuckin' head off—y'all gonna be alright with that?"

Yella Fella clapped his own chest. "We're gonna do all the checkin' for awhile. 'Cause y'all done had it your way for some years now. That shit's over," he swiped his hand in front of his throat. "So, we're gonna check who we want—"

"Fuck that," said Youngbuck.

"—And y'all gots to give us a couple of them punks," said Yella.

"Fuck that, too," said Squirrel.

"'Cause y'all got them hoes when we didn't have a chance at 'em."

Russell hadn't taken a breath in awhile. The adrenaline that had been leaking into his veins began to surge.

Big Body Slim was saying a silent goodbye to his craft shop privileges, and the chance they gave him at gettin' in Nellarosa's pants—penitentiary nirvana—while simultaneously wondering if he should try and get to the shank he had buried in the grass. Damn Fool was taking his measure. None of the Blacks had their hands in their pants, which meant they probably didn't bring their heat... *Did they really think they were gonna drop this on us and get away with it?* Maybe that Henry Rollins–lookin' motherfucker Orton sold them a dream. No telling.

Yella Fella said, "Y'all can holla at ya boy," thumbing towards Orton, "but we done established this."

Youngbuck shook his head and pointed at Orton, "That motherfucker don't speak for nar' sumbitch over here."

The kid, McCann, said, "He just got here. He's not one of us," then cut himself off and looked down. Yella Fella folded his arms, flexing his biceps.

Big Body Slim yanked off the Oakleys and put them in his back pocket. "Y'all gonna get some major shit kicked off—"

"Kick it off, then," said Yella Fella, unfolding his arms and leaning forward. "Y'all ain't gonna do shit, whiteboy."

Big Body said, "Fuck you and everything you stand for, **blackboy**."

Damn Fool charged across the imaginary line between them, chucking haymakers at Big Body Slim. Russell staggered back, eyes wide, praying that it was gonna stay a one-on-one fight... Then Youngbuck blitzed Yella Fella like it was third and long. Yella Fella fired off a couple of punches, then ducked as Youngbuck threw a one-two. Russell took another step back. Sidewinder, Jew Boy, and the other Whites were all paired off with somebody Black and swinging furiously. Russell looked to his left. Itchy Foot was standing with Orton and Ogre. *This ain't my fight. I'm about to be outta here...* Russell felt a jolt. The top half of his body rocked sideways.

Big Body Slim traded homerun swings with Damn Fool... This wasn't working out. They weren't in the same weight class. He was giving up at least fifty pounds and three inches. Big Body Slim dropped his head and rushed in. Damn Fool launched an uppercut that landed, splitting him open above the eye but failing to slow his charge. Big Body Slim felt the heel of a fist hammer into the back of his head, then an elbow in his back snapped a rib bone. He rammed his shoulder into Damn Fool's fleshy midsection, then he got it: his hands locked in an unbreakable grip.

When he was a youngster on the wrestling team, Big Body Slim had multiple ways of intimidating his opponents before a match. His favorite was to greet them cordially with a handshake, then quickly reach behind their back, as if he were trying to hug them, to see if he could clasp his hands. When he did he'd say, "I'm gonna toss you," then immediately do the same thing to the next guy. "I'm gonna toss you... I'm gonna toss you..." to every wrestler in sight.

Damn Fool was too heavy to toss, but if he couldn't get him off the ground, he might be able to swing a leg behind him, take him down, and pin him on his back. Damn Fool knew what he was doing. As soon as the Big Body locked his hands behind his back, Damn Fool grabbed him in an airtight head lock. Sweeping his legs would now get Big Body Slim DDT'ed.

They spun around a couple of times, clutching, jerking, trying to get the upper hand. Damn Fool used his free hand to pulverize Big Body Slim's kidneys. He shuffled left, then right, trying to keep the blows from being direct hits. He needed to swipe the blood from one eye and the sweat from both, and he needed to end this stalemate. They were probably outnumbered three to one, and he was in a vulnerable position. If somebody came with a knife, he'd be in trouble.

Big Body Slim crouched, geared down, then jerked up, thrusting his shoulder into Damn Fool's torso and tightening his grip as he drove him backward toward the concrete wall. About five feet from the wall, Big Body Slim slowed up. He released his grip and re-clinched him below his waist. Damn Fool still had him by the neck, and, lowering his position, he'd practically cut off his air. Big Body Slim bucked, surging with everything he had as he ripped Damn Fool from the ground, plunged his shoulder into his chest, and his right forearm into his throat. He heard the thud of Damn Fool's hand spanking the wall, felt his grip loosen from his neck.

Big Body Slim jerked back. Damn Fool's eyes were hazy. Big Body Slim threw a right to his chin to knock him out, but the blood in his eyes had made him a cyclops, and he had no depth perception. It landed on Damn Fool's forehead, the timing all off. Damn Fool lunged for his neck. Big Body Slim seized upon his wrists and turned sideways, forcing Damn Fool to trip over his extended right leg. He tripped forward and landed face down in a heap. Peter wiped his eyes with his palms, stepped up beside Damn Fool, and began stomping his head with a one-legged goose step. He stopped when Damn Fool finally quit raising his head up.

Russell stumbled to his right. He was pretty sure it was a punch that had the side of his head feeling caved-in. He turned frantically to his left. Another shot, this time to the back of his head, staggered him forward. Russell spun around. C-Life.

The look on his face said he wasn't going to care about Russell trying to make parole. Russell stood, hands at his sides, tears welling, hoping in vain he could avoid this, yet knowing he couldn't. In an instant, as C-Life came at him, he accepted the facts of his predicament and ejected his self-pity, replacing it with a guiltless rage. He stepped his right foot back, tucked his chin, and lifted his hands.

C-Life was on him. Russell dipped and ducked, absorbing the flurry of punches, none of which were landing solidly. He shuffled back a step and peered over the tops of his knuckles. C-Life said, "Don't back up, strawburry blon' bitch." The speed of the punches should've been intimidating, but it's impossible to be intimidated when you're that far past the point of no return.

Russell bound forward, leading with a cluster of jabs. C-Life side-stepped to his right and loaded up. Russell knew he was about to take a shot to the left side of his jaw. He jerked his forearm back and rolled his left shoulder up. C-Life's punch glanced off Russell's wrist and landed on his neck. Russell knew a hook would be coming from the other side immediately. He dipped, bent at the waist, and uncorked an overhand right that caught C-Life's solar plexus. Russell rose with a left uppercut that connected.

"Bitch-ass Whiteboy," said C-Life, as if he were out of breath. C-Life back-pedaled, hand over his solar plexus, and a face that said, *You've done it now.*

Big Body Slim felt for the cracked rib in his back. There was a little pain when he inhaled but the adrenaline was keeping it in check. He scanned the yard, palming the cut above his eye... Youngbuck and Yella Fella were getting their paper. Jew Boy had one about his size. Squirrel was on the grass, wrestling. Sidewinder had two of them on him. Big Body Slim ran their way. He angled to stay out of the one to his left's line of sight.

Most people think that when you're running up behind someone with the element of surprise and a full head of steam, you swing for the fences with a dome call. But the human head, especially when it's attached to a body that's in a fist fight, has a track record of moving at the worst possible time. And if you're 240 pounds of Grade-A Texas beef, you don't want to miss on a swing like that. So you go for the kidney, because its part of the torso, and normally stays put longer.

Big Body Slim planted his feet and leaned into the punch. His target let out a high-pitched cry and crumpled to the ground. The other one Sidewinder was engaged with turned and threw a one-two at Big Body Slim, who ducked his head and punched back. Sidewinder tagged the guy's jaw with a clean right, staggering him. Big Body Slim stepped into an elbow that had all of his weight behind it. He felt the guy's orbital bone crush, dropping him to his hands and knees. Sidewinder set his feet, lined up his target, timed his steps, and drove his foot into the guy's ribs, lifting him up off the ground. Sidewinder's face was pretty bad. His nose was probably broke, and he was gonna have a black eye or two.

Big Body Slim looked around. Almost everybody had two people on them now. Youngbuck and Yella Fella were still both on their feet, one on one. Squirrel and Jew Boy were on the ground.

"Get Squirrel," said Big Body Slim, "I got Jew Boy." Big Body Slim took off running.

In the distance he heard the voices of guards, "Lay it down! *Lay it down!*" and the sound of the "fogger," the most powerful gas gun in the C.O.'s arsenal, with its loud, two-stroke engine revving up. Out of the corners of his eyes he saw more Blacks coming from other parts of the yard.

"Get that big whiteboy," somebody yelled. Big Body Slim slowed and did a three-sixty, looked in the direction from which the voice came... Nobody was there.

He got to Jew Boy. There were two guys standing over him, trying to stomp him out. Jew Boy held one guy by the leg, while he kicked at the other. They both looked up as Big Body Slim arrived. The stomping and attempted stomping stopped. The one to his left stepped over Jew Boy, swinging. Peter stepped to him, firing back. Each man landed a couple of good shots, but Peter had the guy by thirty pounds. Which was probably why the tode put his head down as he kept swinging. Thanks, buddy.

Big Body Slim covered up and rushed in, reaching over and past the guy's shoulders, clasping his hands at his opponent's abdomen. He yanked him from the ground, then slammed him back into it. Lying on top of the guy's back, he dodged a brogan coming at his face. Jew Boy was still holding the guy's other leg but his face was bloody, and Big Body Slim was certain he didn't have much left in the tank.

The guy under him was squirming and cussing. Peter crawled forward and trapped the guy's right leg between his bicep and his torso. "My nigga—*get dis whiteboy off me!*" he yelled as Peter got to his knees, choking down on the guy's shin. Peter stuck his left knee in the guy's asscrack and jerked backwards, taking the leg with him as his back hit the ground behind him. The scream from knee tendons and hip flexors ripping apart was so shrill, Peter actually let go before he planned to. The job was done anyway; ol' boy was completely out of commission, except his vocal chords.

Big Body Slim got to his feet and took a shot in the back of his head. He turned around. Another punch to the back of his head. He trudged forward, feigning a punch to back up the one in front of him. He then pivoted ninety degrees, putting himself perpendicular to, and facing, both of them. He saw Jew Boy struggling to get up and not making much progress.

Neither guy was rushing in. They were bouncing, feigning, looking for a safe port of entry. Big Body Slim slipped backwards, inches at a time, suddenly realizing he was out of breath. The one to his left was edging steadily closer. Peter played his advance off, then feigned a jab at the one on the right before dipping and charging the one on his left. He took a couple of shots to his temples on his way to ramming his shoulder into the guy's gut. He clasped his hands behind his back and held on, holding himself up—more to catch his breath than to gain any advantage over his foe.

The punches to his back were taking their toll. The guy he had a hold of wasn't doing much damage, but the other one was teeing off on his kidneys and ribs. The gas from the fogger had Peter's eyes watering and his nose running. He kept squeezing, scooting his lower body back and forth to avoid the body shots. He looked up and saw the Ninja Turtles, suited and booted, with their gas guns and batons coming down the bowling alley for the rec yard. Unfortunately, a welcome sight.

Big Body Slim quit side-stepping. He widened his stance, prepared to toss his dancing partner, when he saw McCann. The kid had one in front of him, but there was one creeping up from behind, and, even though from this distance Peter couldn't see what was in his hand, he knew what it was.

Peter jerked up and fell backwards. His adversary had him in a head lock but it didn't matter. His position didn't allow him to do anything but go along for the ride into the concrete.

Big Body Slim was on his back, one enemy under him, groaning, the other coming around. Big Body Slim pulled his knees to his chest and kicked both feet at the one standing over him, backed him up. He lodged a couple of elbows into the human pancake beneath him, kicked again, and got up. He lumbered in a trot towards McCann, spinning around every few steps to swing at the tode chasing behind him. He was too far... Jesus fuckin' Christ. "McCann!" he yelled.

Russell saw blood on the back of his hand after he rubbed his fat lip. C-Life's left eye was swollen with pooled blood. They stepped into their punches, locked up, wrestling, and breaking their hold to slip in a punch when possible, like a hockey fight. Russell let every frustration he had gush out through his fists. He landed an undeflected hook on C-Life's temple and felt his grip weaken as soon as the punch connected. Smelling blood, Russell turned loose and wound up, digging deep to launch an uppercut that struck, sending C-Life's head back. A spurt of blood from the cut it opened over his cheekbone dashed Russell's chest.

C-Life faltered backwards. A sliver of euphoria merged with Russell's rage. He bound forward and set himself, cocking back—

"*McCann!*" came a guttural scream.

The I.D. said Thomas Buyers, but he'd been Adisa for the last twenty years. It'd be a couple weeks before he could take a driver's test and get his license. The state I.D. he'd just received didn't look much different than his TDC I.D., which he'd been told was a legit form of I.D. in the state of Texas. And it might have actually been legitimate for all he knew. Regardless, Adisa wasn't going to be caught dead with it. *Insha'Allah,* he was never going back to prison again, and wanted to dispense with anything even remotely connected to it.

He'd moved in with another ex-con, an old friend he'd spent countless hours in the law library with. Texas law forbade two convicts from living together, but Adisa decided he'd rather take his chances with his overextended parole officer finding out his roommate was also a felon than to live one more night in that halfway house. There were more people being raped in that joint than at the prison he'd just left.

He and Alex Whitehurst, a thirty-nine-year-old White con who had two convictions for different types of I.D. theft and liked his nose-candy a little too much, were cruising Houston in a Suburban. The city looked different. Downtown, which used to be a good place to go if you wanted a crack rock or a bullet in your ass, now had the trendiest nightclubs; twenty years ago, they were all on the southwest side of town. While downtown had gone through a metropolis version of extreme makeover, Hiram Clark, the neighborhood he grew up in, was a shell of its former self. He'd been expecting as much. He'd watched youngster after youngster pull up to Acirema screaming about "tha Clark" with so much gold and diamonds on their teeth they couldn't close their mouths. And he'd heard about the Internet video of the kids at his alma mater, Madison High School, engaging in sex acts on the dance floor at their prom. An event that shouldn't have been that shocking considering Usher and Beyonce had a hit song about fornicating in a nightclub that got endless radio play. All of it made for a quick tour of the old neighborhood that ended without a single stop...

The people looked different, too. There were a lot more Hispanics. And regardless of what color they were, the adults seemed to dress more like kids. All t-shirts and shower slides—er, flip-flops. Lots of guys with facial hair that didn't qualify as a beard. Guys and girls with tattoos on their forearms and necks. Little girls, maybe twelve years old, wearing shorts that didn't make it past the middle of their thighs. *Not my daughter,* thought Adisa, *when I have one. And I better make sure not Lane's daughter,* who he was going to meet in a few days and take plenty of pictures to send to the proud papa.

A song by Morris Day and the Time—he couldn't remember the name now—was going off on Magic 102. The DJ Candy Eastman, "the only candy your mother wants you to have," came on as they passed the Summit—or the Compaq Center—or some church or whatever it was now on Buffalo Speedway. Candy's voice and time slot hadn't changed in twenty years. He'd always wondered what she looked like... maybe now with the Internet and websites he could find out... Probably looks like Pam Grier.

He had work with an attorney Alex worked for, drafting filing motions and whatnot. It wasn't enough to make a living on, but it was gainful employment. They were going to drop off another job application at Costco—paying fifteen dollars an hour for night-stockers—before lunch. Alex had been treating him to a different restaurant almost every day since he'd been out. Today he'd let Adisa pick, and he'd chosen Frenchy's Chicken. The one off Scott Street in Third Ward. Adisa wasn't even sure if it was still there.

Not even the thought of that chicken, or how good Candy Eastman must look, could distract him from his Samsung Galaxy S4's screen. The TradePro active trader page was tracking his soybean position in real time, and today, beans were cooperating.

Russell lay in the hospital bed, watching the dust particles fall through the sunlight from the window, trying in vain to ignore the feeling in his gut. The room was smaller than the cells on Acirema. It had one bed, the same steel toilet and sink combo, and an analog TV hung up in the corner above the steel door. He was waiting for the guard to come by with the remote so he could change the channel. Maybe to ESPN... Maybe not. He'd just been moved in that morning from a post-op room where he'd been shackled to a bed for two days. He wasn't sure how long he'd been there. Maybe a week?

Somebody had left the TV on one of the cable news channels. The one he'd heard Slim G-Zus mention before. *Slim G-Zus.* Russell sighed and pressed his head back into the pillow, closed his eyes, and listened.

"...And don't expect to see anyone on the left with a plate of crow in front of them," said a balding middle-aged man in a dark suit.

"No. No, of course not, Tom," said a blonde in a pantsuit.

"I mean, they've had Tawana Brawley, those two Black kids in New York who painted themselves white, Duke Lacrosse—" he threw up his hands.

"And, especially in this case and the Duke Lacrosse team incident." She shook her head. "These were cases where we knew there was going to be DNA evidence, and nobody wanted to wait for that. The Mercenary Reverends and all the other usual suspects were out in full force, telling us about a pickup truck—or the 'history' of South Carolina—"

"What about the history of these hucksters? Do we ever get to consider that?"

"Oh, no. No, they're safely wrapped in the mantle of 'civil rights leaders,'" she mimed quotation marks with her hands.

Tom said, "So, now that we know that none of the DNA recovered from the victim was Caucasian," he held his hands up, "'cause this is a tragic event—not an 'I told you so'—can we begin the conversation about the coarsening of our culture? Maybe the overtly sexual nature of what comes out of Hollywood and the recording studios? Or—"

"I wouldn't bet on it. Our own President said—before the DNA came back—that we needed a conversation on race and the, what was it? 'Historical trends of racism'?"

"Something like that."

"How about a conversation about all the pathologies that're much more likely to occur when a child comes from a single-parent home?"

"Well, Kate, I think that'd make you a racist."

"Ah, yes."

Russell got up. He'd avoided it as long as he could. Still groggy, he negotiated his way to the pisser. He untied the strings and threw the gown back on the bed. He could see a reflection of his V-tapered physique in the toilet's still water... He unlatched the plastic wrap and laid it across the sink. The shit bag came out of his guts easily. His eyes watered, though not because of the smell, as he dumped his shit and hit the button to flush it.

A day after the riot had ended, Elka Salinas was listening to the local American Public Radio affiliate trying to get some details. Nancy Garza filed this report:

> A riot on the Acirema Unit, in the small town of Bee Ef Eee, between White supremacist gangs and Black inmates was said to have been sparked by the recent events in South Carolina. Sources tell me that White gang members were taunting the Black inmates until tensions boiled over. Fourteen inmates were stabbed and two died. Twenty-nine were taken to a local hospital for various injuries. One of those stabbed was Russell McCann, who, along with Cordell Youngblood, a Black man, killed the alleged gunman in a school shooting at a community college in Houston. McCann was operated on and is expected to make a full recovery. The head warden of the Acirema Unit, Arturo Fernandez, released a statement saying that the unit will be on lockdown for ninety days.
>
> After gathering all these facts, I was left wondering, what would all of the defenders of McCann—the gun-rights crowd—as if a gun could have rights—say now? Would they still try to make him out to be a hero? And what about his supposed friend, Cordell? How must he feel as a man of color, knowing McCann was rioting against Black inmates in the wake of what happened in South Carolina?

She droned on...

Elka looked out the window as her eyes moistened. The truck came to a stop at a light. Jamie Johanson snorted, "Stupid-ass whiteboys." She reached over and placed her hand on Elka's thigh. Elka looked down at the freckled, pasty hand. "There's not enough of them," said Jamie.

Elka cursed herself. She knew better, but she got involved with the *gavacho* anyway. Of course, he was in a gang. They all are... and even if he wasn't, he obviously didn't care about her. If he'd have wanted to be with her he wouldn't have got involved, and he'd be making parole. Now he's going to be on B-side for at least a year. The level-1 case he'll get for participating in a riot will make sure he does the entire three year sentence.

She looked up at Jamie and forced a smile to hide what she was feeling on the inside.

Youngbuck wasn't accepting cellies today. You can do that when you're on closed custody, and you don't give a fuck. So he was alone when the guard passed out mail that night. A letter from Slim G-Zus came through the door.

> 'Sup, fella? The Slim G-Zus here. I heard y'all had a rumble in the jungle. Hope everybody's all right. I heard McCann got hit. Let me know ASAP. I ran into a potna of mine from back in the day. He left Acirema before you got there. I ran it down to him about that clown Orton. He knew him from Neal. Which turned out to be a trustee camp! He said Orton got in debt to some Mexicans and caught out by smashing a law. They put him in seg on Darrington where he heard a lotta war stories. He's never done nothing. Nothing, homeboy. He just looks the part and has a little squabble game. And he's a dope fiend. Those Reich clowns should have done a little background check before they hitched their wagons to that clown. The news said it was "White gang members" in that riot, so I'm pretty sure that was Ogre and them and not y'all. Let me know something. Tell the Big Body he'll hear from me soon.
>
> Much love and respect,
> Slim G-Zus

Youngbuck sat down at the desk to write the letter he'd known he'd have to write.

> Hey, bro. News people got it all wrong. Them Reich hoes caught that pussy with Orton. Itchy went with them. They made a deal with that tode Yella. We wasn't trying to hear it. I don't know how else to tell you this, bro, but the Big Body didn't make it. He tried to stop Lee Lo from stickin' McCann. I was going hard in the paint with Yella and, by the time I got there, your boy was already leakin'. Shit was shootin' out of his neck. Big Body got Lee Lo in a headlock and choked him out. Took that fool smooth off the count, but by then he'd already been hit about eighteen times. I tried to stop the bleeding. Every time I covered one, I'd then find him leaking somewhere else. The laws gassed us, I had most of them holes covered up. I'm guessing he bled to death while we was passed out. I'm sorry, bro. I know y'all was tight. I tried. I cut for that fool, too. He was a good motherfucker. That kid McCann made it. I heard he's in the hospital but coming back. They're shippin' a bunch of us. I'm hopin' they leave me and Yella here. He's got something. But so do I. Gotta get another crack at that ho. Thanks for the info about that fool Orton. I knew that ho was fulla shit. Sidewinder and all them's all right. A few bumps and bruises. 'Woods got it worse over here on B-side. Like ten of them got hit. And that's that.
>
>   Much love and respect,
>   Youngbuck

He was sure he still had Salinas, but Russell knew it was going to be difficult to see her. They almost never put women on eight building. He'd figure that out in due time. Right now, he had to deal with the problem in front of him. J-Pod 2 section, closed custody. The other side.

He looked through the plexiglass window. It was dirtier. The closed-custody dayrooms didn't have TVs or tables. There was no dayroom time. You were in your cell twenty-two hours a day, with a five-minute shower and two hours of rec.

Russell didn't know what to expect, especially considering he was just in a race riot. He looked down at his shirt, trying to discern whether or not you could tell the shit bag was under it.

The door hummed open. Somebody hollered from their cell, "Okay," in a Lil John voice. Russell could see shadows in the cells and dark bodies coming to the doors. Another voice hollered, "Whatcha gon' do, whiteboy? Fight, fuck, or bust a ninety-five?"

Epilogue

Just as a physical body can continue to live,
despite containing a certain amount of microorganisms
whose prevalence would destroy it, so a society can survive a
certain amount of forces of disintegration within it. But that is
very different from saying that there is no limit to the amount,
audacity, and ferocity of those disintegrative forces which
a society can survive, without at least the will to resist.

—Thomas Sowell

www.ingramcontent.com/pod-product-compliance
Lightning Source LLC
Chambersburg PA
CBHW030640260626
47157CB00007B/2416